OUR OWN WAY 3
by Misty Vixen

D1523217

CHAPTER ONE

"Don't say it," Gabe murmured as he finished clipping his nails.

"Say *what?* And how did you even know I was here?" Ellen replied, stepping into the doorway behind him.

"I can hear you. Both in general and your thoughts," he said, studying his nails, then replacing the clipper. He stepped in front of the mirror again and studied himself. "You know I never used to do anywhere near this level of prep before," he added quietly.

"I believe it. Most men don't," Ellen replied, stepping into the bathroom and putting her hands on his shoulders. "Trust me, it's appreciated. And I wasn't thinking anything."

"Right. You weren't thinking 'he really needs to relax' or anything like that."

She laughed softly, then grew a little more serious. "Actually, I genuinely was not thinking that. You're pretty relaxed. Or, maybe relaxed isn't the right word. Confident. Calm. You don't seem worried."

"Well, I am," he said, "although admittedly not as much as I'd be if this was a week or two ago."

"Four days ago you were doing this exact same thing to go take a cougar on a date. You were more nervous then."

"It's not quite the same," he murmured. Finally, he looked up at her reflection. "So what *were* you thinking, then?"

"That I was right. When we first started talking, my assessment of you ultimately ended up being that beneath your...cautious exterior was a mostly untapped reservoir of confidence."

"And you tapped it, huh?"

"Oh yes. I very much tapped it. And Holly has helped a lot. You *are* more confident now, Gabe."

"I guess it's finally catching up." He looked down at himself once more. "Should I do more?"

Ellen opened her mouth, then paused, closed it for a moment, and smiled. "What do *you* think?"

"I think...no. I think I'm good."

"Why?"

"Anymore and it starts heading into try hard territory, I think, for Chloe. Any less and I worry about heading into 'I'm too good for you' territory, which isn't the message I want to send for obvious reasons."

Ellen's smile grew and she looked very satisfied. "That's basically what I was going to say."

"Interesting." He turned around and looked up at her, settling his hands on her broad hips. "That being said, I *would* like to know if I'm missing anything obvious."

"Hmm." She looked him up and down. "No. Wait! Yes. One thing. Put on your cologne."

"For real?"

"Yes. Trust me. You want to give her a scent to associate you with, a good one. And that cologne is just...oh my. So good," she replied.

He thought about it, then nodded. "Yeah, that tracks. Although what if she's already been around someone who uses this?"

"That's just a thing we'll have to risk, and this seems kind of obscure."

"It had better be," he muttered as he sprayed some on. "After spending two damn hours hunting it down."

"Oh come on, it wasn't that bad. And it was...ah, mmm. Yeah. So very worth it. That is actually making me horny right now. Because I smell it and I think of you."

"Well...good for me then."

"Very good for you. Now...I do have one piece of advice."

"I'm listening."

"Chloe is a ten out of ten. She's kind of the definition of a big titty goth girl *and* she is a gamer. She's a smoke show. She is obviously, to some extent, aware of this fact. And you feel like she is out of your league. Stop me if I'm wrong."

"You aren't wrong," Gabe replied.

"So then, I advise that you...put this out of your mind. Which I know sounds like advice I always give, but this time it's a little different. I think Chloe wants to go on a date with a guy who won't worship at her feet, but also won't make her feel like she should be lucky for the opportunity...pretty much, what you were saying earlier, but applied to the whole thing." She paused, then sighed and shook her head.

"Okay, I'm a little high right now so it's a little harder to hold onto my thoughts. Um. Okay. Don't laugh at me!"

"I'm not!"

"You're smirking. That's like laughing. Anyway. Basically, be yourself, treat her like you treat us, and uh...fuck it. You know what to do. Go treat that girl to a good date. She needs it," Ellen said.

"I can do that," Gabe replied.

Ellen looked at him for a moment, then hugged him. "I'd make some quip about how you're all grown up but I think that'd be kinda weird given our relationship...unless you're into that."

"Uh...no comment," he replied.

Her eyes flashed. "Wait *what?*"

"What's going on?" Holly called from the bedroom. "What's Gabe into?"

"Nothing that I feel like discussing," he replied firmly.

"Boo! I wanna do weird, freaky shit with you!"

"Oh believe me," he said as he and Ellen stepped out of the bathroom and he poked his head into the bedroom, "you will. Now that things are finally settling down a little, we are going to start experimenting with the part of you that enjoys being held down."

"Really?" she asked, setting her laptop aside and sitting up.

"Oh yes," Ellen agreed. "We're going to do a bit more than hold you down."

"When!?"

"Soon," Gabe replied. He began to say something else and then Holly shifted and the blanket fell away from her, revealing her considerable and bare breasts. He stared at her for a moment before sighing. "I have to get out of here or I'm never going to leave."

"Oh really?" Holly asked, grinning at him. "You want little old me over your shiny new goth girlfriend?"

"First of all, I love you. A lot. Second of all, she's not my girlfriend and you are. Third...um…"

"Third is that he's distracted by whatever tits are in his face," Ellen said. "And you're right, Gabe. You should go because if you don't you're going to pull us into a threesome because we have such a hard time saying no to you and you'll make Chloe very grumpy."

"I wouldn't want her grumpy at me," Holly murmured.

Gabe laughed. "Yes you would."

Holly crossed her arms. "No, I wouldn't. She's not into girls. Which is *fine,* just...disappointing. She's so fucking hot. I'm kinda jealous."

"Same," Ellen agreed.

"Okay, okay, you both are right." He marched over to the bed, leaned down, and kissed her on the mouth. Then hesitated and cupped one of her big, pale breasts.

Holly giggled and rolled her eyes. "*Gabe.* Come on," she murmured. "Don't start what you can't finish."

"Dammit," he whispered. "I love you."

She smiled and touched his cheek. "I love you too, Gabe. Now go have fun."

"Yes, dear."

Holly laughed and shook her head, then picked up her laptop as he straightened back up. He could tell from a glance at her screen that she was working on her pictures again. She hadn't just gotten into the world of photography, she'd dived in headfirst and happily, and he couldn't be happier for her. She was obviously enjoying herself immensely.

Gabe rejoined Ellen and they walked into the living room. He started getting into his shoes.

"What are you gonna do?" he asked.

"I am going to get a little more baked, and then I am going to marathon a cartoon from the nineties that I used to be very, very into it, completely forgot about, and just recently rediscovered. Now that it's official and I no longer have a job and I have actual *time* for myself, I'm catching up on a lot of media that I had to abandon or ignore. So I'm making a pizza and bingeing that shit," she replied.

Gabe pulled his hoodie into place and gave her a hug and a kiss. "Okay then. Have fun and I love you. Let me know if you need or want anything."

She smiled that smile of hers. "So if I want a foot massage or something…"

He sighed. "You know what I mean. And you know better."

"Do I?"

"Yes, you do."

She laughed. "Yeah, don't worry, I'm not going to fuck with you. Go pound a hot goth girl."

"Hopefully. I'm not sure if she wants sex or not."

"I'm pretty confident she wants it, but yes, that is a possibility to keep in mind. I love you too, babe. Have fun."

Gabe kissed her once more and then headed out to his car. As he did, he glanced at the sky and sighed heavily. He could see his breath on the air. It was already pitch dark now, the stars coming out. It was five in the afternoon.

Shaking off the bad feelings that were trying to worm their way into his skull, he got behind the wheel, set his GPS to Chloe's apartment, and started driving.

Although it had been ten days since he'd last seen Chloe, (and first made love with her), it felt like longer. He knew some of that came from the fact that it had snowed lightly a few more times, prompting them to pretty much just chill out in their house.

Besides hanging out with Ellen and Holly, and working on his next project, the biggest thing of note he'd done was go on a date with Isabella a few days ago. Spending the night with a recently divorced cougar who was *amazing* with her mouth had been a study in unusual but blissful wonder.

The whole experience had been odd, but in a good way. For being very smart, very accomplished, and very attractive, Isabella had been surprisingly lacking in confidence. But Ellen had made a really good point when she'd told him: Imagine being with the same person for *twenty five years* and then suddenly breaking up and trying to date again, even casually.

Overall, it had been a great time, and he was hoping that she would ask him on another date. He was reluctant to ask mostly because she was so busy, between being a surgeon and dealing with the aftermath of her divorce as she tried to get her life rearranged.

In truth, Chloe had been on his mind more than anyone or anything else. (Outside of his relationship.)

He hadn't seen her once since they'd had sex and they'd been texting a little. Mostly he'd been giving her space, because that's what she wanted. He was also wondering if maybe they'd gone too far too fast. Not even just that they'd fucked, (twice), but that they had fucked in front of about half a dozen people, all of them mostly strangers to Chloe.

It had seemed like a good idea at the time, and so far nothing she'd said or done had actually strongly indicated that she was freaked out by what had happened, but he was still paranoid. He was a lot less so right now, though, and he felt a bit of weight lifting as he drove through the dark, frigid city.

Chloe had called him up half an hour ago and pretty much out of the blue said she wanted a relaxing date night with him because she was incredibly stressed out. Given he'd been practicing a lot lately in helping women manage their stress levels, and the fact that he wanted to see her again, he'd immediately agreed to come over.

He found himself thinking back to Ellen's assessment as he pulled into the apartment's parking lot. It felt...off.

It didn't seem possible that he could have had this level of confidence back when they'd first met, let alone before that.

There was a parking spot. He supposed this was something he was going to have to wrestle internally with later.

He began to pull out his phone but as soon as he parked, the front door to Chloe's building opened up and she started walking over. She was wearing a long, dark coat and a dark beanie and what looked like heavy dark boots. As she approached, she paused once and squinted into the window, then walked over and got into the passenger's seat.

"Hey...how you doing?" Gabe asked, because he could tell immediately she was in a sour mood still.

Her text had been: *Come save me from my anger before I break something. Or someone.*

"I'll just warn you right now that I'm feeling extra bitchy and not in a fun way," she replied, staring out the front windshield as she dug around in one pocket. Finally, her hand came out with a USB stick. "Can we listen to this? It will calm me down."

"Sure," he replied, pulling his own out of the radio.

"Thank you. Seriously," she muttered, reaching forward, then hesitating. "Don't make fun of me for this."

"I won't," he replied.

"...thanks."

She put the USB in and then fiddled with it for a

moment. Instrumental music soon began playing. It struck him as very fantasy sounding.

"Where are we going?" he asked, his phone out.

"There's a place called Slices I would really like to go to right now," she replied.

He punched it into his GPS and then showed her the most likely result. "This?"

"Yes."

"Okay, then." He set it up and then started backing out.

CHAPTER TWO

"So, uh...what's this from?" Gabe asked.

They had been driving along in silence for about five minutes now and while five minutes normally wouldn't seem like that long, driving in uncomfortable silence made it feel closer to half an hour.

"A video game," Chloe replied after a slight hesitation.

"I thought so. It sounds kind of familiar. Which one?" he asked.

She seemed slightly more relaxed now. "Novis."

"That...seems vaguely familiar, although I'm sure I didn't play it."

"It's from like two thousand five. Didn't get big, never got a sequel or even DLC. Although that wasn't much of a thing back then. At least not for consoles. But I played when I was in middle school and it was just amazing. It was captivating. This beautiful blend of fantasy and horror. You never really see that. I still play it sometimes, and the soundtrack always calms me down."

"I get that."

Another moment of silence passed.

"So...thanks for this," Chloe said awkwardly. "Also, I'm sorry. I know I kind of just bailed after we fucked. And I know I said I didn't freak out after the first time we hooked up, but then I kinda did after we had full on sex. I went through this whole thing, like 'what if I just did something *really* fucking stupid?' and there were all these paranoid thoughts and they wouldn't leave me alone..." she trailed off, frowning as she looked out the windshield again.

"But? I mean, you're here. You reached out to me," Gabe replied.

"Yeah." She sighed and leaned her head against the window beside her, closing her eyes. "I kept sort of waiting for a full freak out to come on. But it didn't. And I sat with it for a while. And I finally narrowed down what exactly my problem was: I trust you. A lot."

"I understand."

"Do you?"

"I think so, at least. I imagine you've trusted your gut up until now and it's served you well. You're probably pretty good at picking out shitty people. And you've probably never trusted someone as quickly as you have me. And now you're wondering if I've somehow managed to slip past your defenses, and I'm actually a huge piece of shit who is going to take advantage of you, or use and abuse you. Is that it?" he asked.

"Pretty much nail on the head, yeah," she replied.

"So where does that leave you now?"

"For now, this is where I am: I'm going to trust my gut. And I'm going to spend more time with you. Also, I just wanna say this now, so you aren't sitting there distracted and wondering all night: I am definitely down to fuck tonight," she said.

"Oh. Awesome."

She laughed. "I was hoping for a stronger response than that, but I guess you've got two noticeably hotter girlfriends waiting for you."

"They are not noticeably hotter than you," he replied.

"I'm telling them you said that." He glanced at her. She grinned, then sighed. "Sorry. I'm not. I'm just feeling...bitchy."

"What's got you so angry?" he asked. "Because you seemed *really* pissed."

Chloe lost her smile and pulled her coat more tightly around her. "It's...a lot of things," she muttered. "I mean I'm already kind of just low-level constantly pissed off because I'm working my fucking ass off to keep up with bills *and* trying to get a new career off the ground." She rolled her eyes suddenly. "Career. Who am I fucking kidding? Playing video games isn't a fucking career."

"I dunno, I mean, is throwing a ball around a career? Or looking really good? Or playing pretend in front of a camera?" he replied.

"I get what you're saying, but they all at least have the benefit of actually working really hard in a noticeable way. They have to train, workout, starve themselves...but also it's winter now and that's depressing. Everything gets dark and cold and dead. And specifically, my job. It's so fucking irritating. Having to deal with morons all fucking day long. And today was just...too much."

"What happened?"

"Woke up to a phone call asking me to come in early because someone called in. I did, because I could use the money. Walked in to chaos. Like twenty people waiting in line. Turns out *another* person called in right after they got off the phone with me. Had to deal with angry, inconsiderate assholes blaming me personally for making them late or the price of the stupid shit they buy.

"And it just built and built and built until finally I get this guy who won't fucking leave me alone. He's just *so* convinced I'm in love with him and he keeps coming around and hitting on me and like Jesus fucking Christ I'm just *not* into him but I have to keep from finally fucking snapping and screaming at him after *seventy nine* attempts to get my number because then *I* would be the asshole. It's just-ugh. Fuck. Fuck it. I don't care. I'm done thinking about this."

Gabe spied the pizza place and pulled into the parking lot. It looked pretty dead, although he imagined that Chloe was probably like him in that this would be a positive thing. There was nothing quite like the enjoyment of being in a restaurant or grocery store when basically no one else was. There was a sense of peace and calm that you couldn't really get at home.

"Okay," he said, parking and killing the engine, then turning in his seat to look at her, "what exactly do you want? I'm not asking because I'm annoyed, I'm asking because I genuinely want to know how to approach tonight."

"Hmm...what do you think I want?" she replied.

He sighed softly. "Question with a question. Fine, I think you want to relax, and you want me to help you relax. Which I can and will totally do."

"That sounds nice," she said. "So yeah, I'd like that. Although I want something a little more specific, but I'll tell you once we place our order."

"Okay then."

They got out and walked into the building. He saw that about a third of it was occupied by a small arcade. They walked up to the counter and ended up settling on a half pepperoni, half supreme pizza and a dozen and a half barbecue wings and a few sodas, then headed for a booth.

She seemed to notice him glancing at the arcade as they settled in.

"So, don't make fun of me, but part of the reason I wanted to come here is because of that arcade. I used to come here a lot when I was growing up and it's one of the few places that is both still around and I enjoyed in my youth," she replied.

"Chloe…" he began, then hesitated, then reconsidered.

"What?" she asked, almost cautiously.

He sighed. "So I was going to say 'you don't have to worry about me making fun of you', but then I remembered that what little relationship we have is built almost entirely on a foundation of snark and brattiness, so…"

She grinned awkwardly and straightened up a little. "Right. First off, sorry, the 'don't make fun of me' is kind of reflexive because a lot of people have made fun of me. Secondly, we should discuss that. I, ah," she chuckled, "I *may* have gone too hard on the brattiness. Sorry if that was kind of a lot. But...how can I describe this? I'm not really sure when exactly I pieced together that I'm...like this, but it was sometime during the tail end of high school. Given I'm twenty five, that means I've been a brat a good seven years.

"And, this is where the problem comes in, it never works out. In the beginning, it was my fault. I came on way too strong and I also confused real arguing for fake arguing. I...refined my process, only then it became a problem from the other side. I haven't found…" she hesitated and then sighed and shook her head, "this is going to sound *really* arrogant, but I haven't found a guy who can handle me in my entirety...what are you smirking at?"

"I'm sorry, it's not you," Gabe replied, "it's just...Ellen basically said the same thing. Like the *exact* same thing almost."

"Huh...interesting. You seem to be handling her

pretty well."

"I'm, well, still figuring it out."

"Hmm. All right, so, I *really* want to fake argue with someone who can throw it right back and, honestly…" She looked around and then cleared her throat and lowered her voice. "Honestly, someone who can...put me in my place. But *without* being an asshole about it. And I am learning that it's just a thing that you either get or you don't. I'm not sure it can be taught. And you...get it. God, there's just so much in my head that wants out all once, I'm losing track...okay, okay. Focus. My point about my brattiness is that I don't want to be bratty or argumentative at all tonight. I want you and I to talk like...regular people. Okay?"

"I can do that," Gabe replied.

"Thank you," she murmured, then took a long drink from her soda. "I think I heard Ellen at the party describe you as 'remarkably uncomplicated' and that is turning out to be an extremely accurate description."

"I try," he replied with a shrug.

Chloe laughed. "Well you're doing a good job at it...so, okay, now that we've set brattiness aside, can we talk about...us?"

"Yes. What do you want to talk about?"

She straightened up a little, a new focus coming into her eyes. "Okay, first thing's first: how many women are you sexually involved with right this moment?"

"Fair question," he replied. "Um…"

"Oh my God, you actually have think about it? *That* many?"

"Not *that* many! Just...give me a second. It's a little more complicated than that."

"...genuinely *how?* Did you fuck or not?"

"There's a couple I *might* fuck in the near future," he replied.

"Wow."

"Hey, you knew this about me when we–"

"I know! Just...shut up and go."

"All right. So obviously Ellen and Holly. And Emily. And maybe Isabella."

"I fucking *knew* it."

"For the record, we actually didn't fuck at the party for...reasons. But we did a few days ago."

"Huh. All right, is that everyone you've actually stuck your cock inside of?" she asked, grinning at him.

"Yes. I mean, not *ever,* but everyone who is in my life right now."

"Uh-huh. Okay, now exactly how long is the list of chicks you will *potentially* stick your cock in?" she asked.

"You're enjoying this," he murmured.

"Maybe."

"Actually pretty curious about why."

"I don't know. I'm trying to figure it out myself. Don't dodge the question."

"Fine. There's a tatted redhead in her mid-thirties who texts me nudes and has straight up told me that if she gets me in a room she will fuck me."

"So what's stopping her?"

"She lives three hours away."

"Ah."

"Other than her, there's a cougar who might...pounce on me at some point in the future. God willing," he said.

Chloe seemed to turn that over in her head for a moment. "Wait...your landlady? Isn't she like...how old is she?"

"She's fifty," he replied. "And it's complicated. I'm not even fully convinced she's into me."

"What? Are you serious? Dude, she watched you screw me. I imagine you didn't just spring that on her, so she showed up at that party–looking hot, I might add–knowing she was going to see your dick going into my vagina. And what about Abby? I kinda thought she was looking at you a certain way…"

"I think she was looking at *you* a certain way," Gabe replied. "Abby's more or less a full lesbian."

"...more or less?"

"I don't know. Ellen seems to think she might be like ninety eight percent lesbian. Which in her mind means there's a slim but real chance she'd jump me. Which, hey, I'd be down for. She's hot as fuck. But I also think that Ellen has a fetish for hooking me up with women. Which I am not complaining about in the slightest," he replied.

"Hmm. Okay. So...I've got six other women to worry about, at least," Chloe muttered.

"No, you have *zero* women to worry about," he replied.

"How do you figure that?" she asked, giving him a hard stare.

"You aren't competing with anyone. No one's going to flip their shit and come after you if we get serious. No one's going to get angry, or jealous, or hurt. We're careful. We don't seriously risk STIs or pregnancy, or someone going insane and trying to burn our house down."

Chloe twisted her lips for a moment as she stared intensely at him, no doubt considering his words. While she was doing that, their pizza and wings came.

She looked at the food for just a moment. "To be continued," she said, and started eating.

Gabe joined her.

CHAPTER THREE

"All right, Gabe," Chloe said after she'd satisfied the most immediate of her craving, "tell me this: let's say you and I get serious. We start dating, it gets intense. What is that going to look like in your mind?"

"You move in with me and Ellen and Holly," he replied. "You would be sharing a bed with all three of us, but not if you don't want to. You can quit your job if you want and focus on streaming. We hang out and have awesome sex and play video games together and watch movies and go on dates. I'll need time to myself, to write, and time for Ellen and Holly. Sometimes I will go fuck other women outside of the three of you. And if we do get serious, you being with other guys is not an option and will break the relationship. And I recognize that this is not fair, but I want you to know it now and not later. If this is a dealbreaker, I will accept that and we can part amicably."

Chloe looked at him for a long time. He had to admit that he wasn't sure how he was going to word it, and he was pretty nervous, because that was a pretty raw thing to just straight up tell someone. Let alone a woman who wanted to date you.

"Huh," she said finally.

Gabe kept waiting, becoming increasingly nervous. This was the kind of thing that could provoke intense results. She might take it fine, she might punch him in the face.

Chloe grabbed a wing and ate it, put the bones aside, then took a long drink and wiped her mouth with her napkin.

"All right," she said finally.

"All right?" he replied.

"I accept. You're right that it's not really fair...but some things aren't necessarily fair in relationships. People are allowed to have deal-breakers and boundaries. And this is yours. And I can accept that."

Now Gabe looked at her for a long moment. "Okay, not to look a gift horse in the mouth, but...you're seriously just cool with that?"

"I'm theoretically cool with it," she replied. "I mean I knew from the beginning that if I chose to pursue this relationship, it was *not* going to be...normal. You're already dating and living with two other girls. So I think that helps. But I also look at it like...pros and cons?

"At a glance, it looks like what I will get out of this relationship, apparently, is a kind, caring, emotionally intelligent, attractive, creative boyfriend, two cool women as roommates, a place to stay apparently for super cheap? And someone who actually *gets* my brattiness on, like, an intuitive level. Most of these things I have *sorely* wanted for years now. And all I have to do get this relationship is: let my boyfriend fuck other women and not be romantically or sexually involved with any other guys? Yeah, that doesn't sound bad."

"I mean I'd say that's accurate," he replied. "It's just...I thought I'd have a harder time of convincing you of that. When people enter into relationships, they typically don't do so for logical reasons, but emotional ones." He paused. "Though that seems less true nowadays. Relationships are a lot more...transactional, it seems. Or that's what I keep hearing whenever people talk about dating apps."

Her expression soured. "Fuck dating apps into the fucking ground. Now, all this being said, I'm still not *sure* about any of this. I need to spend more time with you. And *definitely* I need to see you, in person, having sex with Ellen and then Holly."

"To know if you can handle it?" he asked.

"Basically. But...you know what? I think this might actually work. I'm not really a jealous person. I'm also not the most social of people. I need my alone time. Honestly? Pretty much every relationship I've had in the past, me needing my alone time turned into a problem. The last one, I actually found myself thinking, 'Christ maybe I should just find a side chick for him' because it was just getting to be too much. So the fact that you have two other girlfriends might be perfect for me."

"Well...all right then."

"Don't think you've got me locked in yet, though. I still need to make sure this can actually *work* before we go straight to fucking moving in," she said.

"Oh yeah, no, absolutely. What I have with Ellen and Holly is...*very* good, and I do not want to fuck it up."

Chloe twisted her lips for a moment. "Hmm...if that's true, why do you want to throw me into the mix?"

"I *really* want you. I don't think you'll screw it up, you're really hot, I want to have sex with you on a regular basis, and I think you're cool," he replied.

She snorted. "What's so cool about me? Is it just the fact that I'm a big titty goth girl who's into video games?"

"No. You seem smart, articulate, fun, and caring. You and I are also *very* sexually compatible."

Chloe sighed and blushed, looking down at her food. "Yes, we are," she mumbled.

"Why does that embarrass you?"

"I just...I don't know. Shut up. Eat your food, I want to hit the arcade," she replied.

Gabe laughed. "All right."

...

One thing Gabe discovered was that Chloe had a hard competitive streak in her, just like Ellen.

Another thing he discovered was that she was, in fact, very good at video games.

Even when he was seriously trying, she beat him at everything. They went through two full campaigns of rail shooters, then spent the rest of the time pouring quarters into a racer. He had almost beat her on their third try when she decided she wanted to head home.

"You just wanna leave because you know I'm finally gonna win next time," Gabe said as they walked out of the building.

"No, I want to go home because I'm getting horny," she replied in a low voice.

"Oh."

"And I would've whupped your ass again anyway."

"Uh-huh."

Chloe laughed as they got into his car. As he pulled out of the parking lot and started driving for home, he noticed that she was staring at him in a kind of speculative way.

"What?" he asked finally.

"You're different from a lot of guys," she replied.

"Probably, but how so?"

"Obviously, I play against a lot of people competitively, and most of them are men. And I've run into a lot of guys who are *very* sore losers. And there's a lot more who are middling, they're pretty calm, but I can still kinda tell that it bugged them that I won. Which, you know, I get. I don't like losing. But there's definitely a twist of the knife, apparently, to losing to a *girl*. Which is depressing that that's still a thing in fucking twenty twenty three. But whatever. *You* though...there was some trash talking, but I can tell that it genuinely doesn't bother you that I beat you in every single game we played. And that's rare. Or, at least, it is in my experience," she explained.

"I'm kind of competitive, but I can also turn it off. And I can, with *some* success, separate myself from the results of a video game. Believe me, I've been a sore loser before," he replied.

"Oh yeah, I have, too. I was a little shit when I was younger. Finally got past that stage."

"Uh-huh."

"Oh fuck you. Shut your fucking mouth."

"Clearly you got past it. Definitely."

"Gabe, you motherfucker, I told you–"

"That you don't wanna be a brat. I know. You just...kinda bring that out in me, apparently."

She sighed heavily. "Yeah, and you bring it out in me. This is going to go *great*."

"It probably will be fine. We just need to get attuned to each other, learn when to amp it up, when to knock it off, when we shouldn't fuck with the other at all because they're in a bad mood. Just takes some getting used to," he replied.

"Sounds like you have experience with this already. I really got that vibe from Ellen," she said.

"Oh yeah. Ellen's...complicated. She likes to be

dominant, she likes to be submissive. She likes to argue to be put in her place, and she likes to argue to put others in their place."

"If I really do get involved with you all, it's gonna take some getting used to, living with her and having her as...the woman who is also dating my boyfriend...and the same is true for Holly. She seems like a sweet pea, but she is also just intimidatingly hot. Like she is insanely hot," Chloe muttered.

"They will also have to get used to you. You're going to be first woman I'm involved with on a more serious basis that isn't bisexual," he replied.

"I hope that doesn't complicate things," she murmured. "I imagine it's easier to accept a woman coming into your house and fucking your boyfriend if she also wants to fuck you. And...I don't know, I mean, I've kissed girls at parties before, but who hasn't? But I can't ever see myself eating pussy, for example."

"How about a threesome where you don't actually really do much of anything with the other woman beyond maybe kissing and some light groping?" he asked.

"Mmm...I'd at least give it a shot. I mean I'm a lot closer to that sort of thing after getting fucking railed in front of half a dozen strangers, all of them women," she replied.

They pulled into her parking lot and he parked in front of her building. Gabe killed the engine and they headed inside.

"I'm afraid I live in a basement apartment," she said, leading him downstairs.

"Hey, so did I like two months ago," he replied. "Although admittedly it wasn't for very long."

"Right now it's nice," she said as she unlocked

the door, "because there's no one in the apartment above me and whoever's next to me never really seems to be home. So it's pretty peaceful and it helps with the streaming at least. Which is good because all I have right now is a really shitty mic and webcam. All I can afford."

She let him in and he was immediately struck by how neat the place was. It wasn't a studio apartment, but a one bedroom.

"Here's my home," she said, shutting the door behind him as he walked into the living room.

"This is nice," he replied.

She snorted. "Yeah, I'm sure."

"I'm being serious," he replied. "It's very neat and clean. Why do you think I'm being sarcastic?"

"I guess because I imagine your place must be so much better," she replied. "Here's the kitchen."

He joined her and looked into a small but also very neat and clean kitchen. No dishes in the sink, no stains on the counter. He opened the fridge and found it just as well organized, if a bit barren.

"What exactly are you picturing when you imagine my house?" he asked.

They headed back into the living room and he took a moment to get out of his shoes and hoodie.

"Something like that house you and I had sex in for the first time," Chloe replied.

"Oh dear God," Gabe said with something like real horror. "You are so off base."

"Seriously?" she asked.

"Yeah," he replied, following her down a short hallway. "It's, like, a quarter the size of that house. I mean, it's clean and in good shape, it's just way smaller. We've got two bedrooms, a bathroom, a living room, and a kitchen."

She paused before one of the doors the hallway ended in. "And you want to move *me* in there, too?"

"It's...we're still considering our options," he replied.

"Uh-huh. Anyway. Bathroom," she said, showing him a scrubbed clean bathroom. "Closet. And bedroom."

Her bedroom was taken up by what had to be her work area where she recorded her gaming. It was a nice desk and a decent computer chair. The computer she had looked like by far it was the most expensive thing in the apartment. The bed was a twin size with a big, comfortable looking blue comforter on it.

"So...I guess I don't have a really great grasp of where you're at with your gaming. You said you wanted to get into it, but you clearly are at least somewhat into it…"

"Right. You kinda frazzled me when we were first talking," she murmured. "So, I have a channel that I stream games on. I started doing it just kind of because, about six months ago? I've got like a hundred regulars now. I don't really have a set schedule because I'm so fucking busy, but I want to get more serious about it. But," she said with a certain finality, turning to face him, "I've texted with Ellen a little and there was one thing she said I *had* to get you to do."

"What's that?" he asked.

"Give me a back rub."

CHAPTER FOUR

Gabe grinned. "I can do that. Although I thought it was going to be something else."

"Oh well, she also told me I *had* to get you to eat my pussy," Chloe replied.

"There it is," he said, and she laughed. "I can do both. Take off your shirt."

A look briefly came onto her face, like she wanted to say something cutting, but then it passed and she took off the tight, dark t-shirt she'd been wearing.

"Bra too?" she asked.

"Yep," he replied.

"You just want to see my tits," she murmured, unhooking her bra and working it down her arms.

"Yep."

Chloe laughed. Gabe found himself staring as her big, pale breasts came out. They were even more stunning and beautiful than they were in his memory. She faced him fully, her huge tits swaying and jiggling beautifully as she moved, and put her hands on her hips.

"You're really into these, huh?" she murmured.

"That shouldn't surprise you," Gabe replied, taking off his shirt and tossing it aside.

"I guess not. Ellen's *have* to be bigger and Holly's *have* to be better, though."

"Firstly," he said, walking over to her and gently turning her around, "stop comparing yourself to them. Or stop assuming that I am. Secondly, breasts are just awesome. Full stop, all around. And yours are *particularly* awesome. Thirdly, lay down on your stomach."

"All right," she murmured, and for a moment she sounded a little lost.

He wondered how long it had been since she'd had an intimate interaction that involved no snark, no brattiness.

"How long have you been single? I swear you told me but your tits knocked all the thoughts out of my head," he asked as he got onto the bed with her.

She laughed. "A year," she replied. "Or thereabouts. My last breakup was-I don't want to talk about it."

"Then we won't," he replied.

Gabe settled so that he was sitting on her pleasant ass, which was still clad in a pair of tight black jeans. He laid his hands flat against her back and felt her shiver under his touch. Felt her soft, creamy, smooth skin. Felt her warmth.

He started slowly, dragging his hands up and down her back, keeping the pressure light.

"Your hands are warm," she murmured.

"So is your back. And soft. Your skin is amazing," he replied.

She laughed softly. "That'd sound creepy in almost any other context...this feels fantastic."

"Wait until you feel this," he said, and then switched to dragging just his fingernails over her back.

"Ahhhhhh...oh my God...oh! That's...mmm...oh wow…" she moaned, shuddering and trembling from the pleasure.

"I think people often forget how sensitive backs are," Gabe said.

"Uh-huh," she managed.

He laughed and kept going. After a bit longer, he began kneading her flesh, again starting gently, but slowly working up the pressure.

"You are very tense," he murmured. "I've got a lot of knots here."

"Yeah, I've had to learn to hide it, and it's been a really trying day," she replied.

"You ready for something a little more intense?"

"...yes."

"Okay. I'll give you warnings, but I want to work some of these knots out. That's going to be kind of painful."

"I can take it," she replied a little defensively.

"I guess we'll find out."

"You know I can kick you."

He laughed. "I know. Now..." He rested his thumbs on either side of her lower spine. "These muscles get put to good use every single day when you've got huge tits, which you do. So..."

He started pressing into her muscles there, working the flesh and shoving his thumbs in, pulling back, then repeating a little higher until he reached about six inches up, then going back to the beginning and repeating the process.

"Oh! Ah man! That's-ah! Shit! Yeah, those are tense," she growled.

"I haven't even gotten to the knots yet."

"I thought this was working out the knots!"

"Oh no, no no no. That's a lot more intense."

She sighed heavily. "Great."

"If you can't take it..."

"I can fucking take it!"

Gabe paused for a moment. "Sorry. Shit, you seriously do bring out my antagonistic side. Tell me if you want me to stop."

"Oh believe me, I will," she muttered.

He kept working her muscles and then finally got

to one of her knots. "Okay, here it comes."

"I'm ready," she growled.

He laid his palm flat against, adjusted so that his lower palm was over it, and then pressed down hard and all at once. Something popped loudly in her back and she cried out. He found himself chuckling a little.

"You enjoyed that, you fucker," she whispered, panting a little.

"Did you not?" he replied.

"I...no comment," she growled.

Gabe resumed massaging her, working around the next knot. "Oh man."

"What?" she asked.

"I'm just realizing that if this really does work out we are going to have *so much fun.*"

She chuckled. "What makes you say that?"

"You love being punished, I love punishing. And there are just so many ways in which we can engage with this."

"Yeah, just *so* many ways you can punish me." She hesitated. "You know that was sarcastic but that actually makes me really excited...and horny. Will you–"

"Will I what?" he asked when she paused for too long.

"I'm suddenly embarrassed to talk about this," she muttered.

"You don't have to if you don't want to, but you *can* trust me that I'm not going to hold it against you if you're into something weird. Like, at worst, I will politely decline."

She was quiet for another long moment. He kept working her back while she processed that.

"All right, you've got a point," she said finally. "I *do* trust you. I've trusted you enough to let you in on certain things, to let you in my apartment to spend the night, and to let you inside of me without protection. And I fucking *hate* that women have ruined this phrase, either that or men have ruined it because of what they believe...whatever. I hate that the phrase is ruined *but* I don't normally do that. I'm actually normally a really cautious person, at least when it comes to my love life. So clearly I trust you a *lot*. I've never let someone back in my apartment after just one date. Usually it takes, like, five before I seriously start considering it."

"So...? What do you want me to do?" he asked.

"Spank me," she replied quietly and awkwardly. "Like, with a paddle. From a sex shop. And now I'm extremely embarrassed for asking oh God this sucks I'm so fucking embarrassed now–"

"It's okay, here, knot incoming," he said and pressed down.

"Mother*fucker!*" she snapped as her back popped very loudly.

"Did that derail your embarrassment?" he asked.

"I...yeah, it did actually. What the fuck? How the hell did you know that would work?"

"I figured it'd be really distracting and sometimes I've found that if you can really distract someone at the beginning of a shitty feeling enough, it derails it. It's not a guarantee, but it's decently effective," he replied.

"Man, you really *are* emotionally intelligent. I've never quite put that together before."

"Well, if it makes you feel any better, I will so absolutely spank you with a paddle, or hand, whatever you want, really."

"Will you not tell your girlfriends? I mean, not yet at least. Or is that not a thing? Do you tell each other everything?" she asked.

"So, we tell each other basically everything, but I *do* respect confidentially, even to the women I love with all my heart and soul, provided it does not hurt them to do so," he replied.

"Oh. Well, that's cool." She shifted, then groaned. "How many more?"

"Let's see here…" he murmured, running his hands lightly over her back. "There's like three more. You're *seriously* tensed up." She sighed heavily. "You wanna stop? We can stop."

"No, we've gone this far. And as much as I'm complaining it actually does feel good. So keep going."

"Okay." He resumed massaging one of her knots, trying to get it to relax somewhat before he worked it out. "Anything you want to know? Or talk about?"

"Yeah, actually. Do you want kids?" she asked.

"Uh. Wow."

"I know, big topic for our second 'date', but you dropped your own bomb on me earlier, so I get one, I feel."

"That's fair," he replied. "And…I don't know. Before a few months ago, I was pretty staunchly in the 'fuck no' school of thought. And admittedly there's a lot of me that's still there. But…then I got together with Ellen. And then with Holly. I think they'd both be really excellent mothers."

"I actually feel your dick getting harder," she murmured. "Do pregnant chicks get you hot?"

He laughed. "Yeah, definitely."

"So is it like the idea of getting them pregnant? Or what they look like while they're pregnant? Or what?"

"Both. I *really* would love to get a woman

pregnant. And I *really, really* want to have sex with a woman who is noticeably pregnant. Now, the *reality* of actually raising a child is...something I'm still wrestling with. So that's a big maybe."

"Pretty much the same for me," she muttered. "Sometimes I think 'yeah I'd be a fucking boss mom' and then sometimes I think 'why even bother bringing a child into this nightmare world?', you know?"

"...yeah. Okay, next knot."

"I'm ready."

He worked it for a bit longer, then pressed down. She didn't cry out this time, just grunted loudly. He moved onto the next one.

"Okay," she said, "now, would you seriously be cool with me quitting my job? Because I have to be honest, if you weren't dating two other women, I'd almost certainly tell you to fuck off. I've seen too many women take that deal and then basically be trapped because now they're completely dependent on the guy paying the bills, which was the plan the whole time."

"I would actually be cool with you quitting your job, yes," he replied. "But what do you think of the idea if it's authentic? Because it is. And, in truth, I'm not the one with all the money, that's Ellen right now. Though I imagine that'll slowly change over time. Or maybe it won't. Maybe Holly's photography will take off and she'll be raking in the cash. I don't know, my point is, it's a real offer. Next knot, incoming."

"I'm ready," she said. He popped it and she let out a grunt, then he moved onto the last one. "I mean it sounds like a dream come true? I'd fucking love it? Which is why I'm so uncertain about it. Sounds crazy. Being a...trophy girlfriend? Stay at home girlfriend? Fuck, I don't know."

"You would be my girlfriend who is taking the opportunity to explore her passion without having to worry about bills screaming in the background eternally," Gabe replied. "Okay, last one."

"Ready."

He popped her final knot and she let out a loud groan of satisfaction. "Oh man, that's so much better." Chloe took a deep breath and let it out. "I can see why Ellen suggested this. That was amazing."

"Glad I could help," he replied, running his hands over her back a few more times before getting off her.

"What were we talking about? Oh right. Trophy girlfriend."

"*Regular* girlfriend who doesn't have to pay bills. Or at least not nearly as many. I just am offering to take the pressure off, is all," he replied.

She was quiet for a bit, then she slowly sat up and stretched. Something popped loudly in her back and she moaned. "Fuck, this keeps derailing my train of thought," she muttered. "But *fuck* does it feel better now. That's better for relaxation than a joint...speaking of which...you wanna?"

"Smoke a joint?" he asked.

"Yeah. I've got some."

"Yes I do. Although I need to confirm this now: you *are* offering for me to spend the night?" he asked.

"I am. That is my intent. To keep you here all night and get high with you and fuck you, and then call in tomorrow because the idea of going into work tomorrow makes me want to fucking die and I *need* a day off," Chloe replied.

"Lemme just double check with Ellen," he said, grabbing his phone and texting her.

"Can I see a picture of this redhead who is

apparently super down to fuck? I'm pretty curious," she replied.

"Yeah, hold on…"

Gabe finished texting Ellen, letting her know that he was going to spend the night unless she or Holly needed or wanted otherwise, then he went looking for a picture of Krystal. He'd already gotten her approval to show fuck friends her nudes, so there was no problem there. He settled on one she'd sent him more recently, a full frontal nude pic of her in the mirror.

"Here she is," he said, turning the phone around to Chloe.

She immediately snatched it out of his hand as her eyes went wide and brought it closer to her face. *"Gabe!"*

"What?" he asked.

"How-what-this isn't normal! Are you *fucking with me?"* she asked, looking up at him. She suddenly seemed suspicious. "Okay, this is like a random influencer chick you found online, right? Like you're having some kind of joke, right?"

"Having a *joke?* How is that the way that came out of your mouth? Nevermind. No, I'm not. This is her. This is Krystal."

"I'm admittedly having a hard time with this," Chloe said, looking back down at the picture. "Like, seriously, she's a fucking ten. She's a fifteen. She's a model." She closed her eyes for a moment, then passed the phone back and shook her head. "I'm sorry. I know I'm being a jerk right now, but it's just a lot."

"Why would I lie about this?" he replied.

"I…I don't know! It doesn't make sense."

"Want some proof?" he asked.

"…yes. How do you even know her?"

"She's Ellen's best friend from way back."

Gabe grinned and opened up his and Krystal's text chain: *Hey you busy?*

Her response came back quickly: *No, what's up?*

I'm with a potential girlfriend right now and she doesn't believe you want to fuck me or that you've been sending me nudes. She wants some proof. Can you send a quick video?

The little … appeared, then disappeared, then reappeared, then disappeared, then reappeared again. Finally, she said: *I am offended on your behalf and yes. Just a minute.*

"Oh you did it now," he murmured.

"So she's going to send something? Lemme see the texts," Chloe said, holding her hand out.

"Your face is gonna be red," he said. He began to pass her the phone, then stopped. "What do I get if I prove myself right?"

"...what do you want?" she replied.

"I want you to blow me and take my load on your face," he said.

She pursed her lips, then grinned. "Fine. But in the shower."

"Deal."

He passed her the phone and she looked at it for a long moment, reading over it and slowly losing her smirk. He heard his phone make a noise and she sighed.

"Well?" he asked.

"She sent a vid," she muttered.

"Let's watch it together, shall we?"

"Oh my God, fuck off," Chloe growled, and they sat down together on the bed.

She hit play and Krystal appeared in what appeared to be her bedroom. "Hey Gabe, hello girl who doesn't believe Gabe. This is Krystal, in real life, and I'm saying here and now that I will so totally fuck Gabe raw when I get the chance. And, just to prove it even more, here's my girlfriend."

She turned the camera around to face a bed, where a tall, tanned, toned goddess was laying, reading, wearing little more than a sports bra and panties. She flushed, looking a little awkward, though she did have a smile on her face.

"Well, babe?" Krystal asked.

Her girlfriend laughed and rolled her eyes. "*Yes, for the record, I have given you permission to fuck Ellen's boyfriend. There, happy?*"

"Extremely, thanks babe," Krystal replied, turning the phone back around. She stuck her tongue out and then the video cut out.

"Holy shit, that's her girlfriend? She's fucking cut," Chloe muttered.

"Satisfied?" Gabe asked, taking the phone back and typing a quick *Thank you very much* to Krystal.

"Okay yeah, you win. I guess I gotta get semen on my face," she said. "But in the shower."

"Fine by me," he replied.

Krystal shot him back a response: *It worked, I take it?*

He laughed. *Yep.*

She quickly fired off another text: *I want pix of this chick. Ellen says she's full goth and she's got huge tits.*

He sighed. "Krystal wants pics of you."

"Hmm. Well...okay, hold on," she said, stretching out on the bed and laying an arm over her breasts, leaving them still pretty visible. "Okay, take a pic and then show me."

"Thanks," he replied, snapping a picture of her.

He showed her. "Okay, that's fine. Yeah, you can show her."

"Sweet." He fired it off.

There was a response almost immediately: *GABE YOU FUCKING ASSHOLE HOW THE FUCK DO YOU KEEP FINDING CHICKS THIS FUCKING HOT TO FUCK!?*

He laughed loudly.

"What?" Chloe asked, sitting up.

"I think she's jealous of me," he replied, showing her the response.

Now Chloe laughed. "Wow. Interesting...okay, enough of this. I'm seriously horny. Can we have sex? But like...tender? Or, well, romantic? I mean like no snark, no porn stuff. Like we're dating seriously?"

"I can do that," Gabe replied, putting the phone away and unzipping his jeans.

CHAPTER FIVE

Gabe climbed into bed with Chloe as she finished getting her panties off.

"I'm a little nervous," she murmured softly.

"Any particular reason?" he replied, running his hand slowly down her arm.

She shivered at his touch. "I'm not sure. I think...it was easier, being a brat while you did stuff with me. This is just...this is just *me*. You know? And you're with these fucking amazing women and they're so fucking hot and successful and–"

"Chloe," he said, gently grabbing her chin and turning her towards him so he could look into her eyes, "you did not suffer through all that knot-releasing just to work yourself up again. And I told you, don't compare. I'm not. It's you and me and no one else, right?"

She licked her lips, then slowly nodded. "...right."

He leaned in and kissed her. She moaned and immediately deepened the kiss, responding to it with her whole body. Gabe let his hand run up and down her arm one more time, then cupped one of her big, soft breasts.

"Now," he said, breaking the kiss for a moment, though staying close enough to her that when he spoke his lips brushed hers, "it's just us. Neither of us have anything we need to do tonight. You can sleep in tomorrow. We're going to get high later. We're about to have great sex. If anything goes wrong or anything embarrassing happens, I'm not going to be an asshole about it. You are safe here with me. Let yourself relax."

Chloe stared into his eyes for a long moment. When she closed her own eyes, he pulled back a little to give her some space. She took a deep breath, held it for a moment, then slowly let it out. She opened her eyes again.

"You're right," she whispered. "Thank you. I...have a very hard time letting myself relax."

Then she kissed him, and they were making out. He felt her tongue slip into his mouth, tasted her taste, felt that particular thrill as his tongue touched hers and they twisted together. He massaged her breast slowly for a bit, then ran the pad of his thumb gently over her nipple. She gasped softly.

He kissed her for a time longer, then kissed his way along her jaw, her neck, down across her collarbone, lower to her breasts. He spent some time there, first making a circle with the tip of his tongue around her nipple, then licking across it.

"Ah! Oh my goodness," she whispered, breathing heavily now.

"I remember they're sensitive in the best way," he murmured, then started sucking on her breast.

"Oh my fucking...ahhh yes," she moaned. "That is just fucking amazing."

He switched over to the other breast, giving it similar attention, licking across her bare skin and her nipple several times before sealing his lips around it and gently sucking.

"Yes..." she whispered, putting her hand over the back of his head. "You know the *perfect* amount of sucking. Not too soft, not too hard...that is making me so fucking hot."

"You are *really* going to like this next part," he replied, and went lower.

Chloe was breathing heavily as she watched him,

her eyes wide, her face flushed. He settled down between her thighs.

"You shaved," he murmured as he looked at her bare vagina.

"Yeah. After I knew you were coming."

"I appreciate it."

He leaned in and kissed her bare pussy. She giggled. "Wait did you serious just kiss my pussy?"

"Yep," he replied.

"I...okay then. That's a first. Keep going," she said.

Gabe had to sit on a sudden strong urge to snark at her. He focused on pleasuring her instead. Gently parting her lips, he leaned in and began gently massaging her clit with the tip of his tongue. She inhaled sharply, held her breath, then let out a long moan of bliss as he started eating her out. He listened to her sounds of pleasure as gradually began to go faster, to press harder, to use more of his tongue.

He could feel her writhing around and against him, her thigh muscles tensing and releasing. He could feel the comforter shifting beneath him as she grasped and pulled at it. Her moans became louder, more frantic, more insistent. Soon she was panting and incoherent with pleasure.

She let out a shriek of bliss as he slipped two fingers into her and began fucking her with them in tandem with his oral pleasure.

When the orgasm came, it was *strong*.

She bucked hard enough that she bumped his face with her crotch and he had to grasp her thighs and hold her down as she let out disjointed cries of ecstasy. Her hips jerked and jolted as she orgasmed, and a hot gush of her sex juices hit him in the neck and chest.

It was a full-bodied orgasm, and it was beautiful to behold.

He stayed with her throughout it, though he sat up and kept his hands on her thighs as she jerked and twitched and trembled.

Finally, she went slack, gasping for breath, a fine sheen of sweat on her nude, pale body.

"Oh my fucking shit," she whispered finally. "Gabe. Oh my fucking-*Gabe.*"

"Yeah?" he replied, chuckling.

"That was...*so good.* I fucking came *so* hard...oh man..." she moaned and another post-orgasmic tremor rolled through her beautiful body.

"I need to wash up real quick," he said.

"Oh, uh..." She raised her head and looked at him. "Oh wow, I really got you. Um. Yeah. Sorry. You know where the bathroom is," she murmured, laying her head back down.

He laughed as he stood up. "Don't be sorry. That's exactly what I was going for."

She mumbled something as he slipped out of her bedroom and washed up quickly. As soon as he was dried back off, he hurried back and all but dove into bed with her again.

"Okay," she murmured, "um...oh boy. Do you want me to suck now? Or do you wanna just go?"

"I wanna just go," he replied.

She spread her legs wider. "Then go."

Gabe eagerly got atop her, in between those wonderful pale thighs of her, and rested his head against her glistening, hot opening. He started working his way inside of her and groaned as the pure, raw pleasure of her slick, perfect pussy hit him. She moaned along with him as he penetrated her, grabbing at him and pulling him down against her.

He laid down and kissed her as he got all the way within her. He kissed her deeply, and she embraced him like they were lovers who had been apart for far too long.

Maybe, in some way, that was a shade of true.

He had connected with Ellen and Holly so quickly, it was almost as if they had always been waiting for each other, missing pieces of a broken life, waiting to be fixed by the right person.

He couldn't deny that he was feeling something similar with Chloe.

Staring into her bright, deep green eyes as he made love to her, he felt that connection, and he could tell that she felt the same thing. She embraced him intensely as they kissed, pressing her hips up against him each time he thrust into her, inviting him deeper.

And he accepted that invitation happily, starting to go faster, go harder. She moaned and then yelled in ecstasy as they made love.

It was different from last time, and the manner in which he became lost within her, with her, was so very different, too.

Locked and lost together in a blissful union of lust and love and acceptance and joy.

It was a timeless moment that stretched out.

It went until he felt her begin to orgasm again. Her eyes widened and her mouth opened and it almost looked like it caught her by surprise. Chloe cried out, locking her legs around his midsection and grasping his back and holding her tightly against him as her slick inner muscles began to flutter and clench, and another hot gush of feminine sex juices escaped around his erection. She cried out louder each time he thrust into her.

And then it was his turn, and his own orgasm

burst into existence like a supernova. He heard his own cry of ecstasy as he began to come inside of her. He felt his cock jerking and twitching as his seed burst out of him and began pumping into her, filling her up. He pushed deeper inside of her and the pleasure briefly overwhelmed him.

His hips jerked forward in time with each contraction of their own volition, and he heard her cry out in time with that.

They spent a while longer lost in that pink sea of pure pleasure and raw rapture, and then they were deposited back on the shores of awareness, nude and sweaty and panting heavily.

They stayed like that for a long time, him inside of her, resting his forehead against hers, staring into her eyes.

Chloe was the first to break the silence that fell across them. "Can you get me some toiletpaper?"

"Yeah," he replied, carefully pulling out of her.

He got to his feet, then swayed and staggered a bit as he walked out.

"Holy shit, you okay?" she asked.

"Yeah. Just...overwhelmed," he replied.

"Really?" she called as he headed into the bathroom.

He grabbed some toiletpaper and returned. "Yeah, really. That was absolutely fantastic sex." He passed her the toiletpaper and she held it over her crotch.

"It feels like a lot," she muttered.

"Why don't we take a shower," he replied.

She nodded. He took her free hand and helped her to her feet, then they headed into the bathroom. He started up the water while she did some basic cleanup. As soon as the water was warm enough, they got in. He let her have the water first and watched as she pulled the showerhead down and put it up under herself.

"Are you okay?" he asked.

"What?...yeah. Why?" she replied.

"You just seem kinda...off?"

"Sorry. I'm fine." She hesitated. "I mean mostly."

"Mostly?"

She sighed and replaced the showerhead. "So...I know I asked for intimacy and lovemaking, but that was, um...I mean you felt it too, right? That...connection? It kind of felt like we've been dating for months. Years, even."

"Yeah, I felt it, too," he replied.

"Does that freak you out?"

"No. You?"

"Kind of."

"Sorry."

She laughed softly. "I mean it's not your fault. You gave me what I asked for, but how effective it was, that connection...that has the feel of an event that happened, uncontrolled. Almost like a chemical reaction, or a kinetic one. I've never really felt that before. Not like *that*. Not that...*deeply*. And that's frightening. Or maybe just overwhelming." She frowned and looked at him. "Is that what it's like with Ellen? With Holly?"

He nodded. "Yes." Chloe didn't seem to know what to say to that. "You want a hug?" he asked.

"...yeah."

He stepped forward and embraced her, wrapping his arms around her. She hugged him back, squeezing him tightly and resting her head against him. As he ran his hands up and down her back, she seemed to relax.

"Feel better?" he asked when they let go of each other a few moments later.

"Kind of. But I'm still sort of freaked. I mean, it feels like there's big implications here for me personally that I need to sort through, but now I'm feeling just...*very* weird about being this level of intimate with another woman's boyfriend. Let alone *two* other women. And Ellen is fucking scary. I know she's cool if we have sex, but that wasn't sex. That was making love. That was fucking *intimate.* And that's not the same thing."

"She sent me over here knowing that was on the table," Gabe replied.

"So, to be clear, Ellen and Holly know that you are trying to date me? Like not make me a side chick, but actually date me? Live together? Fall in love?" she asked.

He nodded. "Yes. They know those exact things. And they're happy about it."

"*Happy* about it? Not just tolerant of it?"

"Yes."

She stood there in the falling water for a bit, then finally shook her head. "Okay, I need that joint now. I need to just...I need time to sit with this. I wanna turn my brain off."

"I will gladly join you in that. Although if you're feeling freaked, should I go?"

"No," she said immediately, "don't go. I don't want you to go."

"Okay. I won't go."

She smiled awkwardly, then hugged him again, then pulled back and looked down. "You want that blowjob now?"

"Uh...how about later? I came so fucking hard,

and a lot. And I'm gonna need some time," he replied. "And, if I'm being completely honest, I want more of a nut to bust all over your face."

That finally seemed to break through the tension that had settled over her and she laughed loudly. "What the fuck, dude?! Seriously?!"

"Just being honest," he replied.

She sighed. "Yeah, okay, makes sense. Here, I'm hogging the water. Let's get washed up and then toke up and, I don't know, watch something? Or just talk? Or play a game? I've got some consoles out there…"

"That sounds awesome," he replied.

CHAPTER SIX

"Hopefully this doesn't make me paranoid," Chloe muttered as she finished puffing on the joint.

"Does it normally?" Gabe replied as he accepted it.

"No. Normally it just chills me out. But tonight feels like a night of firsts."

"I guess so."

They sat on her couch together, wrapped up in another comforter, clad in just their underwear. Chloe still looked a little pensive.

"So...is this just like no big deal to you?" she asked after they passed the joint back and forth a few times.

"What? Where did that question come from?" he replied.

"I keep getting hung up on the fact that you have Ellen and Holly to go home to. You have this fucking awesome life, writing books and not having to deal with bills and playing video games and fucking your hot girlfriends all the time–"

Gabe sighed. "Chloe, come on. This matters to me. I mean, am I-does it seem that way? Do I seem bored or something?"

"No, honestly." She shook her head and gave him the joint back. "I'm sorry. Really. I keep asking these mean questions, but you aren't doing anything wrong. Really, you're doing everything right. It's just these thoughts that keep coming to me. And my life feels so fucking boring. All I do is work and play video games. Sometimes I hang out with my friends, but they've got their own lives and...honestly, my life is really boring. I'm sort of just realizing this."

"Why do you think that?" he asked.

She sighed. "I mean I'm not exaggerating, almost all my time is taken up by either working, sleeping, or gaming alone. Either at the coffee place or this apartment or driving between the two. Maybe two or three times a month I get out. Maybe. I used to be a lot more social. But then, I don't know, something changed. I just wanted to be inside more."

"Chloe, I don't think you're boring," he said.

"Why?" she replied.

He pointed at a huge bookshelf that took up most of the wall between the couch they sat on and the TV across the way. "Look at all that. All those books. All those games. All those movies. Life's a little more complicated than 'who parties more'. Interesting is more than how many times you went out or how many people you know. But, even putting that aside, different things are interesting to different people. And so far, based on our time together, I don't think you're boring."

Chloe puffed a few more times on the joint as she stared at him. "How are you doing that?" she muttered finally.

"Doing *what?*" he replied.

"You are so fucking...*real*. Like, you're *so* authentic. I believe everything you say. I tend to distrust people on general principle. So many things I hear from people, in my head I think 'yeah sure okay'. So many people just seem like they're full of shit. And I now some of that is because I'm terminally cynical. But a lot of people have lied to me in my life. And I had...an unhappy experience in school overall. But I fucking *believe* you, Gabe. You tell me something and I buy it. I don't even question it. And I want to know why."

"I don't really have a great answer," Gabe replied.

Her eyebrows raised a little. "So you *do* have an answer? I'll admit, I didn't expect one, because this seems like one of the more intangible things."

"Ellen has told me that I am...very much myself. As in I don't put up any kind of front. I can't help but wear my heart on my sleeve, and I've also gotten comfortable...for the *most* part, with that. And so consequently, I signal to whoever I'm talking with that they don't have to put up a front either. They can just be themselves. And I think this is modified greatly by the fact that I probably tell the truth to a fault. So..." He shrugged. "Yeah, I don't know, that's what I've got."

"Maybe it's the weed, but that makes sense," Chloe murmured. She stared at the joint in her hand for a moment before finally sighing heavily. "I guess...the truth of the situation is that I'm lonely enough to risk it. And you seem like a pretty safe bet. If an unusual one. Here, you want to kill this?"

"Yeah," he said, accepting the joint. He killed it off and put what remained in the ashtray on the coffee table in front of them, then ended up getting resettled with Chloe half in his lap, hugging him tightly against herself.

"I forgot how fucking nice this is," she murmured.

"What? Cuddling?" he asked.

"Yes."

"Me too."

"What? You have to do this every day."

"I mean before that. I was also in a self-imposed sexual and romantic exile before hooking up with Ellen. Not quite a year, but getting there. I know what it is to be touch starved. And saturated in loneliness."

"I'm sorry," she murmured, pulling him closer. "You're a really great guy. I wish you weren't lonely."

"Well, if nothing else, it helped highlight just how fucking awesome relationships that work are."

She laughed, a little bitterly. "Yeah. That work...mmm, I feel it. I'm a little...buzzy."

"What? Buzzy?"

"You don't feel buzzy?"

"...yeah, that's actually pretty accurate. Although I think for me it's closer to...floaty?" He looked at the TV. "So what do you wanna play?"

"Not sure yet," she murmured. "Can we just do this for a while? This is really, really nice."

He turned and kissed the top of her head. "Yeah, we can do that."

"Thank you."

...

Gabe smiled as he saw Ellen's reply: *She fell asleep on you? Honestly that's really cute. How's it going overall?*

He'd never been particularly great at texting one handed but he was managing given Chloe had his other arm.

Good. Food was good. Sex was amazing. Conversation was nice. We really connected. Pretty tired, so I'm gonna go to sleep soon.

She sent a response: *Okay, goodnight babe. Holly says goodnight, too. Should we plan to hang out tomorrow?*

He thought about it. Something told him yes. *Yeah, we'll all hang out. She needs more exposure to you two so she's not so intimidated.*

Ellen sent a laughing emoji. *Think it's gonna take a bit longer. Okay then, see you tomorrow. I love you, Gabe.*

He told her he loved her, and then he wished Holly goodnight and told her he loved her, too. As he was considering how to handle this particular situation, Chloe slowly opened her eyes. For a moment she looked confused, then unhappy.

"Oh no...I fell asleep," she murmured. "Shit man, I'm sorry."

"It's totally fine, Chloe," Gabe replied, taking her hand beneath the blanket and squeezing it gently. "Everything's cool."

"Oh...well, all right." She yawned. "What time is it?"

"Almost eleven."

"Damn. I'm still tired...should we go to bed?" she asked.

"Yeah. We should...you want to be carried to bed?"

She stared at him. "How the fuck did you know?"

He laughed. "I guessed."

"Yes, I would like that very much." He nodded and then got to his feet and scooped her up carefully. "Mmm...you're strong."

"Well, to be fair, you aren't particularly large," he replied, carrying her through the apartment back to the bedroom.

She giggled. "I guess so."

"Is this sweet girl going to disappear tomorrow?" he asked.

"...mostly," she admitted. "Being sleepy and stoned really takes my edge off. But I thought you wanted my bratty side."

"I do. I *really* do, but this is also very nice," he replied. "Here, grab the blanket, pull it back."

She did so and he placed her in the bed, then turned off the light and got in beside her. Immediately she pushed her back against his chest and pulled his arm over her.

"Gabe?" she murmured softly after a moment.

"Yeah?" he replied.

"Thank you."

"For what?"

"For being nice to me."

He kissed the back of her head. "You're welcome, Chloe. Goodnight."

"Goodnight," she whispered.

...

Gabe awoke the next morning with Chloe still pressed up against him.

It felt like a perfect way to wake up. A wonderful, naked woman against him, soft and warm and so very comfortable. He was very tempted to keep laying there, but then Chloe inhaled deeply and came awake, shifting in his embrace.

"I can feel that," she murmured.

"Uh...yeah. Can't help it," he replied awkwardly.

"It's between my thighs," she said softly, and slowly began to rub her thighs together, with his morning wood between it. He let out a small sound. "Does that feel good?"

"Yeah."

"I'm tempted to slip it right up inside me, but I promised you a big, sloppy blowjob."

"I'm horny enough for both," he replied, cupping

one of her breasts.

"You sure?" she asked.

"Oh yeah. And even if I'm wrong, right now, I'd rather come in your pussy than on your face."

She laughed. "Well, in that case," she began to reach down.

"I can handle it," he said, and shifted. She gasped as he penetrated her. "Holy shit you are fucking *wet,* Chloe."

"I'm very horny right now," she muttered.

"You okay with–"

"Good girl is gone, bad girl is here. Don't ask permission," she growled.

"Okay, you fucking asked for it, you slutty brat."

"Don't fucking call me–"

She let out a startled sound as he shoved her over onto her stomach, mounted her from behind, and began fucking her.

It was hard and fast and it didn't last long for either of them. He managed to get an orgasm out of her before he shot his load deep into her sweet goth pussy.

When he pulled out of her and rolled over onto his back, they both laid there panting for a moment. Then they got up and headed to the bathroom.

"Can I use your toothbrush?" he asked.

"Yeah. Will it weird you out if I take a piss?" she replied.

"No."

"Cool."

She turned on the shower, then sat down on the toilet. By the time he had finished brushing his teeth, she was finished, and they ended up in the shower together. Chloe took the water first, cleaning herself up, and then she grabbed a washrag and got down on her knees.

"All right," she murmured as she started rubbing his cock down, "let's see about this blowjob. Huh. You *are* getting hard again…"

"Told you."

She snorted and tossed the rag aside. "I guess you'd have to be pretty horny to keep up with Ellen *and* Holly." She seemed to consider something for a moment. "So does having a ton of sex make you more or less horny?"

"It seems counter-intuitive but more."

She laughed. "Is *that* why you're coming after me?"

"I mean...there's other reasons." Chloe pursed her lips and narrowed her eyes as she looked up at him. Gabe tapped his wrist right in front of her face. "Any day now, Chloe."

A new fire entered her green eyes and she slapped his hand aside. "Oh so *that's* how it's going to be now?"

"That is exactly how it's going to be now," he replied.

"Fucker," she muttered.

"Stop bitching, get to work."

She glared up at him, then gripped his erection, opened her mouth and stuck it in.

Watching her work was a study in arousal and pleasure. Her lips wrapped around his shaft, how smoothly she bobbed her head, the way she closed her eyes, like she was concentrating intensely. And the bliss, the feel of her lips dragging back and forth across his head, the hot, wet pleasure that grew and seeped into him.

She looked almost like a work of art, knelt there before him, nude and wet, her black hair dark and clinging to her head. Her big, pale breasts swaying with the motion of her oral sex. Even the way she posed.

Gabe gave himself up to her. They had shit to do and he didn't even try to hold back. He thought that maybe the fact that they had fucked like fifteen minutes ago would make him take longer, but she managed to get him off pretty fast.

"Going to go soon," he said.

Chloe shifted and upped her game, going faster, focusing on his head, and then right as he started letting off, she took it out of her mouth and started jacking him off. Watching his seed come out of him in hard spurts and spray onto her seductive, pale face was an unreal pleasure. In that moment, it really did come close to feeling like he was living a dream.

Even after being with Ellen and Holly, Emily and Isabella, Chloe's natural and intense beauty still left him thunderstruck.

He sprayed her face down with his seed, her hand working his cock until finally it was left dry-kicking and there was nothing left to give.

"Are you serious?" she asked.

He chuckled as she let go of his dick. "What?"

"This feels like a lot. How the fuck did you have this much left after coming in my pussy?" she replied.

"No idea."

She sighed. "Help me up, you fucking came on my eyes and I can't open them."

"Maybe I'll leave you down there."

"Gabe!"

He laughed again. "All right."

He took her hand and helped her get back to her feet. She turned her face to the showerhead and cleaned herself off. "You are so lucky. That shit is gross," she muttered.

"Can't say I disagree with either of those assessments," he replied.

"You think it's gross but you wanted to put it all over my face," Chloe said, turning back around to face him.

"I mean yeah."

"Why?"

"It feels good."

"It'd feel just as good if I sucked you dry or if you came on the floor here or even on my tits," she replied.

"Yeah, but coming on your face is like...I don't know, kind of like marking my territory?"

She snorted. "I see. So am I your territory now?"

"Yes."

She pursed her lips and crossed her arms and stared at him. He stared back at her. She finally sighed and shook her head. "This is going to take a while to figure out," she muttered.

"At least it'll be fun," he replied.

Chloe regained her grin. "Yeah, that's true." She suddenly froze and her eyes went wide. "Fuck! I forgot to fucking call in! Goddamnit!" she snapped.

She spent a moment hastily cleaning herself up, then got out and quickly dried off.

As she did this, Gabe started cleaning himself, thinking about the day ahead.

CHAPTER SEVEN

"So, everything good?" Gabe asked as he walked into the living room.

"Yeah," Chloe replied. She was sitting on her couch, staring at her phone. "They bitched but whatever. Yesterday was not an isolated incident. I just...fell for the classic trap."

"Which one?" he asked, coming to sit beside her.

"The one where you show what a great, hard worker you are and your reward is just more work and exploitation. Not a raise, not a promotion, not overtime, not benefits. Just exploitation. 'Hey, we could fire this other worker and make Chloe here do twice the work for the same amount of pay!'. Because that's the world we live in."

"Yep," he muttered.

"What makes it suck extra hard is that the woman who is second in command, Linda? She's actually *really* nice. If *she* was in charge, I'd actually be very cool with working there. But she isn't. The woman who actually owns the shop, Janet, is in charge, and she's a fucking bitch. I'll be honest, I hate what we collectively call 'work' so fucking much that your offer of being able to quit and not be homeless is genuinely tempting."

"Well...don't jump into anything before you figure out if you're comfortable with it. Or if *we're* all comfortable with it."

She laughed, a little bitterly. "Don't worry, that won't happen. I don't leap before I look anymore...I think."

They sat there together for a long moment in silence. Chloe seemed to be collecting her thoughts.

Finally, she sighed softly and turned to him. "So, what are we doing?"

"We figured it'd be a decent idea to hang out with Ellen and Holly for a little while. The four of us, out and about, getting to know each other. And Ellen, ever the pragmatist, figured we should start out by doing something annoying and getting it out of the way. Which is laptop shopping. I need a new laptop," he replied. "You cool with that?"

"Yeah, that's fine," she said. "I'm down. Can we get food after the laptop, though?"

"Definitely," he replied. "Come on."

They pulled on their shoes and their coats, (this time Chloe pulled on a lighter hoodie, as it wasn't so brutally cold out today), and headed up and out to his car. As they got in and started driving, he noticed Chloe was quiet and pensive.

"You doing okay?" he asked finally.

She sighed heavily. "Mostly."

"What's wrong?"

"I'm...frustrated. With myself. I've spent what feels like a long time...ugh, as fucking edgelord as it sounds, cultivating a persona. The persona of a person who knows what they're doing and has their shit together and doesn't get particularly bothered by things. And apparently it worked. Too well, if anything. But the reality is that I often feel like I'm just fucking cosplaying a mature adult who knows what the fuck she's doing.

"I'm kind of a bag of nerves right now. There's this part of me screaming in panic, trying to warn me that I'm putting *way* too much trust in you, in Ellen and Holly. That I'm fucking pathetic. I've spent so long trying to be independent and not rely on anyone else and apparently I'm willing to just throw it all away when a hot guy shows up and says the magic words."

Silence filled the car for a moment.

"Nothing to say to that?" she asked.

"This struck me as less results, more rant, unless I misread it," he replied.

She chuckled bitterly. "Spot on, actually. I guess I was just expecting you to defend yourself, even though I'm not attacking you. I'm just...verbally vomiting. But I wouldn't turn away a response."

"All right." Gabe rolled to a stop as the light ahead turned red. He readjusted himself in his seat. "So, do you feel more capable now than you did three years ago? Like in general?"

Chloe frowned, considered it, then slowly nodded. "Yeah, I'd say so."

"That's significant. Feeling like you've got a handle on things takes practice. Conversely, life is inherently chaotic, and most of us are swimming against the current by dint of being not rich. So it's always going to feel like a struggle until you finally make it. But...what I always hear, and I definitely heard this from Ellen, is that 'making it' changes as you succeed and age. What looked like a grand fucking slam success at twenty looks paltry at thirty. Not always, but often enough that it's a problem. But that's not even the most significant thing."

"What's the most significant thing?" she asked.

"You *do* have your shit together."

She didn't respond for a bit, staring out the window. "Do I?" she asked finally.

"Yeah. I mean, you've got your own apartment. As far as I know you're keeping up with your bills. You've got a car. Everything looks pretty neat. You take good care of yourself. You have a job. You're responsible...I don't know. At a glance from the inside, now that I *am* inside, it seems like you've got your shit together. I mean, Christ, just the fact that you've got an apartment all to yourself as a *barista* is pretty significant."

Again she was quiet. They started driving again as the light turned green. For a bit, they just rolled through the city, making their way towards the computer shop Ellen had told him to meet them at.

Finally, she sighed. "That's mostly true, but I don't *feel* like I have my shit together. I guess I should tell you now, I've got debt. Like, real debt. I still owe like fifty grand for college."

"Really? What'd you go to college for?" he replied. "Also, *tons* of people have shitloads of college debt. Or debt in general. College debt is actually pretty reasonable."

"I have a degree in advertising. For all the fucking good it did," she replied. "I don't really wanna talk about it right now."

"All right...feel better?"

"Yeah." She sighed suddenly. "Goddamnit. I'm trying to fucking woo you and you actually come to my apartment and hang out with me and I'm just an irritating bag of fucking nerves that needs to be constantly reassured."

"*Woo me?*" he replied.

She laughed. "Shut up."

"Okay, there's something we should probably talk about now."

"Uh-oh."

"It's not bad. It's good, actually. I've actually been through this with Ellen and Holly. U, how do I put this...? So, I'd say that, in general, I don't mind the uglier emotions. I'm not going to freak out if you start crying. I'm not going to walk away if you have a panic attack. I'm not going to be pissed off if you air out your unhappiness, your bitterness, your anger. And yeah, I'd like to have fun, have a good time, but I'm also all right with you needing a mental health day. Everything doesn't need to be sex and weed and jokes. Okay? You can be real with me, and I'll accept that."

"You might regret that," she replied.

He laughed. "So far I haven't. Ellen and Holly have broken down in front of me. More than once each, actually, because of bad things that happened to them, or because everything was getting to be just too much to handle. My point is that you don't need to be a sexy, mysterious, bratty goth chick all the time for me. It's going to sound so fucking cliched and trite, but...legitimately just be yourself around me."

"What if 'myself' isn't compatible with you?" she murmured.

"Then in all truth? I'd rather find out *now,* as opposed to a year or two down the road. I'm not promising to stick with you no matter what, because sometimes people just aren't meant to be together. Sometimes two awesome people make a terrible couple, or even just a not great couple. If we have to stop seeing each other because who you are isn't compatible with who I am, then so be it. And, to be clear, I'll be really unhappy about that, and I will miss you a lot, but I'm fucking done staying in relationships just because I'm scared of being alone."

"So am I," Chloe murmured. "And...you're right. About all of that. Hmm. You know, every hour we spend together, I see more of why you not only managed to land two *hot* girlfriends, but also Ellen and Holly specifically." She paused. "Well, Ellen.

Holly seems…"

Gabe looked over at her for a moment. "Yes? Holly seems what, Chloe?"

"Ah…thin ice. Sorry. Um, naive? I'm really not trying to talk shit on her."

He chuckled. "Well, you aren't necessarily wrong. Holly's sharp and kind and smart, but…yeah, she's a little naive. Probably less than you think, though. Not that I hold it against her. I still love her."

"Yeah, totally. I mean everyone's got flaws. But my original point is that you are *weirdly* good at navigating emotions. It's like a superpower or something. The amount of people who just *do not get* emotions or social situations is, well, there's a lot of them. Or well, not even don't *get,* more like don't *care.*

"And it's not like I'm not guilty of it. Sometimes I look back on certain things and wonder how the fuck I didn't understand when it should be super obvious…but hindsight is twenty-twenty or whatever they say. Oh! Shit, okay, I keep forgetting to ask this but now I just remembered and you're here: we had that party to celebrate you relaunching your books and launching new books, how is that going?"

"Well, it wasn't quite the lightning strike I had hoped it would be," he replied, "but I can't say it was a failure. Overall, there's an appreciable uptick in sales. But my caveman erotica…those two words sound so stupid together." He shook his head.

"No they don't! I mean it accurately describes it. How's it doing?" she asked.

"Better than anything else so far. It's made like three hundred bucks so far and the few reviews that people have left are all positive, so…" He shrugged.

"Wait, you released a novella about stone age

people fucking and it made three hundred dollars in, what, a week and a half? Two weeks? And you aren't fucking over the moon about that?"

"I mean I don't know, it's okay. And you've also got to understand how erotica books tend to sell. Usually you'll see most of the income that you're going to in the first couple of weeks, then a sharp decline and it becomes a trickle where you're lucky if it makes like ten bucks a month. So it's not like it's going to earn three hundred bucks every two weeks. I'd be a *lot* more excited. Plus it hasn't even cracked any of the top hundred lists for its sub-genres. Though it got close for one of them."

"Gabe! Come on! You were *just* fucking telling me about moving goalposts! Fucking enjoy this! From the outside, this seems like an absolute win. An unquestionable win. Do you know how many people put out a book and are happy to see three hundred dollars in a *year?*"

He sighed. "Okay so I understand what you're saying, but we aren't playing on the same field, if that makes sense? This isn't a hobby for me. This is my job. This is what I've put all my chips on. I need this to work. And I'm fucking twenty six. I could have been doing this like six years ago at least. Eight years, honestly, if I'd known. I'm pretty far behind. The way I see it, I should already be about ten times more successful than I am right now. I'm scrambling to catch up."

Chloe didn't respond for a moment. Gabe focused on driving. He could see the store now.

"Gabe...that's insane," she said finally.

"How? Which part?"

"The expectations of...Gabe! You are *twenty six.* Be happy you aren't trying to start this at thirty six, or forty six, or even older than that. Like, there are probably a lot of writers out there who would want to punch you in the face for saying that. You started doing this *months* ago. Not years, not decades, *months.* And you are already seeing results like this? Where are you going to be a year from now? Or six months? And you've got Ellen, who apparently has a lot of money, and someone's letting you live in their spare house for three hundred bucks a month, like–"

"I also understand what you're saying here, Chloe. But writing is an inherently unstable job. I could lose everything I've built tomorrow. Or what if something goes wrong? One of us gets cancer? Sadie decides she doesn't want us in the house anymore?" He sighed heavily as he pulled into the parking lot.

"I don't know," he said. "You're mostly right. I'm probably being paranoid. But this is *my* damage, or some of it at least. I'm terrified that some event will happen to me, something I have zero control over, and it will just fuck me for the rest of my life. And somehow that will be *my* fault according to a lot of people. I fucking hate capitalism and how it just takes and takes and takes and fuck you if you want something for yourself or your loved ones.

"Fuckheads will seriously sit there and defend this shit, like we should be grateful for the opportunity to be exploited until we fucking die, never being able to retire because greedy rich fucks hold onto every last goddamn cent, legally and illegally." He groaned as he parked in a spot and rubbed his eyes. "Sorry, this is kind of a thing with me."

"I mean I'm not going to disagree. I feel the same way," Chloe muttered.

"I can't believe there are people who claim the

system isn't rigged."

Chloe let out a short growl. "Anyone who says that is either a fucking moron or a liar, or a coward who refuses to see the world for how it really is." Now she sighed and shook her head. "It's kind of a thing with me, too. We should go do this or we'll just sit here in your car ranting about how monumentally fucked civilization is."

He laughed. "Yeah."

Gabe killed the engine and they got out.

CHAPTER EIGHT

Gabe spied Ellen as she and Holly got out of her car not too far away.

He froze. He could tell right away something was wrong.

Several thoughts snapped through his head.

She would have said something to him if something serious had happened last night or this morning. And if for some reason she hadn't, Holly would. But he had checked both their text chains after getting out of the shower and there was nothing.

He and Ellen had texted to set up this very event, and he hadn't sensed anything wrong.

Could something have happened on the way over?

No...couldn't be. Because if it had, Holly would be freaked out. She just didn't have the poker face that Ellen did, and if something had happened to bug Ellen visibly enough that he could tell immediately, then Holly should've been a lot worse.

She *did* seem a little sad, though.

Maybe it was something personal. It probably was, he realized as that thought hit, because she hadn't said anything. Meaning he shouldn't make a deal out of it. Though he fully intended to pursue it as soon as physically possible.

They closed the gap between each other, meeting in front of the main entrance.

He hugged Ellen. "Hey, babe. How you doing?"

She gave him a look that said 'well, cat's out of the bag', but it came and went so fast that he almost thought he'd imagined it. She offered a fairly winning smile. "Kinda tired. Did you two have fun?"

"Oh yeah," Gabe replied, still trying to assess as he shared a hug with Holly. "Hey, pretty girl."

"Hey," she said, kissing him. "Chloe," she added when they parted ways, nodding to her.

"Holly," Chloe replied. "Ellen. We, uh, definitely had fun."

Ellen laughed, and he was immensely relieved to find that it was a very genuine laugh. So, whatever it was, it probably wasn't that she'd suddenly had a change of heart about him fucking the shit out of Chloe.

"Still feeling nervous about this?" she asked.

"Uh...yeah," Chloe replied awkwardly.

"You don't have to. We still don't bite."

"Yeah, it's just, you know, it's gonna take some getting used to."

"I understand. But that's one of the nice things about this sort of thing: we don't have to rush through anything. Come on, I found a laptop online I think would be great for you based on everything you told me," Ellen said, leading them inside.

"Let's see it," he replied, all three of them following her.

Gabe was still trying to figure out how to approach it as they came into the computer store. She seemed a bit more natural now, calmer, and he began to wonder if maybe it was something that could wait. Maybe it really was just something personal and embarrassing that had happened, and she was feeling weird about it.

"Krystal has been complaining at me," Ellen said as she led them through the aisles.

"What about?" Gabe replied.

"You *know* what about."

"Chloe thought I was lying about Krystal." He

heard Chloe sigh softly.

"Really?" Holly asked.

"Oh yeah. We made a little wager."

"*Gabe,*" Chloe whispered harshly.

"What was the wager?" Ellen asked, growing more amused by the second.

"Don't answer her," Chloe growled.

Ellen stopped so abruptly that Gabe very nearly walked into her back. She turned slowly around. She looked...amused and annoyed. And maybe a little dangerous.

She locked eyes with Chloe. "What was that, Chloe?"

Gabe looked at his new goth...friend with benefits. He had heard the phrase 'deer caught in the headlights look' dozens of times throughout his life, but he had never seen it so utterly and perfectly personified as he did in that moment.

"N-nothing," she whispered, her eyes wide.

Ellen simply adjusted her smile to something calmer and turned back around. Looking at Chloe, Gabe couldn't tell if she was terrified or aroused.

In fact, he was confident that she couldn't tell either.

He had known that, at some point, he would see a clash between the two women. Their personalities were simply too strong, too antagonistic (even if it was almost wholly in jest), for it not to happen. He knew that, at some point, Chloe would step on Ellen's toes, even if accidentally. Like she just had.

Had it been an accident though?

...yes, he decided as they resumed following her, it was. She'd just sort of said it, and he could tell it hadn't even been directed at Ellen, simply at him. He suddenly got the idea that this wasn't even about what had happened in this very moment, but more it was an opportunity to set a precedent.

Ellen outranked Chloe when it came to Gabe.

He wondered what that ranking would look like a year from now, provided Chloe decided to join their little romantic circle.

Ellen would still be higher, he surmised. It was just who she was. Her personality was just too strong for any other outcome.

That and the fact that Chloe wanted to be put in her place.

"She had suck me off and let me paint her face," Gabe replied, making sure to keep his voice down.

The place was pretty empty, as it was a Tuesday afternoon, but still.

"Hot," Holly murmured.

"It was actually really hot," Gabe agreed. Chloe sighed again. "Stop complaining. You know you enjoyed yourself, on your knees, where you belong."

"*Fuck you,*" Chloe hissed.

He reached over and squeezed her ass, making her jump slightly. "You will later."

She growled, blushing intensely.

"You two are...um...it's almost like you were made for each other when you're like this," Holly murmured.

"It is seeming that way," Ellen agreed, stopping. "Here, this one. Take a look, tell me what you think."

He took a moment to look over the specs of the laptop on display. Decent RAM, decent storage, good size, not a terrible graphics card...

"Chloe, what do you think?" he asked.

She walked over and studied the specs. "You intending to game on this?"

"Not seriously. I try to keep games off my laptop

since it's for writing, net surfing, and music listening," he replied.

"Then it'll be great. Honestly you could stand to get something less powerful, but it's got an SSD and the specs look good, and that should get the job done just fine," she said.

"Perfect. I'm sold."

He grabbed one of the boxes and they headed for the checkout. They opted in for the warranty, Ellen paid, and then they headed back outside.

"Okay, now what?" Ellen asked.

"It's a decent day out," Gabe replied, "how about we get some burgers for lunch and drive to a park, eat somewhere nice? Talk about things."

"Sounds good to me," Holly said.

"Yeah," Ellen agreed.

"I'm down. I'm starving," Chloe replied.

"Perfect. We'll hit Patties and then figure out where to go from there."

"They have the best fucking fries ever," Holly said.

"I know a really cool park, it has this overlook we can get to pretty easily, and there's a few picnic tables there," Chloe said.

"Perfect. Let's do it," Gabe replied. Then he hesitated. He knew that this was going to bother him if he didn't at least try to do something about it. "Actually, Ellen, come here a minute. Be right back," he said to Holly and Chloe.

He led her far enough away that they could have a private word.

"Is everything okay?" he asked.

She smiled, a little ruefully. "Yeah, I'm fine."

"Something's off, Ellen."

"I know. It's really not a big deal. But I know it's

going to lodge in your mind until we talk about it, so: I had some really bad nightmares last night. That's all it is."

"What about?" he asked.

"That you broke up with me. Also snakes were in there somewhere. And a tornado. It was a really chaotic bout of nightmares. I woke up feeling pretty shitty, but it's fine. I'm okay."

"Why didn't you say something? I would've come home, or talked to you at least. You could've woken me up–"

"Jesus Christ, Gabe, I'm a big girl. I can handle a few nightmares," she said.

"That isn't what this is about, Ellen," he persisted. "This isn't me needing to hover over you and coddle you every time you bump your knee. This is me needing you to understand that if you need me, for whatever reason, even bad nightmares, I will be there. I will pick up the phone, I will text you, I will drive home. I don't care what I'm doing. If you need to talk, about anything, you are the priority in my life. You and Holly. I told her the exact same thing."

She looked at him for a moment, then chewed on her lower lip. "Sorry," she murmured finally. "You're right...and I appreciate it. I *really* appreciate it. Sorry I got defensive. And I hear you, but it really is okay. I wasn't having a panic attack, I didn't break down crying, I didn't freak out. It was just a particularly bad nightmare, and Holly was there, and she was there with me to calm me down. And...if I had really needed you, I would have called."

He nodded and hugged her. She held him tightly. "Okay. I just...sometimes I worry that you've spent so long being independent that you're going to slip into fighting me on taking care of you."

"It's not an unreasonable fear," she muttered. "Traditionally speaking, being weak in front of my significant others has not gone well. But you're right about that, too."

As they pulled back, he looked up at her. "Just to double check, you're still good about me and Chloe, right?"

She laughed easily. "Yes, Gabe. I am. Trust me. The nightmare wasn't even that you left me for Chloe. It was more like...you were just gone? Like I woke up and you weren't there. I think it was just because you weren't in the bed. I had a nightmare when you went to sleep with Isabella. I think it's just...I miss you. But I didn't want to say anything because I don't want you to stop going and spending the night elsewhere just because it kind of freaks me out when I'm sleeping. I've still got Holly and I'll be fine."

"All right...thank you for telling me. I will do my best not to let this have too much of an impact on future decision making," he said.

She laughed. "I swear, sometimes our conversations sound like a generic template for how to talk about your feelings with your spouse."

Gabe considered that for a moment, then shrugged. "Maybe, but it works. And it's not like we've got an audience. I'd rather talk to you in a way that makes sense to us."

"Yep. Now let's get burgers. I kinda want to grill Chloe about her life." He looked at her more closely. "Don't worry, not too much, but I do want to get to know her better."

"Fair," he replied.

They shared a kiss and then headed back to their respective cars. As they pulled out of the parking lot and began making for the burger place, Chloe finally cleared her throat.

"So...was that about, uh, our little interaction in the store?" she asked.

"Oh no, not at all," he replied. "That was completely independent of you."

"Huh. So you're just gonna throw me to the wolves then?"

He laughed. "What?! How is that your takeaway from this?"

"I was mostly joking, just...my life almost legit passed before my eyes. The way she looked at me...that woman would kill for you, Gabe. As in, 'blood splashing her face and soaking her hands, ripping a motherfucker's throat out with her bare fingers' kill for you. I saw it in her eyes. They said: He is *mine,* and nothing on Earth, not God nor Satan, can get between us."

"That's...a little intense, but not entirely inaccurate," he replied. "You still scared of her?"

"Yes...but strangely, less so now? I kinda feel like I saw her at her most intense, just for a second, and...I think I can handle it."

"It's not like you'll be fighting all the time." He paused. "I mean, I hope not."

"Hmm...okay, let's throw out a theoretical. Ellen and I are arguing. Who do you side with?"

He laughed loudly. "Oh dear...Chloe, it doesn't work like that."

"Okay what the fuck does *that* mean?"

"It means that, while I recognize it's a good idea to present a united front in public...I take things on a case-by-case basis. The closest answer I can give you is: I will side with whoever is correct. But it's more complicated than that. I will attempt to defuse the situation and make sure that both you and Ellen are heard by each other. Because in my experience, *too many* arguments sprout from misunderstanding, and then just being stubborn, digging in, and doubling down endlessly. That being said, if you fucked up, I will let you know that you fucked up. And I expect the same thing from you. But this only works if everyone is acting in good faith," he replied.

"Okay holy fuck," Chloe muttered.

"What?"

"Everything you just said just...it sort of brought some of the more unpleasant aspects of myself into focus in a way I've never really been able to fully articulate. That's exactly what I used to do, argue just to win. And sometimes still do. Hmm." She laughed uncomfortably. "You know I've heard the idea of someone 'stealing your heart' and kind of making you fall for them, but I've never...mmm. I need think."

Gabe considered, very briefly, pushing it. Just a little. But he quickly decided against it.

So he drove on in silence.

CHAPTER NINE

"You nervous?" Gabe asked as they pulled into the lot beside the park she'd brought them to.

"Yeah," Chloe replied. "These are pretty uncharted waters for me. I don't know if there might be monsters lurking beneath the waves."

"Fair. But you've got someone you trust with you helping you guide the boat," he said.

"That's true. But...just because I trust doesn't necessarily mean *I* trust you...okay that makes no fucking sense," she muttered.

"No, I get it. Your instincts trust me, but you aren't your instincts."

"Okay, yeah, that. Exactly."

"Well, maybe this'll help: at any moment, you can walk away. Although I would prefer that you not straight up ghost us. We would deeply appreciate a straightforward 'I am walking away' message," he replied.

"Don't worry, I don't plan on ghosting you. But...you're right. I can walk away if I want to."

He parked and turned off the engine, then twisted and looked at her. "Whatever happens, I want you to believe that we like you, and we want this to work. But, more than that, we want this to be a pleasant experience. We don't thrive on making people feel bad. We aren't cruel. We're...cozy." He paused. "Except for when we're engaging with your fucking brattiness."

"Oh fuck off," she replied immediately, rolling her eyes, "pretending like you're annoyed by that."

He laughed softly. "You'd better watch your mouth, Chloe."

She leaned in, her eyes narrowing. "Or *what?*"

"Or I'll put it to use, right here in this car."

"You wouldn't *dare.*"

"Why don't you test me? Find out for yourself?"

She pressed her lips together, glaring at him, then sighed and got out. He laughed and joined her. They took their meals up a short path that led to a shelf of land fringed by a wooden fence and supported a trio of picnic tables.

"Holy shit," Ellen said as she set her food down on one of the tables and slowly walked up to the fence. "This is a fantastic view...I had no idea this was here."

"Yeah…" Holly murmured, joining her, staring almost like she was in a trance.

"Do you want to take a picture?" Gabe asked, standing beside her.

"Yeah." She began pulling her phone out of her purse.

It *was* a fantastic view. They were maybe thirty or forty feet up, and below them was a sprawl of paths and forestry. Dead or dying trees swayed gently in the winds. The pale sunlight painted everything in a faint luminescence that gave it a vaguely surreal edge.

"Oh my God, look," Chloe said, pointing as she joined them. "A deer. No wait, two."

"Deer are so cute," Ellen replied. "I'd give so much to have a deer I could reliably pet. And also it would come and lay down beside me and put its head in my lap. It would be like having a giant dog-cat."

"That would be pretty awesome," Gabe replied.

"You know it just occurred to me that we never really discussed pets," Ellen said.

"How do you feel about it?" he asked.

"I've always wanted a cat but I gave up that dream because I was so busy so often that it just didn't feel fair to the pet," she replied. "But...that's not a factor anymore."

"I'd *love* a cat. A few cats. Or maybe some mice or rats," Holly replied as she lined up her shot. "Honestly anything but fish or birds."

"Why not fish or birds?" Chloe asked.

"It just seems really cruel. I mean a cat or a dog, like they have the whole house and the yard. But you can't really do that with a bird. They have to spend too much time in cages, and they can *fly*. Same concept with fish, only swimming instead of flying, and they have even less freedom unless you get like a massive tank. And they're so expensive, to buy *and* maintain."

"How about you?" Gabe asked, looking at Chloe.

"Me? Um, I'm pretty ambivalent I guess. Well...I guess that's not true. I'd really just be okay with a cat or two. I don't really like dogs." She paused, considered that. "Well, I mean dogs are cool in general, I guess, it's just I've run into too many of them that are just not trained at all. Constantly barking, constantly jumping all over you, constantly tearing shit up, getting into your food," she replied.

"I could see having a few cats," Gabe said after some consideration.

"Should we visit some pet places?" Ellen asked.

"Maybe after winter," he replied. "We're still...figuring things out."

"That's true," Ellen murmured, glancing briefly at Chloe.

Holly took her picture and, after a moment more of marveling at the view, they went back to the table and began eating.

"Okay," Ellen said after a bit, "so, Chloe. Tell us about yourself. I think it's a fair ask, given you've deep-throated our man at least twice now." Holly giggled.

Chloe blushed a little and cleared her throat. "That's fair," she agreed. "Although there's not a lot."

"Oh come on, you're, what, twenty six, twenty seven?" Ellen replied.

"Twenty five."

"Twenty five years old. That's a fair amount of time."

"I guess, but it definitely doesn't feel like my life has been interesting. I was born and raised here, in this city. Had a pretty normal childhood. Both my parents are still alive and together. I've got one older sister. Had what I'd call an upper lower class childhood and there was definitely some struggle there, although it's not like we were ever homeless or anything.

"But there were definitely stretches of time without the phone or electricity or hot water because bills were too high. But then things got better around high school when my dad caught a lucky break and got a better job. I graduated from high school and my mom was pretty on my ass to go to college, so I'd been prepping all through senior year because I figured it made the most sense. And...well, I sure went to college all right," she muttered, rolling her eyes.

"Didn't go well, I take it?" Ellen asked.

"Nope. I got a degree in advertising and now I'm fucking fifty grand in debt and I don't have a job in advertising. And I fucking *tried,* too. The only places where there was even a *chance* of it happening were places I just do not want to live. And so here I am, a couple years later, putting together a living being a barista and trying to be a gamer girl, trademark."

"So you said you stream horror games," Ellen said. Chloe nodded. "I'm kind of surprised you haven't blown up already. It seems like you've got everything the internet loves. I mean, and hates, or loves to hate, but either way: lots of attention."

"In truth, I haven't seriously been trying. And I've only been at it for a few months now. So...that's my application."

Ellen snorted. "Your *application?*"

"Yeah. To be Gabe's girlfriend."

"That seems a little...clinical," Gabe said.

Chloe sighed. "I'm so bad at being sarcastic."

"Or too good at it," Holly said.

"I feel like you're bad at it if no one gets you're being sarcastic," Chloe replied.

"Maybe," Ellen agreed. "You got any questions for us?"

"Yeah, a lot," Chloe replied.

"Fire away."

"Okay. First things first, you both *seriously* don't have any jealousy issues? Because we had *incredible* sex last night. And this morning, actually. And he fucking ate me like I've *never* been eaten before," Chloe said.

Gabe gave her a sidelong glance. It almost seemed like she was actually trying to provoke them. Maybe she was. Or testing them, at least.

"I think that's hot," Holly replied.

"Honestly me too," Ellen said. "But I understand why you're asking. And I can say that I'm not jealous. I look at it like this: jealousy comes from insecurity. It's not always rational. But I'm pretty fucking secure in my relationship with Gabe."

"Hmm. How about you?" Chloe asked, looking at Holly. "It really doesn't bother you? The idea of other girls fucking your boyfriend's brains out?"

"No," Holly replied with a shrug. "I...kinda like it, to be honest."

"Really?"

"Yeah. There's just something about it." She laughed awkwardly. "I can't fully explain it. It's just...impressive? And hot? I never thought I'd like it, but I also didn't really think about it too much before we started dating."

Chloe stared at her for a moment, then slowly nodded. "Yeah, it makes a certain kind of sense. I mean it's certainly impressive. Okay, next question: do you all seriously never fight?"

They all looked at each other for a moment, then nodded.

"Yeah, basically," Gabe replied. "Although admittedly we're kind of early in the relationship."

"We'll get really pissed at each other eventually," Ellen said. "But what matters is how we're going to handle it. And I...probably will need some practice and patience, because I definitely have an unhealthy relationship with arguing. I was taught to go for the fucking throat."

"Oh, wow. Jeez. That's...intense," Chloe murmured.

"Don't worry. I'm not going to go for your throat," Ellen replied. "Or, if I do...Gabe will be disappointed in me, and that will *very much* stop me from doing it again, I imagine."

"We abide by a system of calm resolution," Gabe said.

"That's a way to put it," Ellen murmured. "An

accurate way, to be clear. Just-ignore me. I'm not used to dating someone who is articulate."

"All right. Third question: if I do...pursue this, you both realize that nothing sexy will be happening between us? You both are...*overwhelmingly* beautiful, but I'm pretty straight."

"Yeah, we understand that," Ellen said as Holly nodded.

"Okay, uh...I guess this one is a bit more abstract. I'm kind of goal-oriented, in a broader sense, so let's say I agree to this. I start dating Gabe, I throw my lot in with you guys, what exactly are our plans, like, in general? Like where are we in five years? Because If I *do* decide to do this, it won't be casually."

"Our plan, as a group, is essentially to go our own way. We're aiming to find a way to live on our own, and explore our creative passions, and also be financially stable, and just generally try to live our lives in a way that makes it generally enjoyable. So, I guess, ideally, in five years, I'd see us more or less living the same life we are now, with a bit more stability, and probably a bigger house. Well, ideally a bigger house, anyway," he replied.

"Okay...so, Gabe pretty much offered to have me move in, quit my job, and pursue being a streamer. Which is a pretty big gamble. Would you say that's an accurate portrayal of what's on the table?" she asked.

"Yeah," Holly replied, "although Ellen and Gabe are really the ones in charge. I'm just kind of...you know, figuring things out. I'm happy to let them make choices."

"I'd say it's accurate," Ellen said, "but...hmm. I feel like four people is really pushing it for our place."

"Yeah..." Gabe said. "That's something we'll have to, uh, figure out. Although we've got time."

"About that," Chloe replied awkwardly.

"Yeah?" he asked.

"So my lease is actually up the first of next year. And my apartment is kind of a sweet deal. Like, it took *forever* to find it. And I'm extremely disinclined from moving. And I'll basically be locked in for another year..."

"So we need to figure this out before January first," Ellen murmured.

"Yeah...sorry."

"Well, it's not your fault. Hmm. I think a good next step would be for you to actually *see* our house and see if it's just flat out a non-starter or if you can maybe envision making it work," Ellen said.

"Yes. That's a good idea. I have one more question for now. It's kinda a big one."

"We're listening," Gabe replied.

"How do you all feel about kids? I feel like that's a fair ask, given the potential longevity of what we're discussing."

Gabe happened to be looking at Ellen as she asked that, and something passed across her face. It came and went so quickly he almost missed it, but it was...surprise? No. Not quite surprise. Discomfort? He wasn't sure.

It was *something* though.

"Well, I do not want to be pregnant," Ellen said, "but I would not mind raising children with Gabe and Holly."

"I want to be a mother," Holly replied. "And, as I've told Gabe before, I'd be okay with him getting me very pregnant."

"I think I *heard* your erection pop into place just

now," Ellen said, smirking at him.

Gabe sighed. "Yes. *Any*way, as I said earlier, I'm...uncertain. I know it's not a great idea right now. I'm figuring it out."

"Cool. For the record, I'm about in the same spot myself...well, that's it. That's all I've got for the moment," Chloe said.

"Perfect. So, house?" he asked. They were pretty much finished with their meals by now, and it was starting to get a bit colder.

"Yes...although…" Chloe paused, giving Ellen and Holly an appraising, almost cautious look. They both looked back, waiting. She shifted around awkwardly, then looked at Gabe. "So I know I asked you not to tell them, and I was pretty embarrassed, but...actually being here, I'm weirdly cool with it all of a sudden? So...wanna go to a sex shop?"

"Hell yes," Gabe replied immediately.

"Ooh, what filthy thing do you want from my boyfriend?" Ellen asked, leaning forward.

"I would like him to spank me. With a paddle. And his hand. For being a bad girl," Chloe replied. Despite her assertion, she had begun to blush fiercely again.

"That is *really* hot," Holly murmured.

"Yeah actually it is," Ellen said. "And clearly he's into it."

Gabe stood up and began gathering his trash.

They all laughed. "And he's *eager,*" Ellen added.

"Very," Gabe agreed. "Chloe has such a bitchy mouth and such a fat, spankable ass."

"Oh *fuck* you, asshole," Chloe growled immediately.

"I'm just telling the truth about your huge ass, Chloe. Now," he pulled her to her feet and then gave her ass a smack, "get that big ass in my car."

She glared him for a moment, her lips pressed tightly together. Then, without a word, she grabbed her purse and began walking to his car.

"Chloe," he said, and she stopped. "You forgot to throw away your trash."

She began walking again without saying a word and flipped him off.

"Gabe...you two seriously fit together like two pieces of a puzzle," Ellen murmured as he laughed and gathered up her trash.

"Apparently," he replied, throwing it away in the nearby trashcan. "She's going to get such a fucking spanking."

"Bare ass or with her pants still on?" Holly asked.

"First one, then the other," Gabe replied.

They began heading for their cars.

CHAPTER TEN

"Should've asked this sooner," Chloe said suddenly, "but what's off the table? Like, when we're 'fighting'?"

"Other women I've been emotionally or physically intimate with," Gabe replied. "Don't talk shit on them."

"Okay. Anything else?"

He thought about it. "Honestly nothing springs to mind."

"Interesting. So, for example, if when we're doing our back and forth arguing, I call you fuck ugly…"

"You'd kind of insulting yourself there, dipshit."

"You fucking...you *shit!* Okay, fine! What about your dick? I know that's like *such* a thing for guys. If I tell you that you have an underwhelming cock, what are you going to do about it?"

"Point out your *obvious* lie because it seems to make you scream just fine," Gabe replied. "While I'm spanking the fuck out of you."

She sighed heavily. "You are such a fucking prick."

"Yeah, *I* am the prick here. Maybe if you wouldn't say stupid things I wouldn't have to call you fucking stupid," he replied.

"If you weren't driving I would be genuinely tempted to lay hands on you," she growled.

"Okay, here's a question for *you?* Can I slap you?" he asked.

"Do you want to?"

"Yes."

"You mean like a full-on slap? Like hard?"

"Yes."

"...yeah, you can do that. *Not* in public, though."

"Dear God, Chloe, of *course* not in public. Nothing physical in public. No shouting in public, either."

"Obviously," she muttered. "I'm not fucking trashy."

"Yeah okay."

"I am *not* trashy you fucking shit stain!"

"How about choking?" Gabe asked. Chloe went silent. He glanced quickly over at her. She was blushing fiercely now and not meeting his eyes. "So it seems like you *really* would like it if I wrapped my hands around your throat."

"Yes, but...you *have* to be careful. But yes, I would thoroughly enjoy that. I mean, I think. I've never actually...indulged. But seriously, you'd have to be careful."

"Chloe, I promise that I have your safety in mind above all else whenever we're engaging in anything dangerous. I would never actually hurt you. I mean...beyond whatever you wanted. You know what I mean. I wouldn't do something if I thought there was a *real* risk of you getting genuinely hurt," he said, reaching over and touching her thigh for a moment.

"I know," she murmured. "I wouldn't even be talking about this if I didn't trust you. But it is good to hear it. It's such a thing nowadays, apparently."

"What is?" he asked.

"Choking, hitting, like really rough sex. The amount of stories I've heard from women who've just had that shit sprung on them. Like literally no warning, just straight up *strangulation* out of nowhere. Guys have this fucked idea that apparently every single women secretly wants it and will not only be cool with it being just forced on them, but would be *thrilled* by it, and are actively gagging for it."

"I've heard some of that...fuck, I couldn't imagine just straight up doing that. Just so we're clear, I will *always* ask you before trying something new. Much as it annoys you."

She sighed heavily. "I know I was kind of sending mixed signals, it's just…"

"I get it. I was teasing. Just a little. I understand that this is kind of a weird situation."

"Yeah, that's one way of putting it."

She was quiet for another moment. "Hmm, okay, how about your writing? Would it piss you off if I insulted your writing?"

"Well...I don't know for sure. That's one of those things where I think I'll have to just experience it to find it. I mean, I'll tell you if I realize something's off limits, or if something becomes off limits. But at a guess, I'd say that's farther up the anger spectrum and you should save it for when you *really* want to push my buttons."

"Noted," she said with a devilish smirk.

Gabe glanced at her again, then sighed softly. "Sometimes I think I don't really know what I'm getting into." Chloe laughed. "On the other hand," he murmured, reaching over and laying a hand on her thigh, "sometimes I think *you* don't know what you're getting into."

He gave it a squeeze. She jumped and let out a little shriek. "*Gabe!*"

He laughed exactly as she just had.

...

The sex shop that Chloe led them to turned out to be an inconspicuous little store with a small pink sign and tinted windows.

The woman behind the counter checked all their IDs to make sure they were of legal age, and then they were allowed to peruse as desired. Gabe had to admit that he'd been envisioning something a little different when he'd been on approach. Maybe something seedier, or dimmer, or just generally cheaper.

But it was none of that. The place, which called itself Pink Paradise, was well lit, clean, and quite organized. It was a nice place, and they seemed to have it to themselves. Gabe studied each of his companions as they began moving through the shop.

Holly looked happy, Ellen looked fairly at ease and vaguely calculating, and Chloe looked awkward.

"I've never actually been inside a place like this before," she murmured as they walked along one wall.

"How are you feeling about it?" he replied.

"Awkward."

"I kinda thought you'd be more at home here."

"What gave you that idea?" she muttered.

"I'm not sure, just a little...disappointing."

She shot him a look. "Fuck you," she whispered.

"Later dear," he replied, patting her on her jeans clad ass. She growled something at him and he chuckled. "You want to make scene here?"

"You're so fucking getting it later," Chloe growled under her breath.

"I think you are the one who's going to be getting it later. Now..." he said, stopping as they came before a lot of different paddles, "choose which one you want."

She looked over at him sharply. "Are you serious? You're going to make *me* pick?"

"Yes."

"Do you have any idea—"

He stepped closer to her, looking her in the eye. "You've been a *bad* girl, Chloe, and you are absolutely going to be punished for it later. So you'll do as I tell you and pick which one I'm going to use on you."

She sighed petulantly. "You're too good at this," she muttered, turning to face the paddles.

"Stay," he said, and walked over to Holly. "Hey you."

"Hello, boyfriend," she replied merrily. She was staring at handcuffs.

"You thinking of getting one?"

"I am *definitely* getting two," she replied. "After we started getting into it, I, uh, renewed my interest in looking up BDSM porn. And...pictures of women being cuffed or tied down, uh, it *really* does things to me. And I want you to cuff me. And hold me down. And fuck me. And scream at me," she continued, her voice getting quieter as she went on.

"And pull your hair?" he asked.

She looked at him. "How'd you know?"

"Intuition."

She laughed awkwardly, blushing. "Well...yeah. Yes." She glanced over at Chloe. "It's going well, I take it?"

"Yeah, pretty well," he replied. "She...*really* brings certain aspects out in me that, honestly, before getting together with Ellen, I seriously didn't know were so strong. Or on point."

"It's really nice," she murmured. "So...this really

doesn't weird you out? All the things I want you to do to me?"

"No, Holly," he replied, taking her hand and kissing the back of it. "It really doesn't. Trust me, if you asked me to do something I didn't like, I'd tell you."

"I do trust that, it's just...I don't know, sometimes, well, more than sometimes, this feels *way* too good to be true. And I feel like I'm missing something huge."

"Kind of like this feeling of 'this is way easier than I thought it was going to be...I'm doing it wrong, aren't I?, you mean?"

"Yes, that, exactly," she replied immediately. "I hate it."

"I actually know exactly how you feel. You and Ellen and Chloe are sometimes just too good to be true. I'm waiting for the other shoe to drop. Or I'm wondering how I'm going to fuck this up. But...it's been going away recently."

"Really? Why?"

"I don't know. I think some of it is just time. Time is passing and things are actually going well. You'll feel better as the days pass, babe," Gabe replied.

Holly focused on him suddenly, stared for a few seconds, and then wrapped him in a tight hug. He was a little confused, but he hugged her back, regardless.

"What's this?" he murmured.

"I'm just...suddenly a little overwhelmed by good feelings," she murmured. "I don't know if I've really made it clear but...I haven't really had people in my life who actually, you know, take care of me. Like people who worry about me and try to reassure me and make me feel better if I'm sad. I mean, you met my family. And my friends. Who I have just decided not to be friends with anymore. And I told you about my only boyfriend.

"I had some good friends in school, and there were some nice people in college, but...I haven't had what I would call love in my life for a long time. Not real love, not like this. I'm looking back on, well, my entire fucking life, and I'm realizing that pretty much everyone who was involved with me in any serious way was just trying to get something from me, or use me somehow. And you and Ellen don't do that. At all.

"I can be sad, I can want to be alone, I can be angry, I can be...not perfect, and you will do whatever it is you think will help me, or whatever I ask. And that's a really good feeling, but also, realizing that you've gone most of your life without that, and then finally knowing what it *is?* That's...it's a lot. I guess I'm kind of mourning what could have been, and I'm also just ridiculously grateful for what is now."

Gabe held her a little closer and kissed the top of her head. "I hate that you had to put up with this for so long."

"I know. I'm sorry I'm talking about it again, I know it upsets you a lot, just–"

"No, Holly, it's fine. You should talk about this stuff. I want you to if it'll make you feel better."

"I really appreciate it." They stood there together for a moment more, then she gently disengaged herself from him and smiled. "Thanks," she said. "I feel better now." She glanced over. "I think I want to go talk with Chloe for a little bit about...shared interests."

He laughed softly and kissed her. "Have fun."

She nodded and headed off after grabbing two pairs of cuffs that she'd been eyeing. Gabe watched her go and studied the two women as they began talking. Chloe looked like she was really putting some thought into the paddles.

Gabe looked over at Ellen and found her standing in front of a display that contained a lot of eye-masks. He walked over.

"Hey," she murmured, "everything okay?"

"Yeah. Holly was just a little emotional over how good we treat her," he replied.

"Mmm. I know how she feels."

"Honestly, so do I," Gabe replied. He hesitated a moment, then decided he might as well just push forward. "So...earlier, when Chloe was talking about pregnancy...you had a look."

"Did I?" Ellen murmured.

"Yes. You did."

"Fuck's sake," she whispered after a moment. "I literally cannot keep *anything* from you."

"Is there a problem?" he asked, feeling icy worry flood his gut. "Oh man, tell me there isn't a pregnancy scare with someone."

"No," Ellen said firmly. "It's not that. Believe me, I would've told you if it was that. There's no pregnancy scare, there's no-that's not even on the radar."

"But there *is* something?" he asked.

She sighed, then stepped closer and lowered her voice so much he had to lean in to hear her. "Okay, so...I was going to wait until I heard more, and I *could* be wrong, but I don't think I am. But...ah man, this is kind of awkward...I think Abby and Emily might actually be discussing the possibility of asking you to be a sperm donor. For Abby. To get pregnant."

Gabe was still and silent for several long moments. "And by donor, you mean..."

"I mean have unprotected sex with her until she gets pregnant," Ellen replied softly. "How does that make you feel?"

"Um...honestly? My first reaction is excitement," Gabe admitted.

She laughed and shook her head. "Of course. Kind of a massive fantasy scenario. You get to fuck a new woman, a married woman, and a hot woman, in an attempt to impregnate her with a child you won't have to raise, *and* she's pretty much a lesbian. I know that's, like, a whole thing for a lot of guys."

"It's...a fairly awkward thing," Gabe murmured.

"No, I get it. I mean I'd be a huge hypocrite if I gave you shit for very badly wanting to have sex with a lesbian because I very badly want to have sex with a straight woman right now. If I thought there was a chance, I would so go after Chloe. But it's how we approach it or even if we approach it at all that's the difference.

"There's no harm in asking, typically. But...look, don't bring this up to *anyone,* okay, babe? Not Chloe, not even Holly, especially not Em and Abby. No one. Because she hasn't even directly said anything, she's just...made several statements, asked several questions that makes me believe it. I *could* be wrong."

"Don't worry, I will keep my mouth shut about this," Gabe replied.

"Thank you."

"So how do *you* feel about it?" he asked.

"I feel like it'd be a nice thing to do," she replied.

"You *seriously* wouldn't have a problem with me knocking another woman up?"

"Provided our legal asses are covered and everyone is happy and consenting, no, I don't have a problem with it. I doubt Holly will either, although obviously we'll have a discussion with her. And Chloe."

"Provided she actually joins us," Gabe murmured.

"Oh, she's joining us," Ellen replied.

"You seem really confident still."

"Gabe. She's hooked on you. It's pretty obvious to anyone with eyes. Or ears. I can hear it in her voice. The way she talks with you? Trust me. It's happening."

"That's pretty great to hear because..." He glanced at Chloe. She and Holly seemed to be talking animatedly and happily now. "She is *so* fucking hot. And so compatible with me."

"She really is, on both accounts," Ellen agreed. "Now...I think we should get a few of these masks. Sex and spicy stuff is supposed to be even hotter if you can't see. Also, I want to buy me and Holly some really nice vibrators. I *really* want you to use one on me when you're fucking me, or I want to be able to use it while I watch you and Holly or you and Chloe or you and whatever other women you pull into our bed."

"That sounds good to me," he replied.

"Sweet, come on," Ellen said, grabbing a few of the masks and then leading him elsewhere in the sex shop.

CHAPTER ELEVEN

"Okay, you were right, this is a lot smaller than I was picturing," Chloe murmured as they parked in the driveway of his house.

"Gee thanks," he replied.

"Sorry. I mean, it's nice. I like it, I just clearly had a different idea of how you all were living. But no, this is nice. Honestly I'm jealous. I'd love to have a house instead of an apartment. It's been apartments or dorms ever since I moved out."

"I *really* understand that. The fucking people I lived with up until now…" He shook his head. "Come on, let's give you the tour."

They got out and the four of them headed inside. Holly looked positively ecstatic, peeking into the bag that held her cuffs and the eye mask and the vibrator she'd ended up choosing. Ellen looked rather pleased with herself.

"Okay, living room," Gabe said as they came in and got out of their shoes and coats. "Got the couch recently. And here is my office…"

He led her slowly through the house, showing her every room and trying to gauge her reaction. She looked a little reserved, but he thought that might be because she felt awkward about what she'd said in the car.

By the end of it, they were all gathered in the bedroom. Holly was getting her handcuffs eagerly out of the packaging and Ellen was doing the same with their vibrators. She had gone for the large ones that reminded Gabe of microphones.

"So, what do you think? Do you see it working at all?" he asked as Chloe sat down on the foot of the bed.

"It's definitely not a no," she replied. "This place is kind of cramped, though. But...I mean I did a few years in a dorm room and it didn't bother me that much really. Really, my biggest thing is, where would I set up my gaming rig?"

"Yeah, that's what I've been thinking about," Gabe said. "I feel like, realistically, the only two spots we could do it are either the kitchen or my office."

"I'd feel pretty shitty about stealing your office," she murmured.

"We'd be splitting it, and yeah, it wouldn't be ideal, but I'd rather have you here and give up half my office half the time, if we're being honest."

Chloe's beautiful lips quirked into a smirk. "You want me that bad?"

"Yes. I do."

"Well..." She hesitated as her phone started ringing. She sighed heavily and pulled it out of her purse. "Ugh, great, my mom. Hold on."

She got up and walked into the hallway, then answered the phone.

"Hey, mom. What? No, I'm not..." A sigh. "Of course you'd pick today to-look mom, I just needed a mental health day, okay?...no. Seriously I'm-what? She is? Fucking of course it'd be today. No, I'm-yeah, okay. Yeah...okay. Yes, I'll meet you there. Okay. Love you too, bye."

Chloe sighed heavily, then groaned, then let out a growl of frustration as she came back into the bedroom and marched over to her purse. She shoved her phone back in and picked it up. "So, my mom went by the coffee shop looking for me, of course. And, of course, my sister is in town early for an extended holiday. And I...am not ready to try and explain all this to them. And it actually has been a while since I've seen my sister, so…"

She frowned awkwardly as she looked at them.

"It's fine," Gabe replied. "You actually like your family, you should spend time with them."

"Thanks...wait, do you *all* not get along with your families?" she asked.

"We have all separated from our families because they are horrible people," Ellen replied.

"Really?"

"Yeah. Gabe met my family once and they made him so angry he literally vomited," Holly said.

Chloe's eyes widened a little. "...seriously?"

"Yes, she isn't exaggerating. It was...a deeply unpleasant experience."

"Wow. Jeez, I'm sorry. Um…" She hesitated, then her look of annoyance returned. "Goddamnit! I wanted to get spanked so fucking bad! And then fucked! I'm-ugh! God I want to stay here really fucking bad...maybe I could...no, I can't really get out of this. It'll raise too many questions." She looked longingly at the paddle she'd bought. "Fuck. Will you hold onto it for me? And not use it!? Maybe that's selfish but–"

"That isn't selfish, Chloe," Ellen said. "It's yours. You bought it with your own money for yourself. We will absolutely keep it here for you and not use it."

"Thank you," she replied, then stepped up and gave Gabe a hug, then, after some hesitation, gave him a kiss, pulled back, then leaned in and gave him a longer kiss with some tongue. She pulled back once more, began to go back in for another kiss, then stopped herself. "God-fucking-dammit," she whispered.

"You should probably go now or you'll just keep getting hornier and you'll find it too hard to leave," he said.

"I'd call you an arrogant prick but you're completely right," she growled. "Okay, yeah. I'm going to go."

They followed her out into the living room. She hastily pulled her shoes and coat back on. "All right, um...thanks for everything, all three of you. You're seriously great. And nice. And fun. And I will be back...sometime this week. My sister wasn't supposed to be back in town until next Monday and we've got a lot of catching up to do."

"Do what makes sense to you, Chloe. Just try to keep in touch," Gabe replied.

She nodded. "Definitely. Okay, later."

They wished her farewell and then she was gone.

Gabe sighed heavily. "I was really looking forward to spanking the fuck out of her."

"I was looking forward to watching," Holly murmured.

"Same," Ellen said. "But unlike poor Chloe, who has to go do non-sexy things, the three of us can absolutely do sexy things. And those handcuffs and that mask and my vibrator all need to be broken in. And Holly still needs to get broken in..." she murmured, reaching out and running a finger slowly along her jawline.

"I...really do," Holly whispered huskily.

"This is all true," Gabe agreed.

He took Holly's hand and began leading her back to the bedroom. Ellen followed silently behind them. He brought her to the foot of the bed, then gave her a long, wonderful kiss, hugging her against himself and feeling her soft, warm, amazing body.

"Take off your clothes, Holly," he said, looking into her eyes.

"Yes, sir," she murmured demurely.

He took off his own shirt as she began getting undressed. Their clothes came off quickly, and soon found himself staring at his nude, voluptuous redheaded lover, smiling shyly at him.

"How do you want this to go?" he asked.

"I want you to decide everything," she replied.

"All right. Before we do that though, we need to finally discuss an official safeword. You understand the concept, right?"

"I do. It's the word I say to make you stop completely. And I have thought about it, and I want my safeword to be supernova."

"All right, supernova it is, then. Now…" Gabe stepped up to her and put his hands on her shoulders, then slowly turned her around until she was facing away from him. "Don't move," he murmured in her ear.

She exhaled hard. "Yes, sir," she whispered.

He walked over to the eyemask that she'd bought, a simple black, silky thing, and the two cuffs. He studied them briefly. They seemed pretty straightforward. Solid.

"I'll just hold onto this," Ellen murmured as she held up the keys.

Gabe nodded and walked back over to Holly. He tossed the cuffs onto the bed, then held up the eyemask. He waited for a moment, letting the anticipation stretch out. Holly was breathing more heavily. Finally, when he felt enough time had passed, he settled the eyemask into place, effectively blinding her.

She gasped softly as he did. "What are you going

to do to me?" she whispered.

Gabe leaned in and replied right up against her ear. "You'll find out."

Holly shivered again, harder. He put his hands on her shoulders, then slowly moved them down her arms, enjoying the feel of her soft, hot skin against his own. He leaned in and kissed her neck, then brought his hands back up to cup her big, soft breasts.

"Someone has been a good girl," he murmured.

"Who might that be?" Holly whispered, breathing more heavily than ever.

"You, my love. And when you are a good girl, you get rewarded."

She giggled softly. "Because you want me to keep being a good girl?"

"Well...that and the fact that I love you so much," Gabe replied.

He encircled her nipples with his fingertips and switched to kissing the other side of her neck, eliciting more pleasured sounds from her. After a moment more of this, he guided her carefully to the bed and had her sit down on it. Then he looked over at Ellen and pointed to the vibrator. He made a motion of pushing a switch with his thumb and raised his eyebrows.

She picked it up and studied it quickly, found it to be both battery operated or plug in. She removed the cord and then popped open the side for batteries, grit her teeth a little when she found it empty, then raised a single finger and hurried out of the room.

Gabe laughed softly and climbed onto the bed with Holly.

"Here, farther back, lay your head on the pillows," he said.

"Yes, dear," she replied, grinning and then

moving carefully.

He helped get her in place and then leaned down and began kissing across her breasts while running his fingers gently across her crotch and inner thighs, given he wasn't going to just spring the vibrator on her.

Something he'd learned was that, when it came to pussy, you didn't just up and do things. You had to ease it, whatever it was, even just a little.

Faintly, he heard a click and then a buzzing. Perfect. It turned off and then Ellen came back into the room. He was honestly surprised by how effectively she could move silently if she wanted to. She handed it to him with a smirk and then moved back to her original position, leaning against their dresser and watching.

"Okay, Holly…" he murmured.

"What now?" she whispered.

He responded by laying the big, foamy head of the vibrator against her pussy. She gasped softly.

"What is that?" she asked.

Gabe turned it onto its lowest setting. She let out a sharp gasp and then moaned loudly. Gabe chuckled as he slowly began working it back and forth, making her cry out louder in surprised pleasure.

"What the fuck!?" she yelled, then moaned. "How have I never-*oh fuck yes right there!*" she screamed. "*Fuck that's the spot! Don't fucking stop!*"

Gabe did exactly as she demanded, holding it there, bringing her to an ecstatic orgasm within just a few more moments. She moaned and yelled and cried out, writhing in pleasure and nearly thrumming with sexual ecstasy so intensely that he actually began to worry a little.

But once he pulled the vibrator back and turned it

off, her orgasm ran its course, leaving her with the occasional aftershock of bliss running through her soft, wonderful body, and she went slack, left panting and sweaty.

"What the *fuck!?*" she demanded finally. "I could've been doing that for *years?!*"

"Oh, girl, I know *exactly* how you feel right now," Ellen said.

"You do? Wait, why? I was going to ask why you don't already have one," Holly replied.

Ellen sighed and rolled her eyes. "Blake made me get rid of mine."

"Wait, *why?*" Gabe asked.

She snorted. "I can't remember the excuse he gave but it was pretty obvious that he was threatened by it."

"Lame," he replied.

"Super lame," Holly said. "Because that was fucking *insane.* Holy shit."

"Honestly think I'm gonna masturbate to you two fucking. Babe?" Ellen asked, sticking out her hand.

Gabe laughed and handed her the vibrator.

"Thank you," she murmured, setting it down for a moment and getting out of her pants. She frowned as she looked around the room. "I'll have to lay down beside you. Make some room."

"Gimme a second," Gabe replied.

He grabbed one of the cuffs and then slapped them onto Holly's ankles, affixing her legs together. She let out a little gasp.

"You still okay with this?" he asked.

"Yes," she replied immediately. "I am very okay with this."

"Good." He flipped her over onto her stomach and then put both her wrists behind her back, then cuffed them together.

"Oh my goodness," she gasped.

"What?" he replied, scooting her over a bit more to give Ellen room.

"You're just...really good at that. You're strong."

"Apparently," he murmured, mounting her from behind and propping himself up with one hand while using the other to guide himself into her glistening pink slit. "Now, hold still you little slut," he said, and penetrated her.

Holly gasped and immediately began squirming around and moaning as he pushed his way into her. Gabe used both hands to hold himself up and looked down between them, staring at her thick, pale backside as he watched himself disappear into her again and again.

"Holy shit, this is fucking hot," Ellen whispered, then she let out her own loud moan of pleasure as he heard the buzz of the vibrator again.

He glanced over at her and had to fight to shift his focus back to Holly. She was fantastic to fuck, fantastic to look at, but in that moment, staring at Ellen's long, pale, curvaceous body with her legs spread and her breasts jiggling as she masturbated, a look of unfocused lust on her beautiful face as she stared back at him...

She really did look like some kind of goddess of beauty and lust and love.

He shifted his attention back to Holly. "Fuck, Holly," he groaned.

"What?" she moaned loudly, panting.

"You have got such a fat ass. And your pussy is just...oh my God, it's amazing," he replied, and started going harder and faster. "Are you a good girl, Holly?"

"Yeeeeesss…" she moaned loudly.

"Say it."

"I'm a good girl," she groaned.

"Are you a good little whore?" he asked, and began to go faster, the sound of their skin slapping together louder, more insistent now.

"*Yes! I'm a good little whore!*" she shrieked and began to orgasm once more.

Gabe let out an inarticulate groan of pure pleasure as he felt her inner muscles flutter, growing hotter and wetter as he stroked into her.

She felt like a dream of pleasure and ecstasy.

He went for as long as he could, and he genuinely wasn't sure how long that was, time vanishing like smoke on the wind as they made love.

When he came, it was powerful, and he grunted as he drove deep into her, releasing his seed inside of her and filling her up, pumping her full of it hard and fast and making her shriek and squeal in rapturous bliss.

At some point he became aware of Ellen's moans of pleasure joining their own.

When they were finished, the three of them slicked with sweat, Gabe pulled out of Holly and sat up, looking over at Ellen. She slowly opened her eyes and looked back at him, a look of disbelief coming onto her face.

"Oh my G-are you serious? You want *more!?*"

"I want more," he replied.

She shifted and spread her legs wider, putting aside the vibrator, and he climbed onto her. She moaned loudly as he penetrated her.

CHAPTER TWELVE

"So...how do you feel, babe? How was your first handcuff session?" Gabe asked as he ran the soapy washrag over Holly's bare back, the shower cascading down around them.

"Conflicted," she murmured.

He had noticed she'd been a little off since they'd gotten her out of the cuffs. He'd asked if she was okay watching, still cuffed, and she said she was, but now he wondered if maybe he should've at least taken the time to get her out of them before diving into Ellen.

"What are you thinking?" he asked.

"It was really good. It was so hot. It felt *so* good, and then laying there, watching you have sex with Ellen while I was still all cuffed up...um, that did things to me...that the sex didn't. *Good* things, to be clear, but...I think there's definitely a part of me that, um, wants to be made to watch you have sex with other girls."

"Oh. Wow, really? That's a thing you want to try?" he replied.

"Yes. I do. I want to try it with you and Chloe. I want you to handcuff me to a chair and yell at me and make me watch you fuck Chloe," she murmured.

"This definitely sounds like bad girl territory."

"I know. It is. And I'm...not completely a good girl, apparently. I like being rewarded a lot, but, um, I would like to try out being punished."

"I will be very happy to help you with this...now tell me about the bad feelings."

"Okay...I feel, like...guilty? And ashamed? Like I just did something really bad, and somehow...someone's going to know, and judge me for it...is that normal?"

"I think that's normal. I think it's especially normal if you grew up the way that you did. Honestly...okay, don't take this the wrong way, but I kind of felt that way a little after we had sex the first time."

"Really?" she asked, turning around.

"Yes, but it has nothing to do with you, Holly. Okay? And I don't feel that way at all anymore. I felt like...I had cheated on Ellen. It was a lot worse the first time I did stuff with Emily. I'm saying that I understand how you feel, and it's okay to feel this way. I think it's kind of like...leftover emotions from how we were raised, and the society we were raised in. Do *you* feel bad about what we just did?"

"I mean, I just said–"

"No, no, sweetheart. You. Do *you* feel bad? Not your emotions, not whatever your inner self or whatever the hell it might be is telling you. But you. Or, put it another way, do you *think* you did something wrong?" he asked.

"No," she replied after a few seconds, slowly shaking her head, "no, I don't. I don't think I did anything wrong. I had sex with my boyfriend while I was in handcuffs and I liked it."

"And there's nothing wrong with that."

"There isn't," she agreed, smiling slowly. "Okay, I get it. And you're right." She hugged him, letting out a sound of contentment. "I feel stupidly lucky that I'm in this relationship."

"I think I feel luckier," he murmured.

She giggled. "I guess we're all lucky...you really think Chloe will join us?"

"Maybe. I hope so," he replied.

"You really like her, huh?"

"I do. You two seem to get along pretty well."

"Yeah. She's kind of scary...but then again so was Ellen. I think she's sad, just in general. Like I was. Mmm...I'm worried you and Ellen are right, and it's coming back."

"You can't keep sadness away forever, Holly," he replied, and kissed the top of her head.

"I know...I don't want to go to therapy," she murmured, letting go of him.

They traded places and she took the shower.

"Any particular reason?" he asked.

"I'm just not really comfortable with the idea of telling some stranger all my innermost thoughts. I want to tell them to you or Ellen. Well, most of them. But I'm not saying I won't do it. Ellen's actually got me an assessment set up next week," she replied.

"We'll be there with you, love," he said.

"I'm glad. That'll make it easier."

"So, do you want to do the cuff play again?"

"Oh my fucking God, *yes,*" she replied immediately.

He laughed and kissed her. "Good. Me too. I had a lot of fun."

...

"You're doing it, aren't you?"

Gabe jumped so badly he almost threw the ringbox. He jerked around, still managing to hold onto it, and stared at Holly, who stood in the bedroom doorway with a broad smile.

"Shh!" he whispered sharply.

"She's in the shower," Holly murmured as she walked over.

"She has *excellent* hearing," he whispered, "and if you mess this up, I will be *very* disappointed."

Holly lost her smile. "Okay, okay. Sorry. Just...I'm excited!"

She came to stand before him and held out her hand. He placed the ringbox in it and she brought it closer to her face, studying it.

"It's seriously beautiful," she whispered softly.

"I'm hoping it's...enough," he murmured.

Holly looked up at him. "It's a fake...you know. It's not a real...thing you're doing."

"I mean, yes and no. We're not actually going to get...engaged," he murmured, dropping his voice even lower, "but we kind of are? I mean, it's an actual commitment."

Holly regained her smile and closed the ringbox, then placed it back in his hand. She stepped closer to him. "Gabe, this," she tapped the box, "is not the important thing in the scenario." She tapped his chest. "*This* is. You will do fine and she will be beyond happy."

"I hope so," he murmured.

"Gabe, come on. You make her stupid."

He blinked, refocused on her. "What?"

Holly giggled and shook her head. "I've read a lot of romance novels and I've seen a lot of my lady friends fall in love. Or, at least, in lust, masquerading as love. And when a girl *really* likes a guy, she gets kind of stupid. I mean there's actual scientific evidence I think that a lot of women act a bit dumber or weaker than they really are when they're around a guy they really like. Really, I was just using it as a phrase, as it doesn't really seem like Ellen actually acts stupid around you. But I mean, sometimes I'll be watching the two of you without you realizing it, and just the way she sometimes looks at you when you aren't looking, like...she fucking loves you. Like a *lot*. Also so do I."

"I'm pretty sure Ellen has told me, almost word-for-word, this exact same thing about you. About the watching and the looking," Gabe said, slipping the ringbox deeply and securely into his pocket. "And I love both of you as well. A ridiculous amount."

She smiled and gave him a long kiss. "I can tell you're nervous. Just...do what you did with me, and it'll go totally fine. The deck is completely stacked in your favor, babe. You almost can't fail. I can't imagine you failing. Even if you fuck this up, she'll still be *so* happy."

He actually felt some of the tension go out of his body. "That's a very good point," he said. They both glanced over as the shower turned off. "Okay, I gotta finish getting ready."

Holly smiled, kissed him quickly once more, then stepped back. "Good luck."

"Thank you, dear."

As she left and headed for the living room, Gabe looked around for a moment. He realized that he basically was ready. And it was probably going to take Ellen a bit longer to get dressed. He double-checked that he had the ringbox in his pocket, then quickly pulled it out and looked inside, to double-check that the ring was actually in the box, then hastily put it back. Finally, he walked out of the bedroom and into the kitchen to stare out the back window.

They'd had a slow, pleasant evening together after Chloe had left yesterday, and when he had woken this morning, Gabe had abruptly decided that it was time to pull the trigger on his plan to propose to

Ellen.

It still felt a little weird, because it wasn't a real proposal. Only it was. Just not in the sense that most everyone else thought about it.

He'd been pondering the proposal ever since they'd discussed it, piecing together a game plan to give Ellen a great day. It hadn't been as easy as he'd hoped. Part of the problem was that he wasn't entirely sure what tone to go for. The more time went on, the more Ellen seemed to want almost exactly the same thing that Isabella had told him.

When they'd gone on their date, he had dressed up, and she had dressed down. She'd been a little embarrassed about it and had said 'I want to be nineteen again'. And that actually made a lot of sense. And it made even more sense for Ellen, who had never really gotten to be nineteen even when she'd literally been nineteen.

Because she had been being worked half to death for five years already, with no signs of slowing down.

After twenty solid years of work, she deserved to actually enjoy herself.

As he listened to her leave the bathroom and head into the bedroom to finish getting ready, Gabe tried to comfort himself with the knowledge that if she really wasn't having a good time, or if she truly wanted something else, she'd let him know. He already figured that there was a decent chance she knew that he was going to do the proposal today.

Then again…

Maybe not.

He'd been finding increasingly that where he thought he was as transparent as glass to Ellen, this was not always true. He could actually hide things from her. Not that he particularly wanted to, but there were definitely some situations in which it was a useful talent to have.

Like now.

On the other hand, Holly had figured it out.

In the end, did it really matter? He was going to go through with it regardless, and even if she knew, Ellen wanted this, so she would be happy to go along for the ride, regardless of whether or not she knew which ending was coming.

As he kept looking out onto the backyard, another thought resurfaced.

At some point, it might become prudent to actually get married. But that was going to cause a problem, potentially at least. He could only marry one of them. Who in the hell was he supposed to choose? It was complicated enough right now, although in truth, he imagined that Holly wouldn't mind at all if he and Ellen became officially married.

But Chloe might take issue with it.

And was Chloe even the last woman who might join their household?

It felt impossible to imagine him making this work a *fourth* time, but barely two months ago the idea of dating just Ellen seemed flat out impossible.

He heard the bedroom door swing open again. "All right, babe, I'm ready for our date day."

Gabe made himself relax and, with a surprising ease, slipped his confidence into place. He turned away from the window and joined her in the living room, then paused and smiled when he saw what she had on: a pair of jeans and a simple white t-shirt.

She looked down at herself. "This is okay, right? You said casual, and…"

"It's perfect," he replied.

Ellen got an awkward smile on her face and

blushed a little. "Okay, I love you babe, but don't just say that because you think I look good in apparently everything. I need to know if we're actually going somewhere nice."

"No. I mean, I *do* think that, but no, this really is perfect for today," he replied.

"Okay good."

As she bent over to grab her shoes, he walked up behind her and settled his hands on her hips. "I love what a huge ass you have," he murmured.

She straightened up immediately. "*Gabe.*"

Holly started laughing. "Oh wow, she's blushing *so* bad!"

"Shut up or I'll get the cuffs," Ellen growled.

"That...is not a deterrent," Holly replied.

Ellen stared at her for a second, then sighed heavily. "Chloe is already such a bad influence on you."

"So are *you,* Ellen, if we're going down that road."

Ellen continued staring at her for a second, then shook her head and finished putting her shoes on. She grabbed her hoodie. "I have to get out of here or I'm going to take you and Holly into the bedroom and not leave for the rest of the day, and I want to save that kind of sex for tonight."

"I love you both, have fun," Holly replied.

"I love you too, Holly. I will...do a lot of things to you later," Ellen said.

"Later, babe," Gabe said, ushering Ellen out before she really did drag them both to the bedroom and derail his planned day.

CHAPTER THIRTEEN

"What made you think of this?" Ellen asked as she lined up her shot.

"Well, you really seemed to enjoy it the last time we went mini-golfing, and this one is bigger, but also outdoors, and they'll probably shut it down soon because the real snow's gonna start," Gabe replied.

She took her shot and hit a hole in one.

"You're really good at this," he murmured, putting his own ball down as she moved to retrieve hers.

She laughed. "Yep. You still owe me, you know."

"Do I now?" he replied.

"Yes. I bet you that Chloe would fuck you at that second party and she absolutely fucked you. In front of us all. And you came in her vagina. That is one hundred percent a win on my part," Ellen replied, straightening back up.

"That is a win on your part," he agreed.

"So…?"

"So I owe you an oral orgasm in a bathroom somewhere. Or a changing room. We could do the car, maybe?" he asked.

"No. No way, not the car. Not unless it was like how you made Emily come the first time. I'm too fucking big for anything else," she replied.

"Fair point." He hit his golfball and landed a hole in one. "I'm not too bad, either."

She smirked. "You know normally guys try to reassure their girlfriends when they say they're 'too big' for something."

"I know that you meant too tall," he replied,

joining her and collecting his ball. "And you know that I enjoy this aspect of you. All your...proportions."

Her smirk morphed into that awkward smile she got when he was starting to embarrass her with compliments. She cleared her throat and tried to reassert control. "So, you wanna make it interesting? If you win you get out of our little bet?"

"No," he replied as they walked over to the next hole.

"Why not?" she asked, sounding genuinely curious.

"Because I love eating your pussy."

She shot a look at him, blushing badly now. "*Gabe,*" she hissed.

He laughed. "What?"

"You...are getting too good at this," she muttered, dropping her golfball and lining up her shot.

"This being...?""

"Oh don't fucking-you know exactly what. This...social fencing. You can make me feel exactly what you want me to feel a little too easily nowadays. And we just starting dating fucking not even two months ago!"

"To be fair, we had three years to soak into each other's psyche. And, on top of that, we just get each other on some deeper, intuitive level. You know..." He glanced back at the building housing the other half of the fun center that the outdoors mini-golf course was part of.

"What?" she asked.

"This place has nice bathrooms. And they're individual, too."

Ellen looked over at the building for a long

moment. "Yeah, and it's pretty empty in there…"

"Tempted?" Gabe asked.

Ellen immediately returned her attention to the golf course. "Yes. Very. Let's finish this up."

…

Gabe took another quick look around. "Okay, we're clear, go."

Ellen opened the bathroom door and slipped inside. He followed her in, then shut and locked the door behind them as she flipped on the light.

"Wow, this *is* clean," she muttered, looking around. "How do I wanna do this?"

"Well...you could lean against the wall and put your foot on the toilet seat," Gabe replied.

"Yeah. I could. That's probably best. Okay." She started unzipping her jeans. "Goddamnit, you're so lucky, you know that? If I wanted to blow you all you'd have to do is unzip and whip your cock out and that's it. I gotta take my entire fucking pants *and* panties off."

He laughed. "Yeah...wow."

"What?" she murmured as her jeans came down with her panties.

"Just...your thighs. And hips. I feel like it gets thrown around a lot nowadays, but you seriously would've been worshiped back in the day. Statues everywhere of the tall, thick goddess."

Naked from the waist down now, Ellen seemed more in her element with him. She smirked and it was full of satisfaction.

"Kneel before me," she replied.

"Yes, ma'am," he said, kneeling down as she put one foot up on the closed toilet seat.

He looked at her smooth, bare pussy for a long moment as he ran his hands up and down her generous, pale thighs. He remembered when their positions had been reversed back at the bowling alley, how she'd sucked him dry pretty damn fast.

He wondered how quickly he could get her to orgasm if he was really trying.

And he should be trying, he knew, because this *was* actually risky.

He leaned in and put his tongue to work.

And learned that he needed about sixty seconds flat to bring her to climax. Feeling her hands on his head, hearing her sounds of stifled, barely-contained ecstasy, and then ultimately getting her to orgasm was an experience all its own.

"Gabe, please!" she gasped finally as he kept eating her out while she came.

He relented, falling back and reaching up, helping her keep her balance as the orgasm tore through her body like a wildfire, consuming her. She had one hand clapped firmly over her mouth, her eyes squeezed shut at she nearly convulsed in bliss.

Finally, the pleasure released her and she exhaled hard, her eyes opening but unfocused.

"Here," Gabe murmured, helping her get back into her panties and jeans.

"Wait," she murmured, grabbing at the toiletpaper, "lemme just...clean up a little. Gonna be uncomfortable if I don't."

He helped her when she wanted it and before long they were sneaking back out of the bathroom. They had already paid for and returned everything, so it was pretty easy to just walk out of the place. Although he glanced once at the girl behind the counter. She was pretty cute, maybe Holly's age, blonde hair pulled into a simply ponytail.

She looked at them as they left, a knowing smile on her face, which was just a little red.

Apparently they hadn't gotten away with it completely, but judging from that look, it wasn't going to be a problem.

"Gabe," Ellen said once they were back in the car.

"Yeah?" he replied, turning it on and beginning to get them out of the lot.

"That was seriously amazing oral. That was a really intense orgasm," she murmured. "I've always wanted to do shit like this, but I've never...trusted anyone enough. Which is bothering me an increasing amount."

"You wanna talk about it?" he asked as he began guiding them towards their next destination.

"...maybe. It's been a nice day. But...I guess there's not too much to unpack. It's bothering me how absolutely fucking insane it is that I seriously dated people I didn't fully trust. And I'm looking back on that, wondering how could I have possibly missed that? Because I thought that I *did* trust them. But...I didn't. I mean, I really didn't, not in the most important ways."

"I have something to offer," he replied.

"I am all ears," she said.

"I think there's a good chance that you, on some level, were aware of the fact that you didn't completely trust them, but that you told yourself 'this is how it is, this is how relationships, even marriages, work, there's just always going to be a certain level of distrust there', because I imagine your parents didn't really trust each other."

She was silent for so long that he began to worry

he'd said the wrong thing, but finally she slowly began to nod. "You're right," she murmured. "They didn't. And, whether we like it or not, that's sort of the template we have for our idea of relationships. Which is so fucked. But you're fucking right. You are completely right. Shit." She hugged herself suddenly.

"You okay, babe?" he asked.

"Yeah. I am, actually. I'm...it's just that I'm realizing how all this shit I used to think was so important, was worth sacrificing for, was worth *everything*, just...isn't. It's a really trite thought, but I mean I really was just chasing clout and money. I've even had this thought before, like last month, but I guess I'll have it a few more times and it'll just hit hard each time. It's just that I feel like a different person now. I'm...happy. But it's more than that. I'm secure. It's-I know. I know what it is," she said suddenly, sitting up.

"What?" he asked, because this was obviously very important to her.

"I remember thinking, more than once, 'if I don't do X'–keep in shape, make a certain amount of money, dress a certain way–'then my significant other will leave me'. Not outright, usually, but I knew it was on the table, or it would be that much closer to happening. I was constantly low-level terrified. Of losing my job, of getting out of shape, being boring. And I'm *not* terrified anymore. I mean I'm vaguely terrified of fucking this up somehow, in some way that I have yet to realize, only I'm *not* anymore. I believe that you'll stay with me. I believe that you love me enough to work with me. I believe it in my soul. And I've *never* had that before."

"Jesus, babe," he muttered.

"Have you?" she asked suddenly, looking over at

him. "It's not a trick question, I'm really asking."

Gabe thought about it, but not for long. He shook his head. "No, I haven't. I actually know exactly what you mean. On some level, I did always sort of feel like the woman I was dating was with me for...not me. And that I was on thin ice. If I lost my job, I'd probably lose my girlfriend, too."

"Exactly. Yes. That. It's fucking horrible. And it's *gone now.* I am actually *secure* in my relationship in a way I never have been before. And the enormity of that feeling, of how *good* it feels, how *relieving* it is...it's kind of hitting me, the feeling. It's hit me before, I guess I've just never quite put it together like this. Holy fucking shit I love you."

"I love you too, Ellen."

"You and Holly are so amazing," she whispered. "I'm so lucky."

"So are we."

"If you say so."

"I say so. Basically since the moment we started dating, my life has been the best it's ever been. Ever. Flat out. No contest. You're an amazing person to date, live with, have sex with, do everything with."

"I appreciate that," she murmured, a little awkwardly. "And I'm glad you think so. I think that's another thing that's been missing for a really, really long time. Maybe for my whole life. Being appreciated."

"I appreciate you dearly," he replied. "And it's just one of the reasons I'm taking you out on this date day."

"Speaking of which, we should probably lighten the mood back up. What's next?" she asked.

"Next is that movie Wayward you've been talking about. I've got tickets. And then...more things you'll like," he replied.

She smiled. "You don't want to tell me?"

"Part of the date is surprises. Surprises are good," he replied, and then hoped he hadn't tipped his hand. He still had no idea if she actually knew or even suspected.

"This is true," she agreed, "and I am happy about this. I was pretty close to organizing a date night for us myself for that one."

"Perfect," Gabe replied, and drove on.

CHAPTER FOURTEEN

"There's something special about today," Ellen murmured after she finished off her hot apple cider and tossed the cup into the trashcan as they passed by it.

"Is there?" Gabe replied, doing the same with his hot chocolate.

"Yes. I'm not sure what it is. Just...something. Are you going to give me an early Christmas present or something?" she asked.

He laughed. "I think you just underestimate how good I am with date days."

It was getting really, really close to his time to shine, as it were. The sun was setting and the cold was coming on, but he wanted to do it at a park. After the movie, they'd gone to the mall and wandered for a while. He'd gotten her several books.

It occurred to him, very suddenly, that he didn't actually have a specific place in mind to do the actual proposal beyond 'the park'. Where in the park? He looked around, a little panicked, and his eyes settled on a gazebo not too far away.

He began leading her towards it.

"It's becoming clearer to me that, much as I love you, I *am* underestimating you in some ways. And...it's not necessarily a thing I want to stop."

"Really?"

"Yes. Being pleasantly surprised is...well, pleasant. Also, it's kind of a turn on. Seeing you step up to challenges and face them and overcome them, even relatively mild, day-to-day challenges, is really nice. I'm just really happy right now," she replied.

He took her hand as they walked up into the

gazebo. "Good. That's what I was aiming for."

She laughed softly. They came to stand in the structure and looked out onto the woods. Twilight was falling. He was going to have to do this soon. Was there maybe a better place to do this? Actually, he saw a little river down in the woods they were looking into right now. There was a beautiful clearing beside it. Maybe that would–

"You know," Ellen murmured, "if I had a ring, I think I'd propose to you."

Well fuck.

All doubt that she hadn't picked up on his overall goal evaporated in an instant.

"Seriously?" he asked.

Ellen smiled a bit wider and nodded. "Yes."

Might as well do it here and now.

"In that case…" Gabe reached into his pocket and pulled out the ringbox as he dropped down to one knee. "Ellen," he said, presenting it to her and opening the box, "will you marry me?"

She turned fully to face him and the look one her face was one of utter, startled shock. Her eyes wide, she covered her mouth with one hand and just stared at him for a moment.

"Gabe," she managed finally, and slowly lowered her hand, then reached out for the ring. "*Yes,* Gabe," she said, her voice thick with emotion as she took the ring from the box.

He felt a mix of joy and confusion as he saw the utter bewilderment with which she studied the ring. She slipped it onto the appropriate finger and then brought it closer to her face. So...had she not known? How could she not have known!? Especially after what she'd said.

Well, at least both potential outcomes were good.

"Gabe," she whispered, and she laughed, her smile huge and disbelieving. As he stood up, he saw tears fall down her cheeks. "This is so perfect, honey. I...oh my God. I can't…" She looked down at the ring again, then reached up and wiped at her tears.

Abruptly she wrapped him in a tight hug.

"Yes," she whispered intensely as she squeezed him. "*Yes* I will marry you, Gabe. Yes, I will be your wife."

"I love you, Ellen," he replied.

"I love you, too. *So much.* Oh my goodness," she whispered, laughing and crying.

They stood there in the twilit gazebo, embracing in the cold and not feeling it, just feeling each other, basking in the moment.

It was a very good moment, and even as he experienced and enjoyed it, Gabe knew that this was going to be one of those enduring memories.

After several moments, Ellen finally let go of him and wiped at her eyes and sniffed. "We should, uh, probably get back to the car," she murmured as she began digging around in her purse. "It's getting cold fast."

"Yeah," he agreed.

"Gimme a moment…" She wiped at her eyes with a tissue and then blew her nose. After that, they began walking back.

"Okay, so...cards on the table, I have to know: did you know?" he asked.

"That you were going to propose?"

"Yes."

"No! I had no idea. It wasn't even really on my mind. I thought it was going to be later, closer to Christmas. Although I'm not sure why."

"But...you said–"

She laughed. "I know! I-okay, it's going to sound ridiculous but it was just a thing that came to mind to say. I was really caught up in the moment. It seemed like a perfect day. It just...I don't know! I realize it's an insane coincidence, but I seriously did not suspect that this was going to be the day you fake proposed to me. Although man, Holly was right."

"What about?" he asked.

"It *does* feel real."

"Well...I mean it was, in a way. I really am asking you to basically be my wife, Ellen. Even if we never have some piece of paper recognized by the government that we're married, we basically are. I'm asking you to be my wife, my life partner, my person."

"You're right," she said, grinning broadly, then sighed and reaching up. "Goddamnit, I'm going to be crying all night. I'm *so* happy and overwhelmed. Just...you're right. And I accepted. I guess I shouldn't say fake. It was an authentic proposal and an authentic acceptance." She raised her hand and studied the ring. "Gabe, this is *beautiful*. I'm not much for jewelry, but my goodness. What is this?"

"A sapphire," he replied.

"It's *so* blue! I love it so much."

"I'm really glad, babe."

"Oh my God, you are so getting sucked and fucked like crazy when we get home. I'm getting Holly and we are going to give a great threesome and make you come like five times. Because you fucking *earned* it with today."

He chuckled as they got back into the car. "I very much appreciate that."

As they pulled out of the parking lot and started driving home, he sensed a shift in her mood. She was still studying the ring, but she wasn't smiling anymore.

"Uh-oh, everything okay?" he asked.

"Yeah, it's fine. I'm fine," she replied, then sighed in frustration. "Just...thinking about my past."

"You want to talk about it?"

"Yes. But...before I do, I have a question: do I talk about my exes too much?"

"No."

"You seem really confident in that answer."

"I am...is there...more to that statement? Should I not be?"

"No, it's great. It's appreciated. Just...it feels like too many guys get annoyed or even outright angry if women, let alone women they're *dating,* even acknowledge that they have a past love life. And I mean the thing is, I get not talking about certain aspects of it, I get that a lot of people don't want to hear about certain things, but...I'm realizing that pretty much all of my relationships were unhealthy in one way or another. And I kind of feel the need to talk about them, to...work through them. Or maybe even just to hear someone else say 'yeah wow, that *was* fucked up and you were mistreated', to help combat the idea that I'm just overreacting, or I should just grin and bear it."

"I don't mind talking about this or hearing about it, Ellen. I want to help you feel better," he replied.

"I very much appreciate that...okay. This made me think of, well, obviously, the other proposals. Not counting this one, I've been proposed to seven times."

"Wow. Although I'm not surprised at all. You're a fucking apex girlfriend."

"Yeah...well, the other side of that coin is that it sucks. I know there's this weird narrative that women actually take some sick pleasure in turning down marriage proposals and hey, I'm sure some of them out there do–there are some fucking monster bitches out there–but I am not one of them. I *hated* having to say no. Especially because they *insisted* on doing it fucking public! And I have mixed feelings, looking back.

"Because on the one hand, most of them were...it was obvious that they were doing it mostly for themselves. I mean yeah there was a lot of effort put into it, but I could never escape this feeling that the proposal was for *them* and not *me.* And, not to be a raging narcissist or anything, but I feel like when you propose marriage to someone, you should mostly be doing it for *them.* Right?"

"I'd say yes," Gabe replied.

"Thank you. But the conflict comes in the form of the fact that I know I pretty much set them up to feel like they had to do some big, showy thing, because I thought that's what you were supposed to do. I thought that if a guy was serious, he *had* to spend a lot of time, effort, and, specifically, money on not just the ring but the proposal itself. Which disgusts me to even say that now, but...it is what it is, I guess. It's who I was.

"But all *that* aside, I'm looking back now and feeling like there was just so much...superficiality to everything. I was as much a status symbol as that ring. And again, I can't fully blame them because that was an expectation I set, knowingly or unknowingly...I'm rambling. I guess what really bothers me is how backwards it is, and how the trite notion of 'what *really* matters is *love!*' is actually fucking true! This after school special, bullshit-sounding, trite, worn out, fucking corny-ass nonsense about how 'oh looks don't matter, money doesn't matter, bank accounts and cars and jobs don't matter, all that matters is love!' is *actually fucking true!*"

"You sound really angry about this," Gabe said.

"I am! Because the society I grew up in, the household I was raised in, the media I watched, it's like *all of it* was working in unison to make me roll my fucking eyes at this childish idea that love is enough! I always heard this cheesy BS line about 'oh we could live in a van for all I care as long as I'm with *you*' and I always fucking rolled my eyes and thought *yeah right, the reality is you'd very quickly get sick of living in godforsaken poverty and come to resent this person you 'love' so much,* but fuck me if it isn't true with you, Gabe!

"And I'm just *frustrated* because I spent thirty fucking years with this shit in my head. Do you know I have a very specific memory of watching some TV show with my mom when I was like seven and the characters were getting married and it was the same old same old about 'true love' and my mom very specifically looks at me and says 'Ellen, don't ever marry for love. Love is bullshit. No one really loves each other, they just put up with each other.', she actually said that!"

"Good lord that's a dim, bleak view of humanity," Gabe muttered.

"Yes! It is!" She let out a loud groan. "I actually do seriously, *genuinely* need therapy." She paused for a long moment. "Oh man. So, I feel better, but I also feel *very* guilty now because you just handed me a perfect day and a perfect proposal, one of the best days of my entire life, and this is the fucking reaction you get."

"Oh no, babe, no. Don't feel bad," Gabe replied

quickly.

"Why? Really why?"

"Because it makes complete sense why this happened. You got slammed with this thing that caused you to feel *intense* emotions and emotions are messy and complicated and we don't necessarily get to choose what we feel in abundance. This is related to proposals and marriage, which traditionally have not gone well for you. I'm okay with this, Ellen. And I mean legitimately, I'm not trying to placate you or make you feel better."

"...I know," she murmured, then laughed softly. "We don't really do that with each other, but...it takes a while to deprogram that, I guess." She let out a deep sigh, and this one sounded a lot more content. "Thank you. For everything. I do feel very good, and not guilty anymore...jeez you're getting really good at smoothing things over."

"Apparently," he replied.

She regained her previous grin. "Well, we're almost home now and we can continue the celebration with the extremely fun part."

"That we can," he agreed, and began driving just a bit faster.

CHAPTER FIFTEEN

Gabe groaned as he began coming in Holly's mouth.

He heard her moan quietly beneath his desk as she kept sucking, working his cock with her fingers and thumb just like Ellen had shown her. He could feel his seed leaving him in hard spurts and the feeling of her continuing to suck and drain him dry sent ecstasy careening through him. She kept going until there was nothing left to give, and then she sucked for a bit longer. Finally, she released him.

"So...how much did you get written?" she asked.

"Um. One sentence," Gabe replied as he rolled back to give her some room.

"How much would you normally write in that time?" she replied as she crawled out from under his desk.

"It really depends, but if I'm being productive, like...twenty? Thirty?"

"Oh wow, I didn't realize it was that bad. I guess you really can't mix pleasure and business," she murmured.

Gabe laughed. "Ah...yeah. Not that it isn't appreciated. That was a very good blowjob, Holly. So, thanks for that."

She grinned. "You're welcome. I'm gonna go make some lunch. You want anything?"

"I…" He hesitated as his phone began to ring. He sighed softly and pulled it out. "I need to take this, it's Chloe."

"Ooh, nice. Okay, I'll leave you to it, babe."

She left his office and Gabe answered the phone. He'd gotten a single text from her the day of his proposal to Ellen, and then a little bit more than that the day after, and so far this was her only point of contact today.

"Hey, Chloe," he said.

"Hey, Gabe...um...sorry about basically dropping out of contact. And sorry I don't have a lot of time right now. I swear to God this is not going to be representative of our relationship as a whole. But...I need a favor. And also I am so one hundred percent ready to give you my weekend and let you do whatever you want with me."

"I'm listening," Gabe replied.

"Thank God," she whispered. "So, I'm at work. I need you to come in here about twenty minutes from now. Have lunch with me for my break."

"I will, but why am I doing this?"

"Remember I told you about that fucking guy who comes in, like, all the time and won't leave me alone? I'm hoping he will fuck off if he sees me eating lunch with my boyfriend."

"Why don't you just tell him to fuck off? You are fully capable of it."

"Because my 'fuck off' will get me fired and maybe arrested," she growled.

"Oh. Okay. I will do it, but I would like to know...am I actually your boyfriend?"

"Yes. You are my boyfriend. I have at least decided that I want to date you. I am still trying to figure out how I feel about moving in with you. But my body and mind and heart and soul have all been screaming in unison ever since I last saw you: *make him yours.* So I'm doing that...inasmuch as I can, given you are dating two other women...are you mad?"

"That you decided to actually date me?" he

asked.

"No! That I pretty much went into communications blackout and am still waffling over moving in?"

"No, I'm not mad, Chloe. I mean these are big decisions. Although...you may end up getting spanked extra hard tonight," he replied.

"Oh whatever, give me a break with your fucking twig arms," she muttered.

"Now you're getting spanked *very extra hard* tonight. Your ass is going to be so sore," he replied.

"Fucking try me," she growled. He began to respond but she cursed suddenly. "I'm in the bathroom right now. I've got to get back to work. I'm going to text you the address. Please and thank you."

"Yep, bye."

"Bye."

She hung up. A moment later he got a name and address. Grinning, Gabe got to his feet. He saved his work, shut down his laptop, and marched out into the living room, where Holly and Ellen were sitting together on the couch talking.

"Guess who officially has himself a goth girlfriend," he said.

"She's moving in!?" Holly replied immediately.

He laughed. "She's still waffling on that. But she has decided to date me. Apparently, though, she needs my help right now. Some creep is bothering her relentlessly at her job and can't take a hint, so she wants her new boyfriend to eat lunch with her."

"Ooh...maybe I should come along, too," Ellen murmured.

"I think that might complicate things, or send mixed messages," Gabe replied.

"Yeah, that's a good point. I want to stay here

anyway. Oh! Before you go, I was just about to get up and ask you to help me with something."

"What?" he asked. "I gotta go kinda soon."

"It should go fast. One of the things I've wanted to get a lot more into now that I have way more free time is video games. I used to game some back in the day, but pretty much gave it up entirely beyond some mobile gaming or really basic shit on my laptop. So I want you to help me settle on something. What should be my first game?"

"Well...what do you want?" Gabe asked.

"Something single player, I know that. Something...not too complicated. I like first person stuff, though I'm not very big on shooters. I think, at least. Maybe I'd think they're awesome. Something...not too intense, like not something that's big on reflexes. I'm more interested in the world and the lore than the gameplay," she replied. "Something with a cool world to explore."

Gabe smiled as he walked over to his shelf that had his collection on it. He selected the game he had in mind and walked back over to her.

"Recovery," she murmured, studying the front of the case for a moment before flipping it over. "Oh, it's...old."

"No, it just looks old. It's retro, pixelated on purpose. But it's a *beautiful* aesthetic and it runs so smoothly."

"What's it about?" she asked. "This description seems...vague."

"Basically, it's near-future Earth, like the 2060s. Everything is fucked from climate change, but it's not the end of the world. It's kind of the opposite. It's first person, and there is some combat involved, but mostly you wander around really cool environments as either an engineer or a scientist and you collect data and help people and test out new recycling or terraforming technology. Essentially you're trying to reverse the damage and bring humanity back from the brink. It's a *lot* of fun and there's just so much to get into it."

"This sounds really cool actually, and I do love the look," she murmured. "How long do you think it'll take?"

"Oh, easily a hundred hours."

She looked up. "A *hundred?* Seriously?"

"Yeah, easily. Some of that is the DLC, which I have, but the retro graphics meant that they could spend a lot more resources on producing quality world-building and characters and content. I think you'll love it," he replied.

"Can I watch?" Holly asked.

"Yeah, I'd be fine with that," Ellen said. "Thank you, babe. Oh, also, whenever you get back with Chloe for the night, I want to go bed shopping. If we're going to be having her spending the night and doing sexy things, we need to upgrade sooner rather than later."

"Much agreed," he replied, taking the game and getting it set up for her.

"Are you excited?" she asked. "I know guys get really excited when their girlfriends play video games. Or, that's the general vibe I get, at least."

"It's a mixed bag out in the world, but here? Yes, I am very excited. Although really mostly because I get to introduce you to so much if you discover you like games. This one in particular is one of my all time favorites. Okay, we've gotta go through a little bit of a process to get you an account set up on the console…"

"I can handle that, dear, you should see to Chloe," Ellen replied.

"All right." He passed her the controller, then paused, frowning slightly.

"What's that look for? I promise I won't break your console, babe."

"No, no, it's not that at all. It just occurred to me...I need to make sure to keep an eye on you and Chloe. You're both naturally competitive and Chloe is...*extremely* good at video games. And down that path may lie madness."

"I'm not going to fight your new girlfriend over a video game, Gabe," Ellen replied.

"I know you think that now, it's just...video games are great, but they can open up some seriously wicked anger and vitriol in people who didn't even realize they had it. I don't know what it is precisely, but I have seen friendships and relationships *destroyed* over video games. And I don't think that'll happen here, I just...don't want you two to fight. I mean, not for real."

Ellen smirked. "But fake fighting?"

"Really hot," he replied. "Have fun."

They all said goodbye to each other and then Gabe was out the door.

. . .

The coffee shop that Chloe worked at turned out to be a nice little place tucked away in a quiet part of town called Caffeinaters. He'd driven by it at least a few times over the past few years. It felt a little weird to think that Chloe had been here for a year as a barista, but he was grateful that he didn't have the knowledge.

She was hot enough that she might have overridden logic and shyness and caused him to at least try to get her number.

Maybe it would've worked for him, but then he wouldn't also be dating Ellen and Holly right now.

Gabe parked and headed inside, finding the place middling crowded, about half the seats and booths taken by people reading or working on a laptop or talking quietly. He saw Chloe and a middle-aged woman with a blue streak in her black hair and a tattoo sleeve of vibrant flowers and vines down her right arm behind the counter.

"Oh thank God, I'm taking my break now," Chloe said immediately.

The woman laughed. "Go on, Chloe."

Gabe kept an eye open for anyone paying special attention to Chloe. Several people looked, but no one lingered. That was natural enough, she looked amazing even in a black t-shirt, black jeans, and a black apron.

"Thank you," she said as she walked up to him, kissed him, and then took his hand. He let her lead him over to one of the booths and they sat down across from each other.

"Happy to oblige," Gabe replied.

"I figured you would be...oh, shit, I didn't even think to ask: do you want anything?"

"I'm fine," he said. "How are you doing? You look tired."

"Gee thanks." He just smiled at her. She growled. "Not here," she muttered.

"Fair enough. For real though."

"For real? I am tired. Started my day at seven in the goddamned morning. I'm really glad you're here though. It's...actually a little worrying just how happy it's making me to see your face and hear your voice," she said.

"You seriously don't know what to do with happiness, do you?" he asked.

"You know what, Gabe?" she growled, leaning forward.

"What, Chloe?" he replied.

She opened her mouth, then closed it and looked away. He waited. She frowned, then twisted her lips, like she was tasting something cautiously, prepared to dislike it.

"...you're actually right," she said finally. Then she shook her head. "Whatever, another time. Um. So we're on for tonight? The weekend?"

"Yep," he replied. "Ellen and Holly are very much looking forward to you coming over. Although Ellen has decreed that as soon as you are available, we are to go bed shopping."

"Wait, why?"

"Because if you're going to be involved regularly, we need a bigger bed. Right now it can fit all four of us...if we squeeze in. But we'd like to get it out of the way."

"But beds are like *really* expensive, right? Especially big ones..."

"They are. But Ellen will cover it."

"This feels weird...whatever, it's not like I can talk you or her out of doing anything, especially if it's in your own house. And I can't act like I'd be unhappy with a larger bed." Her smile returned suddenly and she leaned closer. "What was the last sexual thing you did?"

"I got a blowjob at my desk from Holly half an hour ago," he replied.

Her eyes widened and her face flushed a little.

"Seriously?"

"Yep."

"Did you come in her mouth?"

"I did."

"Why at your desk?"

"She wanted to see if I could write while she was blowing me," he replied.

"Could you?"

"Basically no."

She laughed. "That makes sense...aw man, here he comes. It's showtime."

"Great," Gabe muttered.

"Just, you know, act like what you are."

"And that is?"

"My boyfriend, dumbass."

"You're fucking asking for it," he muttered.

She just smiled sweetly at him and reached across the table to take his hand. "Am I, Gabe?" she murmured. "Am I really?"

"Holy shit, you're gagging for it," he replied.

She laughed. "Just...save it for tonight."

"Believe me, I will."

He glanced over as he heard the door ding open. He frowned. Though Chloe hadn't told him anything about the guy in question, Gabe had been envisioning someone...well, kind of like himself. A little scrawny, a lot awkward. The guy who walked in, however, looked closer to the jocks that he'd put up with in high school.

They were about the same height, but this guy was definitely in better shape. Honestly, he was surprised that Chloe had so utterly turned him down. At a glance he seemed like he wouldn't have much of a problem getting her attention. Then again, Chloe was into *him*, so she definitely had some strange tastes.

The guy scanned the coffee shop and zeroed in on Chloe.

Then on Gabe.

They locked eyes and the look that came onto his face told Gabe immediately that this was going to be a problem.

He started walking over.

CHAPTER SIXTEEN

"Chloe," the guy said as he came to stand beside their table, "who is this?"

"This is my boyfriend," Chloe replied. Now she looked nervous.

The atmosphere had changed immediately and Gabe suddenly wondered if he was going to find himself in a Blake situation again.

"You said you were single," the jerk relied, losing all semblance of civility.

"I was the last time we talked. I'm not anymore," Chloe replied, her voice firming up.

"All right, I'm sick of fucking dancing around this. You have got to be shitting me with this guy. *This* guy? You're dating him? Dump this loser and let me show you what a real man can do," he replied.

"Jesus Christ, this is embarrassing. Leave, you're embarrassing yourself," Chloe replied.

A short whistle was let out across the way. "Hey! You! Blue jacket, yeah, you need to get out of here right now."

They all glanced over at the middle aged woman behind the counter. She was leaning forward, both hands on the counter, a deep frown on her face.

"Yes, you. Leave my shop. Now," she said, her voice.

"Fuck you," the asshole replied. "Fuck that and fuck you." He turned back to the booth. "I'm not going anywhere until this fucking bitch–"

A few things happened at once.

The idiot began reaching for Chloe.

The moment that happened, something somewhere inside of Gabe didn't so much snap as shatter. It felt remarkably like a 'break glass in case of emergency' kind of shattering.

Gabe's hand came out and over and grabbed the guy's wrist. Feeling like a different person, his foot shot out from under the table and smashed into the idiot's shin, forcing him to drop into a kneel and yell in pain. At the same time, Gabe yanked him forward and, with his free hand, snatched up the only utensil available to him.

He placed it directly in front of the man's eye, about an inch away.

"Have you ever seen what a spoon does to a human eye? Because I haven't," he said, his voice coming out in a worryingly calm tone.

"Let go of me," the asshole replied, but all his attention was fixated on the spoon and there was no real strength to his words.

"I will, but then you need to get the hell out of here and leave my girlfriend alone," Gabe replied flatly.

"Fine," he growled after a long moment.

Gabe released him and he got back to his feet, absently rubbing his wrist. A long, tense moment passed.

"Hey, asshole. Get the fuck out or I'm calling the cops right now," Chloe's boss said.

The guy looked around, as if suddenly aware of the fact that it had gone silent and everyone was staring at him.

"Fuck you," he snapped, but he walked hurriedly out of the shop.

"You okay?" Gabe asked as he put the spoon down and returned his attention to Chloe. She was staring at him with wide eyes.

"Yes...where the *fuck* did *that* come from? Are

you okay?" she replied.

"I...think so? I'm kinda freaking out a little," he admittedly as he glanced at his hands and saw that they were trembling.

He glanced over as Chloe's boss came over.

"Hey, you all right?" she asked.

"Mostly...sorry for having a fight in your shop," he murmured.

She laughed. "That was *not* a fight. That was a defensive action. And honestly I'm glad. That guy was an asshole and he could definitely stand to be taken down a few pegs...you two wanna go back into the break room?"

"We probably should. Thanks Linda," Chloe replied.

"Yep."

"Come on, babe," Chloe said.

They both got up and she led him deeper into the store, behind the counter, and through a door that led to a small but comfortable break room. As Gabe sat down on a couch, Chloe shut the door and then sat down beside him.

"I'm really, really, *really* sorry," she said. "I did *not* realize it would turn physical. Genuinely. And now I feel like a horrible bitch because it seems like I shoved you into the line of fire and I *promise* I did not do that."

"It's okay, I believe you, Chloe," he replied. "Glad I didn't eat anything. That...is doing some bad things to my stomach."

"I'm sorry, Gabe."

"It's really okay," he said, trying to make himself focus on her.

He felt kind of high, but definitely in a bad way. His brain kept trying to slip away and his head felt a little cloudy, only that wasn't quite right. Maybe foggy was a better word. He'd come down from adrenaline highs a few times before and this was definitely that.

"How did you *do* that, though?" she asked.

"What? Do what?" he replied, blinking a few times. Dammit, there he went drifting again.

"You were *fast*. I had no idea you could move like that. Have you had training or something? Because that was *seriously* just...really fast. And effective."

"So apparently I just naturally have really good reflexes? I had some training from a boxer earlier in my life, and Ellen's been helping me do a bit of self defense training here and there after we made that discovery about my reflexes when her ex came after me," Gabe replied.

"Came after you? Like how?"

"We were in his condo getting her stuff just after she'd broken up with him for cheating and then calling her a fat whore after he got discovered cheating. He showed up in the middle of getting the stuff and...did not react rationally. I'd never been in a fight before, but he swung on me and that was when I learned I have very good reflexes," Gabe replied.

"Holy shit, you've *never* been in a fight? Because those moves looked like you have definitely fought before," Chloe said.

He shook his head and shrugged a little helplessly. "I...I don't know. I don't like it, that's for sure."

She lost the smile she'd been slowly gaining. "I'm still really sorry. I seriously thought he would see us together, assume we were dating, and give up. And I'm not normally so off about stuff like that. I've had to develop a sense to know when to tell a guy to fuck off, when to let him down gently, when to pretend I have a boyfriend, when to just ignore him...fuck, I wish just *no I'm good* would work!" She let out a huff of irritation. "Sorry. So, you're good?"

"Yeah, just need to chill for a bit," Gabe murmured. "Wonder if he's going to wait around."

"God, I hope not. I guess, if we see him around, Linda really will call the cops, and...*hopefully* they will deal with it. But you know how they are nowadays. But, I mean, you can take him right?"

"I have no idea, Chloe," he replied. "Obviously I'll *try,* but that was probably just a really lucky break."

"Maybe...also *where* did that shit with the spoon come from? I saw his face when you said that and, man, he *believed* you."

"So you seem to be having a positive reaction to this," Gabe said. "Just to manage your expectations now, this is not going to be a regular occurrence." He paused. "Well, fuck, I *hope* it isn't."

"Oh no, that's not-trust me, Gabe. I'm not one of those 'fight for me' girls."

"Okay I was very sure that you weren't, because I'd break up immediately if you were, because I don't tolerate that stupid bullshit."

She laughed. "Yeah. I dated exactly *one* guy who wanted excuses to fight and used me as an excuse. God, it was a fucking nightmare. It didn't last long. Every time we went out-nevermind, it doesn't matter. As for how I feel about it, um...well, suffice to say it's admittedly a *little* exciting, but more practically: I am happy that you are capable of that, even if we never need to use it."

"That works for me," he replied.

For a long moment, they both just sat there together, lost in their thoughts. Well, Gabe wasn't thinking much. For the most part he was just trying to wind back down. Although it didn't take too long for the thoughts to start trickling back in.

"Was that guy insane?" he asked suddenly.

"What? I mean, I think so, but why do you ask?" Chloe replied.

"He was willing to apparently grab you and...I'm not sure what he was planning on doing after that part, but he was willing to *lay hands on you* in front of like fifteen people. Like, clear as day. Did he seriously think no one was going to stop him? Or call the police? It just seemed unhinged. Like *deranged*. You know?"

"Yeah...although I guess I've been around more stupid guys? That's not *that* out of the ordinary. I mean there's so many videos of stupid assholes fighting each other in the streets, in the club, at the bar, in restaurants, like *very* public places. And honestly, it *does* seem worse since the pandemic. After everything reopened, it's just felt like...everyone's a little crazier?

"Or, in some cases, a lot crazier. Just the general amount of road rage incidents, shootings, people screaming at each other in extremely public places, it's all gone up. Kinda another reason I want to just...unplug and hide myself away? I've never liked being out in public much, but I definitely hate it more now. Besides being miserable, it's fucking scary."

"No argument from me," he muttered.

A few more moments of silence passed. Chloe sighed again. "I seriously feel like a bitch. I really didn't think it'd get that far."

"Chloe," he said, taking her hand, "I'm not mad.

I forgive you, okay? I accept your apology and I forgive you. I think, *at worst,* it was a little negligent. But in truth, you really can't tell about some people."

"Okay, that *does* make me feel better...huh. I'm just now realizing that I don't actually hear 'I forgive you' that often. Just in general."

"It's a weird part of the social contract," Gabe replied. He groaned and stretched. "I actually think I should go home and just...chill for a bit. I'm mostly calmed back down now, but I still feel jumpy and uncomfortable."

"That's totally cool. I'll walk you out to your car," Chloe said.

"Thanks."

They got up and left the break room. The place was a bit more cleared out, though there was another person behind the counter now, a brunette woman tying her apron into place.

"Oh, Lindsay, hey. I thought it was just me and Linda today," Chloe said.

"I called her in," Linda replied, stepping out from the kitchen area. "She said she wanted more hours. If you want, you can take the rest of the day off. I know you've been...stressed, and this couldn't have helped."

"I..." Chloe looked at Gabe, briefly uncertain. It didn't last long. She nodded and began untying her apron. "Thank you, Linda. I could use a longer weekend."

"You've been working really hard, you deserve it. Go on, have fun," she replied.

Chloe thanked her again and then got her things together quickly. As soon as she had everything gathered, she and Gabe headed back outside. He had an unobtrusive look around, just to see if he saw the idiot from before, or anyone else for that matter, waiting for or watching them. But there didn't seem to be anyone.

They got into their cars and began driving away.

CHAPTER SEVENTEEN

"I'm not trying to be pushy or anything, but could you let me know when you want me to bitch at you? I'd feel bad snarking right now," Chloe said as she stuffed her clothes into the duffel bag she was bringing.

"I'll let you know, but I'm positive it's going to be tonight, probably within the next few hours," Gabe replied.

"...you wanna fuck? Or a blowjob?" she asked suddenly. "I'm already stripped down to my underwear and I'm horny and I wanna take a quick shower anyway..."

"Well..." Gabe was tempted to turn her down, partially because he was a little reluctant to exchange sexual favors if she was feeling guilty and also because he wanted to save it for tonight. But looking her pale body and her big breasts, barely contained by the bra she was wearing, proved to be too much. "All right."

She laughed and stood up. "I knew you couldn't resist. How do you want it?" she asked as she unhooked her bra, slid it down her arms, freed her huge tits, and tossed it aside.

"Ride me until I come," he replied, laying down on her bed.

"Oh yes, sir," she said, taking off her panties. "Do you want regular or reverse?"

"Reverse," he replied.

"All right then."

Gabe felt that wonderful, familiar excitement beginning to grow as he laid down on her bed. She walked over, completely naked now, and put her hands on her hips. "You aren't even going to take anything off?"

"Nope," he replied. "Pull my dick out and get to work."

She sighed heavily. "You fucker. I can't snark at you right now."

Gabe put his hands behind his head. "I know."

"You fucking..." she let out a short growl and then got onto the bed.

Within a few seconds she had his cock out. She leaned down and put it in her mouth, bobbing her head smoothly and coating it with her saliva. From there, she swung a leg over him, showing him her big, wonderful ass and her glistening pink pussy.

She reached back between her legs, grasped his erection, and guided him smoothly into herself. She gasped and shuddered, then started riding him.

"Your tits are amazing, but your ass is pretty fantastic, too," he murmured as she fucked him.

"Good to know," she replied. "I actually-ah yeah, right there, mmm...do some exercise."

"It's working. Because you are stupidly hot."

She laughed and then moaned, riding him a bit faster.

"Come on, Chloe, any day now," he said after a minute or so of enjoying her fucking him.

"Hey! You can't snark at me if I can't snark at you!" she snapped.

"I dunno, I think that makes it interesting," he replied, then reached out and slapped her ass.

"Hey!"

"Pick up the pace, Chloe, we've got a bed to buy so that you can more effectively service me like the whore you are."

She let out a low growl and then started going

even faster and harder, aggressively fucking him.

"Ah, Chloe, maybe–" he grunted.

"Nope!" she snapped. "You fucking asked for this! Fucking come already!"

"I'm about...to...oh fuck yeah!" he groaned grasping her hips and yanking her down into his lap.

She cried out as he thrust up into her, pushing his dick as deep into her as he could as he began coming inside of her. He filled her up, pleasure blasting his body, radiating wildly out from his core and filling him with nothing but good feelings.

When he finished, he let go of her and she sighed heavily.

"You're welcome," she growled as she got off him.

"Thank you," he replied.

"Feel any better?" she asked, cupping a hand over her crotch.

"I do actually. You'd probably better go clean yourself up before you drip everywhere like a slut," he said.

She stopped in her doorway and glared daggers at him. "I am going to...you are going to *get it* later," she snapped, and then headed into the bathroom.

Gabe *almost* said 'that's the plan' but held back, as he didn't think she'd caught onto it yet. He was hoping to get her riled up so that she'd be particularly bratty and bad, and then get *him* riled up so that he spanked the living fuck out of her and gave her a good experience.

And, well, himself too.

After a moment, he heard the shower start up. Gabe laid there for a bit, thinking of ways to bug her, and then smiled suddenly as an idea occurred to him. He got up and walked to the bathroom, then took a leak.

Then flushed the toilet.

Chloe let out a shriek of surprise. "*Gabe!*"

"Oops," he replied.

"You-are you *kidding me!?* You did that on purpose you fucking asshole!"

"No, you're being paranoid. Didn't I tell you I wasn't ready for snark, Chloe?" he replied.

"I'm going to fucking strangle you," she muttered finally.

"I'm not into being strangled," he replied. "Now, hurry up and finish your shower, it's definitely taking too long."

"Get out of the bathroom or I'll strange you *right now,*" she snapped.

"All right, I'm going."

He stepped out, listening to her mutter angrily under her breath. He wondered if that had been a little too far, but she didn't seem *genuinely* angry. Although he probably shouldn't push it much further for the moment.

Gabe walked into the living room and sat down, waiting. This new relationship, (and he had a moment of surprised glee over the fact that this was, in fact, officially a relationship now), was really catching him off guard. He'd been aware of sub/dom stuff, of brats and the basic notion of how the relationship worked, he just wasn't sure it would ever be a thing he could do.

And yet here he was, meshing with Chloe especially well. It was strange but he thought that her earlier assertion–that he understood it on a deep, intuitive level–was dead on. He just *got* it. He always seemed to know what to say and how to react to her when she was like that. And it felt damn good, too.

He was already very much looking forward to their session tonight, and not just because it was sex.

That handcuff session with Holly had been exciting in a way he wasn't very used to.

He wondered suddenly if Ellen would let him spank her.

He heard the shower shut off and then a moment later came the sounds of Chloe moving through the apartment. She was still muttering angrily to herself, although it sounded largely performative. Gabe hesitated as he wondered how he knew that.

"Okay," she said, emerging after a bit longer with her duffel bag, "I am ready to be whisked away to your home and see what it's like to be your girlfriend staying over at your place."

Gabe got to his feet. "Let's do it."

. . .

"...what happened?" Ellen asked the moment he actually looked at her.

He sighed. "How the fuck did you know something happened?"

"The look in your eyes, like you're about to tell me something you know I don't want to hear. And Chloe looks...guilty. Did you hurt my husband?" she asked.

Chloe's eyes bulged. "*Husband?*"

"*Our* husband," Holly said.

"Holly shit, I *just* realized you guys are wearing rings," Chloe murmured.

"How did you miss that?" Gabe asked, raising his hand.

"I don't know!"

"What. Happened?" Ellen asked firmly.

"I got into a little...scuffle, with the guy who was bothering Chloe," he replied.

"Are you hurt?" Ellen asked, walking over to him.

"No, I'm completely fine," Gabe replied.

"Seriously, he is. He kicked the guy's ass," Chloe said.

"That's not-that is *definitely* not what happened."

"What *exactly* happened? I need a clear, concise layout of facts. This is seriously important," Ellen said, her voice flat. They told her. She relaxed after that. "Well...good. I guess if there *had* to be a fight, this was probably the best way it could have turned out."

"I'm sorry," Chloe said. "But holy shit, Gabe is *fast.*"

"He really is," Ellen murmured, studying him. She tilted her head just a little. "...with a *spoon?*"

"It was the only thing on the table," he replied. "But the point is, I'm fine, the guy should be fine, the cops shouldn't be involved, and this should be behind us. And the point after that is: we have Chloe for the whole weekend, and she officially is my girlfriend."

"That's fair," Ellen said, but she pursed her lips and stared at Chloe. Who actually stepped behind Gabe and gripped the back of his shirt. "You got my man into a fight," she said finally.

"I apologized many times! And I offered him pussy and he took the offer and I fucked him better," Chloe replied.

"Hmm."

"Ellen, please drop it," Gabe said.

"...all right. Consider it dropped. So...what do you want to do?" she replied.

"Relax for a bit, maybe an hour at most, then go

bed shopping, then spank the living fuck out of Chloe's fat ass," he said.

"It is not *that* fat," she muttered, coming back to stand beside him.

"I dunno," Gabe replied, reaching back and grasping her ass, "feels pretty fat." She sighed and blushed, but otherwise said nothing.

"That sounds like a plan to me," Ellen said.

"Same! It's supposed to snow overnight," Holly said. "We can just be in this house together all weekend long with nothing to do but each other."

"You are such a little slut," Gabe replied.

She smiled at him sweetly. "You like that about me."

"I do, in fact…" He looked at the TV. "Oh hey, looks like you got into it."

"What are you playing? I definitely recognize that pause menu," Chloe said.

"Recovery," Ellen replied, sitting back down. "It's fascinating. I am hooked. Actually, I kind of don't want to go shopping anymore, because I want to just keep playing this, but...that would be irresponsible."

"Well, you can play for an hour, go shopping quickly with us, then play some more, then watch Chloe get fucked and spanked, then play all night long until the sun rises," Gabe replied.

"Holy shit, I can actually do that," Ellen murmured.

"Wait is that-oh, dude! You got a physical copy?!" Chloe asked, walking over to the coffee table and picking up the case for Recovery. "This is amazing."

"Why is that significant?" Ellen asked.

"Recovery was an indie title, made on a budget,

and so consequently, they didn't have a physical release. It was purely digital. However, there exist a few companies that like to give physical releases to such games, and Recovery got that treatment. It was my present to myself last year. Honestly, Ellen, you're really lucky. This game came out three years ago, and it has all the DLC it's going to get, and the sequel has been being worked on ever since. You're only going to have to wait maybe a year, probably less, for the sequel, whereas I've been waiting for almost three years now," Gabe replied.

"I guess I am lucky," she said.

"Can I watch?" Chloe asked.

"Yeah, sure. Babe?" Ellen replied, looking to Gabe.

"Let me check a few things on my laptop and then I will join you all," he replied.

They nodded and began getting situated on the couch. He headed into his office and fired up his laptop. He checked over his social media and his email, and was surprised to find that he actually had some new followers and a message.

He read it, feeling a bit strange as he realized it was basically someone telling him that they'd read By the Hearthfire's Light and it had moved them, being surprisingly emotional for not just an erotica, but a *caveman* erotica, and they were especially eager to the sequel.

He thought for a moment about how to reply, then fired off an appreciative response worded as well as he could make it, then he sat back in his chair and considered the whole situation. It wasn't his first fan letter, but it almost was. He could count on one hand how many he'd gotten so far. He thought it would feel more unambiguously good, but it felt kind of weird. Not that he didn't appreciate it, more that he just wasn't sure how it actually made him feel.

In the end, he sighed and shook his head. He was probably still kind of frazzled. He checked his sales. Fifty bucks for the day so far, altogether. That felt...not bad, at least. Gabe then checked how much he'd made for the month so far.

As of right now, the month was basically half over.

And his grand total earnings so far for the month were…

"Wow," he muttered.

About nine hundred bucks.

Gabe knew that he had gotten lucky. Chloe was right: there were a *lot* of people out there who didn't see nine hundred bucks from self-publishing in a whole year. He tried to take that into account, but honestly, he just felt behind, like he desperately needed to catch up. He'd researched his ass off and felt like he'd avoided most of the pitfalls that newbies fell into, but there were people doing what he was doing making *ten times* this amount, easily.

He quickly double checked his numbers. In October, he'd scraped together about seven hundred bucks. Not terrible. Then last month, he'd managed to hit a thousand. That felt kind of significant. His first four figure month, even if it just barely cleared the bar.

But here it was December, the month only half over, and he'd nearly almost broken that record. It was almost a certainty that he'd earn more than last month, and he knew that Christmas was supposed to be a really, really big time. Lots of people getting gift cards and new eReaders, excited to dive into the digital world and buy some new books.

Or, in his case, some new smut.

He had been spending all this month preparing to try and take advantage of that fact. He wanted By the Hearthfire's Light finished as a trilogy, and to launch the trilogy pack on Christmas Day. Theoretically, if he could get a bunch of people to buy it at once, that *should* propel it up the charts and give it more visibility, which would then, hopefully, cause more people the buy it. He was also working on a Christmas themed erotic short, but that one was more of a quickie than anything else.

Could he make it work?

By the Hearthfire's Light II was just about done, and he knew exactly what he wanted to do for the third and final installment, so he was fully ready to dive into the writing while Ellen and Holly did their editing.

He probably could manage it, but it was going to take some balancing. Which was going to be harder than ever now that he had *three* amazing girlfriends.

Speaking of which...

Gabe shut his laptop back down and got up. This could wait. For now, he just wanted to be with them. He headed back out to the living room.

CHAPTER EIGHTEEN

"You know, I never thought I'd actually be in a position where I really, *really* wanted to get back to playing a video game," Ellen murmured as they approached the mattress store.

"Were you not into them?" Chloe asked.

"No, not really, not beyond a very casual sense. I've never been...compelled by a video game. Until now. Recovery is compelling."

"It is. I love it. I went through a phase where I played the *fuck* out of it and even–"

"Even what?" Gabe asked, glancing at her.

"Nothing."

They parked outside the store and got out of the car, but then stopped before actually walking inside.

"Okay, now you have my attention. I want to know. I think I know what it is you were about to say, but I'm not sure," he said.

Chloe stared at him. He had yet to give her permission to snark at him. "Will you make me?" she asked finally.

"No, I won't," he replied.

"What do you think it is?"

"I think you wrote fan fiction for it."

She looked down for a moment and slowly began to blush. "Yes," she muttered.

"Why are you embarrassed of that?" he asked.

"Because so many people think fan fiction is fucking cringe as shit and honestly I kind of suck at writing. I was never going to tell anyone. I just posted it online to fangate and it's not like it had that much of a community, there were barely a hundred stories there...I guess you'd probably be better about fan fiction. I think? Because you're a writer? You get it?"

"For the record," Gabe replied, "I am nice about fan fiction because I am not a judgmental person. But also, yes, I get it. And also, I don't think there's much to 'get'. The urge to write fan fiction is really common. I wasn't going to give you shit for it. I actually wrote some fan fiction for Recovery and posted it there a while back. I never finished it, but it got pretty long...should probably go back and finish that at some point."

"Wait," Chloe said, her eyes slowly widening. "Wait, hold on...did you write Recovery Echo Four?"

"Uh...yeah, that was me," he replied.

"*What?!* You're telling me that *you* are Ghostpunk84?" she snapped.

"Yes, that was my handle...wait hold on, are you fucking GothicIce?" he asked, his eyes widening.

She moaned and hid her face. "...yes."

Gabe started laughing. Then he started laughing harder. "Holy *shit!*"

"I take it you two knew each other then?" Ellen asked.

"Yes! Oh man, she left me the fucking *snarkiest* reviews! And when I stopped updating, she sent me so many angry messages!"

"You asshole!" Chloe snapped, stepping closer to him and staring into his eyes. "Do you have *any* idea what kind of torture you put me through? I *loved* that story. I *loved* Recovery Echo Four! And you didn't finish it!"

"I'm sorry! I got depressed! I stopped seeing the point in finishing it," Gabe replied.

"...so are you going to finish it?" she asked.

"I kind of have a lot on my plate right now," he replied. "I'll...see what I can do."

"This is extremely entertaining," Holly murmured.

"Yes, but let's get inside and get this mattress because I want to go play Recovery," Ellen said, leading them into the store.

"I can really relate to that. Now that I'm thinking about it again, I should give it another playthrough," Chloe murmured.

As they began walking around the store, seeing what was on offer, Gabe noticed Chloe seemed increasingly distracted. And then that turned into it the expression of someone who wants to ask something, but is embarrassed.

"What?" he asked finally as they stopped at a king size and Ellen began checking it out.

"I noticed that your protagonist definitely, um, hooked up with several women. Including some of the characters from the game. And…" she hesitated, looking around while chewing on her lower lip.

"And what?"

"It was always fade to black."

"I mean yeah. I wasn't really about the sex scenes back then."

"Well…would you consider, um, maybe writing out those scenes? In detail? Stop grinning like that! This is embarrassing enough as it is!"

"So what I'm hearing," Gabe replied, settling hand on her hip, "is that you want to commission me to write fan fiction smut."

She sighed heavily, glaring furiously at him. "You are just loving this."

"I mean who wouldn't?"

"Yes. If that's what you want to hear, yes, that is exactly what I'm doing."

"What are you prepared to give me?" he asked.

She raised an eyebrow. "...what do you want?"

"I think you know *exactly* what I want, Chloe."

She swallowed and looked around. Holly was watching them intently. Ellen had the appearance of someone who was pretending not to listen.

"You seriously want me to trade sexual favors for fan fiction?" Chloe murmured, leaning in. "Because, for the record, I will definitely do that for you. And I'd like to emphasize *for you,* because I'd never in my whole *life* make this deal with anyone else on Earth."

"Good. That's a deal we can work out," he replied.

"What do you actually want?" she whispered.

"I want to humiliate you, Chloe."

Something a lot like lust flashed in her eyes. "You sick fuck, why do you want that?!" she demanded, her voice a harsh whisper.

"Come on, Chloe, who *doesn't* want to humiliate a bratty goth bitch who thinks she's so great? Who needs to be taken down a few pegs."

"All right, this is fun, but rein it in," Ellen murmured.

Gabe glanced at her. She was sitting on the bed now, staring at them intently. He looked at Holly. Their redheaded lover was blushing intently and panting a little, a strange smile on her face. He realized Chloe was blushing badly, too.

"Point taken," he agreed, relaxing.

If they weren't careful, he might actually start trying to find some way to fuck Chloe right here, right now, hidden away somehow in the mattress store. And that was *stupidly* risky. Way riskier than what he and Ellen had done on their proposal day.

"Yeah, okay," Chloe murmured, taking a step

back.

"Is this bed good?" Gabe asked.

"It's fine, but not the one I'm looking for," she replied. "Come on."

They kept going, and Gabe found himself getting increasingly distracted by Chloe. She kept poking him or touching his hand or brushing up against him, staring at him. It occurred to him, suddenly, that he still hadn't give her permission to snark at him. He almost brought it up, but decided to keep it going just a little longer.

"Okay," Ellen said as she finished laying on a huge mattress they called a king plus, "I think this is it. Bigger than a king size, memory foam, extremely comfortable. Give it a try because this is what I'm throwing my weight behind."

"It's got my vote," Holly said as she touched it.

"That was fast," Gabe replied, sitting down.

"I mean it feels comfy and honestly I'm more concerned about who's in the bed with me than the bed itself," she said.

"You'll definitely feel differently in ten years," Ellen muttered. "You are definitely in for lower back problems, my love."

"Yeah...I'm not looking forward to my thirties, either," Chloe said, looking down at her chest.

"I'm fine with this bed, it does feel really comfy," Gabe said after sitting on it for a moment.

"Chloe?" Ellen asked.

"Feels kind weird weighing in on something like this, but...I *do* have a vested interest," she murmured, sitting beside Gabe.

"That's right, you *will* be getting pounded into this on a regular basis," he replied, patting the mattress between them.

She had just stopped blushing but now she started again. "*Gabe.* You *fuck,*" she hissed.

"I'm just being honest, Chloe. If you can't handle that, I'm not sure if this is going to work."

She stared at him, gritting her teeth and clenching her fists.

"I like the bed," she said finally.

"Okay then, it's settled," Ellen replied. "We're getting it."

"Just like that? Seriously? You're going to drop..." She looked at the pricetag and her eyes bulged a little. "Over two grand?"

"A bed is worth investing in, and right now I can afford to invest," she replied. "And this thing is gonna last at least a decade."

"Not if we're the ones using it," Holly murmured.

Gabe chuckled. "She has a point."

"Well, let's buy it so that it can be delivered and broken in later," Ellen said.

"Aw man. I just realized we aren't getting this tonight. It's going to have to be delivered probably next week, right?" Chloe asked.

"Yes, sweetheart," Gabe replied, grinning at her and patting her on the head, "that's very good! That's exactly what's going to happen."

"Her eyes might start actually glowing with hellfire if you keep this up," Ellen murmured.

"Gabe, I didn't know you had this in you," Holly said.

"Can we fucking go home now?" Chloe growled. "Or can you *please* give me goddamned permission to bitch at you?"

"Oh yeah, I guess I haven't given that permission. I guess I forgot," he replied, grinning at her.

Her eyes widened a bit more. "You have been-*ooh!* You fucking prick!" she whispered harshly.

"You have my permission to be a snotty little bitch," Gabe said.

Chloe rose to her feet and turned fully to face him.

"Oh you've done it now," Ellen said.

"Your Recovery fan fiction was mediocre, but your other fan fictions fucking *sucked dick.* I read every last one of them and they were fucking trash," she said.

"Uh-huh," Gabe replied, standing as well. "If that's how we're gonna play it, we should wrap this up."

"Yep," Ellen agreed. "I really want to see you two in our bedroom together. Come on."

As they began heading for the exit, Gabe suddenly stumbled and then tripped. He managed to catch himself pretty well but ended up on his knees. He twisted back around and stared at Chloe, who was smiling sweetly at him.

"You...are you serious?" he asked.

"What? You should watch where you're going," she replied.

"You have no idea what you're in for," he growled, getting back to his feet.

Chloe shrugged easily and resumed walking. "Whatever you say. Keep up, you're being slow."

"You're fucking *getting it* when we get home, Chloe."

"Getting what? A *real* orgasm? Because that would be a nice change of pace," she said.

"Oh-ho-ho, *wow,* girl," Ellen said.

"Let's hurry this along," Gabe replied, his voice

flat.

Ellen did a good, but not perfect, job of containing her laughter as they went through the process of purchasing the bed. Altogether, with the bed and the frame and the delivery and warranty, it was almost three grand.

That seemed to throw Chloe off her game, but it definitely did not last. Once they had everything wrapped up, they hurried back out to the parking lot.

"I am going to drive," Ellen said, "because clearly you are too distracted."

"I've got a goth bitch complaining pathetically at me, of course I'm distracted," he replied.

"Hey, babe, you should probably sit in the front seat," Ellen said as they began getting into the car.

"...why?"

"Because I don't want Chloe provoking you into ripping her clothes off and fucking in my backseat," Ellen replied.

He sighed heavily. "Fine."

Chloe barely waited for them to get their seatbelts on before she began unleashing a torrent of irritating questions on him.

"Hey Gabe, do you actually care about what you're writing about or are you phoning it in? Wait, actually, before I forget, I noticed a bunch of errors in that one story I read. I can't remember which one, people were having sex in it, they all kind of run together. Oh! Also, I think you should have a better name for your main character in that caveman one. And–"

"Chloe!" Ellen cried, laughing. "You are going to give him a heart attack!"

"He brought it on himself! I was *very* reasonable and agreed not to bitch at him after the whole thing with the stupid asshole at my job! And then he treated me like a fucking brat even though I was being real nice, knowing I couldn't respond appropriately!" she replied.

"So *that's* what was going on?" Ellen asked. "Oh babe, you brought this on yourself. Nevermind, fire away, Chloe."

"Wow, thanks, Ellen. I love you so much, too," Gabe groaned.

"Hey, we all agreed, if you fucked up, it's on you, and that...well, you knew what you were doing," she replied.

"Thank you, Ellen. Gabe, I have this idea for a story I think you should write!" Chloe said, grabbing the back of his seat.

He groaned.

It was going to be a really long ride home.

CHAPTER NINETEEN

"Look at Gabe, he's all quiet and annoyed," Chloe said as they walked up to the house.

"I think you pushed his button too hard," Ellen murmured. "And that's gonna be on you."

"I can take it," Chloe replied as Gabe silently unlocked the front door. "Whatever it is that he thinks he's gonna do, I can completely handle it. He doesn't scare me."

Gabe took off his shoes and then his hoodie. He made sure everyone was inside the house, then he closed and locked the door. Chloe was wearing the strongest smirk he'd ever seen. She'd been almost nonstop on the ride home and he was actually really annoyed, but also not in a bad way? It was very strongly mixed up with arousal.

Though at this point they were both so off the scale it was a little hard to tell the difference.

Well, they had their safeword.

"I mean come on, how hard can he spank anyway? He's got jellyfish arms," she said, her grin growing somehow even wider. "Do you like having jellyfish-oh!"

When Gabe moved, it was fast.

He grasped her wrist and began pulling her towards the bedroom unerringly.

"Oh here we go girls," Chloe said, breathing more heavily. "Gabe's gonna show us what a bring, strong-ah!"

He shoved her across the room as soon as they got into the bedroom. She went stumbling, flailed, and fell onto the bed. Then popped right back, staring at him, her face red.

"What are you gonna fucking do, huh?" she asked. "Come on, Gabe. You think you're scaring me? You think you're really a dom?"

He walked over to the dresser and grabbed the handcuffs, then walked over to her. Holly had already told him she was very fine with him using them on Chloe.

"Are you serious? Fucking handcuffs? That's so fucking lame-*oh!*" she cried as he shoved her onto her back and then rolled her over onto her stomach.

He grabbed both of her hands and cuffed them in one smooth motion.

"You've been a bad girl, Chloe," he replied, holding her down with something like ease. He really was a lot stronger than her. That was going to make this easier.

"Don't call me that!" she snapped.

"Oh you don't like that?" he asked, running his hands over her jeans-clad ass. "You don't like being called a bad girl?"

"No! Don't call me girl at all, but *especially* don't you fucking dare call me a bad girl-*GABE!*" she shrieked as he brought his hand back and then brought it as hard as he could against her ass.

It made a very loud sound.

"I think the neighbors heard that one," Ellen murmured as she and Holly walked inside.

"You fucking...asshole," Chloe whispered, staring back at him with wide eyes.

"We haven't even begun," Gabe replied, sitting down at the foot of the bed and then wrestling her so that she was on his lap.

"Don't you *dare,*" she growled.

Gabe spanked her ass.

"Shut *up,* Chloe. I told you, you've been a bad

girl and the more you bitch and complain the harder I'm going to go," he replied.

She began to speak again and he cut her off with another very hard smack to her ass. Whatever she was about to say became a yell of surprise. She started wriggling around in his lap but he held onto her firmly.

"Stop! Moving! Around!" he yelled, spanking her ass hard with each word. "Take! Your fucking! Punishment! Like the *bratty! Little! Slut! You are!*"

She let out a shriek as he spanked her hard again, then she was left panting on his lap. She looked back over her shoulder at him again, red in the face, her hair becoming messy.

"That was it?" she asked.

"I haven't even begun," he replied, and pushed her back onto the bed.

Getting her on her back, he unbuttoned and unzipped her jeans, then pulled them and her panties down around her ankles, got them off and tossed them away.

"Holly, get me some scissors," Gabe said.

"Yes, sir," she replied demurely, hurrying off.

"Why do you need scissors?" Ellen murmured.

"Yeah, what the fuck?" Chloe asked.

"Shut your whore mouth," he replied, and spanked her bare ass, making her shriek again.

He kept at it, pushing her down into the mattress with one hand while using the other to spank her big, pale ass. He was a little worried he might've done it some damage, but besides being a little red, it seemed fine. And, well, at this point he trusted Chloe to let him know if he was going too far.

Holly returned with the scissors and handed them to him. He accepted them and flipped her over onto her back again.

"What are you doing?" she growled.

Gabe grabbed the bottom of her shirt and placed the fabric between the blades.

Chloe's eyes widened. "Don't you *dare,*" she hissed.

"I'll stop...if I hear the magic word," he replied, knowing that could be interpreted two ways. Either their safeword or please.

"Fuck you," she snapped.

"Okay then, I warned you."

He paused, just for a bit, and then began cutting her t-shirt.

"You bastard!" she cried. "You fucking asshole! I love this shirt!"

"That's why I'm doing this," he replied, cutting it up right through the middle, then cutting carefully along the sleeves, given her hands were cuffed behind her back and this was the only way he was getting it off without taking them off and putting them back on. "It's a punishment, you bad girl. Now…"

He gripped her bra and fit the little bit between the two cups in between the blades.

"You wouldn't fucking dare!" she whispered. "Not my bra!"

"Magic words?" he asked. "Do you submit to me, Chloe? Do you admit that you're a bad girl and will you apologize?"

"No! Fuck you!" she yelled.

"Okay then."

She gasped as he cut her bra off of her in a series of quick, economical snips. He tossed the remains away, knowing that he'd probably have to buy her a new one, but oh well. This was more than worth it. Her big, white tits were exposed now.

All of her was exposed now, her body nude and glorious.

Gabe suddenly felt like pushing this further. He gripped some of her hair and brought the scissors closer. "Maybe I should–"

"No! Safeword!" Chloe replied immediately. "Do *not* cut my hair!"

"I figured that was too much," Gabe replied, handing the scissors back to Holly and then getting Chloe onto her stomach again. "Now...back to the fun part. Punishing you for being an annoying, bratty little bitch and forcing you to submit to me."

"I will fucking *never* submit to you!" she snapped.

Gabe held out his hand. "Paddle."

Ellen apparently had it ready. He gripped it and studied it for a moment. Chloe had gone silent, no doubt waiting. He let the anticipation build, wondering if she would actually demand that he do it. Gabe reached out and laid it gently against her bare ass. She shuddered hard.

"Admit that you're a bad girl," he said.

"Fuck–"

He brought the paddle against her ass. She let out a surprised shriek and he waited to see if it was too much for her.

A moment passed.

Panting, she finally said, "Is that all you've got?"

He spanked her ass with the paddle again, harder, and then again, and again, and kept at it, making her moan and scream. He kept at it, trying to get a feel for when it would make the most sense to switch to full-on sex, and finally decided *fuck it*.

Gabe tossed aside the paddle suddenly and she gasped. He laid down on his back and pulled his dick out.

"What are you doing?" she panted. "What the fuck are you-ah! Gabe!"

He grabbed her, got her onto her side, laid on his, and then jammed his dick in her mouth started fucking her mouth with it. He did it just for a few seconds, then pulled it out.

"You like that, you little whore?" he asked, giving her a chance to stop if it was too much.

Chloe panted and coughed for a moment. "Eat me!" she snapped finally.

He chuckled and resumed fucking her in the mouth. She seemed *absurdly* turned on by all this, and he definitely was.

It was not going to be a long session once the actual pussy pounding started.

Honestly it was kind of hard not to just blow off in her mouth right then and there. She'd fucking got him so wound up in the car.

He was actually tempted to just fuck her fast, come in her quickly and be done with it, but that felt like it was blurring the line of punishment. All of this was ultimately in service to pleasure and gratification, for both of them.

Then again, she was pretty keyed up, too…

Gabe yanked her face into his crotch and pushed forward with his hips, pushing his cock as far as it would go into her throat. He held it there for a moment, then let go of her.

"You! Fuck!" she gasped, coughing.

"I told you that you were going to be humiliated, Chloe," he replied mildly. "Speaking of which…"

"Wait," she said as he pushed her back onto her stomach. She startled wriggling around again but he grasped her ankles and yanked her to the edge of the bed. "I'm not on my birth control."

"That sounds like a you problem, Chloe," he replied.

"You fucker! I swear to God if you fucking get me pregnant..." she growled.

She got her feet on the floor, now effectively bent over the bed, her hands still secured firmly behind her back.

"Go get a condom!" she yelled as he stood behind her.

"Don't have any," he replied, running his hands over her reddened ass, then moving to her hips. He rested his head against her glistening opening.

"Don't you *dare*-" she paused and shuddered hard, momentarily losing control and making a strange sound, "-*dare* put that small dick in me!"

"Holy fucking shit you are *seriously* looking to be broken, aren't you, you little slut? As for this, well, your mouth says no, but your body..."

He pushed his way inside of her and found her to be ridiculously hot and wet inside. Chloe tried to speak but lost her articulation to a loud, long, impassioned moan of pure bliss.

"That's what I thought you little piece of fuckmeat," he growled, grabbing her hips and immediately starting to drive into her, to pound her sweet pussy.

"Don't you...ah! Oh fuck..." she moaned.

"Submit, Chloe," he said.

"No!"

He reached forward and grabbed a handful of her hair by the roots and yanked. "Submit!"

"Ah! Fuck you!"

"Submit to me or I won't let you orgasm! I'll stop right here, right now, and I'll fuck Ellen or Holly and make you watch," he said.

"No!" she cried. "No, please!"

"Then you'd better fucking submit."

"I submit," she moaned, going limp.

"Admit that you're a bad girl."

"I admit it," she groaned.

"Say it!"

He slapped her ass and she cried out.

"I'm a bad girl! I'm a bad, filthy slut!" she screamed and started to come.

Gabe groaned loudly and began going even harder and faster, really pounding her brains out, making her shriek as she twisted and thrashed and twitched with the power of a full-bodied climax. He could feel her fluttering madly inside, her inner muscles massaging his cock as she got hotter and wetter.

He started coming, pushing deep within her and releasing his seed into her bare pussy, pumping it full, hard and fast.

It felt like an orgasm for the ages.

The pleasure blasted through his body like a seismic event, like a supernova erupting in deep space. He hunched over her, having to hold himself up as he started to lose control. His body felt like it was being bathed in pure rapture, his hips jerking, his lower stomach roiling wildly, his cock jerking like crazy inside of her as he spewed out his seed like a firehose.

Some time later, they were both finished, and all that was left was the sound of them panting and Ellen's and Holly's heavy breathing. He glanced over at them. They were by his dresser, Ellen leaning against it, Holly sitting on it, both staring with wide eyes.

Well, that was a good reaction at least.

He returned his attention to the woman who most needed it right now. Carefully extracting himself from her, he straightened up and undid the cuffs.

"Come on, sweetheart, let's get you taken care of," he murmured, leaning down and kissing the back of her head quickly before backing off and giving her some space.

For a moment Chloe laid there, then rolled over and looked at him. She seemed dazed and a little bewildered.

"Uh...you're being nice now?" she murmured.

"Well yes," Gabe replied, offering her his hand.

"Why?"

"Aftercare, Chloe. Unless...you don't want any? I can leave you alone, too, if you want that."

"No, no," she said, coming back to herself a little, "no, that's fine. Um...can we take a shower?"

"Yeah."

She took his hand and let him help her up.

CHAPTER TWENTY

"So...how you doing?" Gabe asked as he ran the soapy washcloth slowly and methodically over her back.

"Um...my ass hurts," she replied.

He laughed. "Well...you *did* ask for it. You actually demanded it."

She chuckled. "I know, it's on me. You did...a *really* good job. How's it look?"

"Red," he replied.

"After the shower, will you take a picture of it?"

"Sure."

"Sorry if that's kinda weird, but...I dunno, there's some people out there who actually like getting marked up with bruises and apparently I'm one of them? But I've never actually done this kind of thing before..."

"It's fine, Chloe," he said.

Gabe gently embraced her from behind and she leaned into it. He was being very careful to read everything. Her tone, her expression (when she faced him), her body language most importantly. She'd just done something not only sexual, not only for the first time, but something that was intense, physically and psychologically.

It was hard to predict how you'd react to that, even if it was what you wanted and had gone into enthusiastically.

"I'm not mad," she said after a bit, almost like she could read his mind. "I feel good about that. All of it. Honestly...I'm surprised."

"At what?" he asked.

"You...please don't take this the wrong way, but

you just really don't seem like a dom. Like, you surprised me so far, and it's not like you were doing a bad job before, I was just...there was a part of me that thought you'd probably do an adequate job when it was time to get *really* rough. But, like, Gabe."

Here, she turned around and looked directly at him. "That was *incredible*. Everything about it felt amazing. If you told me right now that you were some kind of professional, or you'd been doing this for years with submissive girls, I would absolutely believe you."

He laughed softly. "I'm afraid not. I have *some* more experience now thanks to Ellen and especially Holly, but I'm not experienced."

"Apparently you're just a fucking savant at it," she murmured. "That was...it was exactly what I was hoping for. It was better, even. When I orgasmed...that was probably one of the best orgasms of my entire life. And the actual spanking, just...it was perfect. It kind of felt like I was...I dunno, in a movie? Like it just seemed perfect."

"I'm glad," he replied. "Sorry about your shirt...and your bra. But I figured you would've stopped me if you seriously wanted to."

"Yeah, I wore my clothes knowing there was a good chance they'd get ruined by you giving me exactly what I was gagging for. They were both pretty old, so I don't mind losing them...would you really have done it? Would you really have cut my hair?"

"...I don't know," he admitted. "It was incredibly tempting in the moment. Probably not. But I was basically completely sure you'd stop me."

"Then why bother?" she asked.

"Partially to get you even more excited. I mean, I bet your heart jumped and your stomach dropped

OUR OWN WAY 3

when you thought I was actually going to do it," he replied.

She nodded. "Yeah, that *did* feel even more intense than what was already going on."

"I also want to get you more comfortable with using the safeword and saying no," he said.

"I can say no, Gabe," she replied, a little dryly.

"I know, Chloe, but this is...different. I'm not some dumbass catcalling you on the street. I am your boyfriend. You *obviously* have very strong feelings for me. I just, I would never want to be in a position where I'm taking advantage of you during one of the most vulnerable acts. I don't want you doing things or letting me do things just because you don't want to tell me no," he replied.

"That...is incredibly sweet. And I appreciate it."

She hugged him suddenly, and he wrapped his arms around her. They stood together for a time.

"This is special," she whispered.

"Why do you say that? I mean it is, but what do you mean specifically?" he replied.

"This feeling that I'm experiencing right now. I'm happy, and I'm comfortable, and I'm pretty satisfied. But the thing that matters the most to me right now is that...I feel safe. I actually feel truly safe here with you, after everything that we did. And that is special. It's very special."

"It is," he said, and kissed the side of her head.

After a while, they got back to cleaning up. He continued gently rubbing her body with the washcloth. Her smile was more subdued, more relaxed now. Everything about her was. They finished washing and, when she felt ready, turned off the water and began drying. Chloe kept looking at him and grinning.

"What?" he asked.

She laughed softly. "I'm just happy, is all. Seeing you makes me happy. Like it's just a shot of joy."

"That's pretty good to hear," he replied.

"It had better be."

They finished drying off and then headed back into the bedroom, then paused as they found Ellen and Holly naked and on the bed together.

"If you think you're getting away with not fucking us after a performance like that, you have another thing coming," Ellen said.

"Uh...I will do my best," Gabe replied. He looked at Chloe. "You said you wanted to see me doing it with them."

"I would love to see this," she replied.

"Perfect."

Gabe began walking towards the bed.

...

Gabe glanced over as Ellen paused the game.

He found her looking over at them, smiling a little.

"What?" he asked.

"Besides the fact that this is ridiculously cute, I'm also just remembering something. I had this idea of basically living like this when I was a teenager. Just this really cool, laid back, environment. I'd be with a guy and a girl, romantically, and we'd all date each other and be nice to each other, take care of each other, and sometimes we'd have other girls over to...have fun with. It's just sort of coming back to me right now. I thought about it a lot when I was miserable," she replied.

"Oh, wow. Yeah, this must be a dream come

true," he murmured, glancing down.

He was on the big couch and Ellen had taken the loveseat. Holly had stretched out so that she could put her head in his lap and Chloe had wedged herself between his other side and the armrest. Both of them had fallen asleep.

It had been a nice, relaxing day. After...satisfying Ellen and Holly, they'd made a large pizza and watched a movie. Then Ellen had pretty much demanded to get back to playing Recovery, and he'd relaxed with Holly and Chloe, talking about whatever came to mind until eventually Chloe had become aware of the fact that they had edibles.

"It's good you talked her into just a quarter of a gummy," Ellen murmured.

Gabe looked over at Chloe. "Yeah. She's lucky, she seems pretty susceptible to weed. She drifts right off pretty fast."

"I'm not sleeping," Chloe mumbled, slowly opening her eyes, "I'm just resting my eyes."

"Yeah okay, grandma," Ellen replied.

"Eat me," she growled.

"You'd best watch where you put some of your words," Ellen said, "because I actually will."

Chloe came more awake. "Uh...yeah that's a good point," she murmured.

"You two probably shouldn't argue," Gabe said, "given what you're hoping for when you argue with me."

Chloe sighed and stretched. "Yeah. Good point." She frowned for a second. "I gotta piss."

"And maybe sleep."

"No, I'm actually not that sleepy anymore," she replied, carefully getting up.

"All right. Holly...clearly is though," he said,

looking down. She hadn't stirred at all during this. "I think it's time to put her to bed."

"You want my help?" Ellen asked.

"I got her," Gabe replied.

He carefully got to his feet and then gathered Holly up in his arms and carried her to the bedroom while Chloe disappeared into the bathroom. Holly came awake as he finished getting her settled into bed beneath the blankets.

"Hey," she mumbled, "um...I'm in bed?"

Gabe chuckled and ran his fingers through her red hair. "Yeah, babe. You fell asleep on the couch. It's fine, it's late. You should go back to sleep."

"Okay," she replied. "I love you."

He gave her a kiss. "I love you too, Holly. Goodnight."

"Night," she murmured, closing her eyes.

Gabe slipped back out and almost bumped into Chloe.

"Hey," she said, "um...you wanna talk?" She did seem more awake.

"Yeah, sure," he replied, stepping over to the living room doorway. Ellen was playing again. "We're gonna hang out in my office."

"Sounds good, I'll be out here," she replied.

He grinned slightly and then led Chloe into his office, closing the door behind them. He sat down and put his back to the wall. After a moment of consideration, she sat beside him and did the same.

"You look amused," she said.

"Just...I definitely went through a period where I'd be really absorbed in games. The few women that I dated before Ellen were...mostly tolerant of it, but none of them were gamers themselves. And I was just thinking that it's a little funny, being on the other side of that for once," he replied.

"Gonna be true from me, too. I get *really* into games..." She slowly lost her smile. "So...there's one other thing I should mention. About myself. That I should've mentioned earlier, but I'm...I don't like talking about it."

"I thought something was bothering you," he replied. "I'm listening."

She pulled her knees to her chest and hugged them, frowning as she rested her chin on her knee. "It's not all the time, but I get really down sometimes. Depression, basically. I don't know why. Definitely it's worst in winter, but I don't know, it happens maybe once or twice a month. I'll just get really sad and bitchy and low energy and I'm difficult to deal with. Just really miserable. So...yeah. That's what I wanted to say."

"I understand," Gabe replied. "And I accept this about you. And I'll help how I can."

"You haven't put up with it yet," she muttered, then sighed. "Are you mad?"

"No, not at all. I mean it's reasonable to be reluctant to talk about mental health problems. Honestly, I appreciate the fact that you recognized it enough to tell me. And also that you chose to tell me. And me and Ellen and Holly also have problems. I've definitely got a nice little blend of anxiety and depression, Holly deals with depression too, and Ellen...has a lot to work through." He paused. "Okay, we *all* have a lot to work through, but she and Holly really do. Their families...are monsters. Mine too, but yeah. So it's fine."

"Okay...I feel bad now. Like there's this part of me that is feeling like I don't deserve this. You and Ellen and Holly are really nice. I kind of keep an eye out for people's natural...kindness level, I guess? If you know what to look for, you can't figure it out *for sure,* but you can get an idea. People give themselves away in little ways. And everything I see about you three interacting with each other, interacting with me, all says you three are actually genuinely nice people. And...it kind of feels like it's being wasted on me."

"Chloe," Gabe replied, and took her hand, "it is not being wasted on you. You're a good person, all right? You deserve to be treated, at the very least, not like shit."

She laughed softly. "We don't even know each other that well. I've definitely been a bad person before. I've been needlessly cruel. I was such a bitch in high school."

"Reconciling who you used to be, with who you are now, and who you want to be...is a complicated subject. It has a lot of...facets, honestly. And levels. And interpretations. I definitely have some hard lines I won't cross, in terms of putting up with things that people have done, but I also have to believe in bettering yourself, and, if not making up for the past, then at least making a better future.

"And, more significantly, I pursued you. You accepted. We are dating, right this very moment. You are my girlfriend and I am your boyfriend, and I accepted all of you. I'm not just dating a big titty goth girl or a gamer girl or a snarky bitch who is *amazing* in bed, I am dating all of you. And I realize it's going to take time to get to know each other, but I really don't want you hiding your bad emotions or insecurities from me. Also, as an aside...everyone is a shithead in high school to some degree."

She started laughing and then hugged him suddenly. "This is sort of just intensifying those emotions," she murmured. "But thank you. I...oh come on, you're kidding me."

"What?" he asked.

"I'm…" She sighed heavily. "Gonna cry apparently. Why? I'm fucking high and relaxed and happy, but you're telling me you accept me and are going to take care of me and that's just-that's a lot, and I'm having all these feelings–"

"Chloe...it's okay to cry," he said.

She was silent for a moment, then she started crying against him, squeezing him more tightly against her. They rearranged themselves a little, so they could more comfortably hold each other, and he held her as she cried.

It wasn't physically intense, she wasn't sobbing, but it did feel emotionally intense.

They sat there together and she cried and he did his best to comfort her. After several minutes, she stopped, and then slowly disengaged herself from him.

Pulling back, she blinked a few times, wiping at her face. "I feel better," she murmured. "Like a *lot* better."

"That *is* what crying is for," he replied.

She laughed. "Um...thank you. For that." She sniffed. "God, my last boyfriend fucking hated it when I cried. His idea of handling it basically boiled down to telling me 'deal with this on your own'. This...is *so* much better. And that fear isn't coming."

"Fear?" he asked.

"It got to the point where every time I cried, or started to cry, or wanted to cry, I got afraid that he was going to leave me, and that became other things, like if my friends ever saw it they'd decide to stop being my friends, or if my boss ever found me crying

I'd get fired...that one might be true. She seriously does not like me and I don't know why..." She sniffed again. "Ugh, I need to blow my nose. Thank you, seriously, for that."

"You're welcome, Chloe."

She got up and left the office, then came back a few moments later and came to sit back down, but hesitated, looking out the window.

"Wow..." she murmured.

"What?" he asked, getting to his feet and joining her. "Oh wow, it's snowing."

"Yeah...it's so pretty. You wanna go out into your backyard and just kind of be there in it?" she asked suddenly.

"Do you? It sounds like you do," he replied.

"I do. I'll understand if you don't want to."

"No, you know what, let's do it."

"Really?" she asked, smiling a little as she turned to look at him.

"Yeah, come on."

He took her hand and led her back out into the living room. Ellen glanced over.

"Hey you two, what's up? You look like you're going somewhere," she said.

"It's snowing and I, for some reason, want to be out in it just for a little bit, and Gabe is indulging me," Chloe replied.

Ellen glanced out the window behind her. "Oh shit, it is...well, have fun. Gabe *does* do that a lot, I'm coming to learn."

"Do what?" he asked as he finished zipping up his hoodie.

"Indulge our whims. It's very appreciated."

"Well, I do like making you all happy," he replied.

"And that's appreciated," Chloe said.

They headed out through the back door in the kitchen and came out onto the tiny patio the backyard came with. It wasn't a very impressive backyard, just a fenced-in square of now dead grass and just a single small tree in the back corner.

Now, though…

"Wow," Chloe whispered.

"It's so quiet," Gabe murmured as he watched the big flakes drift down in perfect silence. All he could hear was the very distant, occasional sound of a vehicle and nothing else.

"Snow has always been so wondrous to me. I don't really know why, there's just something that seems...I don't know, magical about it. As dumb as that sounds."

"I don't think it sounds dumb. There *is* something about it. It's like...this force of nature that seems so weird. Stuff usually doesn't fall from the sky and even when it does, it's often rain. This just…" He raised one hand. "Drifts."

"Yeah. And it can be like this, or it can be a shrieking storm that blinds and ultimately kills you if you can't get away from it. Or it can even be an avalanche. I've always loved things set in snowy places. And," she chuckled, "despite what we're doing literally this very moment, I love being inside when it snows. I just get this warm, protective, carefree feeling. Like it's okay if I lose the entire day to gaming in my underwear."

"It's reminiscent of childhood and snow days and Christmas vacation," he said. "Holly said something similar."

They stood there together for a few moments longer, and then Chloe took his hand. "Okay, I'm ready to go in now. It's actually really cold out here...will you give me a backrub if I give you a blowjob?"

"I definitely will," Gabe replied.

They headed back inside.

CHAPTER TWENTY ONE

There was a knock at his door.

"Come in," Gabe replied, spinning around in his chair.

The door opened and Chloe stepped in. She looked...both hesitant and resolute, which was a curious combination of emotions to display at the same time.

"Everything okay?" he asked.

"Yes. I just need to talk to, um...everyone," she replied. "If it's not a bad time?"

"No, it's perfect. I literally just finished sending off my current project for edits," he said, getting to his feet and walking over to her.

As they headed into the living room, where Ellen was playing Recovery and Holly was watching, Gabe considered the weekend so far. After that soul-searching talk they'd had Friday night, they'd had a long, pleasant sleep and then a long, lazy, snowy Saturday. He'd woken up earlier than he'd intended today probably because he was feeling the pressure of getting projects done on time more than ever and had gone to finish up By the Hearthfire's Light II while everyone was sleeping.

And now he had, and now he got to find time to juggle three more projects.

"What's going on? You've got an 'I have something really important to say' look on your face," Ellen asked as she paused the game.

"I do," Chloe replied, and motioned for Gabe to sit down, which he did. She stood before the three of them in one of his t-shirts and possibly no panties. "So...I woke up with this feeling. Except it wasn't really a feeling so much as it was knowledge. You know how you just...*know* something?"

Ellen smiled. "I know exactly that feeling."

"Yep," Holly agreed.

"Well...I know. I am definitely falling in love with Gabe. But somewhere in the back of my head I've known that since we first had that conversation. Ever since I first saw him, and he looked me right in the eye, there was just...this spark. This intense...*event.* And I knew. I was frightened and dismissive and told myself I was just really horny, but...after this weekend, no. Not after the things he said to me in the shower, and in his office Friday night."

"Goodness, what did he say?" Holly murmured.

"A lot of things, but mostly that he would protect me, and he would watch out for me, and he would take care of me. He made me feel..." She hesitated and looked up suddenly, blinking several times. She sniffed. "Goddamnit," she whispered, and cleared her throat. "He made me feel loved. He made me feel like he actually really cares about me. And to be honest, that was kind of the final barrier that needed to be broken.

"I knew that I was falling in love, but I also know that this isn't enough. Love is a two-way street. I was worried...that there wouldn't be enough for me, not with him so clearly loving the two of you. But I now feel confident that I was wrong about that, thankfully. Beyond that, though, I also love this place. This atmosphere. Like...Gabe, you're amazing. Truly. Alone you would be more than enough. But this house, you and Ellen and Holly together, it's just...

"It's perfect. I'm completely at ease here. I feel safe. I feel comfortable. I feel happy. The past forty eight hours have felt like getting something I never knew was missing or that I so desperately needed. But if you're seriously extending an offer to live here and be your girlfriend and housemate, then I want to take it."

Ellen sat up. "I am extremely glad to hear this, but...I want to caution you. I've made decisions before when I was deliriously happy and then came to regret them later. And I'm not saying that we are necessarily a bad bet for happiness, but..."

"I hear you, and I appreciate it. But, well, let me put it this way: I want this so bad that I'm willing to risk a *lot*. I am willing to risk giving up my apartment and some of my stuff and stability to try and make this work. This feels like...one of those chances, you know, one of those one in a million shots that comes your way once, maybe twice in a lifetime, and I'd be a moron not to pursue it aggressively. I need this in my life."

She fell silent and stared at them, looking more anxious than ever. Slowly, Ellen and Holly looked over at Gabe, and then Chloe did, too.

"Well obviously it's a yes from me," he said. "I want you in my bed, I want you in my house, I want you in my life. I am very willing to make sacrifices to make this work, and I'm convinced it can work after seeing how you fit within our household. Ellen? Holly?"

"I'm happy with it," Holly replied.

"Nothing else?" Ellen asked.

"Nope. I like Chloe. We get along really well. I want her around and in the house so we can hang out and have fun."

"Okay then. I guess it's on me...hmm. Honestly, I don't have any sort of immediate objections to this happening, I've been predicting that it would happen almost since the first night you two met. I guess my only thought is that you have a kind of...individualistic personality, or at least individualistic tendencies, and I know this because I have the same tendencies. And I would ask that you come into the household understanding that we work as a team, we consult each other about things, we think about how our decisions will affect the other two, and I would ask that you agree to abide by this."

"I understand and I agree to do so," Chloe replied.

"Then I'm game. This weekend has been great. That being said, we need some kind of timeline. How soon were you hoping to move in with us?" she asked.

"Immediately. Literally as soon as possible," Chloe said.

"Oh wow," Ellen murmured.

"I told you, I am *desperate* to be a part of this household. I'm, like, deliriously happy here. This place feels like what a vacation *should* feel like, and I don't want to let that go."

"Before we go even one step further," Gabe said, pulling out his phone and getting up, "there is one phone call we need to make."

"Ah, yes. Sadie," Ellen murmured.

"Do you think she'll be okay with it?" Chloe asked, looking worried suddenly.

"Almost certainly," Gabe replied, walking towards his office as he called up Sadie.

She answered in the middle of the second ring. "Hello, Gabe."

"Hi, Sadie. Um…"

"That goth girl wants to move in with you,

doesn't she?" Sadie asked, sounding amused.

"...*how* did you know?"

She laughed. "I knew the two of you were destined to be together after I watched you...interacting at that party. I didn't think it'd be quite so soon, but it makes sense. Although you must be getting pretty crowded at this point..."

"Yeah."

"I may be able to help. I'm going to send you an address, can all four of you come see me?" she asked.

"Yes, we can do that," Gabe replied.

"Perfect. I think you'll be pleasantly surprised. And, I think it's also time that you and I had...the talk."

"The talk, huh? You mean you're finally going to let me in on the thing you keep pulling my girlfriends aside to talk about?" he asked.

"...yes. Do you not know what it is?"

"No, I don't. They refused to tell me."

"Interesting. Also, appreciated. Also, from what I understand, you will be quite happy to have this conversation." A moment of awkward silence went by. "Well, ah, if there's nothing else...?"

"Nope, that's it," he replied.

"Perfect. Then will you please meet me at the specified address in about forty five minutes?"

"We will. Thank you again, Sadie, for...everything."

"You're welcome, Gabe. I'll see you soon."

They said goodbye and hung up. He stared at the phone for a moment, then walked back out to the others.

"Well?" Ellen asked.

"So, she said yes, first of all. Second of all, she wants us to meet her somewhere, she wouldn't say where, just an address. And finally, she says it's time she and I had the talk. Whatever that means."

Ellen and Holly looked at each other and grinned broadly.

"Finally," Ellen muttered.

"What's the talk?" Chloe asked.

"It's...did she tell you what it pertains to, dear?" Ellen asked.

He sighed. "Nope."

"Good. Although I feel like you should have figured it out by now. But, if you haven't, Chloe, come here."

Chloe came over and Ellen whispered something into her ear. "Oh. Well of course it's that."

"Don't tell him, and Sadie will want to know...how you feel about it," Ellen said.

"I'm fine with it. Honestly I thought it had happened already and Gabe was just weird about it for some reason."

"Okay, well, shall we start getting ready?" Ellen asked.

"Yeah, hold on...lemme see how far away this place is," he replied, feeding the address she'd given him into his GPS. "Huh, about fifteen minutes away. Probably closer to twenty minutes with the snow. The roads aren't all clear yet but it should be fine. So we should leave in about twenty minutes."

"Well then, I'll just play a little more," Ellen said, picking back up her controller.

"So, like...we're good? I can move in, effective immediately?" Chloe asked.

"Yep," Ellen replied, and Holly nodded.

Chloe looked to Gabe. He smiled and nodded. She hesitated, then let out a crazy little laugh and almost knocked him over as she hugged him. "I have a boyfriend! And we're moving in together!" She groaned suddenly. "I'm going to have to explain this to my parents…"

"Huh. Gonna be kinda weird, especially if they come over here. Like...oh yes, these are my boyfriend's roommates...yeah there's only one bed…" Gabe replied.

"They can*not* come over here," Chloe said. Then she sighed. "Fuck, it sounds like I'm ashamed to be with you or something but I swear to God I'm not, it's just...I don't know if they could handle it, the idea that I met a guy, fell in love in three weeks, moved in with him, *and* he's dating two other girls? And not casually, either. Two side chicks would be hard enough to explain, but dating me *and* two girls seriously?"

"We aren't just dating, we are functionally married," Ellen said.

"Yep," Holly agreed immediately.

"Um...that reminds me. No pressure at all, but...do you want me to propose to you?" Gabe asked.

Chloe pulled back and stared at him. "Wait, so, you did *actual* proposals? For both of them?"

"I literally dropped to one knee, pulled out a ringbox, and asked them if they would marry me. Both of them, yes."

"...and you'd do that for me?"

"Hell yes, I would."

"I…" She hesitated, a grin slowly spreading across her face. "No one's ever proposed to me before…"

"It's actually really magical when he does it," Holly said.

"Having been proposed to, like, six times, she's right. There's something special about Gabe doing it," Ellen agreed.

"Huh...yeah. Yes. I want that."

"Do you want to choose the ring or the location or...?"

"No," she replied. "I don't want to know. Surprise me. I want to be surprised."

"You got it...what's your favorite color?" he asked.

"I mean do you even need to ask?"

He laughed. "All right, that's fair, but it might've been something else besides black. I had to be sure, Chloe."

"Dumbass."

"Hey, do *not* fucking wind me up before I have to go somewhere. Because I can, and will, fuck you fast and hard, come inside you, and not let you come, just to prove a point," he replied.

She stared at him, flushing a little. "You wouldn't *dare,*" she said finally.

"Chloe...not right now," Ellen said with a surprising firmness in her voice.

Chloe sighed heavily. "Fine, whatever."

"This is definitely going to take some getting used to," Gabe muttered.

"We still haven't solved the problem of the house, though," Chloe said, looking around. "I mean, I *like* this place, it's just...I'm not sure if it's sustainable."

"Maybe that's where she's having us go," Ellen said. "If she's got two properties, it's a safe bet that she's got three. Maybe she's got a bigger, better house to offer us."

"Hopefully," Gabe said. "I finished Hearthfire Two by the way. Sent it to you two."

"Can I get a copy? I want to do editing," Chloe

asked.

"...yes."

"You hesitated there," she said, smirking.

"I'm concerned your natural brattiness will leak in too much," he replied.

"I'll keep it in check. You can trust me."

"Uh-huh."

"I'll get to work on it tonight babe, once we get back," Ellen said.

"Thank you, love. All right, lemme take a piss and then we can start getting ready," Gabe replied, heading for the bathroom.

CHAPTER TWENTY TWO

"Chloe, I swear to fucking God..." Gabe muttered.

"You shouldn't do that," Chloe replied.

"Okay, you two are going to have to work out some kind of 'no brattiness in the car' rule because I don't think I can trust Gabe to drive you anywhere based on what I've seen so far," Ellen said as they turned onto another street, heading deeper into what was arguably a pretty nice part of town.

"She's right, your sheer fucking stupidity is going to distract me into crashing," Gabe agreed.

"Fuck you!" Chloe yelled and kicked his seat again.

He sighed heavily. "You are such a mouthy bitch."

He expected something particularly cutting from her, but there was nothing. He glanced back at her behind him and she just stared at him with a smile that seemed more genuine than anything else.

"...you okay?"

"Yes," she replied, blushing. "Just...happy. I really love throwing these curve balls at you and the way you just effortlessly snatch them out of the air and throw them right back. You really do get me on some deeper level."

"I'm glad it makes you happy," he said, and she just looked down and blushed worse.

"You two are ridiculously cute together," Holly murmured.

"I think that's true of us all," Gabe replied.

"Here we are...wow, this is a nice house," Ellen murmured as she pulled into the driveway of a two story house, parking beside Sadie's car.

They all got out and joined her near the back of her car.

"Thank you all for indulging me," she said, leading them towards the front door.

"Honestly I feel like you're indulging us," Gabe replied.

"I suppose it goes both ways," she agreed. "Anyway, this is also my property. In truth, I would have offered it to you first but it's in need of renovation. Now that you're moving up to four, I'm thinking that perhaps I should get around to said renovation and then offer it to you."

"That's...quite the kindness, Sadie," Ellen replied.

"After a lifetime of being a curt and at times bitchy woman thanks to my job and my marriage, I have discovered that it is a very good time for kindness. Especially considering the current...climate we all find ourselves living in."

They all murmured in agreement as she unlocked the door and let them inside. From what she had said about renovation, Gabe had been expecting something worse. There were definitely some damage, he saw as she walked them through the first floor, but nothing terrible. The carpets were stained and torn up in several places, the wallpaper was peeling in several other places, and a few of the windows had plastic over them, but overall, it wasn't too bad.

"What made you buy properties?" Chloe asked as she took them upstairs.

"Initially it was just something I always wanted to at least try, and these two houses were in some rare circumstances where they were relatively cheap, as far as houses go. I fixed up the current one first and then began to lose taste for it. I got some preliminary work done here and even got a quote from a contractor to tear up the carpet, replace it, fix some plumbing and electric issues, basically give it a makeover, but then he got busy and we sort of lost track of each other. That being said, I can make it happen if you want this place," she explained.

"I think we want this place," Gabe murmured as they walked around the upstairs.

There was a master bedroom with a master bathroom that had an actually big tub and a separate shower stall, three other empty rooms, and another bathroom. Downstairs was a kitchen and three good-sized empty rooms.

"Before you decide, you should see the basement," Sadie said, leading them back downstairs. "Although I personally think it's rather nice."

"This place is honestly great," Holly said.

"Yeah, I love it already," Chloe agreed.

They headed downstairs into the basement. The stairs led into a big, open area with a sliding glass door that let out onto the backyard, which had an upper deck and a patio, as well as several trees. Gabe checked out the handful of doors along the basement walls. One led to a little closet, one led to a full bathroom, one led to a laundry room, and one led to an empty room where one whole wall was covered in a mirror.

"This kinda looks like a workout room," he said.

"I believe that's what it was," Sadie replied, "though I don't know for sure."

"This is a really nice basement. It's *finished*," Chloe said. "It's rare that I've seen those."

"It seems really big," Gabe murmured. "Not that

I'm complaining, it's just...it seems like a lot for four people."

"Well...you never know if it's going to *stay* four," Ellen murmured.

"I suppose you have a point, although it seems unlikely," he replied.

Ellen snorted. "Right. So, I'm in favor of moving in here."

"Same," Holly replied immediately.

"Yeah I love this place already," Chloe said.

They all looked to Gabe. He nodded, looking around for a moment. "I'm with them, this place is great. How long do you think it'll take to get it set up and also can we store a bed here?"

"Yes you can, I'll give you a key before we part ways," Sadie replied. "As for how long, it's very hard to determine, but I would say probably not until February."

"If we *do* move in after you renovate the place, what exactly would the rent situation be?" Ellen asked.

"Hmm. I guess bump it up to five hundred a month?" she asked.

"Are you serious? *Five hundred* a month for this whole house?" Chloe asked.

"Yes, I'd be willing to do that."

"Does it still include utilities?" Gabe asked.

"Yes," Sadie replied.

"Holy fucking *what?!* Seriously?! Aren't you...I don't know, more concerned about not losing money on this property?" Chloe asked. "I mean not to look a gift horse in the mouth, but…"

"I understand," Sadie replied. "The truth is that I'm lucky enough to have money. I'm very good for money. And I have ways of getting more if I truly need it. You all are such a nice group of people, and the knowledge that I am providing a home for people such as yourselves is genuinely worth more than two thousand dollars a month in rent."

"Well...thanks," Chloe murmured awkwardly.

"You're welcome. Now, ah...about the other thing. I hate to keep you all in suspense, but could we have this conversation at my house? I actually only live a few blocks over," Sadie asked.

Ellen's and Holly's eyes lit up with excitement. "Yes," Ellen said, "let's go now."

"Oh. I didn't realize you'd be so...eager," Sadie murmured as they headed back upstairs.

"Then you have *not* been paying attention," Ellen replied, and Sadie chuckled.

...

"I actually don't believe you," Chloe said as they followed Sadie's car down the road.

"About what?" Gabe replied.

"That you don't know what's coming. I mean, there's no way you can't know."

"Chloe..." Ellen murmured.

"I won't say anything specific, just...it seems *very* unlikely," she said.

"I have suspicions about what she wants to talk about, but...I'm reluctant to give myself too much hope. Or apply too much pressure to her, in case I'm completely wrong. Although given everything that's happened so far, I'm less inclined to believe that now. But all that aside...Sadie obviously wants to tell me, and even the appearance of springing a pleasant surprise on someone can be a joy to experience," he replied.

"That's...a good point," Chloe murmured.

"Regardless, we seem to be here," Ellen said. "Now, Sadie is a *very* nice woman, so don't snark at her."

"I won't," Chloe replied. "I know better than that. She's...intimidating."

"I don't mean don't snark at her just because she's our landlady and she's offering us a ridiculous deal, I mean don't because she's a very kind person who has clearly been through some shit and she wouldn't really know how to take it," Ellen said.

"Noted."

They parked and got out and followed Sadie up to a modest but nice single story house with light blue siding and a chimney. She led them inside and they got out of their coats and shoes. Once they were within, Gabe immediately got a sense of calm in the house. It was hard to describe properly, but he'd always thought that who a person was tended to be reflected in how they organized and decorated their house, but in ways that they didn't fully realize.

He had been in very neat, very decked out homes that felt extremely unwelcoming.

He'd been in messes of homes that felt very cozy and calming.

At a glance, Sadie's home felt a bit sparse, very tidy, and also welcoming and relaxed.

"You have a very nice home, Sadie," Holly murmured as she led them into the living room.

"Thank you," Sadie replied. "Please, uh...have a seat."

Two couches sat facing each other with a coffee table between them. Most of one whole wall was taken up by a bookshelf packed with books. He noticed she had no TV. The four of them sat down on one couch and she sat on the other, facing them all, looking vaguely nervous.

"So, ah, before we begin, Chloe...has Ellen or Holly spoken to you about...the nature of the conversation we're about to have?" Sadie asked.

"Yes," Chloe replied.

"And you are...comfortable with it?"

"I am. If I wasn't, I wouldn't be in this relationship."

Sadie chuckled. "That's a good point. All right, I guess it's finally time to discuss this with you directly, Gabe. Although I will be legitimately surprised if you have no idea of what's about to come out of my mouth."

"I think I do, but...life has cautioned me against getting my hopes up," he replied.

Sadie smiled, then laughed awkwardly and cleared her throat. "I see. Well, I suppose I've beaten around the bush beyond the point of reason, given all that's...gone on so far. This is the situation: I want to have sex with you, Gabe."

"Oh thank God," he whispered, and immediately everyone else began laughing.

"That was about the reaction I was hoping to get," Sadie said.

"So, hold on, let me get this straight: way back then, when we first met, you pulled Ellen aside and asked her if...what? You could fuck me?" Gabe asked.

"More or less," Sadie replied.

"You are extremely brave, I would have been terrified to ask Ellen that if I didn't already pretty much know for sure what the answer would be," Chloe said.

"It was...an emotionally taxing conversation, I

must admit. Not that Ellen did anything to make it that way, to be clear. I will also say that this is not...as I imagined it would go," she murmured.

"So, let me just ask: when did you decide you wanted to have sex with me?"

"As soon as I saw you, but I was...okay, I should probably just start at the beginning. After my divorce, I spent some time alone, and then I tried dating again. And it...did not go well. Dating as a woman in her late forties is evidently quite difficult. Although admittedly some of that is on me because I decided after my divorce I would never tolerate being treated with disrespect again."

"You fucking go, girl," Ellen replied immediately.

Sadie smiled. "Yes, well...life has taught us all hard lessons, I suppose. Anyway, after a while, I sort of gave up and shifted my focus elsewhere. And then, eventually, the idea of being a patron of the arts occurred to me. And then it also occurred to me that I was...fantasizing about a handsome young man, an artist or author or musician. I thought that perhaps we might have a...mutually beneficial relationship, even a casual one. I thought, if there can be sugar daddies, why not sugar mommies? So I began the process, put out the ad, and...then you called."

"This is really interesting," Chloe murmured when Sadie paused for a bit. She was blushing now.

"I always thought that phone call was...a little off. Not necessarily in a bad way," Gabe replied.

"Yes. I was...admittedly, as soon as I heard your voice, I reacted rather strongly to it. But naturally, given the fact that you were already in a relationship, and in a relationship with *Ellen,* I was...well, very cautious. I almost didn't say anything when we actually met."

"What changed your mind?" Ellen asked.

"In truth, I'm not sure. Just...something about the two of you. That's as far as I can quantify it," Sadie replied.

"I want to know how that conversation actually went," Chloe said suddenly.

"Honestly so do I," Gabe agreed.

"She was very straightforward," Ellen replied. "She pretty much told me that she was interested in potentially pursuing a sexual but casual relationship with Gabe, but that if I was not comfortable with this it wouldn't impact the offer. She was very adamant about that."

"I'm...not interested in any kind of coercion. *Especially* if it's sexual," Sadie said.

"And I appreciate that deeply," Ellen replied. "I told her I was comfortable with it, provided she remembered whose territory she was stepping into."

"How about you?" Gabe asked, looking at Holly.

"Oh. Well," Holly murmured, smiling a little, "it was basically the same. Very quick and blunt. And naturally I said yes."

"Your lovers have been...very accommodating. Especially considering how long it's taken me to consider it. I almost jumped you then and there, when Ellen first said yes," Sadie admitted. "It's been...a while. And I haven't done anything with anyone, physically speaking, since my divorce. In truth, though, after the initial emotions and...desires had time to settle, I decided to let myself sit with the notion.

"I had in my grasp, it seemed, access to an attractive young man who was a safe option that I wanted to have sex with and who, Ellen assured me, wanted to have sex with me, as well. I could do it at any moment. I've grown more cautious as my life has gone on, and so I decided to wait. I sat with it, with the possibility of getting exactly what I wanted, and now that enough time has passed, I've found that I still want it, and, very specifically, I want *you,* Gabe.

"But, I want to be clear, I don't think I'm looking for a relationship, per se. I want sex, I know that. And just with Gabe. You three ladies are just...*achingly* gorgeous, but I'm afraid my lust lies only in men. And I trust you all enough that I don't mind forgoing protection. The thing is, I'm still...nervous about all this. Not so much because of you, but because of me. I feel like I can't quite escape my anxiety about...intimacy. That's why I've been so slowly involving myself...what do you think of all this, Gabe?" she asked.

"I think that I am *extremely* excited and aroused by the idea of having sex with you, and that you are a *very* beautiful woman, I absolutely want to do this, and I also very much want you to set the pace for this. I don't want you doing anything you're uncomfortable with," he replied.

"I very much appreciate that," Sadie said. "I'm not quite ready for full on sex, but...if everyone is comfortable with it, I would like...I can't believe I'm going to just say this out loud to you all, but I *do* trust you...I would like for both you and I, Gabe, to get naked right here and now, and take turns pleasuring each other with our mouths until we orgasm."

"Does that mean we get to watch?" Ellen asked.

"Yes, you all can watch. Although, I will be honest, when we have sex, I would like that to be...private," Sadie replied.

"Not a problem," Ellen said, and Holly nodded.

Sadie looked to Chloe. "Oh yeah, I'm cool with this. You seem really nice and Gabe seems, like, *really* into you and honestly I understand wanting to have Gabe all alone and all to yourself."

"Well, thank you," Sadie replied, and stood up. "Shall we, um...proceed?"

Gabe stood up as well. "Yes."

CHAPTER TWENTY THREE

"Do you want to do it here?" Gabe asked as he took his shirt off.

"Yes, I'm fine with here if you are," Sadie replied, unbuttoning the jeans she wore.

"Yeah, I'm good. This seems fine for oral."

"I'm admittedly kind of nervous," she murmured. "I feel like my thighs have held up pretty well, all things considered, but overall...I'm not the woman I once was. And even back during my 'peak' I always felt like I wasn't too much to look at."

"Oh my God, Sadie," Ellen replied, "I know I can't just say 'stop feeling that way', but...you're really hot. As a woman, and as a bisexual, I feel like I can say that with confidence."

"Yep," Holly agreed.

"Honestly…" Chloe said as Sadie's shirt came off, revealing that she was not wear a bra, "I *pray* I look this good when I'm fifty."

"Really?" Sadie murmured, looking down at herself, now clad only in a pair of panties.

"Good lord, *yes,*" Chloe replied. "I would not have guessed fifty. Honestly you could say thirty nine and I'd have believed you. Not that it matters, I mean I feel like we put *way* too much emphasis on age as we get older, but...really, yes, you look great."

"Well, um, thank you," she said, then cleared her throat. "Um, who should go first?"

"Do you want to kiss first?" he asked.

"Oh...yes. I would like that. I would also like your boxers to come off, although I suppose it would only be fair that I also take my own underwear off…"

"At the same time?" Gabe replied.

She chuckled softly. "Yes, that would be good."

They each slipped their thumbs into the waistband of their respective underwear and slipped them down, then took a moment to study each other.

"I, um, trimmed," Sadie said.

"You did a nice job," he replied, looking at the collection of dark stubble above her pussy.

"Thank you."

They sat down on the couch beside each other, continuing to look at everything that was on display. She really did have nice thighs, just the right amount of extra padding, and the same was true of her smooth hips. Her breasts were pretty damn nice. Definitely not as firm or perky as a younger woman's, but Gabe found that, like with Isabella, he genuinely didn't care.

He just loved seeing her naked.

And kissing her.

She seemed to want him to take the initiative, so he did, pressing his lips slowly against her own. He took it slowly, and she seemed grateful for that. He kissed her and then pulled back just a little, waiting to see how she would respond to it. She smiled a little and then she kissed him.

Kissing Sadie was...

It was intensely arousing. There was something about her austere maturity, her ice queen veneer that remained even though he had seen behind the curtain to a closer version of who she was: a somewhat awkward, nervous, kind, quiet woman looking for, if not acceptance, then at least some safe and carefree fun.

That being said, she had not lost her somewhat intense maturity. In some way, she was kind of like what he imagined a powerful CEO or queen of a minor country might be like behind the scenes.

He felt her tongue gently probe his mouth and moved his own to touch hers. As they made contact, she hesitated briefly and then let out a soft moan. She took one of his hands and brought it to her breast. He eagerly began to massage it, taking into his grasp, enjoying the soft weight of it, the feel of her nipple against his palm.

They scooted closer and deepened the kiss. Sadie was breathing more heavily now. She leaned into him even more and he could feel an intense hunger, a desperate need in her movements. Had she said how long it had been since she had divorced? He couldn't remember, he didn't think it had been more than a few years, but he also knew that unhappy marriages that ended in divorce tended to have been void of physical intimacy for a while.

It might have been a very long time since she'd been anything more than hugged.

He groped her breast for a bit longer, then put his hand on her back, ran it down slowly and rested it in the small of her back. He pulled her a little closer and she moved with him, deepening the kissing even further.

After some time, she finally pulled back, panting and a little flushed.

"Goodness," she whispered, then laughed softly, her eyes a little wide. "It's been...a long time since I've kissed someone. Let alone with that much passion. You are *quite* the kisser."

"So are you," he replied. "Also, I can do you first."

"You are also very much the gentleman."

"He really is," Chloe murmured.

"I have *one* quick question," Ellen said.

"I'm listening," Sadie replied.

"Can we get pictures of this magical moment? Because I really want pictures. Also, completely fine if the answer is no."

Sadie thought about it, but not for long. "Today feels like an adventurous day, so yes. But I would like to see them after."

"Of course. Don't mind me..." Ellen murmured as she and Holly pulled out their phones.

"Would you like it now?" Gabe asked.

"I very much would, yes," she replied, nodding earnestly.

"Well, all right then. Lemme just..."

He got onto the floor and crouched before her. Sadie quickly readjusted herself, spreading her legs open wider. He made a faint noise of mild interest as he got into position and laid his hands on her thighs.

"What?" she murmured, a little nervously.

"Oh, nothing, just...it occurred to me that this isn't a tan. Unless you tan naked and frequently," he replied.

"Oh." She laughed. "No. I'm a quarter Hispanic," she replied, looking down at herself. "My grandmother was from Spain."

Gabe thought for a moment about how to respond, decided he didn't want any further conversation in general, and began eating her out. She gasped loudly and then moaned even louder as he began massaging her clit with the tip of his tongue. The sound was, as he imagined more than once, beautiful music to his ears.

He had wanted to hear Sadie moaning in sexual gratification since he'd first heard her voice and finally it had arrived. He worked her pussy slowly at first, trying to get a feel for her and what she wanted, what kind of rhythm was most natural to her, what she might be trying to tell him. That was something he had not quite learned, exactly, but become more aware of after going down on five women in the past few months.

They had ways of telling you things without actually telling you. Ellen, Holly, Chloe, Emily, and even from his one encounter with Isabella, they had all told him things with their movements, the way they shifted, even how fast they were breathing.

It was just a matter of learning how to better read them.

Sadie seemed a little lost in the moment, though, not telling him much, and that made enough sense. Given how long it had been since she'd been gone down on, she was probably overwhelmed by the simple fact that it was happening again.

He knew he'd been basically the same way when Ellen had first blown him.

Sadie moaned loudly as he slipped a finger into her. She was marvelously slick and hot inside and he couldn't help but imagine what it might feel like to slide his cock in there, nothing between them as they fucked until they both orgasmed.

"Oh *GABE!*" she screamed in what sounded like surprised pleasure as he pressed up into her most sensitive spot, first once, twice, then several times, much faster.

And then she began to orgasm.

She twitched and spasmed, and he continued eating and finger her when she didn't try to stop him. He kept pleasuring her throughout the whole experience, seeing what he could from his position down on his knees, his face buried in her crotch.

The sounds she made were those of pure ecstasy.

She twitched and thrashed around him as she came, and finally, as it came to an end, she went slack and he sat up.

"So...how was that?" he asked.

Sadie let out a weak laugh, her eyes closed, her face flushed and a little sweaty. "Do you even need to ask, Gabe?"

He chuckled. "Sort of a reflex."

"Well...whew, my goodness," she whispered, fanning herself with her hand, "that was...I think that might have been the best oral sex I've had in my life. It's admittedly been...*years,* but I honestly can't remember better...okay." She opened her eyes and sat up. "Your turn."

"Awesome," Gabe replied, standing up.

They traded places and he watched intently as Sadie got down onto her knees. She brushed her hair back, then sighed softly.

"Here, I've got you," Chloe said, and tossed her a hair tie.

"Thank you," Sadie said, gathering her hair up into a ponytail. "Wow, there's a situation I never thought I would ever, in my entire life, find myself in: a woman actually assisting me, in a nonsexual way, so that I can suck her boyfriend's dick."

"I can relate," Ellen said, and Holly and Chloe both agreed.

"There have been several...firsts for me lately," Holly said.

"Same," Gabe agreed.

"Your firsts mostly include 'do this sex thing but with *two* women' and 'do this sex thing with another woman while my girlfriend watches or is elsewhere but consenting'," Ellen replied.

"That doesn't make it any less amazing," he said.

She chuckled. "Fair point."

"There we go," Sadie muttered as she finished.

"Oh wow," Gabe said.

"What?" she asked.

"You look *really* hot with a ponytail," he replied.

She laughed softly and got settled. "Thank you," she murmured, then reached out and grasped his erection. "You are...thicker than I saw in the pictures."

"You sound a little nervous."

"Well...I *do* mean to have sex with you, and pretty much all my, um, experience for over half my life now was with one person. Who was *definitely* not this thick. I'm...hoping we can have sex without, uh, complications."

"I think we'll make it work, but if not, at least we know we can do oral pretty well."

She chuckled, a little ruefully. "Well, *you* certainly can. I...am out of practice. It's been seven years since I've done this. So, I guess, I would appreciate some kindness in that regard."

"You will probably do fine," Gabe replied, "but to be honest, I'm still just absolutely over the moon that I got to see you naked, make out with you, pleasure you, and then have you put my dick in your mouth."

Sadie looked up at him. "Ellen was right, you *do* have a way of putting women at ease."

"Apparently," he replied.

"Told you," Ellen murmured.

"Okay, I'm going to just…" She leaned in and licked slowly across his head.

"Ah...fuck yes," Gabe whispered, shivering.

She seemed emboldened by that and continued licking, adjusting and shifting so that she could get every part of his head covered in her spit. She kept licking for a good, long time, and then pressed her closed lips to the tip of his cock and gradually slipped it into her mouth. Gabe watched his dick disappear inch by inch in between those lips.

Closing her eyes, Sadie put her lips all the way down to the bottom and held them there. Abruptly she pulled back and started coughing.

"Oh, goodness," she said when she was finished, "definitely longer than I'm used to."

"Don't try to take on too much," he replied.

She nodded and put his dick back in her mouth, then started bob her head. She went slowly at first, but as time passed and she continued working his cock, she seemed to find her rhythm and it made her more confident. She closed her eyes again and for a while, he simply stared at her, basking in the pleasure that was the experience of Sadie, naked and on her knees, sucking him off, while his *three* girlfriends watched, and took pictures.

The bliss came on in waves as she kept sucking, moving her head, her luscious, wet lips gliding up and down his shaft, slowing as they reached his head and came back down again. For a time she simply paused there and used her tongue and her lips on his head.

"Oh man...just realized...forgot to ask..." he panted. "Can I come in your mouth?"

"Man, he can barely get the words out, you are *not* rusty, girl," Ellen murmured.

Sadie gave him a thumps up. He let out a quick sigh of relief. "Thank you. I *really* want to come in your mouth...and I'm about to."

She started bobbing her head again, going faster now, and he popped shortly thereafter. Gabe groaned as a hot pulse of utter rapture slammed into him, blasting out from his cock as it jerked in her mouth and started unleashing his seed. He came, intensely, and she kept sucking. She sucked out everything he had to give and the bliss was raw and potent and powerful. He felt like he was bathing in it as she sucked him dry.

When she was finished, she sat up and wiped her mouth on the back of her hand. "That went quite well," she murmured.

Gabe laughed. "Uh...yeah, that's one way of putting it," he replied. "Holy shit, Ellen was very correct, you are *not* rusty. You can seriously suck some dick."

She laughed as she got to her feet. "Well, it's nice to be appreciated. If you don't mind, I need a drink."

"Not a problem," he replied.

For the first time, he got a real look at her ass as she walked away. It was a very nice ass, generously padded, probably the part of her that had the most extra weight.

"Goddamn," he muttered.

"I know, right?" Ellen replied. "That is one hot ass."

"Yeah..." Holly murmured. "I wish she was into girls."

"Same," Ellen said.

"Yep," Gabe agreed. "What'd you think of that, Chloe?" he asked when he saw that she was just kind of staring at him.

"Um...I'm deeply aroused," she replied. "I didn't realize it was going to turn me on that much." She shifted in her seat. "Like...goddamn. I think I get it now? There *is* something to the age gap. Noticeably younger guy with noticeably older woman is...*quite* hot."

"Yep," Ellen said.

Sadie came back and started pulling her clothes on. "How did the pictures come out? I noticed one of you got some more extensive shots."

"That was me," Holly said, standing up and offering her phone.

Once she had her panties and shirt on, she took it and studied them. "Wow. I...didn't realize it would look so good. Some of these are also surprisingly tasteful, given how lewd the act is. What filters have you put on these?" she murmured.

"I haven't had time to make any changes," Holly replied.

"Seriously? I kind of assumed you must have done something because I look...much better than I thought I would."

"Told you," Gabe said. "You are one seriously hot cougar."

Sadie blushed and passed the phone back. "I suppose so." She looked around at them all. "So, um, now what?"

"What would you like?" Ellen asked.

"I...think I would like some alone time to process this. It was rather intense," Sadie replied.

"Then that is what we'll give you," Gabe said, standing up. "And, again, thank you for that. That was a very good blowjob."

Sadie grinned awkwardly. "I'm glad. Thank you all for indulging me. Also...I don't mind if you show those pictures to your...inner circle. I don't know what you call them, your friends that you have sex with. Just...nothing beyond that."

"Not a problem, Sadie," Ellen replied. "So far we've been very good about nudes. Really the only people I know who we'd be sharing it with are Em and Abby, and probably Krystal and her girlfriend, Liz."

"That sounds fine by me," Sadie said. She twisted her lips for a moment, then seemed to come to a decision. "Can I have a moment alone with Gabe?"

"Of course, we'll go wait in the car," Ellen replied.

Gabe watched them go as he pulled his own clothes back on, then turned his attention to Sadie. "What's up?" he asked.

"I wanted to say that I really appreciate this...experience. I haven't been emotionally or physically vulnerable with another person for a long time now. In truth, I was beginning to wonder if perhaps that part of my life was over. I don't...yearn for it nearly as much as I did when I was younger. I like the solitude more now. But I'm finding that I don't want it to be absolute, and...well, finding someone that I can have safe and *good* sex with, it kind of felt like an impossible task. But now I've found you."

"I'm glad I could help," he replied, "and I am also extremely grateful."

She regained some of her sly smile. "You *really* wanted to bang a cougar that bad?"

"I really wanted to bang *you* that bad. And also, yes."

"Am I your first cougar?" she asked.

"Ah...no."

"Well now I'm curious."

"A woman named Isabella. Met her through a friend of Ellen's, she's celebrating the end of a rather nasty divorce, and...well, same thing really: she wanted someone a lot younger than her who was a safe bet."

"Interesting...so it *genuinely* doesn't bother? Me being fifty years old? Looking like I do? I've wanted to go after a younger man for some time now, but even in my fantasies I figured he would be...putting up with certain aspects of aging."

"I don't care," Gabe replied with a shrug. "You're just really beautiful to me. Aging doesn't bother me, apparently."

"Well, given how intensely you went while eating me out and making out, I'm inclined to believe you...so I know I said I want this to be casual, but...would you be willing to take me out on a date when it comes time to have sex? Or is that too intimate? Will the others have a problem with it?"

"I know Ellen and Holly won't, and I'm fairly sure Chloe won't. And I certainly don't. I would love to take you on a date, Sadie. It just might have to wait a bit, probably next month, I have, just...a *lot* of writing to squeeze in," he replied.

"That's not a problem. I really appreciate it. I'll get you updates on the renovations when I have them," she said.

"Thanks."

They hugged, wished each other farewell, then she remembered to give him the key to the other house at the last moment, and then he was out the door.

CHAPTER TWENTY FOUR

"So...is this going to be, like, a regular thing in my life now?" Chloe asked after they'd driven for a few moments.

"I'd say yes," Ellen replied.

"How do you feel about that?" Gabe asked.

"So...I'm liking it," Chloe replied. "I thought I would at worst tolerate it, at best enjoy watching you indulge in it sometimes, but, um...that was really hot. I've never really been a porn kind of person, but seeing it happen live, in front of me? Yes, evidently that does things for me. Watching you intimately swap oral with a fifty year old ice queen was...um...can we have sex as soon as we get home? I would like that a lot."

Gabe laughed. "Yes, we can do that. But we should probably discuss more immediate plans. Like, how we're going to go forward with our life kind of plans. From where I stand, it seems as though we are getting a new bed on Monday, uh tomorrow, and Chloe wants to move in with us, even though it'll be a crowded couple of months, right? That's all correct?"

"Correct," Ellen said.

"Yep," Chloe agreed. "That's what I want."

"Okay, good. And we have about...what, two weeks to get you moved out of your apartment?"

"Correct. It's the...seventeenth now, and I have to be out by five PM on the thirty first if I choose not to renew."

"All right. We should get some coordination figured out. I say tomorrow, when the bed shows up, two of us go to rent a moving van. From there, we load up the queen size in the van and drop it off at the new house, then we go to Chloe's apartment and move all the big stuff that needs moving. Either to our place or to the new house. Still track?" he asked.

"Yes," Chloe said. "Although I've got a four hour shift tomorrow, so I won't be free until around four PM. And maybe we should hit up my apartment tonight and do some packing…"

"Probably prudent," Gabe replied. "I will say, though, that once we get this moving sorted out, I need to kind of…sequester myself in my office. I have a lot I need to get written before the end of the year. And that means I'll need your help with editing, Ellen and Holly, as in, getting it back to me a little quickly."

"I will finish the edits tonight," Ellen said.

"Same," Holly agreed. "It's a lot easier now that we both have access to the same document simultaneously thanks to that online thing."

"I really appreciate it. Chloe, I sent you an invite if you still want in," Gabe said.

"Actually, I…think I'll pass. For now at least. I didn't fully realize how time sensitive it was. I don't want my distracted ass fucking up your plans," she replied.

"What's got you so distracted?" he asked.

"…um, *you?* I thought that would be obvious. In case it isn't clear: I am definitely falling in love with you. And that is *extremely* distracting."

"Yeah…" Ellen murmured.

"Mmm-hmm," Holly agreed with a small grin.

"Oh. Um…well, awesome then," he replied awkwardly.

"Yeah, *I* don't know what to do with happiness," she muttered.

"I mean…falling in love and being fallen in love

with is spectacular on its own. I...am now doing it for a third time. While still in a relationship with the first two women. It's kind of overwhelming at times," Gabe replied.

"That's a good point," Holly murmured.

"Hmm," Ellen said.

"Uh-oh, I know that tone," Gabe said, looking over at her.

"I'm feeling...feisty right now."

"Oh shit," he muttered.

"Uh, should I be worried?" Chloe asked.

"It really depends," Ellen replied.

"On *what?*"

"On what kind of woman you are. If you knew that there was a woman somewhere nearby who Gabe had asked out earlier this year and her response was to *laugh in his face,* how would that make you feel?"

"Oh no…" Gabe groaned.

"Really pissed off," Chloe replied. "Why? Who?"

"Let's just make a little pit stop at Becky's. It's a grocery store," Ellen said.

"Ellen…" Gabe replied.

"We need milk and bread."

"Is there some bitch who laughed in Gabe's face working there?" Chloe asked.

"That is exactly the tone I was hoping for, and yes," Ellen replied.

"She might not be working right now," Gabe said.

"Then you have nothing to worry about," Ellen said.

He sighed heavily. "This doesn't seem like a path we want to go down."

"I just want you to go in there with Chloe all up

on you, buy some groceries, and leave," Ellen replied with a shrug.

"Then she'll think I'm cheating on you," he said.

"Exactly. And I'm very curious to see if she'll tattle on you to me, because she has tried to reach me through social media as recently as this month. Holly already went in with Gabe recently, though she wasn't 'all up on him'," Ellen replied. "She sent me a pic asking 'do you know what Gabe is doing when you aren't around?'."

"What'd you say?" Chloe asked.

"That Holly's our roommate."

"Come on, Gabe, you don't want to fuck with her just a *little?* She laughed in your fucking face. Like that had to hurt," Chloe said.

He sighed. "I mean *yes,* I do, and *yes,* it did, but honestly I feel like Ellen made a very good point when she told me that Sandy actually saved me a lot of trouble by showing me who she was immediately, instead of making me date her for three months before figuring out she's a bitch. That being said...yes, part of me wants to do this."

"The question is, will you?" Ellen replied, pulling into the parking lot of Becky's.

"Yes," he said.

"Okay then." She parked. "Chloe, go in there with Gabe and act like exactly what you are: his girlfriend."

"Can do," Chloe replied with a grin.

"Don't...do anything crazy," Gabe said as they got out.

"I won't," Chloe said.

"We'll be here, lovebirds," Ellen said.

Gabe sighed and took Chloe's hand. "We're keeping it simple. We get one of those small baskets, grab some basic shit, go through the checkout lane, and leave."

"Go through *her* checkout lane," Chloe said.

Gabe sighed again but said nothing. They walked inside. He looked around.

Sandy was at one of the checkout lanes.

Great.

She looked right at them as Chloe grabbed a basket. She stared at them silently as they began walking deeper into the store. Chloe paused and gave him a long, lingering kiss on the mouth before they disappeared into one of the aisles.

"So that was her, right? Tell me that was her, the skinny blonde?" Chloe asked.

"Yes, that was her," Gabe replied.

Chloe chuckled deviously as they walked on. "That bitch."

"Why are you so into this? I swear, you and Ellen are taking it very personally. Holly too, actually, now that I think about it…"

"Gabe, come on, are you fucking with me right now? Of course I'm taking it personally. And not just because we're dating now. You're a *great person,* okay? That much is obvious to me. A great boyfriend and a great person. You're kind, thoughtful, hardworking, smart, dominating without being a douche about it, easy to live with...you're amazing. And someone *laughed in your face* when you *handed them the opportunity to date you?* Yeah no, fuck that. Fuck that hard. Fuck that stupid bitch in her stupid fucking face. The fucking *arrogance* of it."

"I mean it's not like she knew, Chloe," he replied. "It's not like she had that entire picture when she made that decision to turn me down. And people are allowed to turn other people down."

"She didn't just *turn you down*, Gabe, she fucking spit in your face. Do you know what that kind of response is, Gabe? It's the kind of response that says 'I'm offended you thought you were good enough to even *look at me* you fucking peasant'. It's arrogance and I fucking hate arrogance."

"Jeez, you are *really* fired up about this...this might be a stupid idea," he muttered.

"I know how to control myself," Chloe replied. "And, I mean, am I wrong? After what you did back at the coffee shop? Or to Ellen's ex?"

"Those were both *reactionary*," Gabe replied. "But I get it. You have a point. When that shit for brains tried to lay hands on you...something definitely activated in my head. But I'm not necessarily convinced it's something we should...feed."

"Think of it less as feeding and more as...sharpening," Chloe replied. "I don't advocate pulling a knife on every rude shithead, but...having a particularly sharp knife for the handful of times it's necessary to use *is* a good idea."

"...maybe," he murmured. "I'm not really a naturally aggressive person."

"And I appreciate that about you. Now...let's wrap this up and go see what Little Miss Prissy Bitch has to say."

Gabe was still a little reluctant as they finished by grabbing some bread and then headed for the checkout lanes. He had to admit that his curiosity was more powerful. And yes, his pettiness. He still wasn't completely over the whole thing because *damn* did that memory still sting. He still thought that, on the whole, too many guys overreacted to being turned down. As *clearly* evidenced by his interaction in the coffee shop earlier.

But Sandy didn't have to laugh in his goddamn face about it. She didn't even say yes or no. She just laughed, *loudly*, and then had walked away.

It just seemed unnecessarily cruel.

Chloe made no effort to hide their relationship status as they approached the checkout lane. She was clinging onto him and she even kissed his cheek as they walked up. He saw Sandy snap a quick photo of them and then text rapidly.

Oh yeah, she was definitely sending that to Ellen.

He kind of felt a little bad about that, because that wasn't a bad instinct. But he knew it was bullshit. She wasn't telling Ellen because she cared about Ellen, she was telling her to try and get in her good graces. She'd fuck Ellen over in a heartbeat if it suited her.

Sandy took a quick look around as they approached, then glared at him as they put their stuff on the conveyor belt. He thought it interesting that, in the exchange that followed, she didn't stop ringing up or bagging items.

"I can't believe you," she whispered, her voice low and angry. "Cheating on Ellen?"

"I'm not cheating on Ellen," Gabe replied. "And what fucking business is it of yours?"

"Ellen is my *friend,* you piece of shit. And you're not cheating on her? I saw you two kiss! I took a picture and let her know. Don't try to give me some bullshit about how you're just friends–"

"She's my girlfriend," Gabe said.

"So, what, Ellen dumped your ass finally?"

"You are *such* a bitch," Chloe snapped suddenly.

"Oh fuck you, you fucking goth whore–"

Chloe leaned forward suddenly and put her hands down roughly on the conveyor belt, which had stopped moving, and Sandy's eyes widened as she leaned back in surprise. "Bitch, call me a whore again and I'll jump right over this thing and put your face in that fucking cash register. I *don't give a FUCK,* do you understand me?" she growled, her voice low and dangerous.

"Chloe," Gabe said, putting a hand on her shoulder. "Again, not that it's any of your business, but I'm dating Chloe *and* Ellen. And you need to stop pretending you're friends with Ellen. Now will you finish the transaction?"

Sandy looked at him, then back at Chloe, then back to him, then finally punched something quickly into the register. She angrily spat out the amount and Gabe paid in cash. He and Chloe each took a bag and walked away.

"That was *not* calm," he muttered as they walked out.

"She called me a whore," Chloe replied.

"You called her a bitch," he pointed out.

"After she jumped down your fucking throat about me, trying to pretend she was looking out for Ellen-fuck that bitch," she growled.

Gabe tried to think of something to say in response, then just found himself laughing softly and shaking his head as they got back out into the parking lot. They got in the car and buckled in.

"So...you both seem kind of tense," Ellen said. "I got a message from Sandy."

"Yeah...Chloe sort of escalated quickly," Gabe replied. "She's also proven that she can be really fucking scary when she wants to be."

"What'd you *say* to her?" Holly asked.

"Let's start driving and I'll tell you," Gabe replied.

CHAPTER TWENTY FIVE

"Hey, Gabe…"

"Yeah, Chloe?"

He looked over when she didn't say anything. She was by her dresser and her closet, both of them open, clothes everywhere. She'd been going through them for half an hour now.

"I was just wondering...does it freak you out? Me telling you that I'm falling in love with you? I mean, it doesn't seem to, but...I guess I was thinking about if our positions were reversed. It would kind of freak me out. It's just, three relationships seems like a lot of pressure," she said finally, looking over at him.

"You telling me that you're falling in love with me doesn't freak me out," he replied, "but you have a point: it is a lot of responsibility. And it makes me nervous sometimes. But generally it doesn't."

"Why not?" she asked, turning to face him a bit more.

"I guess because it's going so smoothly. We don't really fight, we don't even really argue. The way in which we live our lives seems to mostly align. All of us seem to be introverts, with varying levels of 'wanting to go out sometimes'. We all pretty much want the same things. Also, Ellen is, like, *really* smart and responsible. I'm not relying on her completely to be the 'adult', but I at least feel like I can count her on, most of the time, to let me know if I'm making a stupid decision. And you seem to fit in very nicely with us as well," he replied.

"That all makes a lot of sense, actually," she murmured. "Okay, one other question that's been on my mind for a little bit now...how far do you intend to take this whole thing?"

"What whole thing?" he replied.

"The relationships. I mean, you're dating and living with three women right now. *Clearly* there are going to be more side chicks, based off your interaction with Sadie today, but that's not really the same thing. How many girls are you planning on seducing and moving in with us? Because that house had like...seven bedrooms."

Gabe frowned as he considered that. "Well...it's something I think about, too," he murmured. "I mean there probably should be a cutoff point. Honestly, if circumstances were a little different, I probably would say you're the last one."

"...but?"

"But Krystal exists. And so does her girlfriend, Liz. And they each seem like not only would they fit pretty well with us and our lifestyle, but they're both *super* hot. And Ellen seems convinced that moving them in with us might be a remote possibility," Gabe replied.

"Ugh, you're telling me I'll be living alongside *two* absurdly hot redheads? Seriously? Like, I get it, you tell me we're not competing, but, like...mmm. It's tough. It's tough sometimes seeing Ellen and Holly and knowing I'm not that."

"What the fuck are you talking about?" he asked.

"Look, I know you respect me and are really attracted to me, but I mean there's obviously a hotness hierarchy going on, and I'm at the bottom," Chloe replied.

"What the fuck? No you aren't. Also, no there isn't."

She frowned and crossed her arms. "Okay, so if you were suddenly told you could only fuck one of us, who would you choose?"

"That isn't fair! And I don't know! Chloe, come on, you can't keep being like this. You can't keep feeding this. I know you're paranoid and anxious and depressed, but...I am *not* tacitly judging your looks and ranking you in hotness." He sighed suddenly. "Okay, look, I'll put it like this: you're all tens for me, for different reasons, but you're all tens. You're all ridiculously and equally beautiful and sexually attractive. And that's not some bullshit answer I'm giving you to soothe your ego or try to avoid a fight, it's my authentic answer," he said.

Chloe stared at him like she was prepared to fight, but she suddenly lost the expression. "Fuck, I'm sorry. That was kind of mean. I'm sorry, I just…" she sighed and shook her head, looking suddenly tired.

"I forgive you," he replied. "I just wish you'd...I don't know, accept it a little more permanently when I told you this things? But at the same time, I get it. The damage is done, we just have to live with it and repair it as best we can. We've all been raised to think we're unattractive because that makes more money for stupid assholes up top, and that shit leaves a stain."

"It does," she said. "I hate it. And I hate it when people basically just shit on anyone who feels ugly by saying 'oh just stop buying into the stereotypical beauty standards', like I can just *do* that! Like fucking anyone can just *stop!* Literally it wouldn't be a problem if we could." She shook her head and started sorting her clothes again. "Sorry. I'm grumpy. I don't know why. Actually, I wasn't even grumpy like five minutes ago, but I guess it's just really easy for me to slip into that mindset?"

"It *truly* is when you're depressed. Bad thoughts

take swings at us like passing meteors, but the more depressed you are, the more 'gravity' there is to suck those bad thoughts in and give them a place to land, where they burst and take root and get powerful, and then it's a whole thing you've got to either dig out or wait out," he replied.

"That...is a very good way to put it." She fell silent for a few seconds, pausing in her actions and apparently just staring at the t-shirt in her hands. She turned to face him again. "So this is a different train of thought, but it's also a weird one, and...I kind of need to talk about it, but given it's about you, it feels really weird to talk about it."

"I will help however I can," Gabe replied.

"Okay good, I really appreciate it. Um." She twisted her lips, looking away for a moment, sorting through her thoughts. "Okay," she said, refocusing on him, "is this insane? Am I being insane? We met, like, less than a month ago. I actually looked it up, because I was texting my friend about that party where you and I met that night. We met on the twenty fourth of November. It's now the seventeenth of December. And I am moving in with you...if I had been told this before we met, that it was about to happen, I would assume that I was suffering from a brain tumor. The fact that I'm not really questioning this is...making me question it." She sighed. "I sound insane."

"No," Gabe said, getting up and then sitting down on the floor across from her, "you don't sound insane. I understand. Changes are scary, and we also have *way* too many examples of people meeting, hooking up, and deciding they have met their soulmates immediately, only to have their lives shattered three months later."

"Yeah...ugh, we're going to have to wait a bit to tell my parents...will you meet my family at some point? I guess you've gotten off kind of easy with Holly and Ellen, you don't have to worry about in-laws with them because they hate their families I guess, but I actually like mine and they're at least somewhat in my life still…"

"Yes, I will meet your family and do my best to get along with them," Gabe replied. "Although I think a reality you're going to have to face is that at some point they're going to find out. They're going to discover that...I am also with two other women. And we're all living together."

"I know," Chloe replied, sighing. "I'm not naive enough to think I can keep them in the dark forever. Although I do think it's possible that, if I can keep them in the dark about it until we move, then I can get them to think that Ellen and Holly are roommates…" Her eyes widened a little. "Oh man, is this a super shitty thing to say? Or try and do? I'm not embarrassed about the relationship, I just...don't know how my parents will react. I can't imagine they'll react well. And I don't want to have to choose between them and you...fuck. Are you mad?"

"No," he replied, "I'm not mad. This is...a thing I've never had to deal with before. Because you're right in that with Ellen and Holly and myself, we don't have anyone in our lives who we need to hide the more...controversial aspects of how we choose to live from. And I have to respect the fact that you value your relationship with your family."

"I mean you don't necessarily *have* to...not that it isn't appreciated," she replied.

"Maybe *have to* isn't the right phrase. Choose to. But I feel like choosing to pursue you like this and *not* accepting this about you would be really shitty."

"That doesn't seem to stop a lot of people from pulling that shit...so thank you. Too many people just assume problems or differences will sort themselves out when they start dating someone new," she said.

"Yeah, I've noticed that. I think it's more a thing that people don't realize they're doing. But I want you to feel comfortable enmeshing your life with mine. You're going to have to make some changes to fit into my life, and I want to make whatever changes I can to rearrange my life so that you fit more easily into it. I know I'm asking for a lot. So...keep talking. Tell me more. Tell me about your concerns."

"I feel like we've covered most of it," she murmured. "Mostly I'm just afraid I'm seriously fucking my life up because I'm in lust with a boy. I'm giving up my apartment, I'm giving up my job, I'm moving in with you..."

"If it all goes to hell, you could move back in with your parents, right?" he asked.

She nodded slowly. "Yeah. It wouldn't be ideal, but yeah." She laughed suddenly. "My dad never admitted to it and actually lied about it, but he and mom met...kind of similarly. My mom is a lot more, um, open. If one of them is going to understand about this whole relationship, it's going to be her. I guess they hooked up kind of fast after meeting at a party, and he spent the night at her place, and just...slotted right into her life? They just started dating the next morning and they were moved in together in like three weeks and then married after three months, and then a few years later they had my sister."

"What does your dad say about it?" Gabe asked.

She laughed and rolled her eyes. "That he 'courted' her. They went on several dates and they were so romantic and it was true love and whatever. I could always tell *something* was off about it, because whenever my mom overheard it, she always rolled her eyes, so I figured it was more, I don't know, mundane than that?

"I think the main reason she allowed the fiction was because she didn't want to encourage me to just dive headfirst into relationships. But they're still together, and actually love each other and built a life together, so it obviously *is* possible." She slowly lost her smile, then sighed. "I'm sorry I'm so insecure about all this stuff, it *has* to be annoying and unattractive."

"It's less annoying and unattractive and more...a thing most people have to deal with. Both in themselves and in others. Confidence and security are really weird and inconsistent. But...lemme try to help. So, the relationship feels good, right?"

She nodded. "Yeah, definitely. But it always feels good in the beginning."

"The sex is good, right?"

She laughed. "Duh."

"The communication so far is good. The dom and brat relationship is good in a way hitherto not experienced, right?"

"Did you seriously just use the word 'hitherto'?"

"Answer the question, Chloe."

She sighed heavily. "Yes! You get me in a way that, *hitherto,* no one else has. And that feels really goddamned good. And the spanking...my ass is still kind of sore. You need to not go so hard next time," she muttered.

"You need to not fucking bitch at me so effectively then," he replied. "Or use your damn safeword."

"I was having too much fun! Anyway, what's your point?"

"My point is that you are moving as quickly as you are because everything is going *really* well. I'm treating you with kindness, respect, openness, I'm communicating with you effectively. As far as I can tell you feel heard, you feel seen, you feel taken care of and understood. Right?"

"Yes. But what if I'm being blinded by good emotion chemicals?" she replied, then sighed. "I *hate* how awkward this is! How can you be so calm when I'm legitimately asking you 'Hey this is great and all but what if you're actually a massive piece of shit who's taking advantage of me?'?! I don't get it."

"Probably because this doesn't feel like an accusation? Are you *accusing* me of being a piece of shit who is taking advantage of you?" he asked.

"No."

"Exactly. You're worried about it and I want to help you with your worries. You are suspicious because you're good at picking up on things, and this situation seems way too good to be true, and I'm guessing you probably haven't picked up on even a single thing to subtly hint at the fact that we're somehow trying to fuck you over. And that bothers you."

"Yes, it does. It really does feel too good to be true," she muttered.

"And I *truly* respect that feeling. I get it, like on a cellular level. But I have three thoughts that can help you out. Well...two thoughts that can help you and one that *might* help you."

"I'm listening."

"Okay. The first is this: whatever you think about the situation, I think you feel more comfortable about it because of Ellen and Holly. They'd let you know, either consciously or subconsciously, that everything wasn't on the level. Second thing: If this all goes to hell, if you decide this isn't working out, you can walk away, move in your parents, find a new job. You have an out. Third thing...I think you don't trust happiness."

He waited to see how she'd react to that. Chloe began to respond, then stopped, slowly falling into a thoughtful silence. She frowned and stared at the floor they both sat on for a long moment.

"I think you're right," she murmured finally. "It does feel like that. Like I'm always waiting for a bad thing to happen, or for the thing I'm enjoying to break, or disappear, or end, or be revealed to actually be somehow fucking me over. Because it feels like that's been my fucking life. Which I now feel like shit saying, because it seems like you three have had much worse lives."

"Well...that's not really a road we want to go down," Gabe said.

"Why? Just to make me feel better?"

"No. Because down this road lies nothing but misery. I think it's all right to recognize if someone generally had a shitty situation. Like...it's not a great idea to complain about a paper cut to someone who has a broken arm. But in general it's not a great idea to dismiss suffering on the sheer basis that it's less than someone else's," he replied. "There's a difference between maintaining perspective and unhealthily pretending something isn't real."

"...yeah, that's a fair point. It's just harder when it's about yourself. I just feel like I'm fucking whining."

"You aren't whining, you're talking about your

problems."

"Which doesn't help."

"Doesn't it? I mean, you don't feel better after we discuss how you feel?"

She was silent for moment. "...okay, you have a point."

"It's like lancing a wound, it helps get the bad shit out. Same thing but for emotions."

"Emotional painkillers," she muttered, then laughed. "Okay, you have a point, about all of this. And that I don't trust happiness. I guess I don't. Should I, though?"

"I mean, somewhat at least. I think, at a certain point, you need to just...let yourself be happy, Chloe. You're trying to stave off happiness because you're afraid it will somehow hurt you. I'm not saying that everyone should care about everything all the time, but actively trying to care less indiscriminately doesn't seem like a great way to go through life, because at the end of it all, what's it going to get you? You're going to be hurt, regardless. Suffering comes pre-packaged with life. It's impossibly entangled with being human. Nobody gets out undamaged."

"Wow, and I thought *I* was dark."

Gabe laughed. "I'm saying that if suffering is already a forgone conclusion, then you should take whatever opportunities you can, *within reason,* to enjoy yourself."

"Oh, so I should just give in to you and do whatever you want and 'be happy' then?" she asked, raising an eyebrow.

"Well, I mean, I'd appreciate it if you struggled some first, but yes," he replied.

She heaved a heavy sigh and threw a pair of panties at his head. "Fuck you!" she said, and laughed. "You are so weirdly arrogant sometimes."

"Only when I'm certain that it will make you angry, which turns you on," he replied.

"Oh my fucking God," she muttered, then sighed and shook her head. "Okay, *don't* provoke me into angry, rough sex. I really gotta get this done because unlike *you*, I have work in the morning and I'm kinda tired already."

"All right. Are you really going to quit your job?" he asked.

"Yes," she replied, going back to sorting her clothes. "I am. Tomorrow, I am putting in my two weeks. And then I am going to finish them out. And then I am going to relax for a while. And then I am going to focus on becoming a streamer, because that's what I want to do."

"And, during all this, you'll be bending over, spreading your legs, or dropping to your knees for me," he said.

"Oh my-you are being such a prick! Also, I expect you to drop to *your* knees for me, too! In fact, I want oral tonight. I want you to lick my clit until I orgasm," she replied.

"All right, but you're going to have to earn it."

She stopped sorting and glared at him. "We'll just see about that," she growled.

"I guess we will," Gabe replied.

Chloe stared intently at him for another long moment, then went back to sorting her clothes.

CHAPTER TWENTY SIX

"I just had a funny thought," Chloe murmured.

"What's that?" Gabe replied, distracted.

"If Krystal *does* ever come down here, we should send her into that store, too. That chick's head will fucking explode. Or maybe we could send Sadie in, hanging on your arm," she said, then laughed softly.

Gabe paused in his writing and glanced over at her. After finishing packing up her clothes and her games, they'd gotten them over to the house and then he'd gone to work writing Hearthfire Three. After a few hours, Chloe had sought him out and he'd gone down on her like he had promised, then had gone back to work.

But after a bit longer she'd asked him to come lay in bed with her while she fell asleep. They'd compromised and he'd brought his laptop to bed to keep writing.

"I think it might be best if we, um...stopped with that," he replied.

She sighed. "Probably. I'm still really pissed, though."

"You're kind of territorial, you know that?"

"It isn't a territory thing," she replied, rolling over. "You are my *boyfriend*. My very serious boyfriend who I respect a lot, and she fucking insulted you."

"Okay, I get that, and I'd feel similarly if our positions were reversed, but at a certain point I think it becomes kind of damaging to keep going with something like this," he said.

She looked at him for a moment, then sighed softly and rolled back over. "Yeah."

"Hey now, I *do* appreciate it," he said, leaning down and kissing the back of her head. She inhaled deeply and released a contented sigh as he went back to work. After a moment, he asked, "This really doesn't bother you?"

"No," she replied. "I want you here. Being around you is...intoxicating. Just knowing you're near. I feel safe. And happy."

"That's all good to hear...and the lo-fi?" he asked, glancing at the dresser.

"It's not what I'm used to, but I'm finding that I like it." She yawned. "I don't want to go to work tomorrow."

"I don't blame you, but at least you've only got two weeks left," he replied.

"Yes. Two weeks until freedom." She chuckled. "My parents are going to find out. And think I'm insane. Ugh."

"We'll get it sorted out, babe," Gabe replied, reaching over beneath the blanket and placing his hand against her back, rubbing it gently.

After a moment, he slipped it around to her side, then to her front and cupped her bare breast for a moment.

She laughed. "Seriously?"

"Yep," he replied.

"I don't know how you aren't bored by these at this point," she murmured.

"That's just not a thing that's going to happen," Gabe said. "Tits will never stop being amazing to me. Especially your tits, or Ellen's or Holly's."

"I'd say you were full of it but...guys do seem, just...eternally obsessed with boobs."

"They're just that captivating," he replied.

She laughed, then yawned again. "All right, well,

I should sleep. You can leave if you want to get back to your desk or do something else."

"This is pretty comfy," he said. "I'll stay here for a while longer, at least until I'm sure you're asleep."

"Thank you...goodnight."

"Goodnight, Chloe."

Gabe continued writing.

...

It was happening.

Gabe and Holly were driving off to pick up a moving van while Ellen was waiting at the house for them to deliver the bed. He felt pretty accomplished right now. Between the work he'd gotten done last night and all he'd done after waking up early today, he'd cleared over half of Hearthfire Three by now, *and* had managed to get started on his erotic Christmas short. If all went well, he might actually finish it off tonight, although it seemed unlikely given how long this all might take.

Then again, it hadn't really taken him and Ellen all that long when it was just them, now they had two other people helping out.

"You seem especially happy today," Gabe said as they drove through town towards the rental place.

"I am," she replied. "I'm really happy about Chloe moving in, and I've also decided that I'm going to quit my remaining job."

"Really? What prompted that? Not that I'm complaining," he asked.

"The last time I was there, it just kind of struck me that I'm not really doing the job for...anyone. I mean, I'm not doing the job for myself. I'm not doing it for the customers. I'm not doing it for my employers or coworkers. I'm not doing it for you or Ellen. And really that in and of itself probably wouldn't have affected me *too* much, or at least provoked me into quitting. It was the misery.

"The exact moment that I had this thought was right as I walked up to a table that had been utterly trashed by a group of college students. It was such an awful mess. Like *aggressively* awful, like they'd done it on purpose. I looked at that mess and this thought just came to me so clearly, almost as if someone had spoken it aloud: *Why am I doing this?*"

"That's an important question," he murmured.

"Right, exactly. I went back and forth as I finished my shift and then over the next few days, and then this morning I woke up and just knew. I knew that I was going to quit. Effective immediately. I'm going to call up tomorrow and tell them that I quit," she replied.

"You aren't putting in your two weeks?"

"No. I'm not. I would, but they actively disrespect me up there. Being with you and Ellen has made me realize that's what was happening. Really, it'd be better if there was just an absence of respect. Not all of them, but enough of them. And at this point it seems obvious that they consider me a lost cause anyway. It's like I'm not even there half the time to them, ever since I dropped to part time."

"Good, then. I'm glad. I want you to be happy."

She regained her smile. "And I really appreciate that." She grinned wider suddenly. "And now Chloe is moving in with us. I'm really excited about that."

"You don't worry about it getting crowded?" he asked.

"No. I don't care about crowding. I'd put up with a place half the size of our home if it meant living with you all. I always felt...really alone when I was growing up. Home never felt like, you know, *home.* But this does. This feels like my home. And honestly I like having people around. I didn't realize just how *crazy* lonely I'd gotten over the past year, living by myself in that apartment. And besides, we're moving soon, and that house is big. And then Krystal and Liz will come to live with us."

"You seem very confident about that," he said.

"I am. I've been talking with both of them. Krystal is apparently *very* into me. She very much wants to have a threesome with you and me. And Liz is also apparently into me. And I am...they're both *very* attractive and friendly. And Krystal is a little crazy about you," Holly replied.

"Why do you say that?"

"Just in the way she talks about you. She asks a lot of questions about you. Apparently she's read everything of yours, although you might want to tell her about the fan fiction. She's been asking for more stuff."

"...well hopefully it doesn't upset her girlfriend," he muttered.

"Yeah, hopefully not, but Liz seems really nice, and shy, and not jealous. It's kind of funny that she's the one who's shy. She's got actual abs. Not like crazy defined or anything, but you can see them. She just looks like a hardass."

"Yeah...still though, it seems like a lot. I mean do you really think they'll like us so much they'll be willing to move three hours?"

"Maybe. I think so. I mean, I would for you," she said.

He chuckled. "Yeah but you already know that this is a great relationship." He paused for a few seconds, considering. "I'm actually pretty curious about how that would work out exactly, bringing two women who are already dating each other into the relationship."

"I think it would work out fantastically," she replied.

"Well, here's hoping. All right, here we are."

Gabe pulled into the parking lot of the van rental place. He and Holly got out and went inside, then went through the process of filling out the paperwork and paying and getting the keys for the van. As soon as they were done, they came back out.

"Okay," Gabe murmured, pulling out his phone.

He paused and then grinned as he saw he had another text from Chloe. She was mad that he was ignoring her. They'd had some innocuous texting at the beginning of the day, but then she'd started getting snarky and he'd decided that was the best way to piss her off. He took a moment to check her most recent text.

DON'T FUCKING IGNORE ME YOU PIECE OF SHIT!

He laughed and then called up Ellen. "Hey, babe," she said.

"Hey. Got the truck," he replied.

"Oh perfect. The movers just got here. They'll probably be done by the time you come back, and then we get this queen bed out of here," she said.

"Perfect, see you there. Love you."

"Love you too, honey."

He looked to Holly. "We're all set, meet me at our house."

"Got it," she replied and got back into his car.

Gabe began to put his phone away but hesitated as he got another text.

GABE I WILL FUCKING END YOU FUCKFACE UR DRIVING ME CRAZY!

He considered it for a moment before finally responding: *Why are you being so needy today? This is not attractive.*

He put his phone away and got into the van, then paused again as his phone began buzzing and then kept on buzzing over and over. He pulled it out, checked it, and immediately started laughing. Chloe was sending him *FUCK YOU FUCK YOU* texts over and over again. When they stopped, he shot back his own response.

Babe I know you're gagging to fuck me but this is just ridiculous.

He put his phone away and as he started up the van and began driving back home, felt it immediately begin to start buzzing again.

...

Ellen was right, by the time he and Holly got back the movers were just leaving.

Gabe backed into the driveway, making sure to leave enough room between the van and the house to maneuver the queen size into it, and then got out. He and Holly headed inside and found Ellen looking at the bed.

"Is it everything you hoped for?" Gabe asked, coming into the bedroom.

"I don't know yet," she replied, "but I will find out tonight, provided you and Holly help me."

"We have a hard time saying no to you," he said.

"Yeah," Holly murmured.

Ellen laughed. "That's good to hear. Also, by the way, I got the edits done for Hearthfire Two, and I should be able to finish putting the cover together tonight."

"I finished mine last night," Holly said. "Also...who is blowing up your phone?"

Gabe chuckled and checked it. "Uh, Chloe. She's...grumpy."

"What is she saying *so* many times? Because your phone has buzzed like five times already, and you just walked in the room?" Ellen asked. Gabe turned the phone around to face her. She started laughing. "What did you *say* to her?!"

"It's more what I didn't say," he replied, putting his phone back into his pocket. "I've been ignoring her for most of the day. I did also finally fuck with her a little just before now."

"Wow. You two are...definitely something else," Ellen said. "Is she about done with work? Because we have shit to do."

"Lemme see if I can get through this tidal wave of fake anger," Gabe muttered as he began responding to her. She had at least stopped texting.

Serious question: are you almost done with work? We have the van.

"Either way, let's load up the queen," he said.

"Yep," Ellen replied.

"What should I do?" Holly asked, following them into Gabe's office, where Ellen had already moved the bed.

"Open doors for us," Gabe replied.

"Can do."

Between the two of them, he and Ellen managed to get the mattress, the frame, and then the headboard loaded up. Once they had it secured, Gabe shut and locked the back door and then checked his phone again.

"Okay, she's getting off work in about ten minutes, and she'll meet us at her place," he said. "Holly why don't you hop in with me and you can take my car, Ellen...what?" he asked when he saw her looking at him with a small smile on her face.

"What made you make those decisions?" she asked.

"Uh, well...you like driving, and Holly doesn't, and it makes more sense to use my crap car rather than your nice one for moving things. Why?"

She laughed softly. "I'm just happy that you know this stuff. Okay, I love you both, I'll meet you at the new house."

They parted ways, started up their respective vehicles, and began driving.

CHAPTER TWENTY SEVEN

Here he was again.

As Gabe studied himself in the bathroom mirror, it occurred to him, not for the first time, that he was ending up here more often than ever before in his life.

The past few days had been very busy.

Moving Chloe into their home, and their lives, had been a surprisingly smooth and easy process. Throughout it all, Gabe kept expecting something to go wrong. For a time, he hadn't really understood why, but finally he'd realized that it was Chloe. Despite her assertions, she was clearly still at least somewhat nervous about this move.

He could understand. Every time he'd had some kind of big life change, it was nerve-wracking.

They'd ended up shifting pretty much all her furniture to the new house, got the van returned, and then finished moving her small stuff in their cars. After having something of a celebration, both for moving in and for her putting in her two weeks' notice, he'd pretty much just been working. Writing. Editing. Prepping.

He'd spent most of yesterday and the day before that in his office.

And he had something to show for his efforts. Hearthfire Two was published. His erotic short for Christmas was, as of half an hour ago, publishing. He'd made a bit more progress on Hearthfire Three, but most of his time had gone into his Christmas present for Chloe.

He was rereading and touching up everything he'd written for Recovery Echo Four. He wanted to both refresh himself on it and figure out where he needed to expand on the fade-to-black moments Chloe had been complaining about.

In truth, back when he'd been writing them, he *had* been tempted to write the sex scenes, but had ultimately held back mostly because he was afraid that they'd come out stupid and embarrassing.

He still felt weird and uncertain about writing sex scenes now, but apparently he was good enough to at least get the job done, so that's what he was doing. By the time Christmas came, he wanted to have all the fade-to-black sex scenes written and have a minimum of one new chapter for the primary story. Really, he was maybe five chapters away from finishing it, but he knew that a sequel was already demanded by the narrative.

Hopefully it would make Chloe happy, but he also didn't know if she'd be disappointed. She'd clearly indicated she wanted it, but was it actually a good Christmas present? Or would it seem like a lame cop out?

Probably not, but he still felt on shaky ground with Chloe.

Interestingly, and maybe this was an unfair thought–certainly it wasn't one he wanted to share out loud–she seemed the most emotionally unstable out of them all, despite the fact that she seemed to have the best upbringing. It made him genuinely afraid of meeting her family on some level, because if he did and discovered they were actually fucking horrible people, it was going to cause a huge problem.

It seemed unlikely, but tons of people put up with or endured abuse from their family simply because 'they're family'.

As if that was an excuse to abuse, or to tolerate it.

He sighed and tried to clear his head. Right *now*

he had somewhere he needed to be.

Gabe finished up and left the bathroom, heading right to the living room and pulling on his shoes and hoodie.

"Where are you off to?" Chloe asked.

"You know where I'm off to," he replied.

"I don't remember you telling me."

"That sounds like a you problem, Chloe."

He heard Ellen laugh very softly. All three of them were in the living room, Holly and Chloe watching Ellen play Recovery.

"Are you going to see another woman?" Chloe asked.

"Yes."

"Gabe!"

"Well, Chloe, if you actually knew how to suck dick, maybe I wouldn't have to go out and meet other women," he replied.

"Wow," Holly whispered.

"That...that is *bullshit!*" she cried, sitting up straighter and glaring daggers at him.

"Hey, you've let it be known that outright fabrication is on the table."

"When the *fuck* did I say that!?" she demanded.

"You told me, not too long ago, that I don't make you orgasm. Which is *clearly* a lie. So." He shrugged.

"He's got you there," Ellen murmured.

Chloe sighed heavily and frowned. "I actually did forget where you're going," she admitted finally.

He laughed and walked over. "I'm going to take Sadie on a, uh...soft date."

"What the hell does that mean?" Chloe replied.

"I'm honestly not sure, it was her term, not mine," he said. "Now hug me and kiss me and tell me goodbye, I gotta go."

"Are you gonna fuck her?" Holly asked as she got up.

"No," he replied. "She's still not ready for that."

He hugged and kissed all of his wonderful girlfriends, they wished each other farewell, and then he was out the door.

Getting into his car, he started driving. It had snowed a little during the night, but it hadn't even really stuck to the roads by the time noon rolled around. He regretted this a little, as evidently Chloe had only a half day of work and he had been intending to spend more time with her, but he really needed to get this done and out of the way.

In truth, he was buying Christmas presents.

Something he probably should have done a while ago, given how close the day actually was. He'd already put in an order for a new bookshelf for Holly and it was being shipped now, but the rest he knew he could buy at the mall. Only he'd realized that he actually had a hard time just going out by himself anymore.

If he was going pretty much anywhere, at least one of the women he now shared his house with wanted to come along.

And that was great. He loved the company.

But he was trying to buy presents for them.

So he'd asked Sadie if she'd meet him at the mall for a sort-of date, because he'd also been meaning to spend more time with her, and she'd agreed. He was still kind of worried that things might be weird between them now, but admittedly less so now that she made it clear she was happy to spend time together.

And now here he was.

Gabe pulled into the parking lot and eventually

found a space far from the entrance. There were a lot of people out today. Great. He tried to put that thought aside, knowing it to be a selfish one. Couldn't expect to have the whole mall to himself.

But he did hate crowds.

He shivered and pulled his hoodie more tightly about him as he walked hurried through the parking lot, along rows of cars glinting in the winter sun. It was a good hoodie, but he knew he should be pulling on a real coat over it by this point.

The winter had been mild so far, the snows light and far between, but it was definitely getting colder. Even with the sun it was barely thirty degrees right now.

And he knew that some much bigger snowstorm was coming, something that would immobilize the city, or at least keep most everyone in their homes for a few days. He remembered hoping for such a storm every winter, though he was particularly bitter if it happened during winter vacation. He was already off then and it felt like such a waste.

Didn't really matter now, though. For him at least.

Gabe reached the entrance and walked inside. He saw Sadie waiting for him on one of the benches. Her hair was done up in a simple bun and she wore a pair of bluejeans and a navy blue sweater.

"Hello," she said as he walked up.

"Hi, Sadie. You look...really damn good," he replied.

She paused, then sighed softly, her cheeks reddening. "You definitely have a way of making an old woman feel attractive," she murmured finally.

"You are *not* an old woman," he replied.

Sadie looked at him, twisting her lips a little, and

then abruptly leaned in and kissed him on the mouth. It was an extremely pleasant, lingering kiss. When she pulled back from it (after giving him just a little tongue), she looked satisfied and a little amused.

"That look is rather something," she murmured.

"...what look?" he replied.

She laughed. "That one. The grin. I'm reluctant to call it a foolish grin because I don't want it to seem like I'm making fun of you, but...there's something so pure about it. You can't help it. You look...thunderstruck, in a very pleasant way."

"I feel thunderstruck in a very pleasant way," he replied.

She laughed. "Exactly. It's nice to be able to provoke that kind of reaction. It's a pure reaction, that's what's great about it. Well, the fact that it's *good,* but also pure. You can't help it, that smile. I saw it on your face when you first saw my breasts," she said, lowering her voice. "And the first time we kissed. Just this...heavenly smile. It's nice to be able to make that happen. I imagine it's what you feel when you make a girl blush after complimenting her."

"Uh...yeah, that makes sense," he replied, then cleared his throat. "That wasn't an idle compliment, though. You look really damn good right now. Something about your hair, and your hips in those jeans..."

"All right, come on, let's start walking before your mouth writes something that your...the rest of you can't cash," she muttered, looping her arm through his.

They began walking into the mall, carefully navigating the crowds.

"What's *that* suppose to mean? Because I can absolutely cash any check I can write," he said.

She laughed. "That wasn't a shot, dear. I meant...well, I suppose I should say write something *I* can't cash. Because I am *sorely* tempted to invite you back to my house. But I also know that it's not quite time yet."

"I've been meaning to ask...how *exactly* do you feel about...what happened?" he asked.

"Oh, wonderful," she replied, then chuckled. "It was amazing. The encounter was, shall we say, deeply invigorating and satisfying. And there's a strong part of me that wants to rush things forward, but I've often found that listening to that part isn't quite the best idea. I've had to learn the hard way to take my time with things. But another part of it is that I am leaving tomorrow to see my family for the holidays and that's always a very busy time of year."

"Fair point," he replied. "Where are you going?"

"Arizona," she said. "I've got two sisters and we all moved kind of far away from each other, so we rotate the holidays. My older sister is in Arizona, my younger sister is in Maine. You can guess who I prefer to see more."

"I mean, Maine is supposed to be beautiful," Gabe replied.

She snorted. "But you knew that it was Maine. It *is* beautiful, but yes, it's...not the most pleasant place to be. Mostly, though, it's the snow. It gets so much harder to do anything. How about you? What are you going to do? Mmm...I just realized, how do you explain your relationship to your family?" she asked.

"Me and my family aren't on speaking terms so..." He shrugged.

She laughed. "Well, that makes it easier." Then she hesitated. "I'm sorry, that was kind of crass."

"No, it's fine. It's the reaction I was hoping for.

I've pushed my family out of my life and, you know, moved on. For the most part. Although it's about to get complicated now that we've brought Chloe in. Ellen and Holly are both in basically the same boat as me, family-wise, but Chloe is very much not."

Sadie looked amused again. "So what are you going to do?"

"Uh...try to hide it for now. So far, they don't even know that we're dating. But I imagine there's a good chance they'd flip out on the simple basis that I've convinced her to move in with me *and* quit her job. I mean that has to look like classic abuser behavior from the outside."

"Mmm...yes. That is a problem."

"And then it gets *far* more complicated by the fact that I'm also dating two other women. It'll be easier to, um...deal with, once we move into the big house. Not that I want to put any pressure on you about that. We dearly appreciate what you've done for us already, and are going to do," he said.

"I'm glad, Gabe, but it's all right. I don't feel pressured. And, in truth, I couldn't hurry it up much more than I already am," she replied.

"Well, that's good...any advice?" he asked, stopping and heading into the bookstore as they reached it.

"Not really. I don't have know how to handle this. But I guess I'd say let your instincts guide you. They seem to be particularly keen. Speaking of which, how are things with your...flock?" she asked.

"My *what?*"

"I don't know, isn't that what men sometimes refer to women as? Birds?"

He looked at her. "...I seriously can't tell if you're messing with me or not."

She smiled. "Good."

"My girlfriends are fine," he said. "And things are going well. Holly quit her second job and is diving into photography. Ellen has discovered the joy of video gaming. Chloe is...settling in. She's a little...mmm, neurotic sounds like too strong a word, but she's sort of vacillating between overwhelming happiness and deep worry that she's fucking her life up."

"Does that offend you?" Sadie asked.

"No. She's worried that it does, though, and I'm just not saying so. I get where she's coming from, it's a massive change, and at the end of the day, I and Ellen and Holly are asking her to trust us, essentially with her life." He paused, stopping before a display of books. "Is this weird?" he asked suddenly, facing Sadie. "Is what we're doing insane? I mean, even if it is, we'll still keep doing it, but how does it look from the outside?"

Sadie gave a slightly sardonic laugh. "Oh dear...lots of things look insane from the outside. And lots more looks utterly sane from the outside, but aren't. I'm a lot less concerned with how things look nowadays, and more about how things *are*. But that's not the most helpful answer. From the outside, it seems like there's something that's being missed, I think. Your relationship, well relationships, isn't common."

"What do you think is missing?" he asked. "Or, rather, perceived as missing?"

"Some aspect of you. Although I now understand why your relationship is the way it is, I think to an outsider, you don't seem like the kind of person who would have three girlfriends. Let alone three girlfriends who are so breathtakingly gorgeous...is this coming off as insulting?" she asked.

"No," he replied. "I mean, you're right. I'm pretty far from what I imagine if I were told to picture a dude with three really hot girlfriends."

"Yes. We're a very looks oriented civilization. But...that's what I think," she said.

"Hmm. Well, thanks for discussing it with me. Now...can I buy you a book or two to take with you? I'm assuming you're flying," he asked.

"I..." She smiled and her cheeks flushed a little. "Yes, I would appreciate that greatly. Thank you."

"You're welcome. I consider it an early Christmas present."

"I feel bad I don't have one for you," she murmured.

"Oh, you don't have to. Honestly, everything that we...um, that happened earlier, well, you can coast on that for quite a while."

She laughed. "Fair enough."

"Also," he said as they continued moving through the bookstore, "so we're both on the same page, I don't think this qualifies as a date. Like a full date."

"I figured that was the case, but I appreciate you specifying it," Sadie replied.

"Perfect. Now, let's find some books..."

CHAPTER TWENTY EIGHT

"You look like something's bugging you," Gabe said as they walked out into the parking lot.

"Not bugging, exactly, but I did have a thought and now I'm not sure about it," Sadie replied.

They'd had a good soft date. He'd bought her three books, (and a dozen for Holly and one for Chloe and one for Ellen), and then they'd bought a painter's easel for Ellen, and then they'd had a small lunch in the food court.

"Anything I can help with?" he asked.

They came to stop behind her vehicle. "I'm afraid it's potentially a little...insulting. Only mildly, though...I think. I'm not sure. I probably shouldn't have said anything."

"Now I'm really curious."

Sadie looked at him, then nodded. "Well, all right. I'm still having a little difficulty believing that you have no problems with our age difference or, I suppose more specifically, that you find me genuinely attractive. I can acknowledge at this point that I'm in good shape for my age, but there's no denying that when the clothes come off, I will never be mistaken for being under thirty. I'm wondering if maybe you feel this way because we've hooked up, and it's a sort of denial you may not even realize you're engaging with."

"Hmm." Gabe thought about it. "So you're saying that when I'm complimenting you, in my head there's this sort of behind-the-scenes process of: 'I'm attracted to hot women, here is this fifty year old cougar I can have sex with, she must be hot otherwise I wouldn't be attracted to her, fifty isn't *that* old...', or something like that?"

"Yes, roughly," she replied.

"That's not what's happening," Gabe said.

"You're sure?"

"Yes. I'm sure. My *immediate* reaction, inside my head, when I first laid eyes on you was: *I want to fuck her so badly, holy shit she's hot.*"

"So if I were to cold approach you, hit on you totally at random as a stranger…"

"I'd be just as into you and all over you as I have been," he replied.

"…all right," she said finally, then sighed softly. "I'm sorry, this has to be annoying."

"Mostly I just wish you didn't feel unattractive, because I know what that feels like, and it's awful."

"I appreciate it, Gabe. And I appreciate your patience. Although I imagine you must have a lot, dating three women," she murmured.

He chuckled. "Yeah, although honestly? They don't really try my patience…for the most part. Chloe does, but that's kind of by design. We're all pretty low maintenance."

"I imagine that makes it easier…okay, I have to go. I have more things I need to do, and I imagine you have much to do, as well. Thank you for inviting me out, I had a very nice time. You really are quite a gentleman, and I'm grateful," she said.

"I had a good time too, Sadie," he replied.

She paused briefly, then gave him a hug and a kiss on the mouth. It started out as something simple but then she lingered and he kissed her a little more intensely, and she leaned into it and slipped her tongue into his mouth.

After a moment, she pulled back. "You also really are a *very* good kisser," she murmured.

He chuckled. "You are, too."
"See you later, Gabe."
"See you later, Sadie."
He headed for his own car.

…

"So I'm still a little confused on why you aren't working. Not that I'm complaining. You know, for the most part, I *was* hoping to get some more time away from your bitching," Gabe said, rolling to a stop at a light.

"Fuck off," Chloe growled, then grinned, then laughed. "My boss. I think she's panicking because I've put my two weeks in. I am actually a very hard worker, and I help out a lot, and I show up for shifts when other people don't. She relies on me more than she cares to admit because she's so shitty and abusive that most other people refuse to take it and leave."

"So...wait, why does this make sense?" Holly asked.

Chloe laughed. "It doesn't, really. But I think she's freaking out and trying different things that probably she's tried on other people and have worked in the past. Right *now* she's trying the whole 'oh, if you want to quit so bad, then I guess you won't mind if I take your half-day and give it to someone who *really* wants to work, will you?' game and it backfired rather hard on her. She called me up and basically said that while you were out at the mall, and the girl she brought in clearly doesn't give a shit about actually doing a decent job."

"Oh, she was pulling reverse psychology," Holly said. "That's...disappointing."

"I know, right? Fucking basic bitch. I mean the

frustrating thing about this whole situation is that if she had just treated me like a fucking person I probably would keep working, at least for a while longer, until they had replaced me. But no, she comes from the 'we aren't here to be nice to each other' mindset.

"Which, honestly, I could *kind of* get, because I get it. No one's going to be in a good mood and be one hundred percent kind and respectful *all* the time. God knows I'm not. But even in my shittiest moods I can still dole out a fucking baseline level of respect for literal strangers, even when they're being shitheads to me.

"But I swear to fucking God, every person who has that mentality of 'we aren't here to say please' or however they want to phrase it now, is a fucking shithead. They pretty much take it to mean 'I'm paying you money so that means I get to be as cruel and spiteful and dehumanizing to you as I want, which is a lot because I'm a fucking miserable asshole who insists on making it everyone's problem'. It's not even like people asking for respect are asking for *that much*." She paused and looked at Gabe, then into the backseat at Holly. "I feel like I'm bringing the mood down."

"I dunno, I don't think so," Holly replied. "I'm down for a good rant-fest. And I know how you feel. I think we all do."

"I appreciate it," she murmured, settling back into her seat. "Where are we actually going?"

"You never pay attention to anything," Gabe muttered.

"Oh eat me," she growled.

"Only if you're good." Chloe sighed heavily and dramatically. "We're going to a park. Sunrise Lake

Park, I think is the official name."

"I didn't realize there were so many parks in the city," Chloe said.

"There aren't *that* many, but it's nice that there are as many as there are," Holly replied. "I went by a few months ago and I saw a cool looking abandoned gas station near the back, through some trees. With the dusting of snow, I want to get some shots."

"You're braver than I thought you'd be," Chloe said. "And I don't mean that in a bad way. It's just...you look like the sweetest of all sweet peas."

Holly giggled. "Do I really?"

"Yeah, you do," Gabe said.

"You look like you breathe sunshine and your veins flow with honey and sugar. I mean obviously you're fucking ridiculously beautiful, but you also just look, I don't know, almost *aggressively* sweet. Like if a company was designing a mascot to be innocent and cute and sweet, and someone pulled out a picture of you, it would be rejected for being *too* sweet."

"If I wasn't sure you were straight, I'd be pretty convinced you were coming onto me," Holly replied.

"Oh. Um. Sorry," Chloe said awkwardly.

Holly laughed. "It's okay. I mean I'm not offended. As for my bravery of breaking into abandoned places...I'm not sure I'd call it bravery. It's less that I'm brave and more that...how do I describe this? It's more like I realized at some point that not doing it just wasn't on the table. Like I saw an abandoned house a long time ago and I just *really* wanted to see what was inside and it was so overpowering that I knew I wouldn't be able to fight it?"

"Huh. That's an interesting way to put it," Chloe

said.

"It's just how it is. How *I* am. I'm really grateful that Gabe is so...enabling."

"I'd prefer the term supportive," Gabe replied. "And you both need to understand that we follow rules anytime we do this."

"What kind of rules?" Chloe asked.

"Don't take any risks. Make sure we're alone before entering. Be prepared to run at any moment. Don't touch anything. I think that about covers it. Also, this is nonnegotiable. You don't get to argue about or compromise on this. You do it or you don't go," he replied.

"...that's something else," Chloe muttered after a moment.

"What?" Gabe asked.

"The way you are able to differentiate between telling me what to do in hopes of provoking a reaction and telling me what to do but for real. I didn't even want to argue with you when you were laying that down, and I don't think I've ever encountered someone like that, who did it so effectively."

"Interesting. I'm glad about it, at least. So, you got all that?" he asked.

"Yes."

"Good. Because we're about there."

They pulled into the parking lot and found a place to park. There was just one other car in the lot. Everything was covered with a thin layer of snow and the sun was muted behind a gray cloud cover that hid the horizons. Staring at the park stretched out before them, for a moment it felt like he was looking at another world.

"How'd your date with Sadie go?" Chloe asked as he killed the engine.

"Very well," he replied.

"What does a soft date actually entail?" Holly asked.

Gabe got out with them and pulled his coat on more tightly. "In this case, wandering around a mall, talking about stuff, and eating a light lunch. I think she called it that because it was recognized as a date where no sex was on the table."

"That's too bad," Chloe murmured.

"It's all right," Gabe replied. "It helps a lot that I know it's almost certainly going to happen later. It really takes the pressure off."

"I imagine it must," Chloe said.

They started walking, leaving the lot behind and getting onto a path that, after a time, broke away into a lightly wooded area. The three of them fell into silence as they began moving through the dead trees. The sounds of the city seemed distant and somehow insubstantial. The light layer of snow quieted everything and softened the world into an old oil painting.

Birds flitted among the branches overhead, chirping and singing. Squirrels crawled along the forest floor or up the trees. He hesitated as he spotted something surprisingly nearby.

"Holly...look," he whispered, pointing slowly.

Holly gasped softly, raising her camera. "Nobody move or speak."

He waited as she lined up her shot on the rabbit that was perhaps a dozen feet away. It was frozen, ears perked up, staring at them. Holly finished lining up the shot and snapped a few pictures. Abruptly, the bunny turned tail and ran, vanishing into the dead vegetation farther on.

"Did you get it?" Chloe asked.

"Yep," Holly replied, calling up one of the pictures on the display.

"Oh my God, bunnies are ridiculous cute," Chloe murmured as they looked at it. "I think if I *did* get a pet, it'd be a bunny. But then it'd be my responsibility and...well, I'm not going to let my inattentive self result in a poor bunny's suffering, so yeah."

"I know how you feel," Gabe said. "Damn, that is a really good shot."

"Thank you," Holly murmured. "Let's keep going. I remember this place looking *really* cool and I really want to see it."

"Lead on," Gabe replied, and she led them on down the snowy path.

CHAPTER TWENTY NINE

"Okay, you were right, Holly, this does actually look awesome," Chloe murmured as they stood at the edge of the clearing.

"It looks like something out of Recovery," Gabe said.

The gas station looked like it was originally built in the sixties or fifties, maybe even earlier than that, and then had been abandoned sometime in the nineties. It had obviously been left to go to rot and ruin years and years ago.

They were at the back of it and from what he could see, all the windows were broken out. A few were boarded over. There was no paint left anywhere on the exterior and any visible metal was pretty rusted.

From what he could see, there was a dirt road in front of it and, beyond that, a huge, empty field.

"Now what?" Chloe murmured.

"Now we make sure that no one's around," Gabe replied, "and you both make sure to keep the route directly back to the parking lot firmly in your mind. If we *do* need to run away in a panic, it'll be easy to get lost."

"That's a good point," Chloe said. "Have you had to run before?"

"No, I just overthink things," he replied. "Now, don't go inside. Come with me."

He didn't see any clear signs of recent activity, and the snow helped a *lot* with that, but he wanted to feel more certain about it. They got up to the back wall without running into any problems or hearing anything. Gabe waited and listened.

All he could hear was the occasional whisper of wind and the distant sounds of the city.

"Wait here and don't move," he murmured, and walked over to one of the windows that wasn't boarded up.

Peering within, he was glad to see that it wasn't too dark inside, at least. He looked carefully around and although he could see a few empty cans of what looked like cheap beer on the floor, he didn't see anything to indicate someone was presently in there. He checked it out a little bit more, then slowly moved around the building.

Coming to the front, Gabe saw that the dirt road ahead of them was unbroken, the snow undisturbed by either tire tracks or footprints. He peered into the other windows as he made a complete circle of the structure and came back to the girls.

"Anything?" Holly asked.

"Nothing," he replied. "Let's do this."

They walked up to the back door and found it open. Gabe went inside and took another quick look around, then invited them in. The place was definitely old. There was a long faded poster on the wall that was advertising a soda that hadn't been around for at least as long as Gabe had been alive, probably as long as Sadie had been.

"Wow, this place is amazing," Holly whispered as they started poking around.

"Yeah, definitely some post-apocalyptic vibes," Chloe murmured. "Definitely reminds me of a game I played last year."

"What game?" Gabe asked.

"It's called Irradiated. It was small, indie, only on PC. Kind of a survival-horror title with low-rez graphics. Which were pretty effective. It was in a post nuclear fallout apocalypse and there were these mutant people around, everywhere. They were fast and strong and if they found you then you were probably dead. The point was you were trying to find crucial resources to keep your enclave alive and you had to sneak into old abandoned places like this," she replied.

"That sounds fucking awesome," he said.

"It was, although it was pretty small in scope. They've been adding to it, putting in new maps, stuff like that, but it finally hit that invisible threshold where I guess the algorithm discovers you and shows you to way more people, so now it's popular all of a sudden. Which is great, because it means the little team who made it suddenly has money and they want to do a sequel and I am so fucking ready for Irradiated Two. I should check on it, I haven't in a while...why do you like these places, Holly?" Chloe asked suddenly.

"What?" Holly replied, sounding more than a little distracted.

"Why do you like abandoned places? I mean, I *get* why, they're weirdly beautiful, but why these out of...everything else?" Chloe asked.

Holly seemed to think about it. "Uh, hold on," she said, and then lined up and snapped a photo of some of the windows. "There we go. I'm not sure, really. I think it's sort of like the other thing you asked me. About bravery? I just...I see places like this, and they just call to me, you know? They just captivate me like nothing else does." She paused and looked at Gabe. "Well, almost nothing."

He chuckled. "You're pretty captivating yourself."

She grinned and shuffled her feet a little.

"Thanks," she murmured, then cleared her throat. "But yeah, I think that's why. I didn't really choose them, they chose me sort of thing. I also really love taking nature pics, but these places...they're amazing. It's hard to put into words."

"Yeah, I think I kinda know what you mean," Chloe said. "I feel the same way about horror games and movies and books. I care about them and engage with them in a way I don't really do with any other genre. For the most part."

Holly began raising her camera, then stopped and looked at Gabe. She walked over suddenly and hugged him tightly. "Thank you for caring about me enough to help me with this."

"You're welcome, love," Gabe murmured, hugging her back and kissing the top of her head. "I want you to be happy, and this obviously makes you happy."

"It just...means a lot. I mean, a *lot*. After everything that happened...it feels especially good to do this now, especially when you're around," she said.

Gabe glanced over and saw Chloe with an awkward expression on her face. He realized that they had suddenly wandered into some unique social territory. Typically speaking, intimate or deeply personal or emotional things were shared just between partners. Only Chloe was also his partner.

"Pretty much everyone in Holly's life was against her pursuing photography," he offered.

"Oh, wow, that's bullshit," Chloe replied.

Holly disengaged herself from the hug and turned to Chloe. "I guess you don't know. Yeah, my family, my only other boyfriend, they were all pretty actively against me trying to get better at it or even just doing it as a hobby."

"Why?" Chloe asked.

"Mostly because they thought it was a waste of time. Also because it wasn't...a woman's place," she murmured.

"Oh my fucking God, are you serious with that shit?"

"Unfortunately, yes," Holly said. She sighed and went back to taking pictures.

"Her family had...um, 'traditional' ideas," Gabe said.

"Uh-huh. Man, no wonder you vomited," she muttered. "Every time I get another piece of your guys' puzzle, the reasons why you wanted to just...cut out and make your own life gets clearer. I'd want that, too."

"What matters is we're doing it," Gabe said, walking over to the front window and looking out onto the decayed covering that once presided over half a dozen gas pumps.

Now they were gone, only faint outlines on the cracked asphalt left to show they had ever been there to begin with. Besides the skeletal, rusty remains of a long since stripped car, there was nothing else out there in the front lot.

It was a beautiful but lonely view.

Or, at least, it would be without the others.

Gabe sensed Chloe moving up behind him and then she put her hands on his shoulders. "Guess what?" she whispered.

"What?" he replied.

"You're supposed to guess...whatever, I'm not patient enough. I'm horny."

"Oh really?" he asked, turning around and grinning at her.

"Yes. And I would like to be...satisfied."

"*Here?*"

"Yes. Here. Now. Fuck me," she replied, grinning devilishly at him.

"Well how can I refuse a command like that?" he said, grasping her by the belt loops in her jeans and pulling her a little closer. "We'll have to be careful not to touch anything...what?" he asked as he saw her look off to her left, her eyes widening a little.

"Someone's coming," she whispered.

Gabe looked over. Two people were walking up the dirt road. They were still pretty far off, but it was obvious they were headed this way.

"Fuck, let's go. Holly, come on," he replied.

She finished snapping the photo she'd been lining up and hurriedly moved to join them. He led her and Chloe back through the door. He made sure to push them on ahead of him, watching their backs as they ran across the open area between the old gas station and the treeline. It seemed to take longer than it should but finally they were among the trees again, back on the path, and hurrying along it.

"Keep going," Gabe said when they began to slow down.

"Fuck," Chloe muttered, and they picked back up the pace.

He was careful not to go too fast, lest they slip and fall in the snow, and when they were about halfway back to where they had parked, he had them slow down back to a walk.

"Why were we running exactly?" Chloe asked.

"Technically speaking, getting into old buildings is illegal," Gabe replied. "But, more significantly, we have no idea who those people were. And honestly, that place reminds me too much of the set of a horror movie. Probably I'm being paranoid, but I'd rather be safe than sorry in these particular instances."

"Works for me," Holly said, "I got everything I needed. Although I was definitely going to photograph and film you two fucking."

"Would've been hot," Chloe muttered.

"Well, thankfully for us, we've got a nice, big, warm, comfortable bed waiting for us at home," Gabe replied.

"Yeah, it's not quite the same though," Chloe said.

"You're really that hard up to get fucked in a seventy year old abandoned gas station?" he asked.

She sighed. "It isn't the building, you idiot, it's the thrill. I've never really...you know, done stuff in a public place. And I've kind of been hoping to after hearing about what you and Ellen get up to."

"We'll figure something out, babe," Gabe replied. "Now, let's get home, I've got shit I need to be doing."

...

"You know, babe," Ellen said as they got out of their coats and shoes, "I think I'm going to need to read this fan fiction, too. Because this game is...very engaging."

"Hopefully you'll find it enjoyable. I wrote it a while ago," he replied. "Let's see, you're in...Cyprus. That level is pretty cool. I'd say it's really beautiful but honestly the whole damn game is. They were fucking *on* that aesthetic and art direction."

"Yeah. Is there another snow level?" she asked. "I did everything I could in Alaska."

"There is, in fact. A big one. It's DLC, should

become available somewhere in the second half of the game," he replied.

"I love that second snow level," Chloe said. She looked impatiently at Gabe. "Can we do it? I'm still kinda...fired up."

"From a walk in the park?" Ellen asked.

"A little more happened," Chloe replied.

"I...really appreciate it, but I have some things I need to do that I've been putting off, so...we will absolutely fuck later."

She sighed heavily. "Fine...maybe I should finally put that vibrator to use."

"I'm sorry, I just...there's a time crunch," he replied.

"Yeah, all right, I get it."

"Thank you."

He kissed each of them and then headed into his office. Settling down into his chair, Gabe fired up his laptop and then checked over his inbox. Ellen had sent over the finalized cover art for both Hearthfire Three and the Hearthfire collection. He felt a surge of elation. He might actually manage to get this out and done before Christmas.

He paused as he considered that. He really needed to thank her more than he already had, she was proving essential to his continued career.

Gabe settled in to get some more written for Hearthfire III.

There was a knock at his door.

He sighed. "Yes?"

"I'm sorry," Chloe said, opening it up and poking her head in, "but I'm *really* horny." She bit her lip and then opened the door the rest of the way, revealing her nude, pale body.

He stared at her for a moment. She stared back.

Well, his work could wait.
Gabe stood up and Chloe grinned.

CHAPTER THIRTY

Gabe quickly saved and closed out the Recovery fan fiction he was working on as he heard a quick, sharp knock at the door and Chloe's voice.

"Uh, babe, we need to talk."

"Come in," he replied, spinning around and facing the door. Even before he saw her face he could tell something was wrong. "What happened?"

"So, uh...my family knows," she said, looking more pale than usual.

"What exactly do they know?" he asked, standing.

"They know that I have a boyfriend." She paused. "Okay, yeah, I should've specified a little more. They know I have a boyfriend, but they don't know that I've moved in or about Ellen and Holly or that I'm quitting...shit, do they know that?"

"How did they find out?"

"I guess my mom stopped in at my job after I left for the day today and she's friendly with Linda and well, naturally, they got to talking and that came up. I...should have told her not to mention it, but in all the chaos it kind of slipped my mind," Chloe replied.

"Well...great," Gabe murmured, considering it.

"I don't think we're fucked yet," Chloe replied. "I...need your help."

"I'm listening, although we should involve Ellen and Holly in this," he said.

"Appreciated," Ellen said from the living room.

"Oh...yeah. Sorry. I'm a little...panicky," Chloe murmured, letting Gabe take her hand and lead her into the living room where Ellen and Holly were hanging out.

"It's okay, babe," he said, kissing the back of her hand, "you don't have to deal with this on your own. You've got three people who want to help you."

"Right...right. Um, give me a moment to gather my thoughts," she muttered, frowning and staring at the floor.

Gabe waited. After getting the presents and going to that abandoned gas station yesterday, he had been hoping that they were basically home free and in the clear for stuff happening. He kind of wanted to just put his head down and work until he was finished with his projects. Hearthfire II and the short were both officially published and out, and he was most of the way through Hearthfire III. He'd caught up on editing his Recovery fan fiction at least.

"All right," she said. "So–" She paused as her phone vibrated. She sighed and checked it. "Oh great, they want us to come over for dinner in an hour."

"That's not actually bad, I think," Ellen said.

"Yeah, unless I'm missing something, this works to our benefit. They aren't looking to come here, which makes the...more complicated aspects of our lives easier to get around," Gabe agreed. "I just dress up, we go over, have dinner, answer some questions, make chitchat, leave."

"...yeah," Chloe murmured. "I think that could work. Ugh, I'm bad at lying to my family." She paused. "Well, I'm good at lying to my dad, I can never tell with my mom. Mostly I think she just lets me avoid things I don't want to talk about by usually accepting my lie. My sister, though...I swear she's like a human lie detector. And she's gonna be there."

"Gabe's pretty good at these sorts of things," Holly said.

"I mean...probably," he muttered.

"You handled my family pretty well," she replied.

"That was different. Once we got your shit, we could basically have walked out of there flipping everyone off and telling them to suck dicks forever and it would've been basically fine for us," he said. "Chloe likes her family and wants to stay on good terms with them."

"I probably should've talked more about this," she muttered. "Is it...offensive, or rude, or *whatever* that I'm trying to hide aspects of our relationship? Gabe and I have talked about it, but I'm still kind of feeling out where...*we* are? You and me, Ellen, and Holly and I, you know?"

"I totally get that," Ellen replied. "And no, I'm not offended."

"I'm not," Holly agreed. "It's a thing we can work with."

"Exactly. This relationship is new territory for all of us," Ellen said. "Typical relationships take a while to sort of settle down and figure out, so this one is probably going to take longer, even with all the communicating we do."

"Okay good," Chloe whispered. "Um...this plan makes sense to me. Should I tell her we'll be over then? What time is it?" she muttered, staring at her phone again. "Okay, it's four o'clock. That's fine. Right?"

"Yes, tell her that you and I will be over in about an hour," Gabe said.

Chloe still looked freaked out as she fired off a response. She groaned. "I feel like I'm gonna lose my shit. I'm sorry, this just...happens sometimes. Fucking hooray for anxiety. I don't like shit just getting thrown at me, especially not like *this*."

"Maybe you could smoke a quarter of a joint?" Gabe suggested.

"You think so? Well, my sister and my mom know that I smoke weed. I mean, they both do it sometimes. My dad...tolerates it, I guess."

"I can drive us," Gabe said. "Maybe just do, like, two puffs and see where that gets you. We just need something to take the edge off."

"I know what would do that," Ellen murmured.

Gabe raised his eyebrows. "She has a point, you want to fuck? You do seem pretty relaxed after normally."

"Um...yes. But it's gotta be a quickie, I gotta sort through my clothes and find something that looks good and not goth." She paused. "No wait fuck that. I'm just going to goth out hard."

"Is there a reason that was your first instinct?" Gabe replied as she grabbed him and started pulling him back to the bedroom.

"Yes, my dad fucking complains all the time about it, giving me shit about needing to grow up, and my mom says I'm never going to attract a serious boyfriend looking like that but clearly they were fucking wrong!"

"Clearly," he replied.

She dragged him into the bedroom and pushed him onto the bed. "Take your pants off so we can have amazing sex while I go find the weed," she said.

Gabe laughed. "I seriously love the conversations we have."

...

"Okay, okay, okay," Chloe muttered, digging through her purse, "ugh, where the *fuck* is my phone?"

"Here, babe," Gabe said, picking it up off the dresser and passing it to her.

"Oh. Thanks."

"I'm not convinced the sex and the weed help," he said, studying her.

"It did, I'm okay," she replied distractedly, setting her purse aside and then grabbing her makeup mirror and studying herself in it. "Okay...how do I look?"

"Like I'm not going to be able to keep my hands off you," he replied.

"Gabe, *no,*" she said firmly, taking his hand when he started groping her ass. "I'm just going to say it now: safeword. No nonsense, no flirting, no brat-dom stuff. Just flat out *no,* not while we're around my family."

"I wasn't actually being serious," he replied. She glared at him. He raised his hands. "Okay, loud and clear, I hear you: no fucking around. Believe it or not I'm actually *not* one of those guys who grabs his girlfriend's ass in front of her parents."

Chloe relaxed a little. "Yeah, you're right...sorry. I'm still kinda freaked out."

"I can tell. But you look good."

And she did.

She was wearing a black t-shirt and black jeans that showed off her figure but honestly wasn't all that revealing. Really, it was pretty toned down for her. She'd put on a fair amount of makeup though, including black lipstick. Her eyes really popped, too.

"You gonna wear your choker collar?" he asked.

"Duh," she replied, grabbing it off the dresser and putting it on. "Are you *really* going to get us nametags that say 'Gabe's Girl' to wear?"

"Would you wear that?" he asked.

"Well...yes," she replied, smiling demurely, "it's true, isn't it?"

"That's awesome And yes, I am." He checked his phone. "We should probably get going." He looked down at himself. "How do *I* look?"

"Perfect," she replied, finishing with the choker. "Now come on."

"You two make such a cute couple," Ellen murmured as they came into the living room.

"Kind of feels like we're cosplaying a cute couple," Chloe muttered, pulling on her coat.

"We kind of are," Gabe said.

Holly giggled. "Well, we had to do it."

"Also true," he replied.

"Just don't fuck it up," Chloe said.

"Yeah, I'm really so comfortable with the relationships now that if I get a text from Ellen or Holly I'll just casually say 'that was my other girlfriend', or if Sadie texts something 'sorry that was my side cougar'," he replied.

"...were you being sarcastic or not?" Chloe asked.

"I was being sarcastic, yes. Trust me, I can handle it."

"Yeah, don't let them look at any photos," Ellen said. "I feel like it'd be *way* too easy to accidentally swipe over to a picture of me or Holly butt naked gagging on your dick or something."

"That's...a good point," he murmured. "I really need to sit down and organize everything better."

"You haven't done that already?!" Chloe replied.

"New pictures keep cropping up!" he said. "Can we go? We're going to be late."

Chloe sighed explosively. "Yes, fine. Yes. Let's

go. Um...thanks for helping me, all of you."

Ellen laughed softly, looking like she was trying to hold back more laughter. "You're welcome and good luck."

"Have fun," Holly said.

"Right," Chloe groused, heading out the front door.

"Bye, love you," Gabe said, following her.

"Holy *fuck me* it got cold!" Chloe snapped as they hurried over to his car. "When did this happen!?"

"I mean it *is* winter," Gabe replied.

"I know but this is bullshit. It's fucking not even five o'clock and it's pretty much nighttime. I fucking *hate* winter. I hate being cold. Which is good for you since it makes me want to be around you and touching you all the time," she said.

They got into the car and Gabe started driving them. "Yeah," he said, "*that's* what keeps you on your back with your legs spread for me."

"Oh fuck off," she growled. "I said no snarking."

"I can't help it! I really feel like a certain level of snark is kind of going to always be present when we're together," he replied.

She laughed suddenly. "What, like the background radiation of the universe? Or a natural chemical reaction? We can't be around each other without creating this vaguely angry sexual tension?"

"Yes."

"*Maybe* you might have something there, but I need you to can it for now."

"All right but it's probably going to come out a lot stronger at some future date and you fucking *bitched* last time I used the paddle."

Chloe stared at him and he had just enough of her in his peripheral vision to see she had that 'I cannot believe you just said that' smile on her face. "You *suck* at this," she said finally.

"It's your fault...sorry. I'm here. I'm focused. No snark," he replied, making himself focus. "I *do* take this seriously, and I will make a genuine effort."

"Thank you," she said. "I deeply appreciate that. Also, it's nice to have a boyfriend who can actually get serious when the situation calls for it. *Two* of my friends are tied to guys that are just fucking clowns. Like I get being funny, but for Christ's sake they can*not* fucking turn it off and it just gets more and more irritating every time they try to get a cheap laugh...is there some reason that's more specific to guys instead of girls? Or am I biased?"

"Women, on the whole, seem to respond well to being made to laugh. A lot of guys seem to feel that comedy is easy, so they try to be comedians and fail to recognize that comedy is only easy to fuck up. And the consequences of a joke not landing are extreme embarrassment. Except a lot of them are idiots and don't really feel embarrassment, so they keep going. Or that's my read on it, at least," Gabe replied.

"That makes sense to me." She looked over at him. "I'm glad you're not all super serious all the time. Really, you seem to have a bizarrely strong ability to sort of just adjust on the fly? I feel too many people just have two ways of being and it takes all day to switch from one to another. Although it clearly goes out the window if you're faced with a hot woman coming onto you."

"Oh give me a break, I fucking owned you the first time we hooked up," Gabe replied. "And that isn't snark."

"Fucking bullshit," she snapped.

"I definitely had you wrapped around my finger."

"I'm going to crash this car," Chloe growled.

"No you aren't, dear."

She stared at him for a long moment, then sighed in frustration and looked back out the window. "Fine, maybe that's true." A long moment of silence passed, the only sound that of the car and the GPS giving instructions on how to get to Chloe's parent's house. "I'm sorry," she said finally.

"For what?" he asked.

"Dumping this in your lap. Being complicated. The more I spend time around you three, the more obvious it becomes that I'm the 'difficult' girlfriend."

"What? Come on, no you aren't," Gabe replied.

"Give me a break, Gabe."

"Chloe, I've had to do something like this for both Holly *and* Ellen."

"Really?...oh, well, I yeah I guess you had to go to her parent's house."

"To get her papers. Birth certificate, social security card, the important stuff. She'd left it behind because she didn't think she really needed them and she felt *really* bad about it. Ellen needed to get some stuff from her condo. Let me tell you, *that* caused some problems," he replied.

"That's where you fought her ex, right?" Chloe asked, slowly turning back to face him again.

"Yes, but that isn't the problem I'm referring to."

"Wait so what else happened?"

He sighed. "It's...something I'm still dealing with. I'm a lot closer to being able to just let it go, but...it's probably less obvious for you, but Ellen comes from money. In that she had worked for twenty *years* to earn a lot of cash and her condo fucking reflected that. I mean I know we're not doing super great for cash right now, but I was even more broke when we first got together. As in, I literally just had debt, maxed out credit cards and a negative amount in the bank. I had basically put *all* my chips on this writing thing working out, and soon."

"Oh. Wow...yeah, I guess it'd be pretty strange seeing what she'd walked out of if there was *that* much of a difference," she murmured.

"Yeah. I mean her TV by itself was worth more than literally everything in my entire apartment. She had *nice* stuff, and a really damn nice condo. And she walked away from that for my broke, starving artist ass?"

"I mean...she did. Yes. That's romantic, right?" Chloe asked.

"Yes, it is. And I'm very happy about how this has all turned out. I love her, she loves me, she loves seeing me fuck other women, we're in a great rental situation, money is basically good, but...that's all on the surface. In the bedrock, though…"

"What?" she pressed. "I think I'm missing something."

"It's probably just super obvious so you're passing it out of hand," he replied. "Despite our relationship, despite everything Ellen's done to reassure me, despite my own beliefs on the subject...I can't completely escape the notion that I'm failing by not being more successful right now. Also, just to be clear, I can absolutely handle it if one or all of you end up making more money than me in the future. But, yeah, it's that. Really cliched."

"I mean it's cliched for a reason," Chloe murmured. "But Ellen's *clearly* happy. She's over the fucking moon with you, that much is obvious as hell. More money won't really help that, I think."

"I know. It's just one of those things that won't

leave me alone."

"Oh...I suddenly understand your insane standards for your writing. I mean it's still completely unreasonable but it at least makes more sense...would it help if I said I thought you were doing great and you don't need to worry about that with me?"

"Some, yeah," he replied.

"Huh. I thought it'd help more than that at least."

"Well, okay, put it like this: I understand that it's not quite the same thing, but it's kind of like saying 'I promise not to cheat', you know? Like, it really shouldn't need to be said that you won't just dump my ass if I stop making money...not that it isn't appreciate that you *did* say it, but does that make sense?"

"Yes, it makes sense. I just wish I could help more. Although I guess this must be how you feel whenever I complain about being unattractive or compare myself to Ellen or Holly."

"Basically, yes. We all have things we need to work on."

"Yeah-oh shit, we're almost there. Okay, um, just...be cool," she said.

CHAPTER THIRTY ONE

Chloe's parents had a modest two-story house on a quiet street.

Gabe pulled into the driveway and killed the engine, looking out the windshield at it.

"So, are you ready for this?" he asked.

"Yes," Chloe replied. "I mean...I think so."

"Is there something you're not telling me about your family or are you just really this nervous?" he asked.

"I'm just really this nervous. I don't know why I'm freaking out so much recently. I'm sorry."

"It's all right, Chloe," he said, taking her hand. "You're probably freaking out because of all the changes you're making."

"Yeah...fuck. I'm honestly just being shoved between 'am I somehow completely fucking myself over and just not seeing it?' and 'this is the best thing that's ever happened to me in my entire life what if I fuck it up?'. It's...exhausting. But, if it helps, it's getting better."

"So Chloe, I appreciate that you're communicating this and I don't want to discourage that, but I also don't want you feeling bad for having emotions. You aren't a bad person and you aren't being unreasonable because you have insecurities and anxiety." He kissed the back of her hand. "All right?"

That seemed to calm her down at least a little. She took a deep breath and let it out, slowly nodding. "Yeah. You're right. Thank you." She laughed, a little bitterly. "Is it annoying? Having to reassure me this much?"

"No," he replied.

"I think you might be lying but I also think maybe that makes the most sense."

"I'm not lying."

She stared at him, then sighed softly. "Either you're telling the truth or you are an *amazing* liar."

"Hopefully you believe I'm telling the truth, now come on, we should be getting inside."

"Yeah, you're right."

They got out and walked up to the front door. Chloe opened it and walked, Gabe trailing behind her. As they stepped inside and started taking off their coats and shoes, he looked around. The little entryway hall they'd come into led into a kitchen to the right and a living room to the left, with a stairway ahead of them.

A moment of tension passed, and then he relaxed.

This place felt...welcoming, and calm, for the most part.

Some old rock was coming from the kitchen and as he followed Chloe in there, he saw her mom in the process of wiping off a counter. She looked over and smiled as they came in, greeting Chloe with a quick hug.

"Mom, this is Gabe. My boyfriend," Chloe said.

"Oh hey, is the sudden mysterious boyfriend here?" another voice asked, getting closer. A moment later her dad stepped into the kitchen.

Gabe sized them up. They both seemed...about how he had expected. Or maybe hoped. Typical looking middle-aged parents. Although her mom was pretty hot, but that wasn't a surprise. He decided to try and maintain initiative.

"Hello, I'm Gabe Harris. It's good to meet you," he said, and shook her dad's hand.

"Good to meet you, too," he replied.

"You have...a wedding ring," her mother said.

For a moment Gabe was completely lost, then he looked down and felt a powerful bolt of frozen fear stab him in the stomach.

"*Shit,*" he whispered, taking it off.

"Wait what? A wedding ring?" another voice asked from behind them. It was accompanied by the sound of someone coming down some stairs. Had to be her sister.

"Not a wedding ring," he replied, slipping it off and pocketing it. "Just my favorite ring. It only fits on that finger."

Her mother looked...amused? "Why not the other hand?" she asked.

"Feels weird on the right hand," he replied, and was mildly concerned by how easy it was getting to lie about things. Apparently effectively.

Her mom shrugged. "Makes sense I guess," she said. "I'm Jennifer, my husband is Paul. And here's Chloe's sister."

Gabe looked back. Her sister stood in the doorway and...she was extremely hot. Of course she was. Great. She looked like a taller, trimmer version of Chloe. Her hair was longer and had a streak of blue through it, and although she was slimmer than Chloe, she apparently had also gotten whatever gene granted large breasts.

This was going to be a little more complicated than he'd hoped.

"Yeah, I'm Vanessa. I thought you weren't real," she replied.

"Piss off, Vanessa," Chloe snapped.

"Now, now, don't fight," her mother said mildly.

"It's just kind of weird. Normally Chloe talks

more about guys as soon she gets interested, but with you...not a word," Vanessa replied. "Is there anything strange about you?"

"Jesus, Vanessa, you can't just *ask that* of my boyfriend," Chloe said. "I just...was feeling vulnerable after what happened last time, and I wanted this to be a little more private."

"Hmm," was all Vanessa said, apparently seeming to relent, but not looking completely convinced.

"Dinner's ready," her mother said diplomatically, "how about we sit down and get to know each other?"

"Sounds fine to me," Gabe said, but inside he was definitely worried.

That ring was a major oversight. It made enough sense that Chloe would miss it, but he should not have. He felt like he'd probably successfully covered his ass, but what else might he be missing? All at once he wondered if he'd walked in here overconfident.

Well, it didn't matter now, he was here and there was no getting out. The only way out was through and he fully intended to make this work.

Dinner turned out to be some extremely good-smelling mashed potatoes and gravy and meatloaf. Gabe got seated, put his napkin in his lap, and they started eating. At least the good food was going to make this easier.

"So how exactly did you two meet?" her dad asked, firing off the first question.

Gabe almost immediately started getting flashbacks to other times he'd had to do this. It was sort of a cliché thanks to rom-coms that meeting your significant other's parents was a nightmare, but in his personal experience it had not gone fantastically before now.

"We met at a party," Chloe replied. "You remember last month how I was complaining that Cindy invited me to that house party and then ditched at the last second? That one. He was there and I was...into him and we started talking and, you know, we clicked pretty fast."

"Interesting...what do you do?" her mom asked.

"I'm a writer," he replied.

"Even more interesting," she said.

"What kind of books do you write?" her sister asked.

"Romance," he said. "And I can't really talk about them much more than that."

"Why?"

"I'm a contract writer, also known as a ghost writer," he lied. "I have to sign non-disclosure agreements, so I'm legally obligated to keep my mouth shut about any of the specifics."

"How'd you end up in that situation? That has to be kind of rare," her mom asked.

Gabe could tell Chloe was anxious, but she seemed to be slowly relaxing as she realized he was handling it well enough. Although he suddenly wondered if she'd put two and two together and realize that yes, in fact, he *was* a very good liar, and then get worried about that.

"Luck, mostly," he replied. "I was getting kind of desperate earlier this year and was looking around for jobs. I found one to ghost write a novel really fast and did it well enough that the guy who put out the job recommended me to an acquaintance of his who manages a few different pen names. They need content, done reliably and relatively quickly, and I guess I can do that."

"Is it going well?" her dad asked.

"Yeah, pretty well," he replied.

Things seemed to calm down a bit more from there as they told them a bit about themselves. It was pretty in line with what Chloe had already told him about her parents. They'd gotten through most of the meal when her dad decided to ask something a little more intense.

"So, Gabe...do you have a rap sheet?" he asked.

"Oh my God, dad, are you serious?" Chloe muttered.

"He's dating my daughter, I have a right to know," he replied firmly.

"I kind of feel like that's debatable," he replied, earning himself an interested look from her mom, "but no, I don't."

"*You* have a 'rap sheet', dad. God, who calls it that anymore? So does mom," Chloe said.

"Those were...stupid accidents," her father replied awkwardly, and her mom laughed.

"What was it...two bar fights? Some drunk and disorderly, disturbing the peace, and breaking and entering for good measure," Chloe said.

"I didn't start those fights," he replied, "and that breaking and entering was legitimately a mistake."

"He was too drunk to realize he wasn't at his own house and figured that, well, a broken window seemed like a small price to pay to get in out of the rain," Vanessa offered, making Chloe and their mom laugh.

"That's...interesting," Gabe replied.

"I was twenty three!"

"He also sliced his hand open and had to go to the ER to get stitches," Chloe murmured. "The police took him, then arrested him."

"Okay, that's enough," he said, but her mom was laughing still. "Thanks, honey."

"Hey, *you* opened this door," Chloe said.

"She's right," her mom agreed.

"Because your last boyfriend had a record and it turned out to be relevant. You could have gone to *prison,* Chloe."

"He's right about that," her mom said, losing her smile.

"What exactly happened there?" Gabe asked.

Chloe sighed heavily. "It's not as big a deal as they think. He was into drug dealing. I didn't *know* this until the end, when I found drugs hidden in my apartment, and asked him about it, and he got angry and we fought about it and I broke up with him. It was just weed and this was shortly before they fully legalized it."

"Huh. All right." He looked at her mom. "What about you? If you feel like discussing it."

"Oh, I burned an abandoned house down when I was eighteen," she replied. "On accident, for the record. But I was being stupid. Getting high with my friends. Given it was an abandoned property and nothing seriously happened besides an old house got burned down, they were willing to be lenient. I got two years' probation."

"Yeah, *I'm* the one who needs supervision," Chloe muttered.

Her mom grew more serious. "We're not trying to smother you, dear. It's just...the world is not the same place it was twenty years ago. It's...more unreasonable out there now. I mean it's always been dangerous, but...it's different now. And we just don't want anything to happen to you, either of you."

"Yes," her father agreed, "we would do a lot to

protect our daughters."

"Subtle, dad," Chloe muttered.

"I understand," Gabe said. "Protectiveness is a fair instinct. I'm admittedly not entirely sure how to respond though, because I can tell you that I have nothing but good intent for Chloe and I respect her and want to make her happy, and I would never hurt her intentionally, but doesn't everyone say something like that?"

"That's a fair point," her mother conceded, and her father just grunted.

"Okay, let's just...get this on the table now: Gabe's a really good guy. You all know that I stopped dating after the last idiot for a long time because I wanted to get my life together. And I did. I wouldn't have broken my ban on dating for just anyone. He treats me really well and he...understands me in a way that, so far, no one else has, and that's extremely valuable to me, but you didn't raise me to be stupid. If this relationship isn't working out, I *will* walk away. Okay?" Chloe asked.

"All right, Chloe," her mom said, "let's not fight. This has been really nice so far."

Chloe looked at her mom for a moment, then at Gabe, then sighed softly. "Yeah...sorry."

"Holy crap," Vanessa said. "Okay, whatever this relationship is it's clearly working because ninety percent of the time Chloe would've just either doubled down and gotten angrier or started in with the pouting."

"Shut up, Vanessa," Chloe growled.

"What are your plans for Christmas?" her mother cut in.

"I was thinking I could do Christmas Eve here and then Christmas day not here," Chloe replied. "If that works."

"That works. Will you be joining us?" her mom asked, looking to Gabe.

"If everyone's cool with that and Chloe wants me to, yeah," Gabe replied.

"Yeah, that'd be nice," Chloe said after a moment's hesitation.

"All right then. We don't really get too complicated. Pretty much just a meal like this, although with a bit more variety, and we sit around and talk while exchanging presents," her mom said.

"Sounds good to me," Gabe replied.

Her dad began to say something, then hesitated as his phone chimed. He pulled it out and studied it, then sighed. "I have to go deal with something."

"Probably a good time for us to leave, too," Chloe said. "We have things we need to do."

"All right then," her mother replied.

Gabe and Chloe stood and began preparing to leave.

CHAPTER THIRTY TWO

"Chloe, there's one other thing I wanted to ask you," her mother said as they headed outside.

"What?" Chloe asked, a little cautiously.

Her mom looked to Gabe. "I need to speak with my daughter alone for a moment."

"Understood," he replied.

Gabe went to his car and started it up, trying not to be too obvious about watching them. From Chloe's reaction when her mom said the first thing to her, it wasn't a great thing. She seemed to fumble for a moment and then seemed to relax slightly. They went back and forth for a moment, then they hugged and Chloe joined him.

"Everything okay?" he asked as he started driving them back home.

"Well, my mom *also* picked up on the fact that I'm quitting my job. I need to have a stern talking to with Linda about sharing my business," she muttered. "She's really great, but she's kind of too free with information."

"What'd you say?"

"I lied and said I was getting another job. I think she bought it but it's hard to tell. My mom's definitely sharper than my dad...so, overall, I think that went well."

"Yeah. Sorry about the ring," he replied.

"I missed it, too."

"Yeah but I should have noticed it. I think your sister knows something's up."

Chloe sighed heavily. "I think so, too. She's also pretty sharp."

"You and sister must be close."

"Why do you say that?"

"She was pushing your buttons and you didn't react all that strongly. With people who've known each other since they were young and they're still in each other's lives, it tends to go a few ways. One of them is it's easy as hell to trigger each other and just go from calm to pissed in nothing flat. The other is you actually like each other and the teasing really is just light teasing with no ill intent and both people realize this," he replied.

"You're right, we're pretty close. I mean less so now that she's moved away, but things are still good. It was...kinda miserable there for a little while when we were growing up. I had such a damn temper. But mom and dad got us some therapy and I realized I was being really mean and we figured out ways to talk more effectively and then everything was really cool after that." She paused for a moment. "Do you think my sister is hot?"

Gabe sighed. "I'm not answering that."

"Come on," Chloe replied.

"Fine. *Obviously* I think she's hot. And before you ask, your mom is a straight up MILF."

She looked over at him. "Are you trying to provoke me right now?"

"No, I just wanted to get that out of the way. I mean it follows pretty well that if I find *you* extremely attractive, there's a really good chance I'll find your mom and sister attractive."

Another moment of silence passed. "Are you going to fuck my sister?"

"This conversation is going in strange places."

"Don't avoid the question!"

"I mean it depends entirely on you and her. Why do you even think that's on the table? Did I miss something during dinner?"

"I mean you obviously are on the lookout for women to sleep with and you're attracted to her and she's single and probably thinks you're hot," Chloe replied.

"Okay but there's a lot more to whether or not I try to fuck a woman," he said.

"Like?"

"Like: Is it irresponsible? Will it cause problems? Not to mention, as fun as it is, I'm not necessarily all that interested in taking it much further than I already have."

"Why?"

"Because every woman that I have sex with is another potential source of massive problems. What if I get an STD? What if I get her pregnant? What if she's not being truthful and there's some guy that's going to come after me now? I don't want to deal with any of that shit," he replied.

"That's...a great point," she murmured. "Okay, do you *want* to fuck my sister?"

"I mean yes and no? Yes, she's hot and she seems nice. No, for the reasons I just said, but also because I imagine it might be a massive problem for you. I'm not going to pursue anyone you have a problem with. You have power over who I fuck."

"So you'd really just not pursue her if I said 'no, she's off the table'? Just like that?"

"Just like that. I'm reasonably sure we discussed this already, but it bears repeating: I will come to you, and Ellen and Holly, *before* I become any level of intimate with another woman and get unequivocal permission from all three of you. If any one of you says no after we've had a discussion about it and I feel like we've communicated everything from both sides, then I will respect that," he replied.

"Yeah, we talked about it before, just...I dunno. I guess I'm still getting used to this whole thing. Sorry."

"It's fine, Chloe. And *I'm* sorry, I guess I get a little frustrated because I forgot to take my damn ring off and that sort of messed with me the whole time. But it's important we have these discussions about the relationship, about anything really. I don't want to just shut you down if I'm feeling annoyed or distracted or angry," he said.

"That's really nice," she replied. "And I'm glad...also, since we talked about it so much, I'm fairly ambivalent about whether or not you sleep with Vanessa."

"It seriously wouldn't bother you?" he asked. "If I fucked your sister?"

"I don't think so. I mean, I'll need to think about it more. We really buried the hatchet and after figuring out how to live with each other, actually got really close. I want good things for her and...well, it's weird to talk about in this specific way, but sex with you is a really good thing. On the other hand...I've always kind of lived in her shadow."

"Really? Why?" he asked.

Chloe sighed. "I mean besides the fact that she went to college and actually succeeded, she got a master's degree in marketing and actually does it for some big company and makes good money...I've always felt like she was kind of the 'fully realized' version of me. She's a little bit taller without being too tall, and a little bit thinner without being too thin, and her face is better proportioned, and I've been used as a gateway to my sister by guys wanting to date *her* instead of me one too many times. But none of that is *her* fault, she doesn't make me feel this way on purpose, and I've mostly gotten past it."

"Okay, I'll say this once, because I'm not interested in the comparison game but...you are the hotter of the two," he replied.

"...are you bullshitting me? No wait, I think I know what it is: you like me more because you like goth chicks more."

"You have to learn how to take a compliment," he muttered.

She sighed. "Okay fine, I accept. Thank you." She smirked suddenly. "Also you definitely threw my parents off their game. The fact that *both* of them somehow managed to go an entire meal with me dressed like *this* without actually saying anything about it? Definitely off their game. Also, you did really well by the way. I know you're upset about the ring but everyone makes mistakes. Otherwise, you handled that all very well."

"So you're happy with how it all went?" he asked.

"Yes. Also...sorry if it'll be weird to come with me on Christmas Eve."

"I'm sure it'll be fine. Just so long as I get you to myself on Christmas itself." He paused. "Well, you along with Ellen and Holly to myself."

"Oh? You have something in mind?" she asked.

"No, but you do."

"Why...do you say that?" she murmured.

"I've seen you and Ellen talking and I overhead *something* about a surprise on Christmas and I have no idea what it is but I'm looking forward to it," he said.

"It's...I mean we got you a present. You'll be really happy with it," she replied.

"I am, and I appreciate it. Also, I got you some presents."

"What? Really?"

"Why are you surprised by that?" he asked.

"I just...figured we hadn't really talked about it. I didn't actually like *get* you anything, like there's nothing to unwrap…"

"Chloe, I'm positive that whatever surprise you're going to give me, it will be fucking amazing."

She laughed. "You're *that* confident in us?"

"Yes."

"Well...good to know."

They parked in their driveway and headed inside. As soon as they got in, he could tell right away that Ellen had something she needed to talk to him about.

"What happened?" he asked.

"Nothing," she replied, standing up from the couch. "I mean, nothing bad. Probably."

"Probably?" he asked.

"I don't know for sure but I doubt it's bad. Abby and Emily want to speak with us. In person. Now, if at all possible," she replied.

"Oh," Gabe said.

"All four of us?" Chloe asked.

"Yes."

"But she didn't say why?"

"No. She said she wanted to discuss something...personal, and in person, and it pertained to all four of us," Ellen replied.

Chloe frowned. "Do you have any idea what it might be?"

"It could be a few different things but I don't want to speculate, in case I'm wrong. Anyway, how did dinner go and will you be able to go over to their place very soon?" Ellen asked.

"Yes," he said, and Chloe nodded, "and, aside from one big fuckup, it went well."

"What was the big fuckup?" Holly asked.

"I left my wedding ring on," he muttered unhappily.

"Oh...did you manage to convince them it wasn't a wedding ring?" Ellen asked.

"Yes, thankfully. But otherwise, it was nice. Her family seems nice. Now let's go see about this thing with Abby and Em."

...

"Oh yeah, I forgot to ask," Gabe said as Ellen drove them through the city in her car, "will it cause any problems if I go with Chloe to her family's house for Christmas Eve?"

"No, it shouldn't. Holly?" Ellen asked.

"Nope," she agreed.

"Just so long as we're clear that *we* get you on Christmas," Ellen said.

"That is clear," he replied.

"Good."

Gabe fell silent, looking out the window, wondering on what the immediate future held. He thought that, realistically, there were two different possibilities as to what Abby and Emily wanted to talk about. It was either that they were no longer happy with the sexual arrangement and wanted to end it, which didn't quite seem likely, because that didn't really feel like an 'all four of you, in person, right now' kind of situation.

Which left the other option, the thing Ellen had warned him about.

Abby wanted to get pregnant, and she wanted

him to be a sperm donor.

On the surface, the idea was obviously very exciting. He really wanted to fuck her, and he really wanted to get a woman pregnant. He just...wasn't really sure he was ready to deal with the actual reality of raising a child.

Only in this case, he wouldn't have to. It wouldn't be his, and he imagined they'd probably not tell the child. It'd be so much easier to adjust the truth a little and say they had artificial insemination done. It was almost the truth.

Deeper than that, though, he was wondering.

Would he really be okay with it? Going his entire life probably being around a kid he knew was, biologically speaking, his?

He tended to think that he was. Not necessarily because he was that eager to just abandon an unwanted pregnancy, but more specifically because he didn't really believe in the whole 'your *real* parents' thing.

Just because someone was a sperm donor, even if it had been done through actual sex, didn't necessarily mean they were the father. Lots of guys walked away and let their kids get raised by someone else. And then somehow felt entitled to a relationship decades later when they got older and suddenly decided they wanted to be a parent.

He trusted Abby and Emily, though. He supposed that's what was really on the table here: were they going to be good parents? And he thought they would be. As they pulled into Em's and Abby's driveway, Gabe realized that he'd been thinking about this in the background ever since Ellen had mentioned it.

Then again, he reminded himself, it was very possible that whatever they wanted to talk about was unrelated to either possibility.

"Okay, let's see what this is all about," he said as they got out and headed for the front door.

CHAPTER THIRTY THREE

The first thing Gabe noticed as they were invited in was that Abby actually seemed nervous.

Which was interesting, given how calm and composed she always was.

"Hey, so, how's everything going?" she asked with that sort of flustered, half-distracted tone.

"Good, Abby," Ellen said, mildly amused. "I'll just save you some trouble now. Obviously whatever it is that you called us over for is weighing heavily on you, so you don't have to make small talk. We can just cut straight to the discussion."

"...all right," she said, relaxing just a little. "Thank you. Um, here, in the living room. Let's sit down and we can...discuss."

Emily laughed softly, equally amused and clearly trying not to laugh harder. They all headed into the living room, and Gabe found himself looking at the spot where he had fucked Chloe. It felt very strange, in some indefinable way, to think that he'd had sex with Chloe here, and Emily upstairs. And also Chloe upstairs in the shower.

They all got settled, Gabe and his lovers on one couch facing Emily and Abby on the other. For a long moment, nobody spoke.

Finally, Abby cleared her throat. "Okay, um, so Emily and I have been discussing this for...quite a while now. I mean we've been talking about it off and on for years, but finally we've gotten serious about it given...where we are in life. And I recognize this is quite a big ask, potentially. And I don't really know how to properly, um...prep this..."

"Whatever it is, just toss it out there," Ellen

replied. "I doubt you're going to ask us for anything that will shatter the friendship."

"...that's a good point," she murmured. "This is just a big deal for me. And for Emily. And I'm kind of nervous. Okay, here it is: Emily and I want to have a child, and I want to get pregnant, and obviously we need a sperm donor. And we've decided that our first choice is...Gabe."

"I thought so," Ellen said.

"What? How could you *possibly* have–" She looked at Emily suddenly. "You said you wouldn't tell anyone until we were ready!"

"I didn't!" Emily replied.

"Abby, Abby! She didn't tell me. No one told me anything," Ellen said. "I just...picked up on the likelihood of this being the thing you wanted to ask from our previous conversations."

"Seriously?" Abby asked.

"Yes. Seriously. You aren't as subtle as you think. Or, at least, not when it comes to this subject."

"Did you tell everyone?" she asked.

"Of course not! I wasn't even going to tell Gabe but he is...remarkably, irritatingly fantastic at picking up on subtle things. The idea of pregnancy got brought up and I had a reaction to it and naturally he got worried if maybe I'd had a pregnancy scare, but I told him that *maybe* it *might* be a possibility that you might ask for this, but to keep it to himself," Ellen replied.

"And I did," he said.

"Yeah, I had no idea this was coming," Holly said.

"Same. This is...not what I was expecting when I got invited over," Chloe replied.

"Oh. All right. Um...sorry, babe," Abby

murmured. She sighed heavily. "Fuck, I'm really sorry. This has me so wound up–"

"Honey, it's fine," Emily said, hugging her suddenly and kissing the side of her head. "I'm not mad, I understand. And if you can tolerate me when I'm being annoying and unreasonable, I can tolerate some anxiety and a short temper sometimes."

"You two are a really cute couple," Holly said.

Abby laughed softly. "Thank you," she replied. "Um, so...there we are. It's out in the open now."

"So what *precisely* are you asking for, because I feel like there's a couple of ways this could go down…" Ellen said.

"Right. Yes. Um, so, what we're specifically asking for is...I want Gabe to have a threesome with me and Emily, and...come inside me. And then again as needed, until I'm pregnant. That's the, uh, nitty gritty of the actual process," Abby replied.

"I thought you were a lesbian," Chloe said, then sighed when everyone glanced at her. "Sorry, that came out...weird, maybe? I don't know. I'm not trying to be rude. I have no idea how to talk about all this."

"No it's a fair observation," Abby replied. "I am...pretty much entirely into women. Except for some men. I'm closer to ninety five percent lesbian. And Gabe...does it for me. Inasmuch as any man does. Enough that I at least want to try it once with him. Now, as for the rest of it, I have written up a legal document that will essentially clear Gabe from being responsible, in any capacity, for our child. And, this obviously leads into: we would ask that Gabe not be involved in the raising of the child. Which, I hope is received without any negative connotations."

"Don't worry, Abby, that's not an unreasonable

request," Gabe replied. "I'm not offended."

"Okay, good. Because, you all are fantastic. You're great to have fun with and hang out with and, according to Emily, Gabe is *really* fun to have sex with, but we...our relationship is about the two of us, and we want to be the parents to our child," Abby said.

"Very fair," he replied. "Um...what do we all think of this?"

"I'm fine with it," Ellen said.

"Really? It's not gonna weird you out at all that your boyfriend knocked up my wife?" Emily asked.

Abby sighed. "Emily…"

She laughed. "I'm sorry, I can't help but snark at Ellen now that we're cool again. It's just...who we are."

"Yeah, *we,*" Ellen muttered, rolling her eyes.

"Oh whatever, bitch, you were fucking *relentless* with your sarcastic, sardonic snark when we were teenagers."

"Yeah, whatever. Also, *husband,* not boyfriend."

"Wait, what?" Emily asked. Ellen raised her hand, showing her ring. "What the fuck!? Did you get married!?"

"No, Emily, not officially," Ellen replied. "You'd obviously have been invited. But we're functionally husband and wife."

"And Holly and Chloe?" she asked.

"Also husband and wife," Holly replied, raising her own hand.

"Still girlfriend and boyfriend but definitely serious," Chloe replied.

"We should focus," Gabe said. "Holly, what do you think?"

"I think it's great," she replied. "I'm all for this

happening. It's sweet."

"Really?" Emily asked. "I mean, I agree, it's just...I feel like a lot of people would look at this particular situation and call it...I dunno, trashy? Degenerate? Not that they're right, but..." She shrugged.

"A lot of people are trashy and degenerate and can fuck off," Holly replied. "You two want a child, you're asking a friend to help. It's sweet."

"Chloe?" Gabe asked.

"Well...I can't say I'm opposed to the idea," she replied. "Really, my biggest concern would be the legality of it. Not that I think you guys are gonna fuck us over or anything, just..."

"Just everyone will feel more comfortable if all our asses are covered," Abby said. "Don't worry, I completely get it. I trust all of you, it's just...we have no idea what the future might bring. Although...the only other thing I wanted to ask is if, Ellen, you would be willing to be our child's godmother? If anything were to happen to both of us...well, it'd just be nice to know that we're covered in that event. But it's totally fine if you don't want to, that's a huge responsibility."

"If everyone's comfortable with it, yes, I would agree to this," Ellen said.

"I think it's a fair ask," Gabe replied, "given the circumstances."

"So, just so I'm completely clear on this...Ellen being the godmother means that if you both die, she becomes responsible for your child?" Chloe asked.

"Yes, that's basically what it boils down to," Abby replied.

"I'm also fine with it," Holly said.

"Uh...yeah, I'd be okay with that," Chloe replied.

"I think."

"Also, to be clear, this isn't a thing we want you all to decide tonight," Abby said. "Sorry, I should've also said that. Even if you decide you're good with it, I want some time to pass, at least a week, for everyone to sort of sit with it, see how it feels, see if we can think of anything else we might be missing. And...if it doesn't interfere with any plans, I would like to spend some time with Gabe tomorrow. Alone. Like going out and spending time together."

"Tomorrow's...God, the twenty third already," Chloe muttered. "Well, I've got a long shift tomorrow so I don't really care."

"I think it would be nice," Holly said.

"I'm still really deep into Recovery so I'll be happy to just keep playing that," Ellen said.

"What's Recovery?" Emily asked.

"A video game Gabe introduced me to," Ellen replied.

"Oh my God, you turned her into a gamer? How the fuck did you manage that!? I tried for *years* to get you into gaming, you blonde bitch!"

Ellen rolled her eyes. "You asked me to play games with you sometimes, that hardly counts as some Herculean effort on your part to get me to play games. And also I'm sorry, I should have tried playing more games with you. I was...um…"

"A stuck up bitch," Emily said.

"Are you *trying* to get me and Gabe to hold you down and dominate the fuck out of you?"

"...well I am *now,*" she muttered.

Ellen laughed. "I will admit to it: yes, I was kind of stuck up and I thought games were...not worth my time. *Clearly,* I was wrong. Although to be fair I think we like different types of games. You always were playing online shit, with the headphones and the screaming and the cursing. I've always more thought about trying single player stuff, with the immersive worlds and interesting characters and exploration."

"Fair point," Emily said. "But congrats on that, Gabe."

"Thank you. Yes, I'm down for hanging out tomorrow," he replied. "Do you want to plan things or should I? I can do both."

"How about we each do one thing and see how that works?" Abby suggested.

"That works fine for me," Gabe replied.

Abby stood. "Perfect. Let me get you the document to read over. It's pretty short and straightforward. I don't mean to haul you over here and just kick you out, but Emily and I have been doing a lot of running around recently and would like to be alone soon, though."

"That's not a problem, Abby," Gabe said as she grabbed a paper and walked it over to them.

"Honestly I would have just called but this seemed significant enough to be done in person," she said, handing it to them.

"Agreed," Gabe said, passing it to Ellen, who began to read over it.

After a few moments, she nodded slowly. "Still as sharp and succinct as ever, Abby. I'm fine with this."

"Figured you would be."

"Let's get out of their hair and you can start thinking about your date day tomorrow," Ellen said, standing up.

As she did, Abby stared up at her. Ellen looked down. Abby had that look on her face, the one that Gabe had come to recognize. The look that said: *Oh my lord, she's so tall and beautiful, I can't believe how tall and amazing she is.*

Even now, after being with her almost nonstop for some two months he was still amazed by her great height when she stood up. And Abby was noticeably shorter. Ellen had over a foot of raw height on the mousy woman.

"Yes?" Ellen asked after a moment with an amused smile.

"I *really* would like you to be involved somehow when I fuck Gabe," she murmured. "You are one of the most stunningly attractive women I've ever seen."

Ellen blushed, losing her composure, and cleared her throat. "I'd be very happy to tag in with Emily when you and her fuck my husband. You are also extremely pretty."

"I'm so looking forward to this," Abby murmured.

"Same," Emily said.

"Hard same," Gabe agreed.

"Okay, let's go before things get anymore distracted," Chloe said, grabbing Gabe's hand.

"Yeah. See you tomorrow," Gabe said.

They said their goodbyes and headed out to the car. Once they were inside, Gabe began reading over the document. It *was* pretty simple and straightforward. It basically said, in so much legalese, that he renounced his legal right as a parent to the child and wouldn't be responsible in any real capacity. He had the impression that it would probably be a little more complicated than that if push ever came to shove, but in truth, he doubted push would ever come to shove.

"Here, give this a read over," he said, passing it back to Holly and Chloe.

"I can't believe you're actually going to impregnate Abby," Chloe murmured.

"He's going to breed her," Ellen said.

"That sounds kind of fucked up but also hot," Holly said.

"A lot of fucked up things are hot," Ellen replied. "Also, I just wanted to say now, to be clear, and this is for Holly, too–although Holly seems pretty happy with this arrangement–if you really are uncomfortable with this, Chloe, don't be afraid to speak up. I don't want you going along with something just because everyone else is."

"Thanks," she said. "I do appreciate that, but...I'm pretty cool with it so far. I'll think about it more, but if I have any problems, I'll let you know. I'm mostly decent nowadays about speaking up."

"Good," Ellen replied. She glanced briefly at Gabe. "How about you, dear?"

"I mean I wasn't holding anything back. I'm down to do this," he replied. "I'll think about it more, but I don't think my opinion's going to change."

"Definitely going to be insanely hot sex," Ellen murmured.

"Yeah, I've never actually tried to get someone pregnant before," he replied.

"You *sound* horny just talking about it," Chloe said.

"I mean it's hot," he replied.

"Yeah...there's definitely a part of you who would get all three of us pregnant if you could, isn't there?" she asked.

"Oh yeah," he replied, then turned around in his seat to look at her. "And I also know that if I told you to, you'd let me get you pregnant."

"Oh what*ever,*" she snapped, rolling her eyes.

"You would. You'd stop taking your birth control and spread your legs and beg me to breed you."

"Dream the fuck *on!*"

"You two fight really well," Holly said.

"Just try not to start actually having angry sex before we get home," Ellen said.

"I don't know, I think Chloe might have a hard time. Look how badly she's gagging to fuck me," Gabe replied.

"Fuck you, you arrogant prick!" she snapped.

"See? She's begging to fuck me."

"Gabe, I am going to fucking–"

"All right you two, relax. I swear to fucking shit I am going to get a spray bottle," Ellen growled as she drove on.

Gabe laughed and settled in for the ride.

CHAPTER THIRTY FOUR

Gabe found himself taking stock as he drove towards Abby.

Overall, he was feeling pretty good.

He'd finished writing Hearthfire III last night and Ellen and Holly had promised to have it edited and back to him by tonight. He'd gotten his first new chapter of Recovery Echo Four written, and he'd also managed to get two erotic scenes written, which he had decided, in an absolutely genius move that Chloe was sure to roast him on, to call it Recovery After Dark. All that was left was editing all that and he'd have everything he needed.

He had the presents bought, wrapped, and hidden. The bookshelf had arrived and he was going to put it together tomorrow night so he could present it to Holly on Christmas.

And...that was it.

He was pretty much caught up with everything in his life and was looking forward to being able to just relax and turn off his brain entirely for at least a few days. Although he felt kind of guilty thinking that, given how easy his life was compared to even just a few months ago. It was more just that he was so...busy.

Things just kept happening, kept cropping up and needing to be dealt with.

But this was the life he'd chosen, and he'd choose it again if he had to.

And it wasn't like he could, in any capacity, complain about what he was doing right now. Going on a date with an attractive, fun, kind woman was always a great pleasure. Maybe it was less that he was complaining and more that he was nervous.

There was the obvious apprehension that came from going on a date with a woman, but now there was an extra layer of...

Awkwardness?

He wasn't sure what exactly to call it, but a mild anxiety about doing something wrong or off-putting because he'd never gone on a date with a married lesbian woman before. Well, almost completely lesbian.

Maybe that's what he was concerned about.

Gabe put the thoughts aside as he neared his destination.

This, at least, he was very excited for. Although he had some mixed feelings. When he'd started researching things to do in driving distance, he'd stumbled upon the fact that, apparently, there was an aquarium about half an hour away. How he had missed this, he had no idea, because aquariums were awesome and he absolutely would have found a way to go if he'd known.

He felt bad because he figured at least one of his girlfriends would enjoy being taken there, but he was going to go with another woman first. He'd asked them about it and they'd all said it was fine, though Holly and Ellen made him promise to take them sometime soon. Chloe seemed largely indifferent to fish.

Gabe found a spot in the mostly empty lot, parked, and texted Abby. Not long after he had, he saw a car door open up and Abby stepped out. He got out and they met in the middle.

She smiled as she looked him up and down. "You look sharp."

"Ellen said you'd appreciate it," he replied.

"I do."

"You also look very nice," he said.

"Thanks." They began walking towards the entrance. "I'll be honest, I'm nervous. I haven't gone on a date with anyone but Emily for...well, years. Since we met and started dating. And, more than that, I've never actually gone on a date with a man."

"Not once?" he asked.

"No. Not once."

"I take it dating was easy for you when you were younger?"

"Well...yes. For me. I knew others who had difficulty. Hitting puberty in the early two thousands was...not easy as a not straight person. But I was very stubborn, and also settled on my look early and I feel like I managed to perfect it quickly. And that helps with dating."

"Yeah, that would. I've not been great about...grooming, I guess? Ellen has helped me out," he said as they walked inside and bought their tickets. "Wow."

"Yes, this is...very beautiful," Abby murmured.

The entryway opened into a huge lobby studded with large, broad glass tubes filled with water and vegetation and fish. They walked up to the nearest one and simply stood there staring for a while. Gabe had never been able to put it into words, but fish always kind of captivated him. It genuinely gave him a burst of happiness to spot one along the shore of a lake or pond.

After a time, they began walking slowly through the aquarium, pausing to look at more fish as they talked.

"Is it hard, dating three women at the same time?" Abby asked.

"I get the feeling that's going to become a common question. I wouldn't say it's hard, but I would also say that certain aspects of it make it so much easier," he replied.

"Such as?"

"Well, the fact that they all know about each other and like each other is a huge one. Normally when people say 'dating multiple women', there's the assumption that they don't know about each other. The fact that they're generally reasonable and kind and low maintenance probably is the glue that mostly holds us together, I think. I mean, beyond, you know, love...living together also helps a lot," he said.

"That makes sense. It *would* cut down on a lot of driving. But it also has to be cramped at this point, unless Ellen has exaggerated the size of your house."

"No, it's...that's accurate. We finally have a big enough bed," he replied.

"Wait, all *four* of you are sharing a bed? Someone doesn't have their own bed elsewhere in the house?"

"Nope. We've all agreed to it."

"That's something else. I have a hard enough time sharing my bed with just Emily. Mostly because she's a restless sleeper, though. Is it weird for Chloe? Or is this getting too personal?"

"No, it's fine. I talked with her about it and she said she's comfortable with it. She's sort of just diving into certain things and discovering that she likes it. Like sleeping naked."

Abby laughed. "Oh yeah. I started doing it after Emily talked me into it and never went back. It's super comfy."

"Yeah, I'm still kind of getting used to it. For a while I began sleeping fully dressed, like in high school? That was...probably kind of weird."

"*Kind of* weird? Gabe, that's like some serial killer shit. That's the kind of thing that comes out in the documentary. 'He slept completely clothed, every single night'."

"Come on, really? Is it *that* weird?" he asked, laughing.

She chuckled. "Okay, an exaggeration. But it's very weird. Or I don't know, maybe it's more common for guys to go through that phase? It sounds insane to me."

"Yeah, looking back on it now, it was kind of weird. But then I got down to t-shirt and boxers. Then boxers. And then Ellen convinced me to just start sleeping naked."

"I imagine it makes middle of the night sex easier," Abby murmured.

"Ah...yes. Yes it does."

"How often does that happen?"

"Basically every night. Ellen is...very needy at night. And so is Chloe, I'm learning."

"You're a lucky boy. There's definitely a part of me that would kill to have those three living with me, fucking me all the time...but I don't think I could handle that many people around regularly. I like when it's just me and Emily."

"Well...I mean you'll definitely get to enjoy some fun with Ellen and Holly. Provided I'm around."

"That will be very nice. I remember Emily describing Ellen to me and I finally got so curious about this six and a half foot blonde who would have absolutely been a fucking Valkyrie or Amazon warrior in a past life and looked her up online and oh my lord, she was *captivating.* I've always wanted to know what it'd be like to be with her. And getting...tag-teamed by both of you will be, I imagine, quite a nice experience," she said quietly, grinning as she looked around.

"Oh yes," he agreed. "So you've never done anything with a man before? At all?"

"Nope. Not even kissed. Nothing beyond hugging," she replied.

"How confident are you that you won't be completely weirded out by...going all the way?" he asked.

"Fairly," she replied. "I *have* watched straight porn. But I'll admit, there can be a world of difference between that and actually doing it. I'm honestly very curious about what it's like. Emily tells me there is a noticeable difference between a fake and a real dick. I'm going to be taking it slow. We'll hang out, we'll kiss, and if that goes well, we can make out, and if that goes well, we can fool around a bit more…"

She frowned and stopped before a large tank containing manta rays. "It's going to require a lot of patience on your part, I imagine. For which I am grateful. I wanted to convey that. I'm well aware of the fact that I could not do this with someone I did not truly trust. A man who will be aware of my needs and my feelings, who will listen, especially if I say 'stop'. Emily has...stories, about that."

"Oh, wow. Fuck. I'm sorry," he replied.

"Well, thankfully none of them were too traumatic. She had to get pretty stern and one time she had to break a guy's nose and another time she had to use mace. But I wanted to say that I appreciate your efforts, and your kindness. I'm glad that you've treated myself, and Emily, as people instead of just...I don't know, fuckmeat. A chance to have sex. As a lawyer, I've heard too many horror stories," she said.

"I imagine. Well, you're welcome. I'm very glad to help, for obvious reasons, but I'm also glad to be a partner to you in all this. I want you to feel safe and heard, and I want you to feel like this is a thing we're navigating together, even if you're in the lead."

She smiled and hugged him suddenly. "That's it right there," she said as he wrapped his own arms around her. "That willingness to work together, that's so significant. So many people say they're willing to work together but then go right off the rails as soon as there's a bump in the road." She pulled back after a moment. "All right, let's keep going. Maybe you could tell me more about yourself. What your life has been like."

He chuckled. "Well, not exactly great, but yes, I would be glad to."

They kept walking and talking.

...

"Interesting choice," Gabe said as they got out of their cars.

"It's not boring, is it?" she asked.

"No. And honestly, even if it was, I'd still go in there with you."

Abby laughed. "Well, I appreciate that, and your candor."

They started walking up the stone steps to the front of the art gallery. The aquarium had gone well, he felt, and Abby seemed more relaxed at least. Ellen had texted him a few times, and Chloe had texted him several times. Mostly to tease him.

He had to admit, this was an aspect of a

relationship that he'd never thought he would be into. Not after his previous girlfriend. She was a little like Chloe in that she liked to tease him, the only problem was that she often seemed to pick stuff that actually bothered him, or did it in such a way that it seemed actually mean and not just in good fun.

During the last few months of their relationship, a common back-and-forth when they'd start fighting was her saying 'Come on, we were having fun!', and him responding 'No, *you* were having fun'.

It hadn't been a good time.

As they headed inside, Gabe found himself mildly struck by the immediate and immense air of quiet. It was like a library, but somehow more intense without being overwhelming. There was almost no one around, which was probably helping that atmosphere a lot.

"I haven't been here in too long," Abby murmured as she guided him deeper into the gallery.

"What about it appeals?" he asked.

"It might sound weird, but the atmosphere. It's so tranquil. It's so calm. I came here on a field trip once in high school and really liked it, but ultimately forgot about it. And then, one day after I'd moved back following law school and I was feeling particularly overwhelmed, I suddenly remembered it. And I came here, and it was just...magical. I started coming here almost every single week during my worst year. Emily...is polite, but this isn't really her thing. I like to come here and look at the pieces and contemplate...and get angry sometimes."

"Angry? That sounds the opposite of peaceful," he said.

She chuckled. "Well, mostly I'd get angry at some of the more modern art. I'll show you some of them. I swear there are some that are just three swipes on a blank canvas and that is apparently *genius*. Genius worth a hundred grand. It's really frustrating."

"Oh...yeah, that does sound like bullshit. Like, *I* could do that. But apparently no one would care, certainly not enough to drop six figures on it."

"But it's not real anger. It's more like...mock anger. Mostly for Emily. I started complaining once about this exact thing and she thought it was funny so I kept it going. But yes, the atmosphere. I think people who visited the place where I used to work would call me crazy because they'd see little difference between here and there.

"But the big difference is the atmosphere itself, the feelings. This is a place of quiet history. Reverence, even, depending on how you feel about art. Whereas where *I* worked, it was like a pressure cooker. The intensity was silent but overwhelming. I think a big part of it was that I knew just how intense things were. Behind every closed door was a person working furiously on something, and sometimes it was a matter of life or death. That shit wears you down."

"I couldn't even imagine having to deal with that," he said.

"Yeah, it takes a specific type of personality to develop the skillset to manage something like that," she replied. "And I have it, but...it extracts a toll. And I saw the road I was walking down and decided...I'd rather step off the road and let someone else do it. As corrupt as the law system is, we do need good people getting in there and doing the ugly work." She paused and looked at him suddenly. "I envy you, in a way."

"What? Seriously? Why?" he asked.

"You're twenty six years old and you've got

what you want to do figured out, and you're doing it," she replied.

"Well...all right, I'll give you that. But it's only working right now because of Sadie and Ellen and luck."

"That's not what I mean. You're in your twenties and you found what you want to do with your life. What to dedicate your life towards. A *lot* of people don't get that. They just...flounder, looking for meaning. And usually they find something they love, but some don't."

"Didn't you find what you want early on?" he asked.

She laughed softly. "That's a fair point. I knew I wanted to help people with legal trouble since high school and I'm still doing that. I suppose what I'm really envious of is that you seem to be engaging with it without all the...sacrifice and suffering. Law school is brutal. And then somehow what comes next is even more brutal. Or maybe I just envy your age. I know it probably seems insane, but twenty six is so much younger than thirty four. Life just fucking...wears you down. It's not even that I feel old, necessarily, just...worn out, stretched thin. And it's better now than it was before I left my job, but that level of intensity leaves it mark on you."

"I can imagine," he said. "Ellen seems in much the same boat."

"Yes. That was my impression." She laughed, a little bitterly. "It's funny. Emily sometimes feels like she can't measure up to me, she feels guilty because she never really got her life together compared to me, but in truth I'd rather have her life some days. She had fun. She remembers great times and fun parties and cool people. I remember being locked in a room with a laptop and a stack of books. I remember parties I *didn't* go to, because I was studying my ass off. Constantly. And then working my ass off, constantly."

"You'd probably want your life if you had Emily's," Gabe pointed out, a little apologetically.

She laughed again. "You're right, I'm sure. Green grass and all that. I'm learning to live with it."

"Any advice? Because I sort of feel like I basically wasted all the time between graduating high school and starting to date Ellen. I just pissed it all away into a black hole working meaningless minimum wage jobs. I could've been writing and building way before now."

"I'm sure Emily and probably Holly would have some nice advice about making peace with the past and learning to live with yourself and your decisions. But in a way, I think you're closer to being like me and Ellen, and probably Chloe. You're a bit more...pragmatic. So what I have to say is this: the past is done. There's literally nothing in the universe that can call it back. So, beyond learning lessons, dwelling on past misery is an exercise in meaninglessness. No amount of consideration or rumination will allow you to change even the tiniest aspect of the tiniest past event. And if it's literally impossible, then you should instead focus on here and now, and tomorrow, if you can."

"Yeah, that's closer to what I tend to think on my better days," he agreed.

"Knew it. All right, we're close to the more recent exhibits. Let's see if there's anything worth getting fired up over."

. . .

After they had finished with the art gallery, they decided to grab some burgers from a nearby hole-in-the-wall restaurant.

"You were right," Gabe said. "That was a good experience, very calming. And funny, at the end."

"I'm glad you enjoyed yourself," Abby replied.

A moment passed and he could tell something was bothering her.

"You don't seem as happy," he said finally.

She looked up. "Sorry. I'm just...thinking about things."

"What things?"

"I have a completely unfair question to ask you."

"I'll answer it if I can..."

She looked at him for a long moment, then sighed softly and tossed the fry she was holding back onto her plate. "Okay. So...do you really think this is going to happen? I know I said we're going to take a week at minimum to think more about this, but there's a part of mc that's really scared that you all have decided you aren't going to do it and you're just waiting to tell me. And this is completely unfair to ask, I know."

"It's understandable," Gabe replied. He considered it for a moment. "I can at least say that no, we haven't decided we're not going to do it and are just waiting to tell you. If you want my honest opinion on whether or not this is going to happen, I think it is. I'm pretty confident it is."

Abby stared at him for what seemed like a long time, then finally seemed to relax. "Thank you," she said. "I know everything might change but that did actually make me feel better."

"Good. I want you to feel better."

She smiled suddenly. "You also want to get me pregnant."

"I mean yeah, who wouldn't? You are *very* attractive and nice and smart."

"I am also happy to be impregnated by you. You seem pretty smart and kind and hardworking yourself."

"I...hope so," he murmured. "I'm also suffering from depression and anxiety half the time."

"Yeah but–and not to minimize that at all–who isn't nowadays?"

"True."

They started chatting about more idle and simple things as they ate. After a while, they finished their meals and then headed back outside.

"It's been fun, Gabe," Abby said.

"It has," he agreed.

"I'll see you...at some point soon, I imagine."

"Yeah. Call or text if you have any other thoughts. I'll have discussions about this with everyone involved, serious ones, and we'll have your answer."

"Thank you. And don't worry about the time crunch too much...although I guess I'd rather not leave it that much longer. I'm hoping to have an autumn birth."

"We'll get it figured out before too long," he replied.

"Again, I really appreciate it."

They hugged, said goodbye, and then got into their respective vehicles and drove away.

CHAPTER THIRTY FIVE

Gabe sat back in his computer chair, took a deep breath, held it, and then slowly let it out.

It was done.

His Christmas short was up, the Hearthfire trilogy was finished and up, including the anthology, (he'd even written some extra content for it, hoping it would make people happy), and he'd managed to get two chapters and three sex scenes written and edited for Recovery Echo Four. And he'd just finished updating his old fan fiction with the newly edited chapters.

Given it might tip Chloe off, he'd waited to do this until the last minute, and even then, he hadn't updated a new chapter yet. He was going to do that tomorrow, or sometime soon. When his brain wasn't scrambled.

He wasn't even sure why he was so mentally fatigued, but what mattered right now was that he'd actually managed to do it.

After his date with Abby, the only thing he'd come up against that made him seriously anxious was going to Chloe's parent's place. But thankfully, it hadn't caused any problems. If anything, it had been boring. They'd had a meal, exchanged gifts (he'd given Chloe the book he'd bought for her at the mall and she had gotten him an online gift card, awkwardly stating that she was terrible at buying gifts for people), and then they'd talked for a few hours.

The only thing that made it difficult was having to dance around a few issues. He could tell her sister was broadly suspicious and her mother wasn't entirely willing to let go of the book thing, trying to determine what it was he really wrote without being direct about it.

Like Chloe, her mother was pretty sharp and Gabe found himself having focus hard to give an answer that sounded satisfactory without being too vague.

But now it was Christmas. He was home. Ellen, Holly, and Chloe were home, elsewhere in the house right now.

They'd all been giggly today, whispering to each other about whatever it was they had planned for him. He still didn't know and in truth, he didn't want to know. Surprises were nice. Well, when they weren't awful surprises.

And now he was free to enjoy that.

As he sat forward again and shut down his laptop for the day, his phone buzzed. He checked it and saw he had a text from Sadie.

Hello, Gabe. This is an unusual and hopefully not unwelcome request, but I have a friend out here who does not believe me that I have a handsome young man that I am involved with. I was hoping you could send me a picture of your dick. If not, that's fine.

Gabe laughed, he couldn't help it.

Although he'd definitely been getting asked for this specific thing more than ever before since he'd begun dating Ellen, ('ever before' being 'not ever'), he wasn't sure he'd yet had a woman ask for a dick pic like Sadie did.

He fired off a quick reply: *Yes, I can do that, just a moment.*

Gabe considered it for a moment, then stood up and unzipped his pants. He frowned and hesitated. He definitely didn't want to send a picture of it when he wasn't hard. He opened up his special folder on his phone (he'd finally gotten around to organizing it) and started looking at pictures he'd taken of Ellen and Holly and Chloe.

After a moment, he realized not enough was happening because now he was kind of nervous.

Gabe frowned as a new thought came to him. He lived in a house with three ridiculously hot women, all of whom were dating him and were experts at giving him an erection.

Gabe headed out into the rest of his house. He heard voices coming from the bedroom and walked there, finding Chloe on the floor, sorting through her clothes, and Ellen sitting at the foot of the bed, a wineglass in hand.

"What's up? Your pants are unzipped," Ellen said.

"Maybe it's time," Chloe murmured.

"Yeah, probably, we need a good one to two hours leeway."

"Time for *what,* exactly?" Gabe asked.

"Your present, silly," Ellen said, standing up.

"Oh. What's it entail?"

"Eating edibles, firstly. I'll go get them."

"Okay, but when you get back I need your help with something. Or Chloe's. Whoever wants to do it," he said.

"With what?" Ellen asked as she headed into the kitchen.

"Getting me hard," he replied.

"I can do that," Chloe said. "Why exactly?"

"Sadie asked for a dick pic."

Ellen laughed as she came back from the kitchen. "*Sadie* did? Really?"

"Yeah. She's got a friend who doesn't believe

she's got a twenty something dude desperate to bang the fuck out of her and I guess a dick pic makes the most sense, and I want to be hard, obviously, and since you all like doing that so much…"

Chloe snorted. "*Like* to do it, uh-huh. More like *deign* to do it."

"Give me a fucking break, you gag to get me hard," Gabe said.

"*I* like doing it," Ellen murmured. "Here, open your hand."

He did and she placed two of the square gummies in it. "This seems like a lot."

"If it's too much just do one, or one and a half, but I've been seeing how much gets you fucked up and how much gets you *really* fucked up, and I think you should be really fucked up to enjoy this particular gift," she said.

"What is it, exactly?" he asked.

"Well it's still a surprise, to be given to you once you're fucked up, so…"

"Does it involve sex?" he asked.

Ellen laughed. "Of course it involves sex."

Gabe thought about it. She had a point. Not only did the gummies make him really horny, but they also made sex feel even better than usual. He'd been experimenting with different dosages and was discovering that while he wasn't as sensitive to it as Chloe, one usually got him pretty good. He shrugged and ate both of them.

"I'm down," he said.

"Hey! You guys are taking a picture of Gabe's dick?" Holly asked, her voice growing closer as she came in from the living room.

"Yep," Ellen replied, pushing him gently back into a sitting position at the foot of the bed. "You want to help? Chloe?"

"I can help, yeah," Chloe said, taking her shirt off.

"Let me take the picture, I can make it look really good," Holly said.

"That makes sense," Gabe agreed, passing her the phone.

Ellen opened up the robe she was wearing, revealing her long, pale, voluptuous nude body beneath, and dropped into a crouch before him.

"You never wear clothes anymore," Gabe murmured as she undid the button on his jeans.

"Are you complaining?" she replied, raising an eyebrow.

"Not at all. Just observing."

"I'm on the way there myself," Chloe muttered as she crouched next to Ellen, fully topless now. "Clothes are restrictive and annoying."

"Agreed, you should definitely take all your clothes off more," Gabe said as Ellen pulled him out of his pants.

"What's this bullshit? You're already most of the way to an erection," she said.

"Well...that's how effective you are," he replied. "But, you know, if both of you wanted to lick it, I wouldn't complain."

"Oh my God, Gabe," Chloe said, rolling her eyes.

"Sorry if my tongue touches yours," Ellen said as she gripped his cock.

"Eh, I don't mind. I've made out with a few girls in my time, tongue included," Chloe replied.

"Good to know."

They both leaned in and began dragging their tongues across his head. He pretty much immediately finished getting hard, especially when Ellen cradled his balls in her soft, hot hand and began to massage them gently.

The two women continued for about thirty seconds before pulling back.

"Oh come on, that's it?" Gabe asked.

"You are *way* too easy to derail," Ellen murmured, smirking, "you already forgot that we're taking a picture."

"I didn't forget, I just...got into the moment," he replied.

Holly got closer. "Okay, out of the way, girls," she murmured, moving around slowly until she seemed to settle on a proper angle and then snapping a picture. "Here."

"That...why does this look as quality as it does? Also, it seems kinda bigger than it should be," he muttered.

"Angle, distance, and lighting are *everything,*" Holly replied.

"Apparently." He sent the picture to Sadie and then set his phone aside and leaned back. "Now, if you wouldn't mind finishing what you started…"

"I'm afraid not, sweetie," Ellen said, standing and pulling her robe back into place.

"Are you serious?" he asked as Chloe pulled her shirt back on.

"Yes, dear. I don't want you orgasming until you're high as fuck. Trust me, this is going to be as much a present for us as it is for you," Ellen replied.

"All right then," he grumbled, putting his dick away. "Well, I'm finished with my work, officially. I'm taking the rest of the year off, and probably a little of the first week of January. So, we can get to the presents if you want."

"I do want," Chloe said. "I'm *so* fucking curious about what you apparently got me."

"Well...I hope you like it. I'm pretty nervous about this, actually," Gabe replied, getting up and heading out into the living room with everyone.

"What's there to be nervous about?" Ellen asked.

"Well, for one, I don't know if Chloe will not like my gift. I mean I know she'll like it, but I don't know if she'll accept it as a *gift,* if that makes sense."

"Gabe, trust me, I'm not going to be mad, whatever it is," she replied. "You gave me...a new life, essentially. I don't know if I can overstate enough how much happier I am already, and how much of a change this is, and how exciting it is. I get to quit my shit job? I get to *stop paying bills?* I get to live in a house with three cool people, and one of them is you? And we can have awesome sex basically whenever I want?

"And I mean, even all that aside, the ability to just fucking...*relax,* that's big. That's like taking off weighted clothes I didn't even realize I was wearing. That's a fucking *relief,* Gabe. That's massive. You can assume that I'm pretty thrilled. Not to downplay anything, but you're sort of playing on easy mode with me right now: basically anything you do makes me happy."

"Wow, I didn't know it was that intense," Gabe murmured.

"That's how I feel," Ellen said.

"Same, basically," Holly agreed.

"Me too," he said. "I guess I just didn't realize how happy I am apparently making you."

"You're way too observant for that," Ellen said, rolling her eyes as she took another drink from her wineglass. "I think you've just come to undervalue how much of an impact you can have on other people."

"I'm...getting better about it," he replied.

"I know, dear. I just wish you didn't feel that way. Now," Ellen said as they all got settled in the living room on the couches, "this is our first Christmas together, and we're all still...finding our footing in general, so I wanted to think of this as a...soft Christmas, I guess? Mmm." She giggled suddenly. "Apparently I'm a little drunker than I thought. Well, you're head of the household anyway, dear, why don't you take over?"

"Am I?" he asked, standing up.

"Oh yeah, without question," Ellen replied.

"Definitely," Holly agreed.

"As annoying as it is to feed your ego, I have to admit that you clearly are the head of the household," Chloe said.

"Was that sarcastic or not?" he asked.

She sighed. "It was sarcastic. You have a surprisingly small ego given your present situation."

"You mean given the fact that I have you three beautiful women wanting to fuck me all the time?" he asked.

Chloe rolled her eyes. "It's getting bigger, though, that ego."

"There are worse things," Ellen murmured.

"Ellen has a good point," Gabe said. "We're still figuring things out, but in general I also don't want to place too much emphasis on gift-giving. I want everyone to feel good and accepted. So, I think we can all agree, if you didn't get anything for someone, that's okay. It won't be taken personally. Right?" They all murmured in agreement. "Good. Now, how do we want to start?"

"Well, I don't have anything for anyone," Chloe said. "So we can just...get that out of the way now. Between how busy I've been and how awful I am at getting gifts..."

"That's fine, Chloe," Gabe replied. "Holly?"

"I've just got one for Ellen. My other gifts are...more experiences than gifts," she replied, handing a slim gift over to Ellen.

"Gifts as in plural? Does that mean something sexy for both me and Ellen, or...multiple sexy things for me or...something else?"

"Stop fishing," Ellen replied, taking the gift and tearing it open. "The Far Quest," she murmured, studying the game box that was revealed. "Thank you, Holly. This looks really interesting."

"I figured it was something you might like, given your love of fantasy and more recent love of video games."

"That one is really cool," Chloe said. "Damn, I should've got you a video game."

"It's fine, Chloe," Ellen replied. "My turn?"

"Yep," Gabe said.

"Well, I'm afraid I just got one for Holly, in the physical sense. Well...I mean the others are physical, too, but...mmm, nevermind. Here, cutie," Ellen said, passing her a gift.

"Thank you!" Holly replied, tearing it open. She looked radiant and marvelously happy as she studied the book that was revealed. "Reading is something I'm going to do *so* much of now that I have time and I'm not sad all the time. Thank you, Ellen!"

"You're welcome, Holly."

"Okay, my turn," Gabe said. "First thing, Chloe, go get your laptop, it's required for your gift."

"Uh, okay," she replied, getting up and heading

to the bedroom.

While she got that, Gabe passed Ellen her present. She grinned, finished off the wine left in her glass, and opened it up. "Thank you, babe," she said, studying the book he'd gotten for her.

"You're welcome, love," he replied. "Now, I'll be right back. I already put together your present, Holly. Well, one of them."

"I'm excited," Holly replied.

Gabe headed back to his office, passing Chloe as she returned with her laptop. He went in and opened up his closet, hoping that Holly hadn't peeked at some point. He grabbed the three-tiered bookshelf that he'd had delivered and carried it out to the living room.

"Oh wow," Holly said, grinning as she got up.

"Yep," Gabe replied, "I figured you'd appreciate it. And…" He pushed the final wrapped gift on the coffee table towards her.

"This feels hefty," she said as she picked it up, then she tore the wrapping paper off and opened up the box that was revealed. "Oh wow, this is a lot of books." She picked a few up out of the box he'd packed them into and studied each quickly, then set them aside and hugged him tightly. "Thank you, Gabe. For this and for everything. And thank you too, Ellen. Chloe's right, both of you changed my life. For the better, obviously, but better than I even really thought it could be changed."

"You're welcome, love," Gabe replied, kissing her.

"I'm very happy to have been involved in that, Holly. You're such a sweet woman and you and Chloe deserve so much happiness," Ellen replied.

"So do you two," Holly said, sitting back down.

"Second to last gift," Gabe said, walking over to the couch and pulling out the slim package he'd put back there. "This is for you."

"Did you seriously hide a present back there?" Ellen asked as she accepted it.

"I seriously did," he replied.

She laughed and unwrapped it, then stared at the box for a moment.

"What is it? I can't tell from here," Chloe asked.

"It's a painter's easel. I...mmm. Goodness. This is...very strong," she murmured.

"Strong?" Gabe asked.

She laughed softly and set it aside. "Sorry, I'm drunk. It had a strong impact on me. *Thank you,* Gabe. I really, really appreciate it. And I don't quite have all the words right now, but this is a big deal. You helping me go after my desire to paint-it's a big deal."

She pulled him down into a hug and a long kiss.

"You're welcome, sweetheart," he replied. "Now, last gift I have on me," Gabe said, pulling a USB drive out of his pocket and passing it to Chloe. "Fire it up."

"I'm so curious," she said as she accepted it and slotted it into her laptop. She spent a moment navigating. "Wait...holy shit, are you serious?"

"I'm curious too, what is it?" Ellen asked.

"It's new content for his fan fic I was raging about," she replied, looking up. "How much? What's different?"

"I reread and edited everything I'd written so far, wrote two brand new chapters, and also wrote three sex scenes," Gabe replied. "And I'm going to finish it, write more sex scenes, and start writing the sequel soon."

"This is...wow, Gabe. I-this means a lot." She laughed suddenly and looked up higher, blinking a few times, then sighed and wiped at her eyes with her thumb. "Goddamnit, are you kidding me? Sorry, this has to be so stupid, crying over a fucking fan fiction."

"It's not stupid. You care about it," Ellen replied.

"I do. I just...I was having a really shit time in general when I found Recovery. I was pretty depressed. But playing it...I don't know. There's just something about it. It has such a message of hope, even in the bleakest of situations, and it seemed to just-I don't know, break through something inside me?

"I went and found fan fics on it and found Gabe's and it just...captivated me. You write people really well, babe. They feel real, the interactions, the emotions, the dialogue. It helped me a lot. And knowing that you're going back and doing more for me is...a lot. It feels like a lot. Although, I don't want this to get in the way of your, you know, bill-paying writing."

"Don't worry about that, Chloe, it won't. Honestly I was glad for the opportunity. Echo Four is probably my favorite thing I've ever written. I had sort of conceded it lost by now, but going back and looking over it again, it really reactivated in my mind. And I probably wouldn't have gone back if not for you, so thank you as well," he replied.

She laughed and set her laptop aside, stood, and hugged him tightly, squeezed him really.

"Oh man, I just realized something amazing," she murmured. "Like it just hit me all at once."

"What?" he asked.

Chloe pulled back a little, looking up at him, grasping his arms. She looked nervous and incredibly vulnerable. "...I love you...I'm sorry if that's too much right now, but–"

Gabe kissed her. She closed her eyes and leaned into it, hugging him again tightly. They embraced like they hadn't seen each other in years and kissed with an intense, intimate passion for a long moment.

Finally, they pulled back, panting a little. "I love you too, Chloe," Gabe murmured, resting his forehead against hers.

"It just hit me all at once," she said softly, staring into his eyes. "You're so nice and thoughtful and you do all these nice things for me and take care of me and we just fit together so well, I...yeah. I love you." She giggled.

They both glanced over as they heard Ellen sniff. "Oh don't mind me," she said, grinning as she wiped at her eyes. "I'm just really happy. This is sweet and wonderful."

"Yeah," Holly murmured, smiling serenely. "This is beautiful. You two are really good together."

"Thank you," Chloe said, and cleared her throat. "Both of you, for allowing me into your home and your lives, and letting me be Gabe's girlfriend."

"You're welcome, Chloe. You're a great person and I'm happy you're part of the relationship," Ellen said, and Holly nodded.

Chloe sniffed, then laughed and wiped at her eyes again. "Well, um, I guess we should move onto the next thing. Whatever that is."

"How about we just relax and talk and see what happens?" Gabe suggested.

"That sounds great," Chloe replied, and they sat down on the loveseat together.

CHAPTER THIRTY SIX

"Oh wow…" Gabe murmured. "Um...it's coming on hard now." He chuckled.

Ellen and Holly looked at each other, grinning, then back at him. Chloe was in his lap. They'd been chatting and relaxing for about an hour now.

"You horny?" Holly asked.

"Oh yeah, he is, I can feel it," Chloe said.

"Well then, it's time for the next part of Christmas," Ellen said, getting up and then stumbling a little. "Goodness, maybe a little too much wine."

"You're drunk," Holly said, and giggled.

"You're stoned," Ellen replied.

Holly giggled again. "Yeah."

"Come on, babe," Chloe said, getting up off his lap and then taking one hand while Holly took the other.

They pulled him up and then cried out as he stumbled and grasped Holly to keep from falling over. All three of them immediately started laughing.

"Ah, Ellen, help! You're strong enough to handle this," Holly cried as she tried to keep him upright.

"Come on, babe," Ellen said, taking hold of him and hugging him to her. "Stay here, right with me, love."

"You're so tall," he murmured.

She laughed. "I am."

"I'm really glad about that. And your ass is so huge."

Ellen started laughing as she guided him towards the bedroom. "Clearly you enjoy that."

"I do. And I love it so much when you ride me. You look amazing. Like an angel...or an Amazon warrior."

"At some point," Chloe said as she and Holly followed them into the bedroom, "I think we need to find, like, a Marine or something to hook him up with. Some chick in the military. A tall one."

"That'd be so fucking amazing," he replied, then grunted as Ellen dropped him onto his back on the bed. "Wow, I'm so high. My head is buzzing like crazy." He chuckled.

"You're actually super cute when you're stoned," Chloe said, taking off her shirt.

"He is," Ellen agreed, shrugging out of her robe.

"Oh my fucking God, your hips," he muttered, staring at her. "And thighs. Holy shit. And...oh wow," he said, shifting focus to Chloe as her pants came off. "Your pussy is so hot."

She laughed. "What?! Specifically my pussy?" She looked down at herself.

"Yeah. It's awesome. And Holly...your tits are way too amazing. And your hair. It's so fucking red and nice."

"Thank you, dear," Holly said, laughing.

"He's so fucking stoned," Chloe muttered.

"He's also rock fucking hard, look at his pants," Ellen said, climbing into the bed. "Come on, babe, clothes off so we can get this present started."

It was an interesting experience, being this high and getting undressed by three naked women that he was in love with.

"There you are," Ellen said as she got his boxers down. "I bet Gabe has never had three women licking his dick at the same time."

"Uh...yeah, that'd definitely be a first," he agreed.

"Then let's make this happen," Holly said.

Gabe watched with rapturous focus as all three of them got into position, Chloe to his right, Ellen to his left, Holly between them over his legs, then as they leaned in, stuck out their tongues and began to lick his cock.

The pleasure started immediately and it seemed to come on in waves. He exhaled sharply as he felt their tongues dragging across his head, up and down his shaft. Holly even leaned down after a bit and began carefully licking his balls.

"Holy fuck," he whispered, and Ellen and Chloe chuckled in response.

"Is it different?" Ellen murmured.

"Uh, yeah. I can't tell if it's that-ah man...ah yeah…" he groaned as Chloe started sucking him off, bobbing her head smoothly, her luscious lips traveling rapidly up and down his shaft. "Can't tell if...it's the weed or...the all three of you at the same time. But it's amazing. Ah fuck, Chloe."

She kept at it for a moment longer, then stopped and passed him to Ellen, who took up the work and slipped her lips all the way down his erection until he could feel the head of his dick poking against the back of her throat. She pushed a bit farther and then swallowed, and the ecstasy came on hard, making him groan loudly.

"Mmm, he likes that," Holly murmured.

"Uh-huh," he managed.

He put his hand on the back of Ellen's head, feeling her soft pale blonde hair. Everything felt amazing right now. He could honestly see why stoners were as into weed as they were. Everything just felt better, and sex felt beyond amazing.

Gabe wasn't sure how long he watched them switch back and forth, or how he managed not to come during all that, but finally Ellen sat up.

"All right, girls, I want to go first. Holly, will you get the little vibe? I think he's gonna pop quick and I'd like to come, too," she said.

"Happy to oblige," Holly replied, hopping up.

"This is the craziest thing I've ever done," Chloe murmured as she shifted to sit beside him.

"Having fun?" Gabe murmured.

"Yeah, definitely. This is really hot. I've always kind of felt like I'd do well in a threesome with another woman and I am very glad to learn that this is true, and that it's actually *really* hot to see my boyfriend fuck other women," she replied.

"As your boyfriend, I can say that I deeply appreciate this fact, too-ohhhh my fucking God, your *pussy* Ellen..." he groaned as she mounted him and slid him into herself. "You're so fucking wet!"

"You aren't the only one who gets fucking horny when you get fucked up," she replied. "Now..." she leaned forward, "suck on my tits."

Gabe did as she told him with glee as her huge breasts swayed before him. He settled his hands on her broad, powerful hips as she fucked him and put his lips around one of her nipples and experienced pure, hedonistic bliss.

"Here, Ellen..." Holly murmured as she got up beside them both.

He heard a buzzing as she turned on the vibrator and held it against Ellen's clit. She cried out, straightening up and repositioning herself a little.

"Oh fuck! Right there!" she moaned.

Gabe continued staring, the bliss not just washing through him but raging through his body now, Ellen's sweet, slick pussy providing it all. Seeing Holly grinning with that slutty smile on her face as she pleasured Ellen, seeing Ellen's face lost completely in bliss, eyes closed and mouth open, seeing Chloe staring at all this, enraptured...

It was everything he had hoped for and it was somehow better than he had imagined it.

Ellen let out a long, loud, impassioned cry of bliss as she began to orgasm. He groaned as she spasmed, moving him around inside of herself furiously. Her climax was a wonder to behold when he was laying beneath her and right as it began tapering off, he found himself triggering. He groaned loudly and pulled her more tightly against him as he started coming inside of her.

The pleasure evolved into rapturous ecstasy, a mind-flaying bliss that seemed to consume his entire universe as he unleashed his seed into Ellen, pumping her full of it. He could feel his whole body convulsing in time with his orgasm, and each successive spasm released even more ecstasy and intense sexual gratification.

Ellen rode him until he was finished, panting and moaning, and when he was done, she looked down at him with a very satisfied smile.

"That's one," she said, and got off of him.

"What?" he managed.

"My turn," Holly said, and took Ellen's place. "I'm going to be number two," she added, smiling down at him.

She took his hands and placed them on her soft, generous breasts, then took him into herself and began to fuck him.

"Ah fuck!" he groaned. "Oh that's intense. Fuck, Holly..." he panted, slowly being rendered delirious by the pleasure.

And then he was lost in her, too.

She grinned seductively, putting her hands over the back of his own and holding them in place, riding him with an increasing intensity. When she released him, his hands wandered over her soft, supple body, feeling her wonderful heat and smooth skin and curves. He reveled in her as they made love. And then, suddenly, the urge to shift position, to be atop her, swept over him.

"Here," he said, hugging her to him.

"Oh my goodness!" she cried as he flipped them over so she was on her back.

Holly let out a long series of pleasured shouts, sticking her legs up in the air as he began driving furiously into her. The bliss of sexual ecstasy continued to consume him as he stroked smoothly into her perfect, slick pussy.

At some point her climax came on, suddenly and swiftly and powerfully, and his groan of bliss as he felt her inner muscles flutter and convulse wildly became lost in her screams of pleasure. He continued fucking her, making her scream louder, and she grasped at him, wrapping her arms and legs around him, kissing him between her cries of rapture.

After she had finished and he'd continued making love to her for a time, Gabe finally got up on his knees, still stroking into her, and reached for Chloe. She eagerly got up on her knees beside him and made out with him. He groped one of her big, pale breasts as he kept screwing Holly.

"I want a turn," she whispered harshly as they broke the kiss.

"On your back, spread your legs," Gabe replied.

She grinned suddenly. "Make me."

Gabe chuckled and pulled out of Holly, then grabbed Chloe and shoved her down onto her back right beside Holly.

"Come on, make me!" she growled, grinning fiercely up at him.

Gabe grabbed her wrists and pressed them into the pillow over her head, then worked himself between her smooth thighs and used his body to get them open wider. She cried out as he slipped inside of her. She fought him a little as he started stroking into her, but quickly lost that particular desire and instead grabbed him and pulled him against her.

"I love you," she panted. "I love you so much, Gabe."

He kissed her and hugged her against him as he continued making love with her. "I love you too, Chloe," he murmured, and kissed her more.

It became increasingly difficult to maintain his focus as his high and the sex eroded it, and at some point he stopped trying to hold onto it. Time seemed to slip and then blur and then vanish like smoke on the wind.

He made love with Chloe until he realized Holly was asking for more attention, and so he switched back to her, kissing Chloe and then pulling out of her and moving over to Holly. She gasped and moaned as he penetrated her once more, then he was within her and lost to her greatness, her sheer desire and bliss.

And then he was switching back to Chloe after a time.

He wasn't sure how long he was at it, going back and forth between them both, but at some point Holly giggled.

"What?" he murmured.

"I know how to make you come right away," she replied.

"How's that?" he asked.

"Come here."

He leaned down closer and she wrapped her legs tightly around him suddenly. "I forgot to take my birth control," she whispered, "if you come inside me, I'll get pregnant, Gabe."

"Oh fuck, Holly…" he groaned, then groaned again, louder, as she squeezed him with her legs, forcing him deeper inside of her.

"Come on," she whispered, releasing him and then squeezing again with her legs, keeping the motion going. "Come on, Gabe, I want to get pregnant. I want you to knock me up. Make me a mother, Gabe. Get me pregnant."

He almost couldn't help himself as he started hammering away at her harder and faster, and then he was coming inside of her. He cried out as the pleasure slammed into him again, picking him and blowing him away like leaves in a hurricane.

He could feel his seed pumping out of him again, going into Holly, filling her up, and he found visions of her pregnant racing through his head as he came into her.

"Holy shit, it *is* like a button you push," Chloe murmured. "He lasted like ten seconds after you said that."

Gabe kept going until he had finished again, then lay panting on top of her.

"There's a good boy," Holly murmured.

"Hey, Gabe…" Chloe murmured. He looked over at her. She was on her hands and knees beside them now. "I want to get pregnant, too."

"Fuck," he groaned.

"Wow, he actually got harder again when you said that," Holly said.

Gabe pulled out of her, quickly got behind Chloe,

and listened to her yell in pleasure as he penetrated her again.

He went until his third, and he was positive final, orgasm came on, grasping Chloe's smooth hips and driving himself as deep into her as he could as he loosed whatever was left within him in her. When he pulled out of her, his head swam worse than ever, the world spinning wildly now, and his cock was so sensitive it hurt.

"Done," he gasped, collapsing between Chloe and Holly.

"You okay there, love?" Ellen asked, giggling.

Gabe tried to sit up. "I think, um, I need to…"

Then he was asleep.

EPILOGUE

Gabe came awake slowly.

He was aware of sunshine, the soft respiration of sleep, and warmth.

For what seemed like a long time, he simply laid where he was, staring at the ceiling. He remembered...a lot of sex. There was the wrapping up of business, and then gift giving, and something to do with Sadie was somewhere in there, and then it all devolved into a wonderful confusion of sex with Ellen and Holly and Chloe.

He felt very cloudy, and slow.

He would have been content to continue laying there for a while yet, but the urge to piss was slowly becoming unbearable. With a sigh, he began to move. He realized that he'd ended up in between Ellen and Holly, both of them naked, Ellen's voluptuous body mostly revealed to the world as the blanket had fallen off of her.

Holly laid on her back, one arm resting across her forehead, giving her a look of comical astonishment in her sleep.

Carefully, he extracted himself from between them, then took a moment to put the blanket back over Ellen, then headed for the bathroom. Something was missing, he thought as he stepped up to the toilet and began taking a long leak.

No, some*one* was missing. Chloe. She had probably just awoken early and was elsewhere in the house. Had she actually taken anything last night? He genuinely couldn't remember, but the fact that they'd fucked for so long seemed to indicate she hadn't. Then again, they could have been screwing for twenty minutes or three hours.

He genuinely didn't know how long it had gone on for.

Gabe finished, flushed, and then washed his hands and face and brushed his teeth. When he was finished, he felt a little better, but still very cloudy. He looked at the shower for a moment, then decided he wanted to see Chloe first and left the bathroom.

Wandering a bit brought him to the living room and he found her stretched out on the couch with her laptop and a pair of headphones with big black cat ears attached to the top.

She smiled when she saw him and took them off.

"You're naked," she said.

Gabe looked down at himself. "Oh. I guess I am."

Chloe laughed. "Are you still baked?"

"I'm...hungover," he replied. "How are you?"

"I'm great. I didn't drink or eat any gummies last night. I just got worn the fuck out by your goddamned cock."

"Did we fuck a really long time?" he asked.

"Gabe! Yes! Between switching back and forth between me and Holly you must've been going at it for like a fucking hour! My pussy is sore!" she replied.

He chuckled. "Well, I seem to remember you asking for it."

"Oh whatever," she said, rolling her eyes. "Why don't you go take a shower and get dressed, and then you can treat me to breakfast? Or lunch, actually."

"Um...okay. But you gotta drive. I'm still...out of it," he replied.

"Yeah all right. Now go," she said.

Gabe hesitated for just a moment. There was

something weirdly insistent about how she was asking for this. Like it wasn't natural, like she was really trying hard to get him to do it. He let it go and walked back to the bathroom. Turning on the shower, he got in and started washing up. Maybe he was just being paranoid.

Or maybe this was the other gift they had been referencing.

Ellen and Holly were going to get something set up, and they needed him out of the house.

Well, that was fine. Gabe could certainly live with another surprise.

He washed up and, once that was done, killed the water and dried off. Heading back into the bedroom, he found Ellen staring groggily at her phone.

"Hey babe," she murmured, putting it aside.

"Hey, how you feeling?" he replied, pulling on some fresh boxers.

"Shitty. I'm kinda hungover. Should've drank more water," she complained.

"Sorry. Normally I remember to remind you, or *make* you drink more water, but I was so fucking stoned last night."

She laughed softly, then groaned and touched her head. "It's fine, Gabe. I'm a big girl, I should've done it myself. But I was having too much fun." She smirked suddenly. "You know, you gave us a little scare."

"I did? How?"

"You passed out in the middle of a sentence, right after you got done coming inside of Chloe. I actually freaked out a little. But you came awake briefly, complained for us to let you sleep, and then passed back out. Thankfully, you were fine."

"Sorry," he said.

"It's fine, it's a fair reaction after creampieing three women."

"That...really happened last night," he murmured, pulling his shirt on.

"Merry Christmas," she replied. "And you're welcome."

"Extreme thank you. That was amazing. Best Christmas ever, by a long shot."

"Good. I'm glad. You deserve it." She sighed heavily and then stretched and winced as she popped something. "Well, go on, babe. I need to get up and shake off this hangover." She grabbed her phone and checked it. "Oh God, it's already just past one."

"We got any plans today?" he asked.

She hesitated for just a fraction of a second too long. "No, just...I don't want to get into the habit of sleeping in too late."

"Fair enough," he replied, and gave her a kiss. "I love you, Ellen."

She smiled merrily. "I love you too, Gabe. So much. I don't know if I say this enough, but you really are an amazing partner."

"You do say it enough, but I won't complain about hearing it. And so are you." He glanced over. "And so if Holly, if she's listening."

Holly said nothing, didn't even shift, and they both laughed softly.

"I'll see to her," Ellen said, "now get going, babe."

"All right."

Definitely she was planning something, and definitely he wanted to be surprised by it. He headed out to the living room, where he found Chloe waiting for him. After getting his shoes and coat on, they headed outside.

"Not bad for the day after Christmas," she said, looking up at the gray skies.

"Too bad it didn't snow," Gabe replied.

They got into Chloe's car and she started driving them. "I don't know, there are worse things."

"Yeah, but it would've made Holly happy."

Chloe laughed. "Trust me, she was *plenty* happy last night."

"I know, I mean...a different kind of happy."

"That's a fair point."

They drove on in silence for a time. Gabe looked out over the city. A strange, vague lassitude settled over him. He remained silent, looking at the gray skies and the buildings and the streets as they drove on.

"You doing okay?" Chloe asked as she pulled into the parking lot of a small diner.

"Yeah...I think," Gabe replied.

"You *think?*" she asked.

"I feel kinda weird. Not sure."

"Well...let's get some food in you."

He nodded and they got out and headed inside. The place wasn't very busy, which made enough sense given it was the day after Christmas. Honestly, Gabe was surprised they were even open, but he supposed he shouldn't be.

Profits marched on eternally.

They ordered food. Chloe got steak and eggs, while Gabe got biscuits and gravy and a side of bacon. Then they settled into a booth, sitting across from each other to wait for their meals. Gabe realized Chloe was staring at him.

"What?" he asked.

"Just realizing you look pretty good like this," she replied.

"Like what?"

"Haggard. Messy hair, stubble. I dunno, I like it. Not sure what that says about me, though."

"Well, we don't exactly get to choose what we like."

"True...so what's on your mind? You look, I dunno, melancholic?"

"I'm not quite that. I'm more just...distant? It's hard to say. I was just thinking that my life is so insanely different from what it was two months ago, but it feels like two years have passed. It's insane how much got crammed into those two months. My life is basically *completely* different. In October, I was still miserable, broke, struggling to sell much of anything, single, living in a pretty crappy apartment. And now none of that is true."

"Why do you sound unhappy about it?" Chloe asked.

He sighed. "I don't know. Maybe it's because...if all this can happen in scarcely two months, if my life can *completely* turn around so abruptly, then it feels just as likely that it can do so again."

"You're afraid of going back," she murmured.

"Of course I am. I'd say that I now fear losing you three more than I fear death."

"Jesus. That's, um, really intense."

"Well, I love you."

She smiled again and he felt her shoe touch his under the table. "I love you, too. And I love saying that. And hearing it. And, Gabe..." She reached out and took his hand. "You're right, that it can all turn around just like that. But that's always been true. And it will always be true. We can build up defenses against it, but at the end of the day, there's only so much you can do. And believe me, I struggle with this a lot, too. But...all that aside, I don't necessarily think it's a bad idea to reflect on this. On how far you've come, and how easy it is to lose."

He nodded slowly. "Yeah. Reaching for the future is all well and good, but appreciating what's happening right here and right now, what could be, what once was...that's a good thing to practice."

Gabe fell silent as their food came. They started to eat.

...

"You know you're pretty good at that," Gabe said as they drove back home.

"What?" Chloe asked.

"Making me feel better. You're good to talk with. I appreciate that," he replied.

"You'd better."

He laughed. "So...now what?"

"Now we go home and, um, relax."

"Right. Relax."

Chloe said nothing, staring ahead as she drove them through the city, gripping the steering wheel a little tightly. She'd gotten a text, presumably from Ellen, about five minutes ago and had decided all at once that they were done and it was time to leave.

He had to admit, he was pretty curious about what was going on. After last night and how amazing it had been, (he was still sorting through those memories and imagined he would be for a long time to come, given how nice they were to revisit), he wasn't sure what else they might possibly have in store for him.

Well, he was about to find out.

There was another car parked on the street in

front of their house. He didn't recognize it at all. He almost said something, but he knew Chloe would brush it off by pointing out that it was probably just someone choosing to park there for some reason, likely unrelated to them at all.

She parked and they got out.

Chloe said nothing as they approached the front door, but he could sense the tension. The time to spring the surprise was at hand.

He walked in and found Ellen standing nearby, blocking the couch from his view.

"Hello, honey," she said, smiling a broad smile. "We have one more present for you."

"What present?" he replied.

Ellen's smile grew just a bit and she stepped aside, revealing a pale, tattooed redhead lounging on their couch.

She smiled. "Hello, Gabe."

"*Krystal!?*"

ABOUT ME

I am Misty Vixen (not my real name obviously), and I imagine that if you're reading this, you want to know a bit more about me.

In the beginning (late 2014), I was an erotica author. I wrote about sex, specifically about human men banging hot inhuman women. Monster girls, alien ladies, paranormal babes. It was a lot of fun, but as the years went on, I realized that I was actually striving to be a harem author. This didn't truly occur to me until late 2019-early 2020. Once the realization fully hit, I began doing research on what it meant to be a harem author. I'm kind of a slow learner, so it's taken me a bit to figure it all out.

That being said, I'm now a harem author!

Just about everything I write nowadays is harem fiction: one man in loving, romantic, highly sexual relationships with several women.

I'd say beyond writing harems, I tend to have themes that I always explore in my fiction, and they encompass things like trust, communication, respect, honesty, dealing with emotional problems in a mature way…basically I like writing about functional and healthy relationships. Not every relationship is perfect, but I don't really do drama unless the story actually calls for it. In total honesty, I hate drama. I hate people lying to each other and I hate needless rom-com bullshit plots that could have been solved by two characters have a goddamned two minute conversation.

Check out my website
www.mistyvixen.com

Here, you can find some free fiction, a monthly
newsletter, alternate versions of my cover art where
the ladies are naked, and more!

Check out my twitter
www.twitter.com/Misty_Vixen

I update fairly regularly and I respond to pretty much
everyone, so feel free to say something!

Finally, if you want to talk to me directly, you can
send me an e-mail at my address:
mistyvixen@outlook.com

Thank you for reading my work! I hope you enjoyed
reading it as much as I enjoyed writing it!

-Misty

Made in the USA
Monee, IL
12 January 2024

51639081R00203